Also by J. N. Duncan

Deadworld

THE VENGEFUL DEAD

J. N. Duncan

KENSINGTON PUBLISHING CORP.
http://www.kensingtonbooks.com

KENSINGTON BOOKS are published by

Kensington Publishing Corp.
119 West 40th Street
New York, NY 10018

All Kensington Titles, Imprints, and Distributed Lines are available at special quantity discounts for bulk purchases for sales promotions, premiums, fund-raising, and educational or institutional use.

Special book excerpts or customized printings can also be created to fit specific needs. For details, write or phone the office of the Kensington special sales manager: Kensington Publishing Corp., 119 West 40th Street, New York, NY 10018, attn: Special Sales Department, Phone: 1-800-221-2647.

ISBN-13: 978-0-7582-5564-8
ISBN-10: 0-7582-5564-0

First Mass Market Printing: October 2011

10 9 8 7 6 5 4 3 2 1

Printed in the United States of America

Acknowledgments

First of all, I'd like to dedicate this book to my wife, a fellow writer, who must put up with all of the vagaries of the writing life times two. It makes some things that much more difficult, and she continues to tolerate and support me on my writing journey. I love you, babe. I would also like to thank all of those involved in getting this story to where it is: my editor, Martin Biro, and all of the good folks at Kensington for handling those difficult aspects that allow me to keep doing the most fun part, which is writing more stories. I would also like to thank Nathan Bransford, who was a great agent and helped to shape this story into what it is. I hope his new endeavors treat him well. And last, but certainly not least, I thank all of the readers out there who have enjoyed *Deadworld* enough to continue the series.

Prologue

Detective Thomas Morgan threw the empty pill bottle out of his cruiser into the manicured hedge separating a pair of half-million-dollar Sterling Heights homes. The bitter pill in his mouth was beginning to dissolve, so he reached and grabbed the cold remnants of his McDonald's coffee and washed it down.

Had to be the last one for a while, if not for good. Beverly had been getting suspicious of late. Money was funneling in and out of the bank account too rapidly, which was gradually working its way toward zero. And let's face it, the shit was too good to be taken indefinitely. Morgan had seen it more times than he cared to remember. He was turning into an addict or maybe he already was one, if truth be told. Perhaps it was pilfering from his daughter's college fund that finally clued him in. Oxycontin was not more important than his daughter's future. Tom had felt disgusted with himself. Desperation was ugly and weak. He was turning into what he dreaded most, a bad cop.

Hopefully leaving all signs of the bad cop stuck in the branches of a boxwood hedge, Morgan turned the corner into a swirl of crime-scene color, strands of yellow crime-scene tape and red-and-blue flashing lights. Four cop cars blocked off the street leading to a two-story, Tudor-style house that looked like every sixth or seventh house in the upscale neighborhood. Small groups of residents clumped together on the sidewalk and across the street, wrapped up in robes, blankets, or jackets, morbid curiosity getting the better of them, despite the cool and damp October morning. Everyone loved a good murder.

And apparently, this one was very good, in the way people judged horror movies based on how disturbing the death scenes were. Morgan pulled up behind the roadblock and got out of his car. On the opposite side, he spotted Frank Wysocki's vehicle. Morgan frowned. Sock would be less than pleased that he had not been immediately available to pick him up. When he found him sitting on the front porch, hands hanging loosely over his knees and looking pale as milk, Morgan figured this murder was not just very good, it was Oscar caliber.

"Sock, man. You lose your lunch?"

"Where the fuck you been, Tom? Don't stick me with this shit." Sock wiped the back of his hand across his mouth and then through his receding, graying hair. "Your jalapeno-eating, hairy, black ass can take the upstairs. I'll take the nice and cheery guy with his brains blown across the wall."

"Hey, no problem. Sorry for the delay. I was away from the phone for a few." He gave Sock a pat on the shoulder and walked up the front step. Worse than a brain mural? He moved quickly to get out of Sock's sight. Morgan did not like the sound of that, because it usually meant children were involved.

"You're always away from the fucking phone,"

Sock said, but Morgan was already through the front door and chose to ignore him.

He pulled a pair of neoprene gloves from his coat pocket and considered stepping back out for a mask, but that would mean raising Sock's ire once again and so he decided to let it slide. It was just a bit of the old blood and death. Just breathe through the mouth and tune the emotions out. It took years of practice to get good at, but was essential for Homicide.

Morgan upgraded his assessment when he reached the end of the foyer, which opened out into a living room to the right. It was a lot of blood, and one could only call it a living room in the loosest of terms. A white male slumped over on a leather sofa in sweats and a U of C T-shirt. He was in decent shape, until someone put a slug in his head and redecorated the wall with bits of his brain matter. The smell of it was thick and pungent, so the guy had been dead a few hours then, at least. As for the rest of the living room, every last piece of furniture and decoration had been smashed to pieces, demonstrating a level of violence far in excess of that needed to just ransack the place.

Initial impression: crime of passion. Someone had been very upset about something or someone. The rest was up to Sock for now. Morgan continued walking toward the staircase and had to stop to get out of the way of a young beat cop hustling to get to the front lawn before he puked. *Welcome to Homicide, kid. Sometimes it ain't cool or fun.* Needless to say, it put Morgan on edge. Even strong stomachs had their limits. He kept his breath coming through his mouth only and climbed the stairs two at a time.

The temperature dropped a good ten degrees by the time he reached the landing. No draft blew through the house, however. If some dumbshit had opened a window to air out a crime scene before the evidence guys had done their job, he was going to give someone a reason to be sick.

Disbelieving voices, low and muttering came from the room at the end of the hall that doubled back from the top of the stairs. John walked by a workout room with weights and a treadmill, and then a spare bedroom. Items were knocked over and broken, more like an afterthought than an actual effort to destroy.

And still the temperature turned colder. Morgan thrust his hands into his leather coat's pockets and forced his breath to slow and get shallower. The stench had taken on a different tone. Someone had spilled their guts onto the floor. He had seen it before with knife and bullet wounds. Gut deaths were some nasty shit.

Morgan paused when he reached the door. Goose bumps ran down his spine. He closed his eyes and tried to will away the nervous knot in his stomach. This had happened a couple of other times when he was on the verge of stepping into a crime scene that he would never truly walk away from. Some crimes had a way of burning themselves indelibly upon your soul, and no effort could scour it clean. They changed you and you had to hope you were strong enough to not let it take you down a dark path that might end your life or at least your career as a cop.

This was going to be one of those crimes.

Both officers had handkerchiefs over their mouths. They were staring across the room, which Morgan found obscured by a corner of wall marking the entry into the room. He cleared his throat and both of them jumped, wide-eyed, glazed with fear and then relief.

"The fucking cavalry has arrived!" one of them said, raising his fists into the air. "This is brutal shit, man. It's all yours, Detective—"

Morgan stuck his arm across the entry, blocking his escape. "I'll need one of you to stay," he replied. "Draw straws or something." He took a step around the corner and stopped dead. "Jesus-mother-fucking-Christ!"

"Brutal, man. I warned you," the first said. The other just nodded, refusing to pull the cloth from his mouth.

Morgan waved at him. "Go. Brutal boy can stay."

"Aww, shit, Detective. Come on."

He narrowed his gaze at the cop, mouth drawing into a thin line. Morgan did angry face very well. "You're staying. Greenie over there can go puke now. Go!" The other hurried out and Morgan slowly turned back around to face the bed on the opposite wall. "What in God's name . . ."

"I told you, Detective," came the muffled reply. "Brutal. Sick fuck."

Morgan swallowed down the bile in his throat. He had abruptly forgotten to watch his breathing and sucked in a lungful of the putrid air. The woman on the bed had been gutted and had the same black dot on her forehead. Dark splotches of blood and matter coated the headboard and wall behind her. The rest of her was just a grizzly mound of red straight out of a horror movie. From the neck down, Morgan hardly recognized the rest as having been human. Whoever had attacked her had not just cut her open. They had actively yanked her insides out.

"You touched anything over there, officer?"

"No sir," he said. "I'm not getting close to that. Blood on the floor around the bed too. Maybe not just hers."

Morgan nodded and stepped toward the end of the bed. The woman lay slumped against the headboard, pillows pushed to the side. Her legs were pushed apart at an uncomfortable looking angle, with her hands clenched in her lap. Likely, she was alive when her gut had been split open. So much for anger. They had a genuine psychopath on their hands. Still, Morgan eyed the mass of organs and entrails spilled out on the bed. They did not look quite right, far more mass than should have been coming out of the human body. Given the blackening, pulpy mass in the chest cavity, the lungs and heart were still tucked up inside. So, why did this look all wrong?

Careful of the blood spatter on the floor, Morgan stepped around the corner of the bed and moved in for a closer look, holding his breath as he did.

"You see something, Detective?"

Morgan waved him off, leaning over the body. He started to reach down, to pull some of the gore aside but froze, inches away. Something tiny and far too recognizable lay buried with the bloody remains. He stood up, staring at it in disbelief. "Ah, fuck me, man."

"What is it?"

It couldn't be. Sweet Lord above let it not be. Morgan leaned back over, his hand with a slight tremble. He slipped his gloved hand beneath what might have been kidney and lifted, exposing a miniature arm and hand with its tiny fingers to go along with the face that he could not believe was what he was seeing. Morgan's heart thumped like a mad drummer in his chest.

Leave my baby alone! The voice burst inside his head, a screaming, rage-filled bomb.

Morgan stumbled back, clutching at his head. "God . . . damn . . ."

"Sir? What the hell?" The officer rushed over to Morgan, gripping an arm to steady him.

He gasped, sucking in the foul air, sure that any moment he would be spewing his coffee all over the floor. "Pregnant," Morgan said, shrugged off the hand and made for the door. "She was pregnant!"

"Ah, shit," the officer said with quiet shock.

Morgan stumbled down the hall, grasping at the rail to keep his balance. He had to get out.

He killed my baby! He killed him. He must die. Must die! Help me kill him. You must!

He tripped and fell going down the stairs, clutched at the hand rail and kept himself from somersaulting down to the bottom, but only managed to delay the fall, and Morgan did a tumbling, rolling slide over the last dozen stairs before thudding onto the hardwood floor of the foyer. Someone had torn the babe right out of her womb, massacred her flesh and left the infant to rot away in the wake of blood. The voice was right. Someone would have to die for this.

Yes. You will help me. He must die.

Morgan struggled back to his hands and knees. "Get out of my head."

No. You will help me. My baby needs justice.

What was this shit? The Oxycontin was fucking with him, causing hallucinations. That had to be it.

Let me in, Detective Thomas Morgan. You will help me get justice.

"Morgan, you OK?" Sock was kneeling beside him. "What the hell is going on?"

Sock's voice sounded hollow, distant. His muscles were weak and trembling. "Sock? She was . . . the vic . . ." Morgan sagged sideways into Sock, who grabbed a hold to keep him upright.

"I know, man. Sucks to be us, huh?"

Sock's voice faded into the distance, coming down a long tunnel. "Sock . . ." *Sweet Jesus, help me.*

You are too weak, Thomas Morgan. I will gut them and

splatter their fucking brains all over their walls. My boy will have justice!

"What is it, Morgan? You need me to get someone in here?" asked Sock.

Morgan sat up and stretched his neck from side to side. He pushed away from Sock and slowly staggered back to his feet. "No. I don't need anyone. I'm good. I'm going to kill them, every last one of them."

"That's the spirit," Sock said, slapping him on the back.

"Yes," he said and grinned. "It is."

Chapter 1

Laurel's accusing finger dripped blood from the puncture wound created when Drake bled her out. No matter what Jackie did, she could not get the apology out of her mouth before the depressing light of day intruded and sent the dream scattering away, back into the foggy recesses of her mind.

Jackie lurched up from the couch, the door buzzer driving tiny little spikes into her throbbing skull. Bickerstaff blinked at her from atop one of the couch cushions.

"Shit. Go away!"

The cat leaped off and jumped for a safer perch atop the piano, hidden among the empty tequila and wine bottles, half-empty glasses, and open Chinese food containers.

"Not you, dummy." The buzzer rang again, followed moments later by her ringing phone. Jackie put her hands to her ears. "Oh, my God."

She swung her feet off the couch and pushed herself up. Her head weighed fifty pounds. The motion knocked over the carton of fried rice in her lap, sending the remains spilling across the floor.

"Damn it!" Jackie brushed rice off the couch. She needed at least one clean spot in her apartment. The answering machine finally picked up.

"Jackie? You awake? I know you're home."

The voice brought Jackie to her feet, feeling like a wobbling, overstuffed bobblehead. It was Belgerman.

"Oh. Oh fuck." Jackie turned, looking quickly around her apartment to see if she might be able to sweep the collected crap of two weeks' worth of slumming and depression out of John's sight. There was shit everywhere. And she realized that the litter box was officially too full. He could not come in. Could. Not. Likely, he'd just fire her on the spot.

Jackie made her way through the clothes on the floor, spilled mail off her entry table, and hit the intercom button for the downstairs entry. "S-Sir?" She was forced to clear her throat to get the word out. "What are you doing here?"

"I stopped by on my way in to give you a file you might want to look at before you come back."

"A file? For what?"

"Your new partner," he said. "Figured you might like to get a head start on him so you can be a bit more up to speed."

Jackie let her head sag against the wall. New partner. Holy hell. The thought had been completely gone from her mind. "Let me get something on and I'll come down and get it."

"Just buzz me up, Jack. I'll hand it to you."

And see my place? I don't think so. "That's OK, sir. Just give me one sec."

"Jack! For Christ's sake. We could have been done already. Buzz me up."

Jackie jumped at the startling loud volume of his voice and hit the button without even thinking. "Shit."

She was standing there in a knee length T-shirt that stated ALL GOOD THINGS COME IN SMALL PACKAGES. Jackie opened the hall closet and pulled out an overcoat, a button-down, belt-at-the-waist, traditional khaki-colored raincoat that had been a gift from Laurel her first day on the job. She couldn't even remember the last time she'd worn it. She yanked it off the hanger and barely got it wrapped around her as Belgerman came up to the door. Jackie stepped halfway out and held the door closed against her foot. A couple inches of space did not afford much of a view, or so she hoped.

"Looks like I woke you up, Rutledge." He smirked at her appearance. "If I didn't know better I'd say you were rather happy to see me."

It took Jackie a moment, looking down at herself, to realize what he was getting at. It looked as though she might be naked beneath the overcoat. She could feel her cheeks begin to flush. "You did, sir, but that's OK. I should probably be getting up now anyway."

He glanced at the door. "Hiding someone in there, are you?"

"What? Oh. God no. I was just sleeping, sir. I'm not much of a morning person. Sorry."

He laughed kindly at her. "Don't be. I was just giving you shit. You going to keep me standing out here in the hall like your local Jehovah's Witness?"

Jackie glanced back into her dumping ground of an apartment. It was not the home of a well-adjusted agent. It was an embarrassment. "The place is kind of trashed. I haven't really done any cleaning since I've been off. If it's all the same, sir, I'd rather you didn't see it this way."

Belgerman looked over her head through the crack in the door. "I've never pictured you as the neat and tidy sort, Jackie. And you're talking to a guy who lived on his own until he was thirty-two. I've seen and lived in my share of trash heaps, so quit worrying."

She winced, keeping a firm grip on the door handle. "I know, but, uh . . . it's bad."

John rolled his eyes. "How many times have I been out here, Jackie?"

"You've never been here, sir."

"Exactly," he said. "I don't care if you've been punching holes in the walls. I know how hard this is. I've been there. I lost a partner to some gunrunners about fifteen years ago. One of the shittiest times of my life. I think I can see past the mess. Honestly, I'm curious. I'm not your father."

Jackie looked up into his very fatherly eyes. He'd always had some of that feel about him. She had more respect and admiration for his work than anyone. And somewhere buried in the vaults of her mind, a twelve-year-old girl desperately wished she could have had a father just like him. Her shoulders slumped and Jackie let go of the door.

"Don't say I didn't warn you," she said and stepped back in to give him access. She wanted to run and hide, shut herself away in her room and make him put the file down and leave. After closing the door, she found him standing at the threshold of the living room.

"So this is the infamous piano," he said.

Jackie leaned against the wall behind him, arms crossed over her chest. *Please, please, please don't ask me to play.* "Yeah, that's it. Doubles as a bar."

There were three empty tequila bottles sitting on top, a half empty bottle of red wine, half a dozen Chinese food cartons, and a mostly eaten package of Oreos. None of this would have been so bad if it weren't for the pair of flies eagerly buzzing around the treasure trove. If he didn't go in any further, he would miss the kitchen, where every last dish and cup sat unwashed in the sink and overflowing onto the counter.

"You have a cat?" Belgerman turned to face her at last. His face was slack, noncommittal.

Jackie looked around but didn't see Bickerstaff. This only meant one thing. He had smelled the cat or, rather, the cat box. Another one of those things she had been meaning to get to, but it had never made it on the to-do list above drinking or channel-surfing. He had to be thinking she was completely disgusting.

"Bickerstaff," she said. "Big, fat tabby."

He smiled. "That's not a name you came up with, is it?"

"He was a gift from Laur."

John nodded. "I figured. Been a rough couple of weeks."

It wasn't a question. He knew. What could she say? "It has. I'm . . . spinning my wheels here, sir. I, um . . . I don't know how not to work."

"You've never taken more than two days vacation in eight years, Jackie."

"Really?" That fact had never occurred to her. Vacations were not something she had needed or wanted.

"It's good to take time away from the Bureau on occasion. Helps maintain perspective," he said. "But losing your partner and friend is not the way to do it."

Where was he going with this? "No. Guess I'm living proof of that."

"It will get easier, Jackie. Not in a few days or even months, but it'll happen."

Months. She could not handle months of this. "How did you deal with it, sir? When you lost your partner, I mean?"

He chuckled. "I worked. A lot."

Jackie nodded and said nothing. Work would be

good. Work would get her out of this depression pit and give her something worth doing. More importantly, work would occupy her brain enough to keep every damn thing from reminding her that Laurel was dead and no longer a part of her everyday life. And where the hell was Laurel anyway? Two weeks and not a peep. She thought she had felt her presence several times, but no appearances. Even a *Hello, how are you?* would have been nice.

"You want to start coming in again, Jackie? Office stuff mind you, no investigating until your thirty days are up, but if you want to be in the office around the guys, I think that might be doable."

"Seriously?" She wanted to hug him. "That would be great. I need to get out of here, and there's plenty for me to do that doesn't involve chasing bad guys."

"Would give you a chance to get used to your new partner also, before you're back out in the field."

"Yeah. That would be a good idea," she said. New partner. The two words sounded completely alien. "So, who is it? Anyone I know?"

Belgerman handed her the file. "His name is Ryan McManus, out of the San Francisco office. Mostly gang enforcement stuff, but wants to do homicides. Steady, levelheaded guy. I think he'll suit you."

Jackie stared at the name printed on the folder tab. It should have said Laurel Carpenter. "Can I come in tomorrow then?"

"This decision isn't entirely mine, Jackie. You need to get Tillie's agreement as well."

Matilda, the office shrink, the wise, old aunt who had the uncanny knack for knowing exactly what you didn't want to talk about, and to whom she owed visits. She had extorted them from Jackie in order to stay on the Drake case. Nobody in the world terrified Jackie more.

"Great. So much for that idea." Jackie made no effort to hide her annoyance.

John laughed. "I think she'll be amenable to the idea, as long as she knows you won't be out in the field. She's dealt with partner loss before. She knows how hard it is, Jackie. Besides, aren't you seeing her today anyway?"

"Shit!" She had completely forgotten. "What time is it?

Belgerman looked at his watch. "Nine forty."

"Fuck! Fifty minutes." Jackie hurried toward her bedroom. "You could have said something sooner! I look like shit."

"You look fine," he said. "You want a ride in?"

"No, I'm good. I'm going to shower right quick. I'll see you there, sir."

He chuckled. "I'll see myself out then. Just remember to remain calm, Jackie. Tillie only needs to see you're not losing it."

"OK, thanks." *So, lie through my teeth,* Jackie thought. For two weeks that was all she had been doing. But this was a chance to get out of the hellhole of her apartment. She needed to work, needed the routine of her life to return, because outside of work, she had nothing, she was nothing. She only had to convince the omniscient, brain-scanning Doctor Erikson that this wasn't the case.

Chapter 2

Nick Anderson woke from a dreamless sleep to the sound of a scream. For a moment he thought it had come from a dream, but it persisted for several seconds after he was sitting up in bed, blinking away the sleep in his eyes. It was not a scream his normally acute hearing could pick up, but one that came from that part of him that was dead and pulled from the energies of Deadworld. He had no ghosts upon his property unless someone had just died, but if someone had the scream would have been far louder and distinct. This was faint, distant, and full of rage. For him to hear a death cry of a spirit from miles away meant death on an order of magnitude he did not wish to imagine.

He did not even get a chance to consider calling Shelby when his phone rang. "Did you fucking hear that, Nick? We need to find her. Pronto."

"Good morning, Shel." He looked at the clock. He had been asleep for an hour and twenty minutes. "Or I guess it's still night. And yes, I heard her. She woke me up. I'll check the news soon and see if anything has happened. I'll pull out the police scanner too. If I get nothing by breakfast, I'll meet you, and we can do a cruise around town."

Nick got up and took a hot shower, brewed four shots of espresso with a dash of cream, put on the local station to check on the news, as well as pulling it up online, and then sat down at his desk to go over some reports from Bloodwork Industries. He had been away from things of late, but the ship was sailing smoothly. The latest developments on his synthetic blood were still being tested, and likely would be for some time. After working on it for twenty years, a few months was a pittance.

Maybe Jackie would like a tour of the labs? Nick dismissed the idea. Science did not strike him as being an interest of hers. Though if her failure to return his calls was an indication, neither was he. Moving on from Laurel had proven more of a challenge than she anticipated. He could have told her that. Look how long he had dragged his dead wife Gwen around, using her to ward off contact with any and everyone who might have even wanted to get close. Then Shelby came along and buried her, for a while.

Nick rubbed his hands over his face. He was too tired still, and his brain had the tendency to be morose and depressed when it was tired. If something did not pop up soon, maybe he would take a swim before heading out to meet Shelby. The early edition of the news ruined his plans.

A white couple had been murdered, according to the reporter, "in a very violent fashion" in a wealthy burb on Chicago's west side. The reporter's choice of terminology is what piqued Nick's interest the most. If it had been gunshots or stab wounds, the reporter would have been specific. There may well have been, but there was something more, and then the young, male reporter convinced him that this was the crime scene they were looking for. The female victim had supposedly been pregnant. He dialed up Shelby, and five minutes later was out the door.

They were at the crime scene by 6:30 AM. The crowds had dispersed though a few straggling neighbors peered on. The entire house was fenced off in yellow tape. There were still two police cars and two unmarked cars parked along the street and a television van from the local FOX affiliate. By and large it seemed that most of the excitement had faded away.

There was no doubt about the ghost either. She had been here. Unfortunately, as far as Nick could sense, she was no longer around, just the lingering sense of something else.

Shelby leaned forward, looking out the front window up at the house. "What is that? Crying? Aww, hell. Is that the damn fetus I hear?"

Nick slowly huffed out a lungful of air. She was right. "Think so. And we've got a very irate mother who is not here."

"Should we try and check on it?"

They had never come across the active ghost of an unborn child. Nick wasn't sure exactly how you dealt with such a situation. Clearly, the mother should be the one. "No, not yet anyway. Maybe the mother needs a chance to get over the initial shock and come back to her babe."

"Maybe she's possessed someone and is hunting down her killer," Shelby said.

The more likely and less desirable scenario. "Probably." From out of the open garage, a recognizable figure in the familiar dark jacket emblazoned with yellow FBI lettering appeared.

"There's Pernetti," Nick said. "Let's go have a word."

Shelby huffed. "Great. Captain Pricktastic."

"At least he's FBI," Nick said. "Rather not be discussing this with any of the local PD around here." He walked through the street, meeting up with Pernetti as he reached the end of the driveway. Given the television crew lounging in their van, things must have been in the cleanup stages already. Pernetti's narrowed eyes and balking step told him just how much his presence was welcomed.

"Mr. Anderson," he said and stopped a good ten feet away. "And hello to you, Ms. Fontaine. What brings Special Investigations out here? I wasn't informed that you were coming."

Shelby crossed her arms over her chest, hip cocked out to one side. Nick answered before she could open her mouth. "We weren't called out here by law enforcement. We believe there may have been some . . . supernatural element involved here."

A smirk etched lines into one side of his face. "Really? Do they carry guns and knives? Cause what we have here is a couple shot in the head and the wife cut open from tit to ass. Poor girl was pregnant, too. No, what we have here is just good old human perversity, Mr. Anderson. I'm sure . . ." Shelby took two steps toward him, and Pernetti shut up, his forehead beginning to turn red.

"Don't say anything regrettable, Pernetti," she said, a sweet smile on her face. "It's been a long night."

"Yeah, whatever you say." The sarcasm was waylaid by him retreating a step. "Not even sure we're going to be involved on this one. Possible it was a gang hit, given the woman's history, but this ain't my scene. Guy named Wysocki is inside if you want to look around. Doubt he'll be giving a couple of PI's free access though. Didn't look the type. And I'm fucking done with this mess. So, just stay behind the tape and behave like . . . normal people."

He sidestepped around them and quickly made for his car. Nick put his hand on Shelby's arm. "Don't, Shel. Not worth the effort."

She shrugged away from his hand. "Love to bitch-slap that twerp right across that glow-in-the-dark forehead." Pernetti, still within hearing distance, flipped her off before getting into his car. "Forget that. I'd love to drain a pint from his flabby fucking ass."

Nick looked down at her. She always had the prettiest flush to her face when she got really irate. "Is that so?"

"Of course not." She rolled her eyes and gave him an exasperated sigh. "Fuck you. Don't give me that look."

"And what look is that?"

"The one you should be having for Jackie," she snapped back.

Nick frowned and pulled out his cell. He was not going to get into that conversation with her again. "John? It's Nick Anderson. I wake you?" Shelby shook her head and walked away, heading toward the lone group of neighbors who still lingered on the edges of the scene.

"No, just eating some breakfast. What can I do for you?"

"Pernetti was out here investigating a murder scene for potential gang involvement," Nick said, "and I'd like to suggest you make this an FBI involved case if at all possible."

Belgerman paused and Nick could hear him swallowing a mouthful of drink. "I'm listening."

"A woman was murdered here," Nick stated. "Her unborn child was cut out of her."

There was a quiet sigh in Nick's ear. "Christ. OK."

"The mother's spirit was a little more than angry, as you might imagine. Both Ms. Fontaine and I heard her ghost's screams, but it is no longer here at the crime scene."

"I'm still not quite following you, Nick. Where is it?"

"That's the important question," he replied. "We suspect that she may be in possession of someone who is at or near the crime scene."

"Hold on. You mean literal possession? She has taken over someone else's body?"

"Yes. Likely she is going after whoever killed her," Nick said.

"I see," John said quietly. "And no way to prove this is going on?"

"No. At least not until we can actually track her down. If we can find who she's in control of, then we should be able to force her back to the other side."

"How sure are you that this is what is happening, Nick?"

"Pretty damn sure. I've seen it before. It's very rare and it's potentially very lethal. Spirits with this much pain and rage have one goal and that is to kill the perpetrator, and while he may have it coming, anyone in the way is going to go down, too. This spirit will probably move quickly as well. If she knows who she is looking for and where they are, you could have another murder on your hands by the end of the day."

"Great," John replied. "I'll look into this soon as I get in and make sure our help is needed. You can brief everyone later about what might be the best way to go about finding this possessed person. I'll let you know what time, Nick."

"Thank you, John. I appreciate this. The police are not easy to work with, in these kinds of matters."

He laughed. "I can imagine. Most FBI aren't either. Laurel changed things around here in that regard. Anyway, I need to go. I'll call you soon."

Nick clicked off and discovered Shelby had found her way to the television van and was talking to the reporter and crew. "Anything useful, Shel?"

"Thanks, guys," she said, and turned to face him. "Not really. This is going to suck. I'll bet there were at least a hundred people in contact with this crime scene today, maybe more. There was a decent crowd here earlier. Belgerman helping out?"

He led her away from the television crew and back toward the car. "Yes. Hopefully it won't take him long to get things organized and then he'll call me in to tell everyone."

"We're going to be lucky to find her before she kills someone."

That's what he was afraid of. "I know. I'm hoping we're lucky. Maybe she didn't know the killer." He sagged down into the car, already tired. It was going to be a long day.

Shelby slammed her door shut and gave him a sardonic look. "The fucker cut her baby out of her body and put a bullet in her head. That was not a stranger. I hope she finds him and rips his goddamned guts out and strangles him with them."

"Odds are she's going to have to go through someone to get to the perp. Innocent people are going to die here, Shel."

She rolled her eyes. "I was expressing outrage, you

stoic old shit. Aren't you just a little bit sympathetic for this girl?"

"Of course I am," he snapped back and gunned the engine on his car. "Just because I'm not stomping around and threatening to bash heads if people don't do something, does not mean I don't see what's happened here."

"Well maybe you should," she said. "A little more motivation and maybe Jackie wouldn't be blowing you off right now."

Nick backed the car around and squealed the tires up the road. "You saying it's my fault Jackie hasn't wanted to see me?"

"No!" She growled in frustration. "How can you be so brilliant and dense at the same time? It's annoying. I'm saying that if you were more proactive about it, she might be more interested in saying yes. If you don't show effort and enthusiasm she's not going to give a shit. I wouldn't either."

"She's got a lot to deal with right now, Shel. You ever consider that she's just not ready to be seeing me for anything close to resembling a date?"

"And she never will be! Fuck, Nick. She's depressed and sad and her esteem is in the dumpster. She needs something or someone to help kick start her in the other direction. Insistence is OK sometimes, babe. Makes us believe you're really interested."

"Or I'll just piss her off and she won't want to bother."

"She spends half her time drooling in front of the TV and the other crying into a tequila bottle. I think she might like a little insistence. Talk to her, hon. You can be very persuasive when you want to be, even without the eyes."

Nick gripped the wheel tightly with both hands and

slid around a corner, doubling back a block over behind the crime scene, keeping his senses open to the spirit. "Shouldn't have to talk her into seeing me," he grumbled.

"Oh, for fuck's sake, lighten up. Enjoy the game a little. You pursued me once upon a time, and rather enjoyed it as I recall."

"It was different—"

"Uh-uh," she said, wagging a finger at him. "Not so different, Sheriff Boy. I was a down-in-the-dumps opium addict at the time, or have you forgotten that?"

No. He had not forgotten. She had been beautiful and broken and angry at the world. Full of fire, and he had been unable to resist her. But one thing had been different. "You weren't afraid of me though, Shel. What I am . . . it still frightens her."

Shelby let out an annoyed bark of laughter. "You scared the hell out of me, Nick. I just didn't give a shit. Jackie cares. She wants to live and she needs someone to be alive with. Be that guy. Act like life is important to you again."

"That's hardly a fair thing—"

"The fuck it isn't!" She turned against the car door and stared at him, her face livid with righteous anger. "You've been a guilt-ridden, depressing, morose son-of-a-bitch for the past thirty years. You've been given a new lease, babe. I suggest you take advantage of it, and you can start by dragging Jackie's ass out of her cave and having a little fun together. Christ! Enjoy your life a little. God knows you deserve it." They drove in silence for a few seconds before she added, "Unless of course you really just aren't interested in her."

He was. He had refrained from calling her each and every day for the past two weeks. He knew she was hurting. He wanted to see her and, if he were totally honest, needed to. Her blood still flowed in his veins, and the feeling of her, the touch of her soul upon him called to him. The question was, did she need him? And was pushing the issue going to motivate her toward him or away?

"Maybe I'll stop by her place and check in," he said. "See how she's doing."

"Maybe?" She huffed at him, shaking her head. "This is not a situation to be wishy-washy, Nick. Take a stand. Tell her you want her. She needs to know."

And if she didn't want to know? He said nothing. She was probably right.

Chapter 3

Fifty-seven minutes later, Jackie found herself stepping into a world only minutely less reviled than Deadworld, sitting in the most dreaded of all places, the office of Matilda Erikson, FBI shrink. Few who entered came out alive or with their identity intact. At least, that was how Jackie always felt upon entering the quiet and peaceful domain of Aunt Tillie, who had promised that one day they would have a real talk about things. And now, thanks to blackmail, Jackie sat stiffly in her chair, trying to figure out just how real things should get.

Never had peace and quiet felt so disturbing. Everything about the room, from the soft, overstuffed chairs to the cool, serene green color scheme made Jackie's gut squirm in abject fear. Seated in the chair opposite the quaint, mahogany coffee table, Tillie sipped at the steaming tea she had just poured for them. Jackie's cooled untouched on the edge of the table.

Tillie set her cup down and sat back, one hand idly playing at the jeweled butterfly dangling from her neck. "You look tired, Jackie."

"I'm fine," she said. "All I do is sleep."

Tillie nodded, her mouth drawing into a tighter line. Jackie realized that had been the wrong thing to say. Off to a great start already. There had to be a way to convince the mind-reading witch that she was well on her way to normal. Two more weeks of exile was going to kill her or at the very least drive her insane.

"Have you done anything else these past two weeks? Have you gone out at all? Visited with friends? Taken in a movie?

Oh, you mean like be social? "No. I'm just trying to relax and move on with things. I haven't been in the mood to go out."

She picked up the tea again and took a quiet sip. "Have you been in the mood to do anything at all?"

"What is this? Twenty questions?"

"It's my job to ask questions, Jackie," she said. "We had a deal, remember? And if you want to come back early as John is suggesting, then you need to be willing to share. This isn't an interrogation."

"Fine." Jackie's fingers dug into the arm of the chair. "I'm still getting over things, but it's getting better. It's just a lot to deal with."

"It is," she replied. "What's been the hardest aspect to deal with?"

Jackie's brain spun in a helpless neutral. She had no gear for emotional sharing. "Um . . . being out of work, I guess." Tillie just stared at her, tea cup held perfectly still in her hands. "You know, you should be an interrogator, not a shrink. All that tea and silence and that damn look you have would break down al-fucking-Qaeda."

Tillie sighed. "Jackie. You're making this harder than it needs to be. Inside these walls, you're safe from everything. I'm not here to judge you. Nothing you say here will ever leave this room. You can be as calm or crazy as you want."

Jackie picked up the tea cup, focusing her will upon it to keep it from quivering in her hands. The warm liquid was strong but it wasn't coffee by any stretch. "Not working really has been the hardest part," she said. "I need it. I'll be saner here than cooped up in my apartment all the time."

"An agent isn't the only thing you are, Jackie."

"But it's the only thing I want. OK? Nothing else matters. Everything else in my life is utter shit. When I'm here, I know what the hell I'm doing. Everything makes some kind of sense. Hell, I'd be happy pushing paperwork."

"I can't OK you coming back," she said, a curtain of stillness against Jackie's rant, "until I'm sure you can go to bed at night without thinking it would be better not to wake up in the morning."

"That's bullshit!" Jackie set the cup down, spilling half of it into the saucer. "I'm not suicidal." God! If she thought that, she would never get her job back.

"But the thought has crossed your mind?"

"Why would I tell you that even if it were true?" Jackie threw up her hands in frustration. "I want my job back, not to be locked up for my own safety."

Tillie leaned forward, elbows resting on her knees. She folded her hands together beneath her chin. "Because it's a normal thought to have, Jackie. I understand you better than you may realize. I know what you lost. The anchor in your life is gone and you've been cast adrift. The tomorrows look just like today, lacking any meaning. You have no idea what direction to set yourself in now."

Jackie cast her eyes down to her lap. The words had gripped her stomach and twisted it into knots. She could feel the tears welling up again. She hadn't cried in three days and she wasn't about to start. "It really isn't fair that you can just look at me and see that."

"It's what I get paid to do," she said, a gentle smile upon her face. "I also spoke to Laurel at great length about your relationship."

"What?" She stared at Tillie in disbelief. "When? Why?"

Tillie laughed softly. "Dear, I saw your friend twice a month for five years. We had a great deal to talk about."

Her mouth worked soundlessly for a moment. She made a quick swipe at her eye with the back of her hand. "I never realized, not until just before . . ." Her voice trailed off, unable to say the words.

"Do you still blame yourself for her death?"

Jackie flung herself back in the chair, letting out the breath she had been holding. No point in lying about that, now that she was a blubbering mess. "What do you think?"

She sat up straight, eyes so full of sympathy and pity that Jackie could not look at her. "I think that if you can't find a way to stop, you'll never be able to come back. It will ruin you as an agent, Jackie."

"What! No! That is so not fair, Tillie. You can't hold me to that." She stood up, hitting the coffee table so hard that her cup fell over, spilling tea across the surface. "Shit. You want me to just forget about what happened in thirty days? You have some nifty little drug that will wipe my memory?" She spun away, walking across to the opposite end of the room by a bookcase stuffed to the brim with psychology books. Jackie stared blankly at the titles. "I can't forget."

"Nor do I expect you to," she said. "What I do expect is for you to talk to me about it, in whatever way you see fit. It doesn't have to make sense, but Jackie?" She waited until Jackie turned around, hands thrust defiantly into her jeans pockets. "If you don't, it will continue to eat at you until there is nothing left." She reached over and grabbed a handful of Kleenex from her desk and soaked up the spilled tea. "Please, sit back down."

Jackie shook her head. "I need to stand." She paced, walking behind her chair to the other side of the room to look out the window at the cloud-shrouded downtown skyline. "What's there to say? You know everything about me already. Why not just tell me what it is I need to do so you can sign off on that dotted line?"

She chuckled. "You think I'd let you off so easily?"

"No, but what's the point of telling you stuff you already know?"

"Because the point is not for me to know it," she replied. "The point is to put your issues into your own words, to let someone else hear them, and know that you aren't so utterly alone and helpless as you feel right now."

"I'm not helpless." Jackie couldn't even convince herself with those words.

"Then do something about it, Jackie," she said. "Get off your butt, put on clothes, and get out. You need to be around other people. You need to do something to get your mind out of this rut you're in. You want me to sign that dotted line? Then show me you're willing to make the effort."

The words stung. Effort. Now there was a laugh. She walked back over to her chair and sagged back into it. "What if there's nothing I want to do?"

"I find that hard to believe."

She let her head rest against her hand, elbow

propped on the arm of the chair. "I mean it. Who the fuck do I do anything with? I'm not going to ask any of the guys here. I don't need their pity. There's no family dinner I can join. The only person I did anything with is, you know . . . dead. I could go down to the pub, but you already know where that leads."

"Dear girl, you can drop the sarcasm." It was the first time Jackie had heard any hint of annoyance out of Tillie.

"I'm serious," Jackie said, pointing an accusing finger. "Laur is the only person I did anything with, the only one I talked to. She's the one I told my story to when I was too drunk to realize that my mother wasn't actually floating in my bathtub. But she probably told you that shit already." Tears were starting to fall now, but Jackie didn't care anymore. "She's . . . she's the only one who wanted to do anything with me. She loved me in spite of all the stupid shit I did. Why? Why would she love me, of all people? Did she tell you that, Tillie? She tell you why she was in love with someone as fucked up as me?" Damn her! How had they gotten on to this? So much for proving she was doing fine.

Tillie grabbed the tissue box off her desk and handed it to Jackie. "And why do you think you're so unlovable? I don't see that at all."

Jackie grabbed a handful of Kleenex and wiped at her running nose. "Do we really have to talk about this now? I just wanted to come back to work. I need my routine back, Tillie. I can't handle being at home all the time."

"What we talk about is up to you, Jackie. I can't make you talk about anything. But this issue is important. It goes back a long way for you."

She could not look Tillie in the eye. "I know. I'm just . . . I'm not ready to talk about that yet."

"Will you when you're ready?"

Did she have a choice? She had promised to talk about her mother's death at the hands of her stepfather, but the mere thought of doing so made her squirm in the chair. "I will."

"And I want your word that you will get out of your apartment and do something social in the next two weeks, anything involving being with other people."

Jackie sighed. She didn't want to go out. "Like what?"

Tillie shrugged. "Dinner? A movie? Maybe a museum? You like music. See if the orchestra is doing anything soon."

"Nobody around here is going to want to go to the orchestra."

"Nonsense." Tillie frowned. "You're assuming. I think you'd be surprised how many people around here might take you up on a night with the Chicago Symphony. Or what about that Nick fellow? He's a good-looking man."

Nick. Three times now she had blown off dinner with him.

Tillie saw the uncertain look on her face. "You don't like him?"

The memory of Nick's mouth against hers in the darkness of the cadaver freezer burst into Jackie's mind. Desire and desperation and fear all swirling together before he'd cut her open and drank her blood. "No, he's fine, I guess. It's just . . . it's because . . ."

"Because he's a vampire?"

"Where did you hear that?" Jackie felt abruptly on the edge of panic. How much did she know?

"John told me, gave me the case file on this Cornelius Drake person you all killed," she said. "Though to be honest, I'm rather curious what really happened. That report has some serious holes."

Jackie breathed a sigh of relief. The less Tillie knew the better. She really would think she was crazy if that all came out. "Fine. He's a vampire. He's a hundred and seventy-six years old. He has like half a dozen degrees or something. He shoots better than I do. He cooks better. He's smarter. He's worth millions of dollars. Only thing I have to offer a guy like that he can get downtown for fifty bucks."

Tillie's eyebrows arched with curiosity. "He sounds fascinating. You aren't the least bit curious about him?"

"No," Jackie stated.

"You're afraid of him?"

"Of course not."

Tillie's knowing smile had her shifting in her chair. "Jackie, quit selling yourself short. You'd have things to offer any man beyond what fifty bucks will buy."

"I'll figure out something else."

She shook her head at Jackie, a far too motherly effect. "You need to take some risks."

"I take risks all the damn time."

"Outside of work, dear. Risks to the heart, not your life." She placed her hand on her chest. "And I know how much scarier that is than dodging bullets."

No argument there. This was embarrassing. Jackie felt like a babbling, clueless, thirteen-year-old. She crossed her arms over her chest. "So, will you sign off?"

"No fieldwork."

Jackie nodded. "No fieldwork."

Tillie settled back and took another sip of tea. "OK. I'll sign off. Two weeks, Jackie, then we'll see how things are. And you need to keep coming to see me."

"Yeah, yeah. Every week. I know." She sat up in her chair. Yes! How the hell had that happened?

"Thank you, dear."

"For what?"

"You opened up a little, and I know how hard this is for you."

"I'd prefer waterboarding," Jackie said with a smirk.

Tillie laughed. "Am I really that bad?

In a word? Yes. "No. I just don't like doing this."

"It's good for you. Trust me, you'll see."

Jackie got up to leave. It was only going to be good in the same way getting a bad tooth pulled was good: painful but necessary.

Chapter 4

In the stairwell leading up to her apartment, Jackie caught the faint whiff of cigarette smoke. None of her three neighbors smoked, and it was not allowed in the hall, as stated quite clearly by the NO SMOKING sign at the base of the stairs. The culprit made himself visible by leaning over the rail, his face shadowed by the overhead light fixture.

"Agent Jackie Rutledge?" It was a curious voice, not hardened with contempt as one might expect from someone lurking in ambush.

Jackie's shoulders slumped. What now? "Who wants to know?"

"Philip Margolin, *Chicago Tribune*," he said. "I was wondering if I could ask you a few questions?"

"No." She stomped up the stairs, shaking her head. Could the day get any worse? "Whatever it is, I'm not interested in talking. So, go away."

He met her at the top of the steps, dressed in jeans, loafers, and a black, leather jacket. He had that disarming, journalist's smile that might lead you to believe they had the best of intentions. He was clean-shaven, blue-eyed, with an unruly wave of dark blond hair.

Jackie didn't return the smile. "I mean it. I've nothing to say." Her impression that he would ignore her proved accurate.

"I wanted to ask you about the incident at the parking garage downtown a couple weeks ago."

That froze Jackie mid-step. She frowned, looking up at the journalist with a contemptuous glare. The information on that incident had supposedly been "cleaned" of any suspicious evidence. "Your comprehension skills seem to be lacking, Mr. Margolin. I said no."

He followed Jackie to her door, speaking quickly. "I was hoping to clear up some confusing information. Witnesses claim the Cadillac Escalade belonging to one Father Stanford Brisby was empty after it crashed, yet official reports have him dying at the scene."

Shit. "You'll have to contact the FBI, Mr. Margolin. I don't give out case information that hasn't been cleared for public consumption."

Again with the smile. Jackie had to admit he had that part of the job down pat. "As you can imagine, I've met with limited success in speaking directly with the FBI."

"And you are expecting me to be otherwise?" Presumptuous prick. "I'm not fond of journalists, and with good reason. I don't talk to them unless absolutely necessary, and you, Philip, aren't necessary. Good-bye." She dug out her keys to unlock the door.

"How is this related to the fire at the Tanenbaum Funeral Home, Agent Rutledge?" He laid his hand over the keys in the lock. "Please. If you could clear this confusion up for me, I'll be on my way."

Jackie stared at the hand covering her keys and closed her eyes for a moment. “Let go of the keys, Margolin or I’ll remove your hand.”

Something in her voice must have alerted him, as he abruptly let go, bracing his hand against her door instead. “No need to get prickly. I’m just doing a follow-up story here, and some facts don’t make sense to me. Why did the FBI raid the funeral home after Brisby was supposedly killed?”

She turned the key in the lock. “You’ve got three seconds to step away before I decide to break your hand. Be kind of hard to write the story then, won’t it?”

“Agent Rutledge,” he said, the smile wiped from his face now. “I’ll keep digging. The FBI is concealing information on this, and I’ll find it. I was hoping to get something clear from a primary source.”

Jackie felt a cold rush of air blow through her before a familiar voice spoke softly from behind.

“Perhaps you should leave Ms. Rutledge alone, sir.”

Jackie spun around, her heart up in her throat. “Nick! What the hell are you doing here?”

“Saving a weary FBI agent from a badgering journalist by the look of it,” he said.

Philip took a step back from Jackie, his bravado vanishing in an instant. “I was just asking the agent a few questions about a case is all, mister.”

“And I suspect she said no.”

Jackie recovered from her initial shock and stepped over to Nick. The day was going from horrid to nightmare before her eyes. “Why are you here?”

“Good morning, Jackie,” he said with a feigned smile. “I was in the area. I tried calling.”

“Yeah, but I thought—”

“Agent Rutledge? Did you have any more to say about the Tanenbaum fire?”

Nick and Jackie replied simultaneously. "No."

"I'll continue to look into this," Margolin said, looking decidedly uncomfortable now as he had no way around them to get to the stairs.

"But you won't be doing it here," Nick said. "You can leave now."

Margolin missed the subtle emphasis on the last word.

Jackie couldn't quite believe what she was hearing. "Nick. I'm fine. I'm handling it."

The disarming smile returned to Philip's face. "She's got a handle on it."

With alarming speed, Nick stepped forward, grabbed him by the front of his jacket and pivoted him around, walking Philip to the top of the stair with the ease of handling a child. "I believe I said *now.*"

"Easy, man," Margolin said, straightening his jacket. "No harm, no foul."

"There will be if you do not leave."

Jackie ran a hand through her disheveled hair. What the hell was he doing? Was he really threatening to beat the guy up if he didn't leave?

He only stood his ground a moment longer, withering quickly under Nick's disturbing stare. "I'm gone," he said, waving them off as he descended the stairs. "I'll be in touch, Agent Rutledge. You can count on that."

Nick stood guard at the top of the stair until Margolin exited. "I truly dislike journalists." He turned back to Jackie. "So. How are you, Jackie? He didn't bother you too much, I hope?"

Panic coursed through her veins. "Damn it, Nick! What are you doing? Why are you here?"

He stuck his hands into his jeans pockets. "I was so

close, it seemed such a waste to not stop by for a minute and say hello."

"Well, hello," she said. "Thanks for stopping by, but I've got a new partner file to look at today thanks to Belgerman."

His eyes narrowed a fraction. "I've only got a few minutes this morning. Have a spirit to track down before it causes trouble. Maybe we could just have a cup of coffee?"

"Thanks, but I've had like four cups already today," she said. Even with the contacts it still proved difficult to look the man in the eye. It didn't help that she was lying through her teeth. "I really did have things under control here."

"I'm sure," he said. "I apologize. You just didn't look in the mood to be dealing with someone like him." His head cocked slightly to one side. "You look tired, Jackie."

"I'm . . ." What was the point? He would know she was lying. "Yeah, I'm tired. I just want to go curl up on the couch and check out what Belgerman gave me."

He looked at her in silence for a moment. "Let me make you some tea then."

You are not coming in, Sheriff. No way in hell. "Think I'm out of tea, actually."

"You have a mini-mart right underneath you." His eyes narrowed. "If you'd rather I didn't come in, just say so, Jackie. I'm pretty sure I can handle it."

Jackie sighed. Why did this have to be so goddamn difficult? "Look, tea would be fine, but my apartment is a disaster zone right now. I don't want anyone to see it."

He studied her and Jackie wondered just what it was he could see. His gaze was as unnerving as ever.

"Haven't done dishes or picked up a thing since you got back from the hospital?"

She tried to look offended. "I'm not that . . . OK, yes. The place is trashed, Nick. Your PI skills win again."

"I'll help you straighten up a bit," he said. "I know how this works, Jackie. I've been there myself, and all it does is help you stay in the rut."

"I don't think you understand," she replied. "It's beyond trashed. I don't want to let you, much less anyone else see me living like that."

"Do you know I once lived in a cave for two years?"

"What? Why do I need to know that?"

"It was back in 1889. There were some people tracking me down. They knew or strongly suspected what I was, so I had to disappear for while. I found a cave and lived alone for almost two years. I used the same pair of clothes for most of it, washing them out occasionally in a nearby stream. Didn't comb my hair once. Had no soap. It wasn't pretty."

Eww. "So you understand."

"I do," he said. "So let's go in and I'll help you out while you check out your file."

"No!" She backed up protectively in front of her door. "That's not what I meant. I can't ask you to do that, Nick."

"You don't have to," he said and motioned at the door. "Come on. Let a friend give you a hand. Trust me. You'll feel a hundred times better when it's cleaned."

Friend. Were they friends? It was both more and less than that. Tillie's words came back to mind. She needed friends, but Nick . . . there was just too much in the mix to easily define him as such. "I'd rather we didn't. Not today."

"Jackie." He looked exasperated. "You can't offend

me. There is nothing in there that I haven't seen or done myself and far worse I may add."

She gave in. Jackie knew she wouldn't be able to out-stubborn him. She didn't have the energy for it. "Fine. Don't say I didn't warn you." She undid the lock but then stopped with her hand on the knob. "One comment and you're gone."

Nick smiled at her. "Of course."

Once the door closed, Jackie wrinkled her nose. She had run off in such a hurry earlier that the litter box had remained unchanged. Nick stood silently at her side, waiting for her to move forward.

"On second thought," Jackie said, "maybe you should leave. This is really bad."

"Nonsense." He pushed the door closed and walked in. "So it's a little cluttered." He stepped over a sweatshirt on the floor and moved toward the kitchen. "You have garbage bags? Cleaner? Paper towels?"

"Um . . ." She tried to picture what lay beneath her sink but could not recall. "I'm not really sure what I have." She followed, picking the sweatshirt up off the floor and clutched it protectively to her chest. "Nick? Really, you don't have to do a damn thing. This is my mess. I need to deal with it."

Nick turned away from the sink and gave her a curious stare. "What would Laurel do?"

"What's that supposed to mean?"

He turned and knelt down, opening the cupboards beneath the sink. "It means Laurel is your friend. If she came home with you to this, what would she do?"

"Besides slapping me upside the head?"

His laughter echoed from under the sink as he rummaged around. "After that?"

"Yeah, but that's different. She's . . ." Jackie was going to say *my friend* but then realized it was a backhanded slap at Nick. What the hell were they anyway? Friends was a stretch by any definition. What did you call someone whom you'd nearly arrested and then had save your life? She gave up and shrugged. "It's just different."

"OK," he replied. "You have nothing useful under here." Nick stood back up and walked over to her. "Jackie. I know this is odd. You don't want anyone to see you living like this. I get that. I've been there, believe me, but I'm going to go out on a limb here and say that you aren't repulsed by my presence."

She took a step back. "No! I didn't mean to imply that at all."

"But . . ." He reached for her, eyeing the sweatshirt, and after a moment Jackie reluctantly handed it over. "Everything that's happened freaks you out a little. I freak you out a little."

Jackie shook her head. "Nick it's not that, it's . . ." She sighed, shoulders slumping. "Yes, I'm sorry. It all freaks me out, more than a little."

"Don't apologize," he said and wagged a finger at her before returning to the kitchen. He opened the fridge and began to look through the depleted shelves. "I'm 176 years old and have to drink blood to stay alive. I'd say that puts me solidly into the freak category."

"You aren't a freak."

"It's OK," he said. "Any normal person should be worried upon encountering someone like me."

"Not sure I'd call me a normal person either."

Silence engulfed them. Jackie glanced around at her shambles of an apartment. Yes, she was perfect date material all right. "So, where does that leave us?"

Nick shrugged. "Beats me. This isn't a game I've ever played well, Jackie. What about friends?"

"What about them?"

He motioned his hand between them. "You and I. I like you. I'd like you as my friend. I could use one."

Jackie rolled her eyes at him. "You have to have friends."

"Who can understand my rather unique situation? And not run screaming in the other direction when they do?"

And he hadn't run screaming from her when the shit hit the fan. "I see your point."

"So, how about we start there?" His voice was earnest. "Can we be friends? I'm known to be useful in a pinch."

Nervous laughter rushed out of her. No dates. Just friends. Maybe she could handle that. And truth be told, she wanted his friendship. "Yes, that's fine. I'm good with that."

"Good." He stepped around her and walked toward the door. "As my first act of friendship, I'm going to go out to the store and get some stuff to clean this place up, and maybe bring back coffee."

Jackie found herself smiling, muscles that hadn't worked in quite some time. "I'd like that. Maybe I'll even help out."

His chuckling faded with the closing door. Bickerstaff gave a disgruntled meow and sauntered out of the bedroom, purring as he rubbed up against her ankles.

She picked him up and then sat down on the couch, nuzzling his face against her cheek. "Just friends, Bickers. Don't you worry."

Chapter 5

Bickerstaff's gentle purr on top of her chest lulled Jackie into a blissful doze, sending her into another disturbing dream. A knock on the door jerked her awake again; Bickerstaff's claws dug into her chest as he jumped to the floor. The disturbing dream of being tethered to Drake by tubes full of blood faded quickly into the recesses of her mind.

She rubbed at her chest. "Fuck. Who is it?"

"It's Nick."

"Oh. Come in," she said. "It should be unlocked."

He entered, coming around the corner with his arms full, numerous plastic bags hooked in each hand. Perched on top of one hand, held by his thumb, was a drink carrier with two Starbucks cups. "Hope I didn't forget anything."

"Jesus Christ, Nick. What did you buy?"

He shuffled into the small kitchen and set the bags down on the floor. There was no room on the counter thanks to the detritus of two weeks of doing absolutely nothing. "Things you were out of, things I thought you could use." He set the drink carrier down and pulled out the coffees, bringing one of them over to her. "Here."

Jackie swung her legs off of the couch and took the cup. "Thanks. What do I owe you for all this?"

"The promise that for the next couple of hours, you'll just sit there and relax and take your mind off of . . . everything."

"Nick . . ."

"I mean it," he said and walked back to the kitchen. "Mindless relaxation. Find something on the TV or play the piano or take a bath. You pick up a single cup and you'll be sorry."

Jackie stared at him in silence and sipped her coffee, hiding the smile that turned up a corner of her mouth. She had never seen this social version of Nick before. He seemed almost . . . normal. She had no energy to argue either. "I'll see what's on TV I guess."

She surfed the channels, found nothing that piqued her interest, and watched Nick move around her apartment and clean. Their conversation was sporadic, superficial even. He asked nothing personal and Jackie felt compelled to do the same. Bickerstaff watched with dignified indifference from his perch atop the piano. She finally stopped apologizing for the mess after he threatened to stop cleaning.

"Would you rather be doing this?" He held out the dishcloth in her direction.

Jackie laughed. "No. I don't like cleaning under any circumstances."

"Works out well then," he said. "I don't mind it at all."

"You want to come over every week and tidy things up for me?"

He closed up the dishwasher and turned it on. "Sure. I'd love to."

Jackie's stomach jumped. "I wasn't serious."

"Good a reason as any for friends to get together, I'd say."

Friends. Yes. Laurel had done the same on many occasions. She had usually sprung for dinner then. If she sprang for dinner with Nick, it would mean they'd be having dinner together, in her place, in private. Maybe not just friends then. "I'm sure you have better things to do than clean my apartment on a regular basis."

He had sprayed down the counter tops and was wiping them clean. "Jackie, my time is pretty much my own these days. I do things more because I want to, not because I have to. What would you do if your time was your own?"

The news on the TV caught her attention while he spoke. She recognized the man being interviewed on the screen. It was Detective Morgan from the Joint Violent Crimes Task Force. His imposing, black body filled the screen. The scrolling caption at the bottom indicated that a woman had been murdered. The volume, however, was too low for her to hear.

"I think I'd still be working at the FBI," she replied. She pointed at the screen. "That is what I do, right there. Catch bad guys. Nothing much compares to that."

"You'd have made a good sheriff, back in the day," he said. Nick caught the picture on the television and stepped closer to turn up the volume on the evening news. "One sec. I want to hear this."

"—bastards will be caught. The people of Chicago will see justice served." The detective waved off the reporter. "Now, get out of my f—ing way."

"Man, Morgan," Jackie said. "He's really ticked about something."

"Shelby and I were at that scene this morning. We think a ghost may have possessed someone."

"No shit?" Great. More supernatural crap. Then again, what was she worried about? She couldn't work cases now anyway. "Is the FBI in on this?"

Nick gave her a hesitant smile. "Maybe. I called Belgerman this morning. I'm hoping he makes it happen, but Shelby is out looking for the ghost now. If we can get to her before anyone else gets in her way, we might be able to send her on."

Jackie's brow furrowed. "Gets in her way? Could this be dangerous?"

Nick walked up to her, drying his hands on a dishcloth. "Possibly. Possessions are never good. For one, it takes a very powerful spirit to possess someone, and the only reason it does happen is to dissipate very strong emotions, like rage or grief."

"Would it try to kill someone?"

"I've seen it once before," he said, "and yes, it did kill someone."

Jackie stared at the newscast, trying to imagine someone walking away from the crime scene with a rage-filled ghost inside them, off to kill their killer and no one the wiser. If she had been taken over by her mother's ghost and gone after her stepfather, Carl, her entire life might be different now.

"Jackie? You OK?"

His hand on her arm startled Jackie's attention back and she pulled away. "Yeah, sorry. Just trying to understand how that would all work out."

"Not well, generally," he replied. "Possessed people don't tend to recover. They're ostracized, institutionalized, or killed. From what I've learned at least."

"Then we need to find out who got possessed."

"Agreed," he said. "But we also need to eat. Can I interest you in dinner?"

Dinner. That had the earmarks of a date and Nick

lingering around into the evening hours. Was that such a good idea? Great food, some wine, and that might lead to other things, things she wanted and yet terrified her at the same time. Any physical thoughts of Nick inevitably turned to his mouth buried in the crook of her arm, drinking away her life. It was irrational and unfair to him, but her mind refused to let it go. "I thought you had a ghost to hunt for."

"If you'd like dinner," he said simply, "I'll stay."

She looked around, stunned at the difference he had made. Things were never this clean. Dinner was the least she could do for him. It just seemed rude to tell him thanks and good-bye. Her answer got waylaid by the sound of the buzzer coming from the outer door.

"Who the hell could that be?"

Nick walked over to the kitchen window that overlooked the street. "Looks like FedEx has something for you."

Jackie marched downstairs and found a FedEx guy standing by the door. "Package for Jackie Rutledge," he said, handing her the electronic box to sign.

Jackie signed and handed it back to him, taking the box in return. She looked at the label and almost dropped the box. The return address read Sam and Beatrice Carpenter, Laurel's parents.

Jackie walked back in, the box gripped in both hands before her. What could they have possibly sent her? Something of Laurel's no doubt. Her heart began to thump hard in her chest, stomach turning to knots. Nick was standing at the door when she returned.

"Anything good?"

She pushed passed him and headed for the kitchen, pulling a knife from the knife block. It trembled in her hand. The blade slid easily through the tape and Jackie set it down, opening up the flap of the box. The item inside was surrounded in bubble wrap.

Nick peered over her shoulder as she slid it out of the box. "A book?"

"I don't know," she whispered. What kind of book could be so important that they would send it to her?

A simple, handwritten note lay on top beneath the wrap. *Jackie. We came across this in Laurel's things and thought it best for you to have it. Hope all is well. Best Regards, B.*

The book was leather-bound, forest green with flowers embossed around the edges. When Jackie picked the note up, the reality of her new possession froze the breath in her lungs. There in large letters, set into the hard, leather cover was a single word. JOURNAL. Her fingers shook as they traced over the white and baby-blue flowers at the edge, then curled around the edge of the cover and lifted it up. They were getting clammy. Part of her wanted to just wrap it back up and shove it into the box, never to be seen again.

On the cover page, Laurel's elegant, flowing script stood out like a neon sign. The note was addressed to her.

Jackie. Inside you'll find my notes and thoughts about our years together. All of the glorious ups and downs, joys and frustrations, laughter and tears reside in here, such as I saw them. I hope you will read them. I hope it will bring you a bit closer to me. This note is only in case I can't give the journal to you personally. If such is the case, know that I shall always be with you in spirit and that I truly loved you with all of my heart. Always, Laur

"Jackie?" Nick's voice was filled with concern.

She closed the book, hands resting on top as though it might open again of its own accord. The salty taste of a tear stung the corner of her mouth. "I'm . . . I'm fine. I just, you know, miss her, even if her ghost is around. Somewhere."

"You all right?"

Jackie felt him standing directly behind her. If she turned, likely her face would be staring into his chest. She could lay her head against him and maybe those arms would enfold her and she could close her eyes and breathe the scent of his leather coat and cry a few tears for the loss of her best friend and guilt she still harbored for not saving her. She could have done a lot of things in that moment.

"I'll be fine. Just need some private . . . space," she said. "Go hunt your ghost, Nick." Jackie took a deep breath and let it out.

His body continued to stand for a long moment behind her. She could feel his gaze bearing down on top of her head, those bright eyes that saw everything. If he would just lay a hand upon her shoulder, the moment would break and she would turn to him, but the seconds passed and then she felt him step back.

Then tension rolled out of her body. "Thanks for everything, Nick."

"Glad I could help," he replied. "I'll let you know if we find her."

Jackie turned around and found him backing away toward the door, his face unreadable. "Be careful."

He smiled. "Always."

A moment later he was gone and Jackie resisted the urge to call him back.

Chapter 6

A chill wind whipped across the sagging porch floorboards, pinning loose newspaper and leaves up against the rail. Rain was coming, with the promise of yanking the beautiful fall colors to the ground to be pressed and stamped under foot. On the porch, Morgan's swayed against the wind, steadying himself before rapping his fist against the screen door. The other hand lay tucked beneath his jacket against the cold.

Rosa! You can't do this. Let's go to the police. Let us help you. The other voice in her head was strained and desperate. The voice that belonged to the weak man she had stepped into and become. His body had been turned into her tool for justice.

Rosa hissed back through clenched teeth with Morgan's voice. "Shut it, pig. You had your chance to stop them before."

Rosa knocked again, harder this time, before the bare bulb above the door flicked on. The deadbolt clicked open, but the chain lock remained in place. A muscular Hispanic man, hair shaved close to his head, tattoos inked down his arm, peered through the crack.

"Yeah? What the fuck you want?"

"I'm looking for Eduardo," Rosa said.

"Who's askin'?"

"So he's here."

"What you want, motherfucker? You looking to fix, go somewhere else."

"Don't want your fucking drugs, Hector," Rosa snapped back. "I want Eduardo."

"I know you, asshole?"

"You did," she said. Rosa took a half step back with one foot and withdrew her hand from the coat, revealing a pistol. Morgan cringed within the depths of his own body, locked away by the sheer force of Rosa's rage as in one swift, sure motion, she brought the muzzle up and fired point-blank at Hector's face before he could move out of the doorway. A spray of blood exploded out the back of his head and he dropped to the floor.

Rosa yanked open the screen door, reared back, and gave the door a swift kick, snapping the chain lock's mount from the door frame. There was a woman's scream in a room to the left. Rosa stepped in and over Hector's body, swinging the gun around in a smooth arc until it found the source, a wide-eyed Hispanic woman, bare-footed, wearing jeans and hoisting a toddler at her hip. The remains of dinner still lay scattered across the dining table she stood beside.

Morgan wailed. *Rosa, no! You can't do this. She's got a kid.*

"Run and you will join Hector." The woman nodded in silence, tears sliding down her cheeks. "Where's Eduardo?"

She shook her head. At the same time there was commotion from the back and the sound of footsteps coming up basement stairs. "Please," she begged. "What do you want?"

"Eduardo." She took three quick steps up to the woman, who cowered back and collapsed down on to one of the dining chairs, the child wailing in her arms. "Don't move." She reached up and pressed her hand to the woman's forehead. "You will forget," she said. The woman's face went slack, her eyes glassy and blank.

At that moment, a man flung open the basement door and stepped into the adjacent kitchen, gun in hand. Rosa stepped away from the woman and fired, tearing a hole through his knee. He screamed in agony and stumbled to the floor, sending his gun sliding across the linoleum floor.

A few quick steps and she was in the kitchen where the man clutched at his shredded left knee, smearing blood across the floor as he writhed in pain.

"Hello, Eduardo."

The man groaned. "What do you want?"

"Payback, you slimy, little fuck."

"What? Who the fuck are you?"

She walked up to Eduardo, pointing the gun at his head. The hands flew up from the ragged knee to his face.

"No! Please, man. What do you want? The money is downstairs. Whatever it is, man. I didn't do it!"

"Yeah, Eddie," she replied, voice soft, grating. "Yeah, you did."

The gun drifted down to Eduardo's crotch and fired again. He doubled up on the floor, screaming. Rosa walked across the kitchen to a knife-block by the sink and withdrew an eight-inch butcher knife. In the dining room, the toddler's screams became piercing. She walked back to the crying Eduardo, whose hands clenched between his thighs, shiny and slick with blood.

She stood over him for a moment, the rage fading into an easy smile. "Hurts, don't it, you fucking prick?" Eduardo screamed in Spanish and Rosa chuckled. "I know the feeling. Burn in hell, Eddie."

When he looked up, eyes wide with terror, Rosa fired a shot through Eddie's forehead, blowing blood and brain matter across the open basement door, and he collapsed to the floor.

In the other room, prayers were being whispered over and over again. Eddie didn't need any praying over, not where he was going. Pulling the arms away from his crotch, Rosa put the gun away and hefted the knife in a fisted, sure-handed grip. The smile twisted back into a mask of rage, and she plunged the knife in to the hilt just above the pubic bone.

Oh, God! Rosa, what are you doing? This isn't the way. Don't do this.

Careful to avoid the spreading pool of blood, she straddled Eduardo's body, adjusted her grip, holding the buried knife with both hands and then gave it one good, hard yank upward. The steaming stench of entrails rose into the air as the pink tangle of intestines spilled onto the floor.

Satisfied with the effort, she went to the back door beyond the kitchen and out into the night, ignoring Morgan's anguished groan.

Chapter 7

Jackie turned, squashing Bickerstaff up against the cushion behind her. He complained and jumped up on to the back of the couch. She sat up and looked around her immaculate apartment. It was hard to imagine she lived in such a place.

The clock on her cable box said 7:24 AM. She had been asleep for over twelve hours, and she felt almost normal. Jackie stretched and stared at the journal resting on the coffee table for a long moment, running Laurel's words through her mind several times.

"Nope," she said and picked up the book. "Not yet. Sorry, Laur. I just can't." Jackie had thought maybe she would be ready to look at Laurel's journal after a night's sleep. She wasn't. It just felt weird with Laurel's ghost still in her life. She carried the journal into the bedroom and put it into the box in her closet containing everything else Laurel-related that had been in her apartment—pictures, gifts, and anything else that sparked a painful memory. Someday they would come back out, but the constant reminders everywhere she turned made existing in her own home nearly unbearable. She wondered what Tillie would say to that?

Jackie closed the door and went to the bathroom to start a shower. Her hair was plastered to her head, eyes heavy with the dark rings of fatigue. God, she looked like shit. How did Nick stand being around her yesterday?

"What in God's name do you see in me, Nick?" Jackie rubbed the sleep out of her eyes and stripped out of her sweats and T-shirt, before stepping into the welcoming steam of the shower. Would they ever go more than two hours together without there being some kind of drama? The bigger question: Did she want to go more than two hours with him? Yes. No. Maybe. Her brain refused to come to any kind of conclusions regarding Nick. Part of her had wanted him to stay last night. The other couldn't get rid of him fast enough.

Jackie scrubbed herself with a loofah. "Face it, Agent Rutledge. You're a big chicken shit."

Then again, she felt fear about everything in her life right now. Afraid to go back to work, afraid to be home alone, and afraid to be around anyone, especially a compelling, good-looking guy who drank blood and was old enough to be her grandfather several times removed. Tillie however, was right. She had to do something, and the safest place to do it was headquarters. It was the only other place she felt comfort, where things were familiar, and in control. She would take in the file on McManus, see what he was all about, and finish putting Laurel's old things away and out of sight.

The problem of her desk still remained. Could she handle anyone else sitting there? Jackie tried to imagine a strange agent sitting across from her, spinning around on Laurel's chair, putting his things into her desk drawer, or typing away on her computer. No. It didn't work. It creeped her out even. The desk would have to be moved. Maybe she could arrange to have it put in storage or disassembled. There were spares around the office. She would call maintenance when she got there.

Cleaned, dried, and feeling the best she had in days, Jackie walked into the kitchen and found that her fridge and pantry had been filled with goodies. Starbucks coffee drinks, bagels, pita and hummus, cinnamon rolls, and other items not deemed terribly healthy by most dieticians. Not a salad item in sight. OK, so maybe having a guy like Nick around wouldn't be such a bad thing. At least she would eat well. Of course, her coffee drink would be sitting right next to that container of synthetic blood he had to drink.

Jackie grabbed an onion bagel and some cream cheese from the fridge and, when she turned, noticed the blinking light on her phone. Someone had called last night. She pulled apart the pre-sliced bagel and dropped it in the toaster before picking up the phone. A moment later, she heard Nick's calm voice. He'd have made the perfect late night radio jockey. Jackie figured it likely that he had done just that at some point in the past.

She listened to his message, her heart skipping a beat when he said he would take her to the first crime scene. Had he talked to Belgerman about doing that? Might be a problem if he hadn't, but did Jackie care? No. Likely best not to inform him until it became necessary. Her brain leaped at the thought while she dialed Nick's number. If they found something, perhaps she could be cleared early to work on the case.

Even if it was just the one case, it would be something for her to take her mind off of everything else.

"Nick!"

"Ah, there you are. Good morning, Jackie," he said. "Was beginning to think you weren't interested in coming."

"You kidding me? Of course I'm coming. I just got your message though. Sorry. Where you at?"

"Annabelle's, having a pastry and coffee and killing time until you dragged your lazy butt out of bed."

"Did you clear this with Belgerman?"

There was a momentary pause. "Shelby went over there last night I think. She would have said if there was an issue."

Jackie laughed. "You're sneaking into a federal crime scene, Mr. Anderson?"

"I'll be with a fed, so I've got an excuse."

"I'll be ready by the time you get here," she said. She almost told him to bring her a chocolate croissant, but balked. He didn't owe her one or have any obligation to bring her one. Of course, Laurel rarely did either. She did it because she wanted to.

"All right. See you soon." He hung up.

Jackie gave an imaginary high five to Bickerstaff who stood on the counter, pacing. All matters were moot in the morning until kibble resided within his belly. "Be excited for me, Bickers baby. I'm going to go break some rules and check out the icky blood stains."

He meowed and rubbed against her arm until she picked him up. Jackie fed him and then walked down to the front walk to wait for Nick, who arrived a few minutes later. He was driving the purple Porsche. Opening the door, Jackie got into the car, feeling mere inches off of the ground.

"You got it fixed," she said.

"I did." His hand rested on the gearshift. "You sure about doing this? I don't want to risk too much trouble for you here."

"Just go." Jackie waved him onward. "You're making me nervous and I'll bail if you wait much longer."

Nick glanced in the side-view mirror. "Fair enough." The Porsche squealed into the street, leaving a fifty-foot skidmark on the pavement. "There's a chocolate croissant in the bag there," he said after the car had settled into its dartlike motion in and out of traffic.

Jackie stared at him. "How'd you know I wanted that?"

"I asked. Tina says hello, by the way. So, do you have any specifics on the crime scene other than the murder victims?"

The bag did indeed contain two chocolate-filled croissants. She bit into one, licking off the chocolate that was about to drip out of the middle. "Thanks. Actually, let me call Denny and see what kind of info he has. He can't say no to me."

"Really? Why's that?"

"Think I scare him a little," Jackie said with a smile, and keyed in Denny's number.

"You?" Nick gave her a disapproving look. "But you're so little."

For about a half second, Jackie thought he was seriously making fun of her. She changed her tone as the words flew out of her mouth. "Fuck you. I pack a mean punch."

"Get no argument from me on that one."

"You know what? I'm tempted to just—Denny? It's Jack."

"Jack?" Denny sounded surprised and a bit cautious. "Good to hear your voice. We miss you around here."

"Believe me, I miss you guys more," she said. "I was

in the office for a few and saw everyone was out on a new case."

"Yep, it's an ugly one too. You back on the job already?"

Jackie winced. "Sort of. I'm allowed to push paper for the next two weeks."

Denny paused. "Not supposed to involve you then, Jack. You know that, right?"

"Den, come on," she pleaded. "Just give me a little something. I'm dying out here."

"Yeah, well," he said, "just don't let any of this get around. It's my ass if it does."

"Mum's the word." Her stomach danced with excitement. Finally, something to focus on.

"I'll send you a couple of crime-scene pics to look at, but what we've got here is a Hispanic male, twenty-seven, with bullet wounds to the knee, head, and groin, as well as a large, vertical knife wound running from groin to sternum. Second vic has a single gunshot wound to the face."

"Ouch. Someone was sure pissed off," she said.

"Wounds are similar to the Hispanic woman and white male killed earlier. All were affiliated gang members except the white guy. I think he was the woman's boyfriend or something. Might just be internal gang violence, but this has marks of some kind of ritual killing. Both vics were eviscerated and shot in the head. I think the other two were just unfortunate enough to get in the way."

Jackie frowned. "Hold on. There's been more? When did this murder happen?"

"Last night, about two AM from what we can tell."

Nick's hands turned white on the steering wheel. "Damn it. It's our ghost. She knows who she's after."

"What? Who?" she asked.

"The ghost. She knows her killer . . . or killers," he said. "They need to figure out who else the vics might be associated with. Fast."

"I got that," Denny said. "I'll pass that along to Pernetti."

She groaned. "Pernetti is in charge of this? Great."

"Sorry." Denny laughed. "Everyone deserves their shot."

"Or not. So what happened at the first one?"

"That one was worse. The vic was pregnant."

Eviscerated a pregnant woman? "Fuck. What's wrong with people?"

"Got me, Jack. Anyway, we're still trying to confirm the connection between the two murders, and I really don't want to be caught feeding you info when you're supposed to be parked at a desk."

"OK, thanks, Den. This is great."

He laughed. "You got a twisted notion of good news there, Jack."

"Just nice to hear some work-related stuff, you know?"

"I know," he said. "I'll tell you if anything else comes up."

"You rock. Talk to you later."

Jackie hung up. It felt good to sink her teeth into something again. Maybe, just maybe if she came up with something useful for them to go on, Belgerman might let her back in to help out, even if on the side. If she could show she was holding things together, he would. Tillie on the other hand—convincing her would take more work. For the Wicked Witch of Illinois, holding it together wasn't enough. She would actually have to talk about shit better left unsaid.

They were winding their way through a wealthy neighborhood, with its groomed and manicured streets of three-hundred-thousand-dollar homes, splashed by the colors of fall leaves. The front of the brown, Tudor-styled home still had crime-scene tape across the front that nobody had bothered to remove. There was a blue van backed into the driveway, its rear opened to the raised garage door. It was a cleaning-service van.

Nick parked the Porsche along the curb in front of the house. "That's convenient. Though I was looking forward to impressing you with my lock-picking skills."

Jackie gave him a questioning look. "Because being a concert pianist, biochemist, and a gourmet cook aren't good enough for me?"

He grinned and those rare lines on his face emerged that made him look all too human and far from dead. "You're a tough woman to please, Agent Rutledge."

"Not really," she said and opened the door. "I'm just a cantankerous bitch, that's all."

Nick laughed and followed her up the driveway to the garage. As she stepped beneath the frame of the garage door, Jackie felt a sudden wash of cold pour over her. She froze. The amused smile and almost decent mood vanished in an instant.

Deadworld. Something was here or had been, and it wasn't Laurel. She licked her lips. "Nick?"

"You feel that?" he asked, surprised.

She nodded. "What the hell? This isn't Laurel."

"No," he said. "It's not. Is it very strong?"

"Faint," she replied. "I'm shocked more than anything. How am I able to feel that? I thought it was only Laurel."

"Interesting," he said. "Perhaps the trip to Deadworld has made it so you can sense the dead."

"Fuck that!" She stared at him in disbelief. "I'm no psychic. One ghost is enough, thank you very much."

A rather round black woman came out of the door to the house carrying an overstuffed green garbage bag. She paused, giving Jackie and Nick a wary eye. "Can I help you with something?"

Jackie pulled out her ID. "FBI, ma'am. Just here to do some follow-up on the crime scene."

"Ugh," she replied, shaking her head. "You folks better catch the sons of bitches who did this. Ain't right."

Jackie nodded. "We will, don't you worry." She stepped around the muttering woman and went inside, where the cold of the dead intensified.

The house had been trashed. Even with the cleanup in progress, there were still broken bits of picture frames, shattered vases, dirt from planters, and assorted other household items strewn around the floors. Dishes were broken in the kitchen, bookcases knocked over in the living room. A lamp base lay on top of a video cabinet beneath a wrecked flat panel television. Behind the sofa against one wall was the dried rust-red blood splatter of one of the victims. The cushions, once a sage green, now sported a splotchy, dark pattern of blood. The sickly sweet smell of blood and death was still faint in the air.

Another cleaner, a rail-thin black man, was randomly tossing the debris into a bag he held in his hand. He nodded at them and continued to work in silence.

"Really wanted to pull off the appearance of a robbery, didn't they?" Nick said as he stepped over and around the debris to get to the bloodstained sofa.

Jackie did not answer. She stood in the main entry, where stairs went up to the second floor and a hallway led down to what appeared to be an office. She had thought she heard something, and it was making her stomach knot up. Jackie closed her eyes and caught it again, this time holding onto the sound, a barely audible keening, almost like a . . . baby.

She whispered. "Nick?"

He stood up from where his hand had come to rest on the couch. "This person has moved on or is no longer around here. What is it?"

"Can you hear that? I swear it sounds like crying."

Nick nodded, his grim face staring at her curiously now. "That's the babe, I think. You can hear that?"

The cleaning man edged around behind Jackie and quickly walked toward the back door. Jackie turned around in a slow circle, until she finally determined a direction. It was above them. She pointed at the ceiling. "It's up there." Jackie then dropped her hand and turned back to Nick. "What's going on here, Nick? Why can I hear that?"

"Not sure," he said and put a hand on her shoulder. "You OK? You're looking pale now."

"'Cause I'm fucking freaking out here, Nick. Why can I hear a crying baby? I don't have psychic abilities. I don't!"

"Maybe you do now," he said. "Let's go up and check things out. This could be very important if it's true." He headed up the stairs, but Jackie balked. Halfway up, Nick turned. "It's safe, Jackie. It'll do little more than scream its lungs out at us. Annoying, but hardly dangerous."

Easy for you to say, Jackie thought. Could something have happened to her on the other side? Could it be more than just Laurel? Could it be every fucking thing out there? "It needs a damn off switch," she said, and marched up to find the screaming dead baby.

The temperature dropped with each step up. The

smell of blood and death ramped up a notch. By the time she reached the landing, it wasn't just cold, it was freezing.

Jackie frowned and began to breathe through her mouth. The odor had grown incessant, cloying at her stomach. If she didn't know better, Jackie would have sworn someone had just been gutted. The landing wrapped around the stairs, the four doors going back all closed. She walked toward the back, feet silent on the runner stretched the length of the floor. There was no doubt where the screaming was coming from. Nick was already there, opening the door, as though it were the most normal thing in the world to do. When he opened the door, Jackie's stomach lurched but nothing changed. The noise level remained constant, and the smell still gnawed at her stomach.

Nick waited for her, just inside the doorway. "Blood-stained bed, Jackie. That's all. A lot of blood though."

She walked up and stopped next to Nick. Even breathing through her mouth wasn't enough. The stench of blood and human insides filled the room like a cloud, thicker than normal air. "God. You'd think we were wading in it the way it smells." She tried to hold her breath.

"Tell me if you see the babe's ghost," he said. "It doesn't seem to be materialized."

The room looked like what you'd expect from any suburban master bedroom: a long dresser against one wall, a queen-size bed with matching head and footboards, matching bedside tables, a chair and ottoman beside the window. From there, the rest was in total disarray. Lamps were broken on the floor. The mirror above the dresser had fallen behind and there were shards of glass strewn over the dresser's top. Pictures were broken and torn on the floor. Someone had taken a knife to the chair and ottoman, with stuffing billowing out of its many wounds. The bed had been stripped, but the bloodstain remained. It was enormous. Blood spatter from the gunshot wound to the head adorned the headboard and splashed the wall behind.

There was no baby to be seen. Yet the muffled wailing continued, persistent and distressing. Jackie squatted down and peered under the bed. Her breath was already beginning to run out and her stomach would not deal with another lungful of the fetid air. She walked quickly over to the dresser, opening the drawers, only to reveal a scattering of rumpled clothes. Jackie could not localize the sound. It emanated from every part of the room. Across the room from the bathroom, the closet door was open, and Jackie ran over to look, only to find a neatly ordered space filled with shoes and suits and dresses.

Finally Jackie had to walk over to one of the windows and slide it open in order to suck in some of the cool fall air. "How the hell am I supposed to investigate crime scenes like this? Walk around with a goddamn gas mask on?"

"You learn how to tune it out. It takes some practice," he said. "Is the smell of blood really that strong?"

Jackie sucked in a lungful of good air. "It's like someone's guts have been baking in the summer sun for the past three days. It's bad."

When she walked back over, her gaze froze upon the middle of the bed. The blood there did not look soaked in but now glistened like it truly had been freshly spilled. Jackie blinked and rubbed at her eyes only to find the stain appeared to be seeping back out of the bed, a fresh pool burgeoning up from within the mattress.

"Jesus-fucking-Christ," she said, staring in rapt horror. A moment later it sank back in, leaving the normal, dark, day-old stain. "Did you see that, Nick?"

"No, but I felt something. The wail is a bit clearer too," he said. "What did you see?"

Jackie pointed at the mattress. "The um, the blood was seeping up out of the bed."

He raised an eyebrow and walked over to the bed. "Curious." Nick reached down and touched the mattress. He closed his eyes for a couple of seconds, his mouth drawing into a thin, grim line. "He's here all right. Just on the other side." He stood back up and looked at Jackie. "Recent deaths tend to make the wall between a bit thinner."

Jackie stared down at the brick-red stain, about four feet across. It took a lot of soaking blood to make a stain that big. "That's nice to know."

"Touch it and see," he said, giving her a nod toward the bed. "Please. I'd like to know if you're able to make any sort of contact."

She took a half step back. *Contact?* "What do you mean?"

"Just if you get any greater sense of the spirit of the babe. Its voice should be sharper, like it literally is just a few feet away. You may almost feel like you can reach out and touch it."

A shiver ran down Jackie's spine. *Touch it? Are you fucking insane?* Despite the apparent ease with which Nick had performed the action, this was not a normal thing to do. This was downright creepy. Jackie slowly leaned forward half expecting the blood to come surging up at her once again, but nothing happened. In what must have looked like slow motion to Nick, Jackie reached down with the tip of her finger and touched a small splotch of blood near the edge of the bed.

The wailing cries pierced her skull in full-on surround sound, eardrum-ringing rage and terror. The blood repooled upon the mattress, churning and splattering across the surface as though something lay there, squirming in the gore.

Jackie staggered back, mouth agape, her ears ringing. The feeling of death swam through her like a tidal surge, colder than ice, and flashes of memory flooded her brain. The bone-eating cold of Deadworld. Her stomach revolted, and Jackie stumbled to her knees, retching up the morning coffee onto the carpet.

Jackie clutched at her head and screamed, "Get out! Get out, get out, get out!"

A moment later Nick was at her side, arms around her. His cool, calm voice in her ear. "It's gone, Jackie. The door's shut. It's gone now."

She wiped the back of her hand across her mouth and tried to listen between her own ragged breaths. The babe's cries were distant once again. "Nick? Can we get the hell out of here? Please? Now?"

He pulled Jackie up to her feet and walked her toward the door until she had regained her equilibrium. At the bottom of the stairs, the cleaning crew stared at her with wide-eyed curiosity. Nothing to see here, not a fucking thing. Jackie hurried past them and out the door into fresh nondead air.

Chapter 8

At the top of the stairs to her apartment, Nick said, "I'll make some coffee or will that be too harsh on your stomach?"

Jackie had not considered that he would want to come in. She thought he was just getting her to the door and making sure she didn't throw up yet again. He had refused to let her pay for getting the floor of the Porsche cleaned. There weren't many things more humiliating than losing it in a guy's car, unless of course you were so drunk you didn't even remember doing it. Regardless, she did not want Nick fussing over her in her apartment. Fussing was the start of a slippery slope that Jackie did not want to consider right now. She just needed some time to collect herself and calm down.

"Nick." She stopped and looked up at him, her hand resting on the doorknob. "I'd rather be by myself for a bit, if you don't mind. My brain is fried. My stomach hates me, and I just need quiet for a while."

"That's fine," he said, with no hint of disappointment. "We should probably talk about what happened some more. Get Shelby and maybe Laurel if she's available. I don't want you running around thinking you've gone insane, Jackie." He offered her a faint, wry smirk. "You're just psychic."

Jackie opened the door. "God. Please don't call me that. I'm not a psychic."

"But you do have some psychic abilities. We can help you figure it all out, Jackie."

She gave him a wan smile. *But I don't want it figured out. I just want the fucking stuff to go away.* "Thanks. I'll call you later, Nick. And I'm really sorry about the car. I still can't believe I did that."

"Don't worry, Jackie. It's fine. Don't hesitate to call if you have any questions or just want to talk about things."

Jackie nodded and closed the door, leaning back against it with a sigh of relief. If he'd pressed, she probably would have let him in. He was just so damn polite about everything. Nothing she said or did or wanted to do put him out of sorts. It made you not want to say no to him, and that feeling had the butterflies in Jackie's stomach doing handsprings. Bickerstaff waltzed up and rubbed himself against her ankles and Jackie picked up the tabby, holding him tightly against her chest and rubbing his ears.

"Hey Bickers, baby. Guess what Mommy saw today?" He purred and rubbed his face against hers. "That's right, a ghost. Can you fucking believe it?" Bickers pulled back to look at her and then rubbed the other side of his face against her. "I know. Freakiest fucking thing ever. Mommy would just as soon never do that shit again." She dropped him down to the floor where he trotted toward the kitchen. "Hungry? Well, let's see what the hunky old vampire has for you today."

She served Bickerstaff up his dinner and grabbed

a beer from the fridge. Probably not the best thing for her stomach, but the tequila would kill it.

"Laur? You around by chance?" she yelled out into her apartment. "Could use your help with this one. Kind of important." The only sound was the cat hungrily slurping up cat food. She could sense no dead people either, but Jackie wasn't sure if that meant anything or not. "Laur!" After a minute, Jackie finished off the first beer and walked to the bathroom. She needed a shower badly. Even though she hadn't vomited on herself, she felt as though the stench of blood still clung to her, had coated her skin and soaked into her clothing.

A shower, another beer, and she was at least cleaner. Still no sign of Laurel. Jackie had really hoped she might hear or at least somehow be aware of what had happened.

"Laurel!" Jackie yelled for the seventh or eighth time. She had lost count. "Where the fuck are you?"

Why wouldn't she come? Jackie needed her now more than ever. She needed someone to explain what the hell had happened back there in that house. She wanted to know if that was a normal experience and more importantly how you stopped doing it. Even after two hours and a hot shower, she could still sense the cold that lingered in her body. Her joints had a faint, arthritic ache to them. It didn't hurt, but she could tell it was there. The dead had seeped into her bones. Pouring herself a glass of wine, Jackie wrapped up in a blanket and flipped through channels on the television, completely at loose ends.

Bottom line, she was terrified. Sensing the dead was Laurel's forte, not hers. The psychic radar she had so fondly poked fun at over the years was not equipment she possessed, nor did she want to. So what the hell had happened back there? How did a visit with the dead make her psychic? What she needed was Laurel, and more information on the crime, neither of which she could just call up. Belgerman would have her flagged on the computer and he would want to know why she was snooping around on a case she was not supposed to be involved in. Hearing dead babies and seeing blood-surging mattresses would not go over well. Hello, loony bin.

She channel-surfed for a few minutes but quickly realized she was in no mood for television. Instead, Jackie got up and walked over to her piano. Bickerstaff quickly joined her, hopping up on top to sit and look down upon her. Something about her fingers moving across the keys enthralled him for some reason.

"What would you like to hear, Bickers? Something slow and relaxing?" She reached up and scratched under his chin. "My thoughts exactly."

Jackie began the single quiet notes of Tchaikovsky's *Romance in F Minor,* remembering how Laurel used to stand beside the piano, leaning over the edge with her chin resting on her hands. She thought the look and smile had been for the playing, but Jackie understood now that the look had been directed at her not the music. A look of love that she had failed to recognize. Nobody had ever looked at her in such a way, so how was she to know what it really meant? She heaved a sigh and continued to play, closing her eyes and letting the notes tumble through her body, letting them take away the stress and anxiety of earlier in the day. Much as she played, however, the music failed to eliminate the image of a squirming, ghostly mass smothered in blood. Like a train wreck, her mind refused to look away.

She stopped and opened her eyes. "Fuck. I can't work like this, Bickers. I can't do it. How the hell did Laur deal with this every day?"

A cold breeze tingled at the marrow of her bones. The familiar ache bloomed inside her once again, and Jackie could almost hear the doorway to the other side opening up. A moment later, Laurel stood in her familiar spot beside the piano, the television screen glaring through her gray, translucent form.

The smile on her face was even more hesitant than her voice. "Hi, hon. I heard your song. I had to come see you."

Jackie blinked a few times to make sure she wasn't just imagining it. Had she come for her song? What about the million other times she had called out for her when she was drowning in tears and cursing the rising sun for letting her see another day? She did not hide the sarcastic bite in her voice. "Hello, stranger. Nice of you to drop in."

Laurel winced. "I'm sorry, Jackie. I am. It's just . . ." She raised her hands in a helpless gesture. "I can't help you right now, but I've missed you so much. I wanted to let you know I'm still here. I'm not going anywhere."

Jackie stared at her best friend, trying to pull apart the feelings of relief and outrage. She didn't try too hard. "Except over to Shelby's maybe? Latch on to those sweet, vampire lips or . . . or just what the hell does a ghost and vampire do together?"

"That's unfair, Jackie, and you know it."

She shrugged. "So? Fairness isn't too high on my list when I'm balling my fucking eyes out because you're dead, only you're not . . . really, but now I get to see dead people every day apparently. Yea, me! Because something happened to me when cowboy vampire saved my sorry ass and I got to play with all the ghost people and now I'm fucked, thank you very much."

Laurel's translucent figure straightened. "My death isn't the real problem. Shelby and I decided—"

"Shelby?" Jackie slammed her hands down on the piano keys and Bickerstaff made a mad dash for the bedroom. "Since when has she got any business deciding anything regarding my life? What the fuck, Laur! Just a little help over the past two weeks would've been nice. Hell, even popping in to say hello. But she's got no right to be deciding anything. She's not my goddamn mother!"

Laurel closed her eyes for two seconds. "She didn't decide anything for you, hon. It was for me. I can't help you get over me. These first steps need to be yours. If I help . . ." She gave Jackie a pained smile, looking on the verge of tears. "I won't stop. I can't be your crutch anymore."

"Crutch." Jackie crossed her arms over her chest and nodded. "I thought you came over to hear me play? Now we're going to talk therapy, which by the way, I didn't need until you died."

"You did," Laurel said, her voice quiet and sad, "but I wanted to be your therapist."

"What? What bullshit is that?"

"I couldn't not help you, Jackie. I wasn't capable of saying no to you. For anything. Don't you see?" Laurel threw up her hands and turned away from the piano. "You're too pissed off at me to see anything."

"Yes, I'm pissed," Jackie yelled. "My best friend said she would stick around for me, make sure my life was back on track, and she's been gone since day one. All it's done is make me more fucking miserable."

She turned back around and gave Jackie a plaintive

smile. "You have to be able to help yourself, Jackie. You need to—"

"Get out," she snapped and waved Laurel off. "I don't need you here if this is what I'm going to get."

The smile faded and Laurel nodded. Her voice was tearful. "I see. It's not the time then."

Jackie didn't look at her. "Good-bye, Laur. Go bonk your vampire."

She said nothing and when Jackie finally looked up Laurel was gone. The mood to play had been stamped out. Jackie got up and went to the kitchen for a sweet, double shot of tequila. Maybe it was time for two or three.

Chapter 9

Whether Jackie wanted to or not, and she clearly didn't, Nick knew something had to be done to address her experience at the crime scene. One hundred and fifty years had not dulled his initial experience with the dead. When he had returned to his home after Drake's massacre to find Gwen and his children's ghosts, his initial thought had been relatively plain. He had lost his mind. Later, he figured God had been punishing him for his crimes. He would not let Jackie go through that.

The obvious manner in which to address the issue would be to repeat the experience, so Nick got out his cell and dialed up Belgerman once again.

"Belgerman. What can I do for you, Mr. Anderson?"

"Sir, I have a favor to ask of you, if you don't mind."

He laughed. "Nick. You're more than a century older than I am. Please. It's John, and what do you need?"

"I'd like to take Jackie to the crime scene you were investigating earlier today."

The pause was long enough that Nick was almost

certain the answer was no. John's voice was suspicious. "What's this pertaining to?"

"I've got reason to suspect that Jackie may have acquired or be experiencing some kind of psychic ability related to her exposure to Deadworld."

There was a spluttering noise on the other end of the line. "Jack's psychic? Oh, I'll bet that went over well."

"Not exactly," Nick said. "I'd like an opportunity to test it though, and a murder scene is fertile ground for psychic energies."

"You going with her?"

"I'll be with her at all times."

"Go ahead then," John said. "Remind Agent Rutledge that this does not mean she's doing fieldwork."

"I will. Thank you, John."

"How's she doing? You've seen her, I assume."

Nick smiled. He wondered what sort of rumor mill was grinding away down at the FBI, but knew that John cared a great deal about the welfare of Jackie. He was almost like a father figure from what he could tell. "She's struggling, I think. It's hard to lose a partner, especially when they were so close, but you throw in what happened and nearly dying? It's a unique situation, but she'll make it through."

"You sound rather sure of that, Nick."

"I am," he said. "She's tougher than she thinks and she's not as alone as she believes."

"Good. Thank you, Nick. You'll keep me apprised of these psychic phenomena? Let me know if there's anything pertinent to the case?"

"I will. Good night, John." Nick hung up the phone and pulled into Shelby's parking lot. Her lights were on, and she'd said she wasn't going out tonight, so Nick had not bothered to call. He let himself into the building with her spare key and walked down to her apartment on the end. It took her nearly two minutes to answer the door. In the meantime, Nick felt the fading presence of Laurel. She didn't need to leave on his account.

Shelby answered the door with her usual eye-popping smile, but Nick could see the tiny stress lines furrowed between her eyes. "Hi, babe. You don't look so annoyed now."

"And you look stressed," he said and stepped into the apartment when Shelby walked away from the door.

"I'm fine. Just a basket case of a girlfriend is all," she said. "I'm ready to smack Jackie."

"They have an argument?"

"Something like that. Jackie is miffed Laurel stopped by to say hello because she missed her, and so Jackie told her to fuck off."

"Did she know Jackie saw a spirit today?"

"What?" Shelby whirled around at the news. "At the crime scene?"

Nick nodded. "She had a full-blown channeling experience. The infant or fetus I suppose, since it hadn't been born yet, came through or what there was of it. It was a bit uncanny, honestly."

"Ugh, Nick! Fuck. No wonder Jackie was wigged out."

"We should take Jackie to the second crime scene and see what we can find out."

"Second? I've missed this bit of news."

"Two victims, one gutted like the first, second shot in the head."

"Think it's our ghost?"

"Who knows, but I think it's worth looking at. We can check for her presence, and Jackie can have a second shot at testing herself at a murder scene. If this is a permanent change, she needs to figure out what it is quickly. I don't think she's equipped to handle it on her own."

Nick walked into Shelby's kitchen and grabbed one of the metal containers from her fridge, kept just for him these days as she had gone back to the real thing since Drake. He didn't know where or how she was siphoning off what she needed, but he was done complaining. It was her choice and her life and if she got busted for it, so be it. For Nick, the residual effects of taking in so much energy to kill Drake had kept him going for days, but he could feel it beginning to wane now just a bit. He would drink the vile tasting synthetic his company made to prolong its effects for as long as he could.

It felt far too good to have the energy of real souls flowing through his blood. Part of him knew he should let it dissipate and get himself back to the normal state of affairs, but there would be no other time to come after, so Nick had decided he would enjoy the luxury for as long as he could.

"She's not equipped to handle it," Shelby agreed. "How's things going with you two, anyway?" She walked up and took the empty container from his hand and rinsed it out in the sink. "Anything I'd like to know about?"

"No," Nick snapped back. "And why would I inform you of those details?"

"That's OK," Shelby said, looking back at him with a smile. "Once Jackie is over being mad at Laurel and me, she'll spill the beans."

"You want to come with me or not, smartass? I'm not sure what we'll find, but I'd like another pair of eyes, especially on Jackie."

"So, I'll look around while you check out her ass?"

"You're just too funny sometimes, you know that?"

"I do," she said. "Let me get my coat and I'll meet you over there. Jackie can ride with you, since I'm not high on her list at the moment."

They arrived at Jackie's to the rumble of thunder. An evening thunderstorm was rolling in. Shelby had held up the picture of the Doppler radar on her phone and proclaimed it was going to be a good one.

Nick buzzed Jackie's apartment from the street-side door. After a minute he buzzed it again. "Think she might have gone to bed? She was pretty wiped out from earlier."

Shelby gave him a look and shook her head. She placed her finger over the buzzer and held it down, giving Nick an impatient look. "Must you always be so fucking polite?"

"It can wait until morning," he said. "I'd just hoped for sooner rather than later."

"It's 7:30, Nick. She's either in the bath or drunk and ignoring us."

About twenty seconds later the window on the far side of Jackie's kitchen slammed up. "What the hell . . . oh. What are you guys doing here?"

Shelby waved. "Can we come up a talk for a few minutes?"

Nick watched her lips tighten in annoyance. "Why?"

Shelby huffed. "Because it's not something to shout up to you in a window about, that's why. Just buzz us up, would you?"

"Can't it wait until tomorrow?"

She turned to Nick. "Explain to me why you like her so much?"

"I'll go with, 'it's complicated,'" he said. He looked up at the ruffled figure sticking out of the window.

"Jackie? We want to take you to the second crime scene."

Her head came up and hit the window frame. "Ow! Shit. Why?"

Shelby rolled her eyes and looked skyward. "Mother above us. Do I deserve this?" She took a step toward Jackie. "Buzz us up, Jackie, or we'll just force our way in." A couple coming out of the grocery started to walk toward them but quickly decided to cross the street instead.

Nick watched Jackie mouth the word *bitch* before ducking back inside. A moment later the latch on the door clicked open. Shelby yanked it open and marched up the stairs.

"Shel, keep it calm, will you? We want—"

"I know, I know," she said, waving him off at the top of the stairs. She stopped before Jackie's door and let him go first. "You talk, so I don't smack her."

She opened the door when Nick stepped up to it. "Hello, Jackie." Her eyes were puffy and dark. Too many tears and too little sleep. She stared at him in silence, exasperated. "We'd like to see if you have any more psychic responses to the scene, and to find out if maybe the spirit of the mother was involved in these murders."

Her shoulders slumped. "Now? It's late."

"There's nobody at the scene. Belgerman gave the okay for you to come check it out."

"Oh. OK." She stepped away from the door and let them inside. "You sure this ghost is involved?"

"We don't know yet, but we'd like to check it out and see. The sooner we make sure this spirit has moved on, the better."

"And what if I find it?"

"We'll be there to deal with it, Jackie. Don't worry."

Shelby walked passed them into the living room and straight over to the coffee table. She grabbed a half empty bottle of tequila and marched it over to the sink and dumped it out. "Get dressed girl. You're coming with."

Jackie gasped at her in disbelief. "You bitch! That was like fifteen bucks of tequila right there."

"Boohoo," Shelby replied. "Get your boots, Jackie. I want to see your psychic powers in action."

"Maybe I don't," she replied, giving Shelby the stare-down, which lasted all of about three seconds. "Maybe I've had enough ghostly bullshit for one day."

Shelby just crossed her arms over her chest and continued to stare in silence until Jackie huffed in frustration and stomped off to her bedroom.

Nick whispered in Shelby's ear. "You're good. I'd have never done that."

She glanced up at him and smirked. "I'm not trying to get in her pants."

Jackie came out a couple minutes later in jeans, sweatshirt, and hiking boots. "I'm half-drunk, you know. You really think this is the best time?"

"Well I can give you a little of the vampire voodoo, if you like," Shelby said, taking a step forward.

"No!" Jackie scooted back on the couch away from her. "Fuck. I'm coming, OK? You know, having gotten Laurel, you'd think you could be nicer to me."

Shelby's hands went from tucked under her arms to poised on her hips. Nick shook his head. *Please don't escalate this. We've almost got her out the door.*

"You'd think," Shelby said. "But is that really where you want to go, hon? Is that the argument you want to have with me?"

Jackie worked her mouth in a tight, squirming

line. Nick tried hard to look noncommittal about the whole thing but was hoping to hell she would suck it up and pick that fight another day. They didn't have time for it. She muttered under her breath, stomping past Shelby and Nick to the hall closet where she grabbed her coat. "Someone better be buying the coffee."

Nick sighed. Thank God. "It's on me," he said.

In the car, Jackie propped her face against her hand and rested her elbow against the door. She sipped at the Starbucks cup in silence. Nick gave her a few more minutes to cool down.

"Jackie."

She didn't look at him. "What."

"You have someone you can call to give us any specifics or anything interesting about the second crime scene?"

"I'll call Denny." Jackie punched in his number as they drove away from the house. "Den, it's Jack. Anything interesting on the second crime scene? I'm heading over there with Anderson and Fontaine right now to check it out."

"Hey, Jack," he said. "One bit of interesting evidence turned up, assuming it's verified, which I expect it will be."

"What's that?"

"The bullets used to kill the vics were police issue."

"No shit?"

"Yeah. Not sure they can trace it to a specific gun, but it sure looks that way."

"A rogue cop would be bad news."

"No kidding. Those never end well."

"So, you guys all done over there for now?"

Denny said, "Pretty much. I don't think anyone is there if you're just going to look around. You got permission for this?"

"John said we could check it out."

"What are you up to, Jack?" His voice was wary.

"Quit worrying, Den. We actually have permission to investigate the scene. I'm taking Anderson and Fontaine over to check for possible supernatural involvement."

"Ah. All right then. Have fun with that. Give my regards to Casper."

"I'll make sure to give him your address. Later, Den." She cut off his laughter and put the phone away. "Does John know why we're doing this?"

"Yes."

"Are we heading into something dangerous?"

"Not likely," he said. "I wanted you to be able to practice some, to see if you can replicate what happened this morning. It's important to find out what your limitations are, Jackie, where the boundaries lie. What exactly you are capable of."

"How the fuck would I know?"

"Exactly. How could you possibly know, without testing yourself?" Nick reached over and laid his hand on Jackie's shoulder. It was little comfort, but he could see beneath that thin veil of annoyance that Jackie was afraid of what was going on. "We'll be with you every step of the way on this, Jackie. There is very little actual knowledge on this kind of thing, so we're kind of winging it." He wasn't about to tell her that she might be unique in the world, as the only living being to cross over to the dead side and return. Vampires didn't exactly count as a living being, not entirely anyway.

"Sorry if your words don't comfort me, Nick. I'd

rather know nothing about it, actually. But I guess I get to whether I want it or not."

If not for me dragging you over there, you might not be in this predicament. Nick gripped the steering wheel a little tighter and kept driving. "I had to save you," he said, his voice barely discernible above the traffic. "I had no choice."

Jackie finally looked at him. "What? Save me from . . . oh! Christ, Nick. I wasn't blaming you. You did what you had to in order to save my life. You didn't know taking me there would have this effect. I'm just pissed that it did. If I thought going back would reverse it, I'd be sorely tempted to have you drag my ass back." She gave him a wry smile. "Almost. I have thanked you for saving my life, haven't I?"

"I believe so, yes," he said, failing to keep himself from chuckling. "I may have one last request of you to make us even."

She eyed him warily. "Not going to take advantage of a drunk girl are you, Sheriff?"

"I could if you prefer," he said. "That's not what I was going to ask for, but if you're offering up something different?"

"Not happening, not now," she said and then winced at her words. "That sounded far harsher than I meant it. I just meant, I'm not . . . fuck. Never mind. What were you going to ask?" She turned and smiled, charming even if it was fake.

"As Nicholas Anderson the philanthropist, I am sometimes asked to give a speech in dedication to something I've donated a sum of money to," he said. He was already picturing Jackie on his arm, walking among the crowd. It was difficult picturing her in a dress and makeup. A look, he decided, that he would very much like to see on her.

"I know," she answered. "I've seen some of the press clippings."

"I have one coming up in a few days." He turned and stared at Jackie with his best, bright-eyed gaze. No influence, just a hopeful, politely imploring look. "I'd like it if you came with me, as my date."

"This sounds like a formal sort of thing, Nick. I'm not really into that stuff."

"It is, but Shelby would help you get something for it if you don't have anything formal to wear. She's very good with clothing, whereas I'd be pleased if you came in jeans and a sweatshirt." *Though you sell yourself short, Ms. Rutledge. You'd be stunning in a strapless dress, and I believe I'd pay money to see you wearing heels. Just once.*

Jackie laughed. "So would I. Do you need an answer now?"

"No," he said. "A couple days. I'll drag Cynthia to it if you can't go, but I would like to take you." He smiled at the look she gave him. She still was having a difficult time with him being interested in her. No pressure though. He had all the time in the world.

The second crime scene took them into a far harsher part of the city, where the overcast skies felt inclined to reach down and mar everything with their bleak and ashen, ever-changing claws. House and yard maintenance did not appear to be a high priority on most resident's lists. Fortunately it was dark and drizzling, so most of the children were off the streets. Nosy kids at a crime scene could be the worst to deal with.

Nick pulled his car into the cracked driveway, two crumbling paths of cement that led to the back of the house and a single car garage with a caved-in door. Shelby parked her Mini at the curb. Rusting, chain-link fence separated them from a backyard that looked surprisingly well kept. A row of azaleas ran along the fence to the back corner of the garage. The lawn was thick and even, looking recently mowed. A grill stood covered on a wooden deck coming off of the back door. Someone wanted a small place of optimism in a very pessimistic neighborhood.

"You want to wait here while I check things out first?" Nick watched her, his hand gripping the door handle.

"No," she said, her mouth turning defiant. "I'm fine. Is there anything I should do if I hear or feel something?"

"Just tell me if you do," Nick said. "Likely it'll be the cold first. Kind of like—"

"I know what it's like. No need to remind me." She opened the door and quickly exited the car, slamming the door behind her.

Careful here, Sheriff. Walking among the lingering dead was habit for him, but for Jackie it was certainly a startling and frightening experience. Seeing them on the other side was one thing. It was over there, away from reality. But on this side, Nick knew full well how that felt. The constant reminder of death had a very unnerving effect. He would attempt to warn Jackie, but she might just as easily sense something at the same time or before him even. No two people's psychic abilities were the same.

Nick opened and stepped through the gate leading to the back porch. He could already feel the faint tug from whomever had died inside. Jackie stood at the base of the porch, seemingly unaware. He pulled out a small box from his coat pocket. She watched with curiosity until she realized what he had.

"Do I want to know where you learned how to use those?"

He smirked. "Taught myself. Not hard really. Just takes a deft touch." Pulling out the correct set, Nick made quick work of the lock. "I didn't want to wait for one of your coworkers to arrange to have the door unlocked." She watched him with a wide, glassy stare, hands crossed tightly over her chest. "You as cold as you look, Jackie?" But it wasn't the cold, at least not the sort made by temperature.

Her gaze snapped back and she sucked in her breath. "What?"

Shelby, who had walked up from the street, stopped behind Jackie. "Can feel it, can't you?"

Jackie looked at each of them and then nodded. Nick said, "Thought so. We're close to whomever it was."

"*Was* is good, long as they're not here. Just hurry it along," she said. "I don't want nosy neighbors wondering why the feds have to break into a crime scene."

The lock clicked before he had even turned back. "Wait here, OK? I don't want any ghostly surprises."

Nick stepped inside. The screen shut behind him but he left the door open. He was in a small utility room with a stacked washer and dryer. A pair of poles mounted across the other interior wall still had freshly washed clothes hung upon them. He found the switch just inside the door and flipped on the light. One door opened on the right, going to the kitchen. Beyond it, he could smell the lingering scent of bleach and household cleaner. Stepping onto the white, speckled linoleum floor, Nick could understand why nobody was staying in the house. The back corner of the kitchen was a surreal painting of blood spatter. Someone at least had cleaned up the vast pool on the floor, though he could still see faint traces of where it had been.

"It's right here by the door." He turned on the harsh, overhead light. "Come on in."

He could hear Jackie muttering under her breath. "Sure. Let me put on my special ghost gloves first."

He poked his head out the kitchen door. "It's safe. Just some blood spatter that didn't get cleaned up. No active spirits around right now."

Jackie opened the screen door, gave a cursory glance at the washed clothing, and stepped up by Nick. "Will they pop in unannounced?"

He had opened the screen for her when she stepped up, and Jackie brushed passed him into the kitchen.

"Not likely," he said.

"You aren't inspiring my confidence, Nick."

"We can deal with whatever may show up. Don't worry."

"Yeah, this is me not worrying here." She stared down at the faint traces of outline from the pool of blood that must have been four feet across. "Remind me never to give Laurel shit about getting spooked again."

Shelby stepped by them, chuckling. "I'm going to check the rest of the house. Be right back."

"Feeling anything beyond the spiritual residue?" Nick asked.

Jackie looked up from the bloodstained floor. "The what?"

"That sense of Deadworld you feel now is basically the leftovers of the ghost's presence here. It's residue of the dead, you might say."

"Lovely." Jackie closed her eyes. Nick watched her trying to take deep breaths, but there was a slight, nervous stutter in her chest. Her hands thrust deep into her pockets. "I'm getting nothing." Nick simply nodded once. It would be some time before her nerves were out of the way. She stared at the dried droplets of blood against the door leading down to the basement. If she was willing, blood might do the trick again.

"This generally works better if the victim is here. It's a more direct connection. Whatever was here had very negative energy though, but I'm not getting much beyond that," he said.

Jackie stepped over to the basement door and squatted down on the balls of her feet. Nick smiled down at the finger that hovered in the space between with the slightest tremble. She glanced back at him with a worried little furrow between her eyes. "I touched blood the last time, but I could hear the baby before that."

"Likely because it still lingered at the scene. The blood allowed you to turn up the volume, so to speak."

"Does it always work like that?"

"I find there are no absolutes," Nick replied, "with the living or the dead. All you can do is try and see. We'll go from there."

Jackie laid her hand down flat on the door, covering some of the blood spatter. A moment later her body went rigid, frozen in place, eyes wide, staring at nothing. Nick could feel the surge coming through from the other side, a wash of energy flooding back through the doorway that had been closed for several hours now, but at the touch of her finger had sprung open. No effort at all. Astonishing. She cried out, stumbling away from the door.

Nick stepped forward, using his leg to block her backward motion and scooped his arms down around her waist. Something not remotely close to surprise or fear boiled up out of her throat.

"Jackie!"

"I . . . will . . . kill you!"

She turned in his grasp, and Nick was so startled

by the twisted snarl that warped her mouth and pulled the lines of her face into something he could have scarcely imagined, that he did little more than take a stunned half-step backward. Consequently, his reactions were all too humanly slow and the swinging roundhouse from her small, but effective fist caught him square in the mouth.

Nick immediately tasted blood. She had got him good, and she was getting ready to come after him with more.

"Nick? What's going on?" Shelby stopped before him, having run back from the front of the house at Jackie's screaming proclamation.

"Jackie!" He grabbed her by the shoulders and gave her a firm shake, but she reached over to clamp down on his hand with her mouth and forced him to let go. The force of whomever had been here was still quite strong and Jackie had soaked it up like a sponge. He had little choice now but to either bind her up until it faded or snap her out of it. Nick, having always found that directness paid off in the long run, brought his hand around and slapped Jackie across the side of the face.

She yelled in pain and Nick pulled her small body against him, wrapping her up in a big, bear hug. "Jackie? You with me?"

The tension washed out of her in a rush. She sagged against his chest, legs barely able to hold her upright. "Nick? Holy shit! What happened? I touched the wall, and now you're crushing me in your arms."

He eased Jackie back on to her feet. "Sorry. I had to keep you from decking me again."

"What?" She turned, looking up at him in wide-eyed disbelief. A tentative finger reached up to his mouth but didn't quite touch, before she withdrew it, followed by a sharp inhalation of breath. "Shit. I did that?"

"Yes." He smiled, splitting his lip open once more and wincing. "Can't say I expected that, or the 'You will die' sentiments either."

"I did not say that."

Shelby, who now stood next to them, took Jackie's face in her hands and looked into her eyes briefly. "I heard you, hon. You were pretty pissed."

Nick realized he should have been looking for any remaining signs of lingering possession, but the fact it had happened at all still was boggling his mind. "It's OK. I've heard far worse."

Jackie glanced over at the dried spatter on the door. Her body began to tremble. "But I didn't say that. I know I didn't. I'd remember saying something like that."

Nick gripped her by the shoulders and turned her around. She had the wide-eyed look of a child on the verge of tears, realizing they're in trouble for something they didn't even know they had done. "Jackie, look at me. You tapped into the energy left by whoever was here. They were pretty angry. It overwhelmed your senses and you spoke through that emotion. I know it wasn't you, but the words did come out of your mouth."

"But . . . but I don't remember," she said helplessly. Her shoulders sagged. She kept darting her gaze back and forth between them, looking for some kind of reassurance that neither of them had to give. Not the sort she wanted anyway.

"I know," he said, trying to sound soothing. "No harm done, though I'd say we've just confirmed that your connection to Deadworld is still quite strong."

"No." She shook her head. "God, no. This isn't happening, not to me."

Shelby laid a soft hand upon her shoulder. "Jackie, it's all right—"

"No!" Jackie pushed herself away and reached for the back door. "I've got to get out of here."

"Jackie," Nick pleaded. "Shit."

The cold air was a relief after the thick, oppressive heat of the house. Jackie ran to the Porsche, flopping down in the seat and slamming the door shut. A moment later, Nick climbed behind the wheel.

"I can't be here right now." Her breath came in ragged gasps. She was close to hyperventilating.

"Deep breaths, Jackie," Nick said, laying a hand upon her knee. "Slow, deep breaths."

She filled her lungs and then let it out in a rush. "No. Just need to get the hell away from here."

Nick nodded. *Fair enough.* It had been a long time, but he could still recall those initial days of terror when he realized what he could do.

Jackie huddled against the door, her head resting against the window. Her voice, quiet and distant, sounded almost like a child. "I never escaped from Deadworld," she said. "We came back, but I never got away."

Chapter 10

Jackie slammed the apartment door behind her, leaning against it as though someone might try to push their way in. Who knew? Maybe whatever that thing was that had usurped her brain and played puppetry with her body had followed them home. Could ghosts move around at will? Drake had seemed to pop back and forth as it suited him, but he hadn't actually been a ghost either. Bickerstaff waltzed up and rubbed himself on Jackie's ankle and she nearly kicked at him in surprise.

"Bickers! Christ. You nut. Can't you see Mommy is freaking out here?" She picked him up, letting him rub his face against hers. The act was instantly soothing. Nothing like a little unconditional love to calm a racing heart. "You don't care if I'm turning into a big, ol' freakish joke, do you, baby?"

Jackie made a beeline for the bathroom, kicking off her shoes along the way. She needed to get the grime of death off her. It was not the usual sort of grime that came from poking and prodding around dead bodies. She could be hip-deep in blood and entrails and not lose her lunch, but this had been different. The death had been inside her somehow, like a poisonous gas that had invaded every cell of her body. Perhaps there could be no getting rid of it once it had entered, fused to one's very DNA.

With the shower spraying the tiled wall with pure hot water, Jackie gave it a few minutes to build up steam before stepping in. She stared at her face in the mirror, grown sharper the past couple of weeks from lack of eating. Her eyes, once proudly intense, looked weary and, dare she think, fearful? If you looked deep enough could you see the dead in her eyes, too?

The steam began to obscure her image and Jackie gladly turned away. She stepped into the shower to breathe deeply of the warm mist, and hoped maybe some of that death that had somehow invaded her earlier might find its way out through her pores. She turned off the water thirty-odd minutes later when she had reached the limits of her water heater. Her muscles had finally begun to relax and the steam did appear to have cleansed some of the bitter aftertaste of death from her body. Now it was time for a glass of wine, maybe two, and her piano. She needed the piano tonight.

Jackie needed some worry-free solace and something capable of driving away the events of the day. That meant either drink or play and Jackie didn't feel so depressed at the moment to chose oblivion over Brahms. Shuffling out in pajama bottoms, socks, and a T-shirt, Jackie opened a bottle of pinot noir, poured a very full glass, and turned on the TV to a blue screen. After turning off the rest of the lights Jackie sat down at the bench. As though the blue lighting were a cue, Bickerstaff sprang up on top of the piano and peered down at her with his lazy gaze.

One huge gulp to warm her belly, and Jackie set her fingers upon the keys to do as they wanted. More often than not, she would pick out snippets of songs and refrains, music with repeating melodies and rolling scales. When stressed, her mind craved hypnotic rhythms, never-ending roads that her mind could wander on and get lost, away from all things.

Exactly nine whole minutes into her playing, just when her brain had taken its first steps out onto that blissful, solitary road, someone knocked at her door. Three soft raps. Jackie paused and held her breath. Either Mr. Chen in the apartment behind her was coming to complain, or Mrs. Galloway had let some fucking solicitor in through the bottom door again.

"Go away," she whispered. "I'm not here."

Three soft raps again upon her door. "Jackie? Are you there?"

The voice was disturbingly familiar. She should know it, so familiar in fact, Jackie knew she was just spacing on who it was.

"Jackie? Please, just a few moments of your time."

Her breath sucked in so quickly she coughed and nearly gagged on her lungs. Tillie! Oh-my-fucking-God Dr. Erikson. Jackie started to scramble off of the bench, and then abruptly realized that her apartment was in damn fine condition for visitors. There wasn't a thing to pick up. One could even say a normal person lived in this apartment. One who didn't hear screaming ghost babies or blackout and sucker-punch people. She reached over and turned on the floor lamp by the piano and walked to the door.

"Dr. Erikson? It's almost ten." She opened the door, leaving the chain guard on. It was indeed Tillie, dressed down in jeans and a smartly fitted cashmere sweater. "Why are you here?"

"Because John told me he had given permission for you to come back to a case on a limited basis. He would not give me a clear answer on your exact status and you didn't return my calls, so I came to see for myself."

She sounded polite. To most, her voice might appear calm and unruffled, but Jackie knew without a doubt she was more than a little upset. That hard sparkle in her eyes might even indicate furious. Reluctant, Jackie unlatched her door and stepped aside.

"I'm not really actively investigating this case," she said, hoping the excuse would waylay her. "I'm just acting as liaison to the Special Investigations team. They think something supernatural might be involved on this case."

"Thank you," she said with a smile and crossed the threshold, a sight Jackie could not have imagined in a million years. Matilda Erikson standing in her home. The world really was conspiring against her.

"Oh, for goodness sake, Jackie. Quit looking at me like that. I'm not upset with you. John is the one who should know better. He didn't even consult me beforehand."

"Would you have said yes?"

Tillie gave a tiny, noncommittal shrug with one shoulder. "The answer is that it always depends, and since I know nothing of his reasoning, I can say that I honestly don't know. Why don't you tell me?"

Jackie found herself grasping for answers. Her mind had begun to drift and now the gears were slipping and clunking, trying to find their rhythm once again. "Um, I'm not sure exactly. Does it really matter?"

Her head tilted at Jackie, an exasperated look that required no words. "May we sit down?"

Do we have to? I really don't want to tell you a damn thing, Tillie. I know I should, but I don't. "Sure. You want something to drink? I don't have tea."

She gave Jackie a faint, amused smile. "I'm fine." She stepped into the living room proper and walked up to the piano. "So this is the famous piano."

"I hardly think so," Jackie said with a snort. "I bought it from a piano store like thousands of other people do."

"It was one of Laurel's favorite things," she said. "To her, it was famous." Her voice had a lilt of sadness to it that brought a lump into Jackie's throat. She really hoped this would not be some sort of sentimental stroll down memory lane. She'd be sobbing in no time for sure. Bickerstaff stared at her from atop, looking decidedly lofty and pensive. "And is this the glorious Mr. Bickerstaff?" She walked up and held out her hand, which Bickerstaff leaned forward to smell and then rub his face against. Jackie had half hoped he would bolt for the bedroom, terrified to death of her. Traitor.

"He apparently believes you're safe," Jackie said.

"Cats are finicky creatures."

Jackie walked around and turned off the television before sitting down in the chair in the corner. Tillie seated herself on the couch, keeping her posture rather straight. This would not be a kicking back with a beer sort of chat. She wondered how much Tillie really knew of her life. How much had Laurel told her? Had every page in her life's book been read through and analyzed, tsk-tsked and laughed over for the past five years? Likely she knew a lot more than Jackie wanted her to know. Hiding out in the shadows was very difficult when the other knew just where to shine the light.

"It's a nice apartment, Jackie. About what I expected, I think."

"Did Laur draw you floor plans?" When Tillie just stared at her with raised eyebrows, Jackie finally slumped back in her chair. "Sorry. This is very disconcerting, having you here in my living room. I can assure you, though, I'm perfectly . . . OK, not perfectly, but I'm doing much better and I feel confident I can do the small job that I've been given."

"You know, dear," she said and folded her hands in her lap, "you are one of the few agents I've ever worked with who has actually made more effort to get back to work than to get out of it."

"Tillie, you know this is no vacation for me. I'm tired of brooding. Being around the action, even if I'm not directly in it, will help keep my mind off things."

"So, why do Mr. Anderson and Ms. Fontaine need a liaison with the murder unit? Can't they just contact one of the team members on this case?"

"I think it's just because I'm familiar with what they do and how they do it and some of the team aren't quite so . . . open-minded I guess you'd say."

"All of them?"

"I don't know," Jackie said, throwing up her hands. "I haven't talked to them all. Mr. Anderson asked John if I could assist them in coordinating with the team on this case until they determined the extent of paranormal involvement."

"The request came from Mr. Anderson, not you?"

"Yes. He called John about it because he said there was the possibility of a very pissed-off spirit being involved."

"Is there?"

"Maybe. It looks like there's something going on, but it's difficult to tell."

"I see."

Her eyes wandered very carefully over Jackie. She felt sure the woman was likely a cyborg from some secret government lab sent to make sure they had no psychos in their midst. Tillie was probably measuring her blood pressure as they spoke.

"Are you enjoying it?"

"What?"

"The work," she said. "I'd always considered you to be the sort who either wanted to be right in there in the muck or not at all."

"I would prefer to be in there, but as you know, I've not been cleared for it."

"Yes, I know." A corner of her mouth curled up and Jackie could hear the gears grinding away. "So what did you get to do today?"

"Today?" And there goes the ballgame, goddamn it. She's going to know I'm lying or covering or something. "I took Nick and Shelby to the crime scenes to see what they could, you know, sense."

"Anything good?"

"You mean did they sense anything?" Her tongue was turning into a dusty, dry snake, the tail of which was squeezing a quick, unsteady beat around her heart.

One of Tillie's eyes narrowed at Jackie. "Yes, dear. Ghosts. Isn't that what they do?"

"Yes, of course. They did sense ghosts." Her smile felt rubbery and fake.

"How fascinating," she said, and sounded genuinely interested. "Did you get to see any?"

Her voice came out too high and too loud. "Why

would I have seen any ghosts?" And why did this demure, middle-aged woman have to make her feel so defenseless? She was the Yoda of shrinks, all seeing and knowing, and it terrified her beyond words.

Tillie smiled her warm, comforting smile. "If they saw a ghost, I just thought you might have got to see it, too, that's all. I think that would be an amazing encounter."

"You really believe all that you've heard about them?"

Her head tilted, the little curl of her mouth flattening out. Tillie's eyebrows, pristinely plucked, rose into perfect question marks. "You know the answer to that as well as I, Jackie. Of course I believe it. Hadn't I been seeing Laurel for the past five years? You two had a couple of cases that involved supernatural phenomena as I recall. You should—" She cut herself off with a wave of her hand. "Why is this making you so nervous? I thought coming here would make you more comfortable talking to me, but you seem less. Did something happen today?"

"No. No! Nothing happened," Jackie snapped back in a rush. "I mean, other than the ghost stuff. It was kind of creepy, but, you know . . ." She shrugged, feeling like a wilted teenager under cross-examination on the witness stand. It just wasn't fair. Nobody should have this kind of effect on someone. She was the mother from hell. "Fine. I saw a ghost. Happy now?"

Tillie laughed. "Oh, Jackie, my dear girl. You need to quit thinking I'm out to get you. I never have been and I never will be. Period. End of story. If you saw a ghost, then you saw a ghost, and I firmly believe that you did."

She laughed along with Tillie. "Dr. Erikson, I don't

think it'll be possible for you to ever not make me nervous."

Her eyes rolled. "I just have an advantage over you because Laurel has spoken about you so often. That's her perspective, mind you, but I get the benefit of insider information."

"It's cheating."

"Agreed, but I'll take it. Otherwise, with your stubbornness, we'd never get anywhere."

"That's not . . . OK, maybe it's a little bit true, but I'd be far more comfortable if I didn't think you knew everything about me."

"I'm sure there are a great many things I don't know about you, Jackie. As I'm sure there are some things I'm aware of that you would prefer I'm not. All I can tell you is that I will never use it against you. My job, and also my desire, is to see you as a functional, healthy, and hopefully reasonably happy member of the FBI."

Jackie rubbed her face with her hands. "I'm just afraid you'll think I'm crazy and want to throw me in a padded room. I never used to see any ghosts, not until all the Drake shit went down."

"Nearly dying can do that," Tillie said. "It changes your perspective on things."

"Oh," Jackie laughed. "It did a lot more than that, I think."

Tillie sat back in the couch. "Will you tell me? What happened I mean. The report is mostly 'need to know' and at this point I apparently am not on the list."

"Will you promise not to freak out and pull me from this case?"

"Can you keep your nosy little hands out of the case and remain a liaison?"

They stared down one another for about ten seconds until Jackie heaved a sigh. "Yes, I can remain a liaison."

"Very well, but I would like coffee to hear this story. If you don't mind."

"You drink coffee?" Jackie blinked in amazement. "But I thought you were the prim and proper tea lady."

"Tea is for the office, dear. Coffee for the real world."

Jackie got to her feet. "Wow. I may almost like you now."

She made strong coffee, and Tillie drank it, even if it was with a couple teaspoons of sugar. And she told the story, from the point when Laurel died until she decked Nick at the crime scene earlier in the evening. It took her nearly an hour. Jackie kept a careful eye on Tillie, watching every facial expression, every blink of the eye, and every quirk of her mouth. She paused at certain points to give Tillie the opportunity to express incredulity, but Tillie only listened in interested silence, hands folded neatly in her lap. In the end, all she could see was that Tillie had been truly intrigued, fascinated, and horrified by what had happened. Jackie had spoken her piece, ready to jump over and throw Tillie out at the first hint that she thought this whole story was ludicrous. But there wasn't one iota of disbelief. Or she was the best liar Jackie had ever seen.

"And so here we are," Jackie said. "The depressed, wacko, circus freak and her shrink."

"Well," Tillie replied and said nothing else for a few moments. "You're neither a wacko nor a freak, Jackie. Depressed? Yes, though you appear to be handling it reasonably well, all things considered. Honestly, I'm in awe. You realize you've likely done something nobody has ever done before."

"I doubt that," Jackie said. "I'm sure it's happened at some point in the past. We've just never heard about it."

"Unlikely, but fine, almost nobody. You've seen ghosts. You've died and come back. It's . . . it's really quite astonishing, Jackie. I believe I'd have had a nervous breakdown."

"Yeah, well I did and I'm still not all the way back, but being around work, even this little bit makes me feel a bit more normal, Tillie. I need it."

"Not too much though," she said. "And if you miss seeing me because of it, that shall be the last day of work you see until I say you come back."

"Christ. You big meanie. I'll come in. I swear, every week. If Laur can see you for five years, I can handle a few weeks."

Tillie's eyes widened and her head tilted a few degrees. "A few weeks? Do you honestly feel you can get all of this sorted out in a few weeks?"

Jackie had no snotty rejoinder for the truth. "How long do you think? Reasonably, I mean, to help sort through my, um, issues."

She raised her hands up, unknowing. "A few months? A few years? It's up to you, Jackie. How long will it take for you to be able to speak about your mother to me without wanting to punch me in the face?"

A tide of heat washed up through her face. "I said I was sorry about that. It's just . . . you know what all my buttons are. It's really not fair."

Tillie smiled and chuckled quietly. "No, it's not, but I'm not paid to play fair, dear. I get paid to help people figure things out and if that means pushing your buttons, then that's what I shall do."

"Deep down, you really are an evil witch, aren't you?"

"Only for you, Jackie. I derive great pleasure in your endless torments."

"I figured as much." Jackie let out a deep breath. "I'll try. Really. I know I've got some shit to deal with."

"I won't make you talk about anything," she replied. "If it's your mother, that's fine. If it's someone else, that's fine too. I just want you to be willing to face some of these things directly. It's time you quit running from your life, Jackie. You can handle these things. I promise."

"Yes, Aunt Tillie."

"I'm serious, Jackie."

"I know you are," Jackie replied. "This talk just makes me nervous and the more nervous I am, the snarkier I get."

"There's no rush. We aren't on a timetable. We'll just talk and see what happens, but you have to be willing to really talk to me. Can you do that?"

"If you don't think I'm crazy already, then I guess I can talk about anything." Or so she hoped. Some things had been buried for so long and so deep, she wasn't even sure she knew where to dig.

"Good." Tillie clapped her hands together and Jackie jumped. "Now then, one last thing. A small favor."

"What?" She prayed for something normal.

"Play a song for me. Anything, but I'd like to hear you play just once."

"I don't really play for other people," she said.

"Laurel spoke of it so often," she said. "I would so love to hear you play something. Five minutes, Jackie. That's all I want."

"I'm not that good," Jackie replied. "Really. It wouldn't be a big deal." She watched Tillie's face sag with each word. Laurel and Tillie had made a very close bond over the years. Jackie had just never realized how much so until recently. And guilt was a wonderful motivator. Nothing like cursing out your shrink to get you doing stuff you really didn't want to do. "OK, fine. One song."

Tillie got up with a little bounce in her step. "Oh, good! Thank you, Jackie. I know it's a lot to ask."

"I should get a free pass card or something for this," she said, shaking her head. She walked over to her piano bench and sat down.

"That's fine," Tillie answered. "Give me five minutes and you get one free call-off, no questions asked."

"You want to come over for dinner every Saturday?"

"Oh, funny girl." She smiled and leaned against the piano, much like Laurel used to do on Saturday nights when they would stay up late and bullshit or talk cases and drink wine. "Let's go with this once and see what happens."

"Any requests?"

She shrugged. "Just play something Laurel liked. I don't care what. This is just a pleasant reminder of her for me."

Jackie took in the soft smile and her now glassy-eyed gaze and realized that Tillie really did love Laurel in that caretaker, mother-daughter sort of way. She thought for a long moment, trying to pick out a favorite that she felt she knew well enough to not sound like a hack. Jackie dramatically flexed her fingers together until a knuckle cracked. "OK, here goes. Do you listen to classical music?"

"Some, yes."

"Then you will likely recognize this one if I don't butcher it all to hell and back."

She took a deep breath and let it out slowly before she began, her fingers playing Beethoven's *Ode to Joy.*

She was pretty sure Laur had only liked it because of the title and the fact it had been in the Gary Oldman movie about the composer. Laurel's tastes though, tended more toward New Agey stuff and classic crooner tunes. She liked this piece, however. The title fit the gradual building of tones to the triumphant, glorious climax. Joy could hit you that way, sneaking up until it suddenly overwhelmed.

The nerves bled away into the notes after the first thirty seconds and she forgot that Tillie was there, chin propped on her hands, eyes closed. *This one is for you, Laur, an* Ode to Joy, *because I think you brought it to everyone you met.* Jackie tried to recall some of those joyous moments she had experienced with Laurel, from graduating, to the first day on the job, to breaking their first case. She caught the sound of Tillie sniffling, which brought tears to her own eyes, and the sense of Laurel was there too, just beyond the veil. She was near and listening in, and then tears began to fall upon the keys while she played.

After a few minutes, a hand came down lightly upon her shoulder. "Thank you, Jackie." The hand wiped at the tears on her cheeks. "You can stop now. That was lovely. Really and truly lovely, but I shall soak my shirt if we keep going."

Jackie wiped at her eyes with the back of her hand. "Sorry. I didn't—"

"Oh, Lord no, dear. No apologies." She sat down on the bench beside Jackie. "Good for us both." She smiled. "Is a hug all right with you? We're not on the clock."

She shrugged a shoulder and didn't say anything, which they both took as a yes. In the middle of it, when Jackie took a moment to breathe in the soft fragrance of Tillie's perfume and the warm, strength of those arms embracing her, a knock came at the door. She reflexively pulled away. "Damn it! Who could that be?"

Three more soft knocks. "Jackie? It's Nick."

Her heart froze for a moment. She glanced back at Tillie, now with a tissue in her hand dabbing at her eyes. "Ah, hell." she muttered and unlatched the door. "Something out there truly hates me."

Chapter 11

"Hey, Nick. Why are you back without calling? Again."

"Sorry, Jackie." He gave her a pained smile. "I . . . are you OK?" His hand rose up between them and then stopped, unsure if he had a right to continue. "You look up—"

"Mr. Anderson, I presume?" Tillie stepped into the entry. "I thought I heard your name." Jackie saw the barely concealed smile on her lips and her shoulders slumped. Lovely, just lovely. "Did you have a previous engagement, Jackie? I didn't mean to interrupt."

"No, Tillie. It's fine. Nick just came by for . . . what exactly?"

"I just had a few things I wished to discuss about . . . well, earlier today."

Jackie waved a hand at him and marched back into the living room. "She knows, Nick. I told her the whole thing."

He nodded. "Ah. I see." He put out his hand to Tillie. "And you must be Dr. Erikson. Jackie has mentioned you."

"And I'm not nearly as evil as she claims," Tillie

said and shook his hand with a nervous laugh. "So, you're the vampire, as it were."

"I am indeed, ma'am." He grasped her hand and glanced over at Jackie who was back on the piano bench. "Am I interrupting an appointment?"

"No, no. Just a friendly chat. I wanted to see how she was doing being back on a case. You'll keep a careful eye on her, won't you?"

Jackie palm-slapped her forehead. "Tillie! Holy crap. That's not his job."

Tillie stepped up close to Nick, staring him directly in the face. "Goodness." She reached up with both hands and held his face. "Look at those eyes! I think, my dear, that it is his job." She came down off her toes and gave one of Nick's cheeks a soft pat. "Yes, I think so."

"Dr. Erikson," Jackie said, exasperated, "what are you talking about?"

"Nothing, Jackie. It's nothing." She beamed at both of them. "I'll let you two discuss whatever it is you need to. Jackie, my dear, that was so lovely, I can't even say. Thank you." She nodded at Nick. "And Mr. Anderson, I do hope we get to speak at some point in the future. I would be very interested to talk about things."

He gave her a sardonic grin. "I'm sure, Dr. Erikson. Perhaps soon."

Tillie walked out, smiling back over her shoulder at Jackie as she closed the door. Jackie shook her head in disbelief. "Un-fucking-believeable." Now she would have Tillie to deal with regarding Nick. "What is it, Nick? Come in. Sit down. Have a beer. Relax and stay awhile."

"I apologize. I should have called."

"Why didn't you?"

"Because, you don't answer your phone," Nick said. "And I wanted to be sure I talked to you tonight about doing any more forays into the supernatural."

"You couldn't just leave a message?"

"About this? No," he said, walking through the living room and toward the kitchen. "It's too important to leave to the whims of technology."

Jackie huffed. "Whatever, Nick. I would have got my messages by morning."

"That was a marvelous 'Ode to Joy' by the way."

The warm flush ran right by her annoyance and heated her face. "Quit changing the subject. Why didn't you just call and save the hassle of coming all the way back over here."

Nick pulled out the espresso cup from a drawer, the grounds from the freezer, and filled a cup with water for the machine. "I don't find it a hassle to come over, nor is it out of my way. I like being here."

Jackie swallowed what felt like a mouthful of dust. It wasn't so much the words but how he had said it, earnest and sincere. Why? When he had that glorious expanse of house out in the country with its sprawling stone fireplace and endless books and the steam bath that melted you down into a gooey puddle.

She propped her elbow on the piano and laid her cheek against her hand. "I just wish you'd called, that's all."

"Because of Dr. Erikson?"

"Yes, because of Dr. Erikson," Jackie snapped. "It'll be the first thing she mentions when I see her next week. So, thanks for that. You and I are not on my list of things to chat about with my shrink."

The espresso machine began to chug under the pressure of the steam and Nick got a carton of milk from the fridge. "Good to know we haven't reached the therapy level yet."

Jackie sighed. "I wouldn't go that far. Our . . . um, friendship hasn't exactly played out like a normal relationship."

"Is that a bad thing?" He turned on the steam and began to froth milk. "You can't exactly say that things have been boring."

"Given the option, I'd take boring over this supernatural crap any day. A plain old normal relationship, thank you very much."

Nick spooned off some foam into the top of a cup. "I understand completely," he said in a far quieter voice. He brought her the cup and sat down on the piano bench, his thigh an inch or two from hers.

Jackie took the warm cup into her hands. "I didn't really ask . . . thanks." She gave Nick a wistful smile and took a sip of the coffee. The man was a genius with an espresso machine.

"I've been dealing with the dead for a very long time, Jackie. It's not easy."

She nodded through another sip of coffee, licking the foam off her lips. "I'm never going to be rid of this, am I?"

He laid his hand on her thigh, the large spread of his fingers reaching nearly from one side of the bench to the other. "No, you won't, which is why you have to be very careful here and try not to do anything without Shelby or me. You've got something . . . I'm not even sure what it is yet, but it's a remarkable ability. It's also potentially very dangerous. Promise me you will be careful with this until we understand it better."

"Nick, I'm a very capable FBI—"

"Promise me." The hand squeezed lightly around her leg. "I mean it."

Some small part of her found the concern sweet, but the rest took offense. "I know how to take care of myself," she said.

"Can't say I'm one to talk about caring for one's own life," he said.

"At least we're not boring."

He gave Jackie that half-cocked grin, the right corner of his mouth curled up which exaggerated the tiny crow's feet around the eye. At that moment, for that second at least, she wanted to kiss him.

His breath huffed out the barest laugh. "Heaven forbid we were ever—"

Jackie reached out with her free hand and cupped his cheek, turning that smirk toward her. The bright, bottomless eyes glowed down at her with something other than laughter. And while her nerve held on to that moment, where she forgot the age and the blood and the dead, Jackie leaned up and kissed Nick, sliding her hand around to the back of his head. The hand upon her leg squeezed more firmly, sending warmth to areas not touched by coffee.

She inhaled sharply, her grip on his head relaxing until his teeth nipped down on her lip, holding her to him, not letting her pull away. Jackie relaxed into it once again, tongue slipping over and around his. Nick's mouth tasted of wine and coffee, disconcertingly cool to the touch, but she didn't care. He liked it here, wanted to be here, and it gave Jackie's heart a flutter of relief to know it really was because of her, even if she still did not understand why. For now, the kiss was enough.

"Thanks for being worried," she said. "And for the coffee."

The hand withdrew from her leg, where Jackie could feel the imprints of his fingers linger for several seconds after. "Welcome. So, it's a promise?"

"I promise to be careful, Nick. As much as I know how anyway."

He laughed. "Guess I can't ask for much more than that."

He seemed pleased and Jackie relaxed. Not a stupid move after all. Maybe she would get the hang of this stuff. Jackie set the coffee down and tucked her hands between her legs to keep them from shaking. She might have been sixteen the last time that happened, and maybe not even then. The thought of asking Nick to stay danced like a fleeting whisper through her head, tantalizing but still out of range. One step at a time. Pour a few drinks down her throat and you could skip all of the steps, but this was real, clearheaded stuff, and Jackie found herself suffering a bad case of nerves over it. A simple kiss. God forbid what would happen if she crawled into bed with him. Jackie smiled, sipped her coffee, and avoided catching Nick's direct gaze.

"You look tired," he said. "Touching the other side can drain you more than you'd think."

"More stressed-out than tired. I don't like this, Nick. It's scary, and I don't scare very easily."

"I know. Go lay down on the sofa." When she made no move, he added, "Please."

Any number of things could happen on a sofa. "For what?"

"Just go. Your *Ode to Joy* has me in the mood to play, and perhaps it will help you relax. If you fall asleep, I'll just let myself out."

Piano. Ah, well, that she could handle. No trembling required. She did as he asked and arranged the throw pillows for her head. One more long draft from her cup and Jackie set it on the coffee table. Nick began with a simple, quiet melody, so soft she could barely hear it. The tune had strength in it though, and it brought to mind the courageous solitude of those who endured and climbed above hardship to eventually reach once unattainable goals. Of a young girl, brought low by betrayal and death only to fight her way back to reach the once far-away goal of justice-bringer.

In the back of her floating, drifting mind, Jackie had the notion that Nick was doing a bit more than just playing the piano, that he had put a little more force behind those notes than just his fingers. She was beyond the point of caring, however. Jackie was riding across the sky on billowy clouds, sailing toward a full moon that beamed down upon her with its cool, tranquil glow.

Chapter 12

Two hours out of Chicago and the cries of her baby boy rang like tornado siren in her head. They had not faded. They never would. Her baby boy would be screaming for justice for all eternity, because the one who should have protected him was as dead as he was. The living had failed as well, incompetent and uncaring for a woman who had tried to do right only to experience a horrible wrong for all of her efforts. The living were not concerned with justice, but the dead cared a great deal. It was the only thing that mattered. There was no tomorrow when you were dead, only the moment. And this moment was consumed in a storm of rage and vindication.

I will get you justice, Morgan's voice pleaded.

"Not strung out on Oxycontin, you won't." Rosa glanced up at the face in the rearview mirror, sallow and pale, with red-rimmed eyes, puffy from a lack of sleep. "Look at you! Sorry-assed nigger detective. Chicago's finest! What a crock of shit. Your kid proud of you? Your mama? Fuck you and your justice." She swept the hand across and broke the mirror off its mount, sending it tumbling to the floor. "I'm doing just fine."

Please! If you let me go, I will bring them down. I'll kill them all. I have the resources.

"You're weak and a man whose begging makes me sick. If you're strong enough, then break free and show me justice. But you're no man, Detective Morgan. You're just a fucking addict!"

No, wait! I'm not. I can prove it.

She pushed his voice back until it faded into her boy's plaintive and angry cries. "Not proving nothing with this body, Detective."

The drive heading back into the trees off the county road was not marked with an address. Of course, it didn't matter that every other drive was. One could never give credit to Rennie Vasquez for being brilliant. Charming and vicious perhaps, but the man's brain only had two gears, fight or fuck. She parked the car and noticed that Morgan's hands had a slight tremble to them. She clenched them for a moment and then relaxed. For now, it was gone, but withdrawal was really starting to wear on Morgan's body. Having kicked over the cocaine bucket three years ago, she knew how quitting was only just the beginning.

The rutted gravel drive disappeared beneath a lightless, cloud-covered sky, and the falling October leaves. Fortunately, she had been down here before and knew more or less how it took a gentle curve to the left through the trees to a clearing. The mobile home on the right was storage, and overflow sleeping when they had more than five or six people down here, but the lights were only on in the one on the left.

She absently rubbed at her belly. "You ready for this, little man? Mama is going to cut open Loopy

Lopez for you, so you can watch him bleed out on the ground like the pig that he is."

Somewhere inside, beyond the raging wail, Morgan screamed out in frustration, unable to stop his body from obeying the invader's commands.

Rosa pulled the Glock from its holster. "Shut it, Detective Morgan. I'm just doing your fucking job."

The leather loafers clung to the soggy drive, making soft, slurping noises as Rosa came out from under the trees and marched toward the lit-up mobile home, the Glock dangling with a deceptive casualness from her hand. Laughter bubbled out of a corner window when she came alongside. A woman, whose voice she did not recognize, giggled and then turned to husky desire. The man, however, she knew. It was Loopy, coked up and screwing his brains out. Rosa paused, hand clenched around the pistol's grip, itching to empty the clip into the thin walls, but then gathered herself once again and continued on to the door.

The stairs creaked beneath her feet, but nobody would be hearing much of anything with the television blaring in the living room. She could sense the souls of two more wretched clones in Rennie's drug-addled army, half-dead already. Rosa pulled open the screen door and stepped up to check the door. Locked. This time around, they would not just walk up to answer the door. They didn't come down to this hole expecting visitors.

Rosa held the screen in one hand and aimed the gun at the lock. Morgan's voice cried out from the depths. *Don't do this! You're ruining my life!*

"Already ruined, Detective," she replied and fired at the door, following it quickly with the heel of her shoe.

The splintered door flew open, giving Rosa a

wide-angled view of the kitchen, living, and dining room area. Someone jumped back from the fridge, while another scrambled off of the couch. She recognized him.

"Hello, Miguel," she said, and turned the gun upon him.

"What the fu—" he began, but never finished, when the bullet caught him just above the ear and sent him flipping backward over the couch.

A scream came from down the hall in the bedroom, and Rosa turned toward the sound. In the kitchen, the other guy had pulled a knife from a block on the counter. His screaming charge made it about three steps when Rosa fired again, blowing out the guy's knee. He stumbled to the floor, the knife bouncing off of the linoleum and stopping at Rosa's feet. She reached down and picked it up; it felt a bit small in Morgan's large hands.

"Thanks," she said, and fired off another round, blowing off the left side of the guy's face.

Behind the closed door at the end of the hall came the sounds muffled hysterics and Loopy's harsh swearing, telling the woman to shut up. Rosa did not pause and marched down the dark, wood-paneled hall, kicking open the hollow door with enough force that the lower hinge broke free.

The skewed door interfered with Loopy's lunging attack, and Rosa found herself knocked back into the doorframe, switchblade buried in Morgan's thigh. She brought the butt of the pistol down on Loopy's head and sent him staggering back into the room. It was accompanied by the women's scream and the shattering of glass. She was attempting to crawl out of the window. Even ghost-powered reflexes were not enough to get off a clean shot, and the bullet pierced clean through the woman's calf before she tumbled out to the ground below.

Loopy struggled to get to his feet in front of her; one carefully placed toe beneath the chin took care of that and sent him sprawling back on the bed. Rosa took three quick steps over to the window and saw the screaming woman attempting to limp away through the mud.

"Lie with the devil, you stupid whore," she said, and calmly buried a slug in the woman's back.

On the bed, Loopy groaned, too dazed to get up. Rosa tucked the gun into the back of Morgan's waistband and flipped the butcher knife around for a more secure grip. "How's it going, Loopy? Miss me?"

His over-dilated, glassy eyes tried to blink away the fog of getting coldcocked. "Wha . . . what? Who are you?"

Rosa reached down and clamped Morgan's hand around Loopy's throat. "It's Rosa, you loaded little shit. My baby boy says you can rot in hell."

He clamped his hands on Morgan's powerful arm, vainly trying to free the pressure off of his throat as Rosa continued to squeeze and push his head down into the mattress. There was a sickening crack from his larynx as it gave way to the crushing force of Morgan's hand being driven with supernatural strength. His scream came out as a gurgling cry and changed abruptly to a grunt when Rosa drove the knife down into his groin.

Chapter 13

Jackie rubbed some gel into her hands and scrunched her hair. It was the first time in months that she had made an effort to do anything with it at all. *Wash and wear* was her hairstyle motto. Scrunching was as far as it would go, however. If she wore any makeup, Belgerman would see through her efforts in an instant. A little deodorant, a spray of perfume that Laurel had bought for her birthday three years before and still was only half empty, a swish of mouthwash, and Jackie was good to go.

She studied her face in the mirror over her bathroom sink. Other than the dark circles under her eyes, she didn't look too bad, did she? "You can do this," she told herself. "You're OK."

Nick had called her at 8:30 AM. "Go see Belgerman," he said. "Tell him everything and that you want to be on this case so you can figure this out." She had still been on the couch. Ten hours of dreamless sleep. She would have to kiss him again for that. "And because of Laurel's abilities, he'll be on board for this. Just look confident and don't give him a reason to say no. Call me when things are situated, and I hope you slept well last night." He clicked off before she could reply. The annoyance of the abrupt cutoff got her up out of bed until she realized he had likely done it on purpose. Bastard already knew her better than he should.

She walked back to the bedroom to get dressed and called Nick back. "He'll call you and want to verify this you know."

"I'll sign a contract if needed. I want to figure this out, Jackie. I feel partly responsible for your situation."

"Well don't," she'd told him. Even though part of her blamed him, she knew this wasn't his fault. "And thanks for helping. You don't have to."

"But I want to."

"Damned if I know why."

She could sense him smiling on the other end of the line. "Your hard edges suit me."

Jackie laughed and Nick chuckled along with her. "You're crazy, Nick. You should be running in the other direction as fast as you can."

His mirthful tone subsided. "Sheriffs don't run from anything, Jackie. Besides, I know a good thing when I see it. Call me when Belgerman gives the OK for us to work this."

A good thing. If she was Nick's notion of a good thing, then he had some issues. Jackie pulled on gray denim jeans and a button-down black blouse. For a moment she pondered digging the dress flats out of their box in the closet, but then went ahead with her boots. After toasting a bagel and feeding Bickerstaff, she was ready to head in.

Normal soon went out the window when Jackie pulled through a Starbucks to get a coffee. She had almost ordered a tea to go with the coffee. The empty seat beside her suddenly became a vast hole. She was going into work alone. The morning banter was gone. Laurel's morning review of the day's activities was no more. And thanks to Jackie's big, fat mouth, who knew when she would be seeing Laurel again.

The silence grew louder with each passing mile. By the time she pulled into her parking space, the meager confidence she had built up was gone. Belgerman would say no. He could be extremely hardheaded about something when he set his mind to it. He would see her desperation and know she wasn't ready for this. Look what had happened the last time he gave in and let her stay on the case. He had nearly lost two agents instead of one. No way would he risk it on the freaky paranormal shit again, not with a basket case of an agent who had inexplicably gained psychic abilities.

Jackie continued the negative thought process on the elevator ride up and was muttering to herself by the time she stepped out on her floor. She took a deep breath. The smells were the same. The sounds were familiar. The row of cubicles and doors opening into conference rooms all looked the same, yet it all felt different. Jackie got the sickening feeling in her gut that she no longer belonged.

Down the aisle a dark-haired head poked around a cubicle wall. A smooth, blue-eyed face looked her way and Jackie's stomach seized for one brief second. The person was seated in Laurel's space.

"Hey," he said. "You look lost. Can I help you with something?"

Jackie took a step forward and then stopped. "What are . . . who the hell are you?"

His eyes narrowed as he studied her. "McManus. You Agent Rutledge by chance?"

The air in the room began to evaporate. Why was

he here? He shouldn't be here already. Couldn't. "Who told you to take that desk?"

"The desk?" He looked confused, looking back as though he might be missing something. "They told me to take it when I came in earlier. You're Agent Rutledge, aren't you?"

"They? What they?" She refused the urge to run up and yank him out of the chair. "That isn't your fucking desk."

"Whoa, hold on," he said and stood up. McManus walked toward her, the easy smile on his face dissipating with each step. He stopped a few feet away. "You're Rutledge, right? Isn't that your desk next to mine? It's my understanding that you're my new partner."

They were doing this to her on purpose. Had to be. Didn't want to even give her a chance to get things situated and put right. Jackie stared at his proffered hand like it was on fire, then at the face now creased with concern. She ignored him and walked past. "That's not your desk."

Jackie stopped at Laurel's cubicle. McManus's jacket lay draped over the back of her chair. A picture of a preteen girl sat in a silver *I Love Dad* frame next to the computer monitor. A black coffee mug steamed away next to it. He was getting settled already and Laurel's boxed up items were now missing from the cubicle's corner.

"Where are the boxes?" she demanded. "Where'd the fucking boxes go that were sitting right there?" Her finger jabbed repeatedly at the empty corner.

"Ms. Carpenter's things?" McManus stood a few feet behind her. "I put them over there by your desk. Figured you'd want to do something with them."

The fact that he knew her name angered Jackie even more for some inexplicable reason. He was invading private space, space that Jackie, unreasonable though she knew it to be, felt should still be under her control. It should have been her job, her goddamn right to complete the closure on Laurel's space.

"Move your shit," she said. "You're getting another desk."

"What?" He looked perplexed. "You're kidding, right? This one of those 'new guy' things you do?"

Jackie stepped over to her desk and picked up the phone. "Get me building maintenance."

She glared at McManus, who looked unsure about the whole situation. He clearly didn't believe she was serious.

"They said you might be a little weird about this."

Weird? "What's that supposed to mean? Who said that?"

"Um, one of the guys. Last night, we were having drinks," he said, measuring his words as he spoke. He knew he was treading on some thin ground.

Jackie's hand clenched around the phone. "What else did they say about . . . Maintenance? This is Agent Rutledge up on Five. I need you to get up here and exchange a desk. No! I don't give a fuck how busy you are. Get up here now or I'm coming down there and dragging your ass up here." She slammed the phone down. "What else did they say?"

He took a step back. "Look. Nothing. It was just the guys having drinks, welcoming the new guy sort of thing."

Jackie's bark of laughter held no humor. "Bullshit. I'm sure they had all kinds of crap to say about Agent Rutledge."

He moved over to his cubicle and grabbed his jacket off the chair. "Ok, I can see there's an issue here. Maybe we should've talked first before I set up shop."

"Fucking bet your ass we should have."

"I'll just go get some more coffee or something while you get things dealt with here." He picked up the nearly full cup and backed away.

"What's going on?" Belgerman stood in his doorway down at the end of the aisle. He took one look at Jackie and his shoulders slumped. "Morning, Jack. There a problem?"

Shit. Her anger twisted into apprehension. "Nothing, sir. I wanted to get things situated for McManus here, but he . . . he's early."

He walked up, forehead wrinkled with curiosity. "Situated? What needs to be situated?"

McManus sipped at his coffee, looked at Jackie, then at Belgerman. "It's all good, sir. Just a little confusion about what to do with Ms. Carpenter's things before I settle in."

"I see." He gave Jackie a wary glance, and then took in the boxes on the floor behind her. "Aren't those her things right there?"

The elevator dinged and one of the maintenance guys stepped out. "Hey," he said, "what's this about needing to exchange a desk?"

Jackie sighed. Fucking-A. Welcome to the Jackie is a lunatic show.

Belgerman frowned. "The desk? What's wrong with the desk?"

McManus said nothing, waiting with cup held to his lips for Jackie's reply.

"He needs a new one," Jackie said. "This one isn't right for him."

The maintenance guy looked confused. "What sort of desk did you have in mind? Aren't they all pretty much the same?"

"Look! He just needs a new desk, OK? Find him

one and switch it," she said. "There's got to be a spare one around here."

More confusion. "You just want me to switch it for another one?"

"Yes! Is it really that hard to explain?"

Belgerman shook his head and walked back toward his office. "Jack, can I talk to you for a moment, please?"

She pointed at the maintenance guy, then at the desk. "You. Just do it." She hurried after Belgerman. He closed the door behind them after she entered.

"What are you doing, Jack?" His voice was filled with more than annoyance. "It's McManus's first day and you're already giving him shit."

"Sorry, sir," she said. "I wasn't expecting him here so soon." Butterflies were doing a jig in her stomach. Her mouth had gone bone dry. Oh, yes. Confidence was the word of the day.

Belgerman turned and leaned against his desk, crossing his arms over his chest. "When were you expecting him? I'm not really expecting you for another two weeks."

"I was expecting . . . I don't know when I was expecting him," she said. "I just thought I'd have more time to prepare."

"You check the file I gave you?"

"No, not yet."

"Be a good place to start."

"I know, I know. I'll get to it today," she replied. Jackie took a deep breath and crossed her arms over her stomach, hoping to calm her nerves. "But McManus isn't what I came in for."

"You're here about your crime scene visits," he stated. "Anderson told me he wanted to test your abilities. He believes your . . . experience may have given you some psychic connection to the spirit world."

Jackie nodded. *How to explain this? How do I not sound like a complete lunatic?* "It would seem so."

He waited while Jackie gave him a halfhearted smile. "And?"

"And . . . well, I don't exactly know how to explain it, sir. It sounds completely crazy."

Belgerman unfolded his arms and braced his hands upon the desk. He gave her that fatherly, *this is me you're talking to* smile. "Any more crazy than chasing vampires and ghosts? Or escaping a burning building by crossing into the realm of the dead?"

Jackie laughed nervously. "I suppose not, if you put it that way."

"So, what happened?"

She let out her breath in a rush. "I heard a ghost at the first crime scene, a screaming baby."

The easy smile vanished. "There was no baby. Wait. You heard the screams of the murdered fetus?"

Jackie nodded. "Yes. When I touched the blood stain on the mattress, something happened. I saw something there, squirming in a pool of blood, and its screams were right inside my head, like it was right there."

"Christ, Jackie. I'm sorry," he said. "That must've been awful."

She blinked. Just like that? No *what the fuck are you talking about?* He didn't even look skeptical. "It was. Sir? You don't find that utterly insane?"

"It is insane," he replied. "That doesn't mean it didn't happen."

"But sir. This is me we're talking about here. The falling apart nutcase who just lost her partner. You don't think it might be the result of . . ." She shrugged helplessly. "Totally losing it?"

"Are you? Losing it, I mean."

"Not like that," she said. "It's been hard, sir, really fucking hard. I can't lie about that."

"Good," he said. "Because I'd know you were lying if you said otherwise."

"But I'm not crazy. It happened. I know it did. I just don't understand it."

"Did you go to the other crime scene?"

"Yes." OK, here came the fun part.

"Same thing?"

"Not exactly." He waited for her in silence again. "I punched Mr. Anderson in the face."

After pausing to make sure she wasn't kidding, Belgerman burst out laughing. "I'd have liked to have seen that. Was it after touching bloodstains again?"

Jackie nodded. "But I couldn't remember doing it. I even screamed at him that I wanted him to die."

Belgerman looked concerned now. "The spirit went through you and attacked Anderson."

"I guess," she said. "I'm not sure what happened."

"What does Anderson have to say about all of this?"

"He says I need to figure out what's going on and learn how to control it."

He rolled his eyes at her. "That kind of goes without saying. Are the two events related, Jackie?"

"Honestly, sir? I don't know. Maybe. I don't know how to deal with any of this. This was all Laurel's area of expertise."

Belgerman sighed, a wave of sadness rolling across his features. "I know. You want in on this case?"

"Sir?" Really? She wasn't even going to have to ask? "I need to figure this out. It's got me scared and freaked out."

"Anderson is on board with this from what I've gathered."

"He said that he and Ms. Fontaine would sign a contract to that effect if needed."

Belgerman nodded. "They will. I'll sign them on as a consult on this case."

Jackie jumped up and down on her toes. "Thank you, sir. Goddamn. Thank you."

"I need to discuss this with Tillie," he said. "She won't be very pleased."

"She came over to my apartment last night," Jackie said. "We had a decent talk, I think. Hopefully she won't be too upset."

He gave Jackie a wry smile. "Tillie doesn't get upset. She gets back at you in other ways."

"No kidding." Jackie chuckled nervously. "That woman scares the hell out of me."

"Really?" Belgerman walked around and sat down at his desk. "She's one of kindest, most intuitive people I've ever met. She's an amazing woman."

"It's that intuitive part. She sees right through everything. It's freaky."

"Makes her very good at her job, Jackie."

"Too good," she said.

"This doesn't excuse you from your weekly visits. I fully expect you to comply with your arrangements with her."

Jackie sighed. "I know. I will."

"I mean it, Jackie," he said, assuming that fatherly tone once again. "You need her right now. Losing a partner, especially one as close as you two were, hits harder than you realize."

"I have a pretty good idea." Jackie licked her lips, her mouth suddenly dry. He was on board with all of this, so he might as well hear it all. "I see her sometimes. Laurel, I mean."

Belgerman's brows arched with surprise. "Her ghost? You've seen her ghost?"

Jackie nodded. "A couple of times. We've talked."

"I see." He pondered this information for a moment. Jackie couldn't tell if he liked that information or not. Maybe that was one step too far. Hearing spirits was one thing, but talking to your dead partner was stepping too far over the crazy line. "Is that making things easier or harder for you?"

She thought about that for a moment. "Both, I guess."

"Fair enough," he replied. "You won't be the lead on this case by the way. Pernetti is handling this one, and we're working closely with Gang Enforcement."

Jackie's heart sunk a bit. "Understood. I'll . . . manage."

He laughed at her deflated expression. "No choice, Jackie. You can opt out if you want."

"Oh, no, no. I'll deal." Taking orders from Pernetti was going to really stick in her craw. It was minor compared to the triumph of actually being able to work again. She almost didn't care what she did.

"And now you can go deal with your new partner," Belgerman said, waving her toward the door. "You didn't exactly get off to the best start."

"Does he know anything about the weird shit we've dealt with around here?"

"No. I want him to get settled in first. I'm sure he's heard some vague information about the Drake case given that he's got the job, but unless someone has broken my gag order, he knows nothing specific."

"Great. Hope he's open-minded."

"One of the reasons I brought him in," he said.

"You can fill him in when you see fit. If you think he's ready."

"And what am I supposed to tell him about why I'm back?"

"Use your best judgment on that. With Anderson on consult, though, you should probably let him in on things pretty quick."

Jackie rolled her eyes. "You see the absurd irony here, don't you? I get to be the weird psychic agent."

"Yes," he replied. "Try not to punch anyone who makes fun of you, Jackie."

She bit off the snappy retort. He knew her too well. "I'll make every effort, sir."

Belgerman laughed. "Of course. Go. There's a briefing this afternoon if you're ready for it."

Jackie opened the door. "Thank you so much. You've saved my life."

He was already on the phone. "Is the doctor in?" He waved and Jackie closed the door.

Chapter 14

Jackie stood in the aisle between her desk and what was formerly Laurel's, her arms folded across her chest, and the fingers of one hand drumming absently against her arm. Ryan McManus looked up from where he was reconnecting his computer, a questioning expression on his baby-soft face.

"McManus," she said, "I'm sorry I freaked out on you earlier. It was uncalled for."

He grinned and waved her off. "No complaints. This desk is better than the old one. You going to retire it or something?"

For a second she thought he was being sarcastic, but then realized it was just innocent humor. "I don't know. It was stupid. It's just a damn desk."

"A very meaningful desk," he said. "I feel bad. It would have been good for them to tell you I was starting today. So, when are you due back? I was told it would be a couple of weeks."

Jackie stepped over to her desk and sat down. He sounded like a nice enough guy. Young too. She hoped he was older than he looked. "Actually, I'm sort of back now. I'm going to be assisting on one case until I'm back full time."

He appeared confused by this. "Really? It's a special case?"

How much to tell him? Jackie decided to wait. "It might be. We need to get up to speed on it quickly though, and I'd like to read through your profile, ask a few questions, get a feel for my . . . new partner." The words stuck in her mouth like a foreign language.

McManus laughed. "Hope I'm not as bad as you make it sound. I'm excited to be in a homicide unit now."

"Not bad. Sorry, didn't mean to make it sound that way. Laur was the only partner I've had since joining the Bureau."

He nodded. "That's rough. I've heard nothing but great things about her. I'll try to live up to her legacy."

If you're half of what she was, I'll consider myself lucky. "Don't. Laurel was unique. Just try to be a damn good fed. That's all I want."

"Works for me," he said. "Anything comes up in my profile, just ask. I need to get this computer back on so I can get back to work."

Jackie flipped open the file she had set on her desk and began to read the vitals on Ryan McManus.

Born and raised outside of Philadelphia, Ryan McManus was apparently a typical, working-class, Irish Catholic kid. Jackie saw that and immediately wondered how he would handle the notion of vampires and ghosts. She didn't need a wooden-stake–wielding partner. He was surprisingly older than her at thirty-five. He could have passed for twenty-one. A cop at twenty-two, married at twenty-three, and a daughter at twenty-four. He had an eleven-year-old kid, which accounted for the picture on his desk. It was just him and his daughter in the picture, however, which explained the divorced at twenty-nine. Four years of Gang Enforcement as a cop in Philly and then recruited into the FBI for the same. He had moved out to the San Francisco office shortly after his divorce. Jackie was curious about that, but that sort of question could wait. He had been trying to get a Homicide job for the past four years.

He had training as a hostage negotiator, was an excellent marksman, and had been involved with law enforcement softball teams.

"Sox or Cubs?" she asked.

"What?"

"Sox or Cubs? Which is your favorite?"

"Um . . . I'm a Phillies fan," he said.

Jackie shook her head. "You're in Chicago now. You have to pick one."

"Do I get bonus points for the right one?"

"No, but you get to be a loser if you pick wrong."

He laughed. "In that case, Sox."

"Good choice. You can still be my partner."

On the other side of her cubicle, Denny, the team's scene photographer, stood up. "What are you doing here, Jack? They let you back already?"

"What do you mean, already? I've been gone two weeks."

He grinned at her. "I know. I was kind of getting used to the quiet time."

"Fuck you, Den. I know you missed me."

"I did, actually," he said, abruptly serious. "How you been doing?"

Jackie shrugged. "Been better. Just glad to be here. I was going stir crazy at home."

"You're back full time then?"

"No, just for this new case," she replied.

"Oh? Something going on with it I don't know about? You dig up something new?"

Jackie glanced over at McManus who was listening with interest. "I'll put it this way. Special Investigations is definitely helping with this one."

He rolled his eyes. "Shit. It's worse than it looks then. Great. Thanks for ruining a perfectly good morning, Jack." He sat back down, muttering to himself.

Jackie turned back to find McManus staring at her. "Special Investigations?"

"They helped us solve the Drake case," she said, hoping he would leave it at that for now.

"Ah, I see." He nodded, obviously pondering more questions. "People have been oddly silent on that one around here."

"And with good reason," she said. "There's a gag order on it."

His mouth formed an *O* of surprise. "That bad?"

"That strange."

"OK, now I'm really curious. Am I one of the 'need to know' people?"

Jackie studied him for a moment. He would need to know. The big question was whether and how he handled it. It wasn't a conversation she relished having, but it would be the one deciding factor in how well they might get along as partners.

"Yeah, you are," Jackie replied. "And I'll tell you right now, how you respond will tell me if we can be partners or not."

"Seriously?" He appeared shocked by the notion that their relationship might hinge on such a specific thing.

"Dead serious." Jackie grabbed her coat and stood up. "Let's go for a ride. I need a coffee and I don't need Denny eavesdropping on us."

"I heard that!" Denny said.

"Go do something useful."

"Yeah, yeah. So glad you're back. Really, I am."

Jackie grinned. She certainly was. It felt really damn good in fact. "Come on, McManus. Let's go see how open-minded you really are."

Denny's voice followed them out. "Good luck with that, McManus."

Once in her Durango, Jackie took them out toward Annabelle's. "Before I say anything, you realize that you are bound by the gag order on this, too. Talk to anyone about it and you're gone."

"I assumed as much," he said.

Jackie took a deep breath. "What do you know about my former partner?"

McManus shrugged a shoulder. "Almost nothing. You came out of training together, were partnered up immediately, and worked together your entire time in the Bureau. She was kidnapped and murdered by a guy named Cornelius Drake. That's pretty much it."

The image of Laurel in the warehouse, glowing beneath the fluorescent lamp, her lifeless arm dangling off the table flared up in Jackie's mind. It was the first time in days she had recalled that image.

Jackie slammed on the brakes to avoid running a red light. "Sorry. Distracted."

McManus's hand came off the dash. "No problem. That stuff is still pretty fresh. I apologize."

She relaxed her grip on the wheel, gave him a faint smile. "Don't. I have to be able to deal with it. You won't be the only one bringing it up." The light turned, and Jackie drove down the block and into the driveway for Annabelle's tiny parking lot. "This . . . this was our favorite place for coffee and food." She suddenly felt choked up and had to force the lump in her throat back down. Maybe Annabelle's wasn't a good idea after all.

After a moment of silence, McManus opened his door. "What do you want? It's on me. New guy pays."

"Tell them the coffee is for Jack, and I want a chocolate croissant."

He nodded and headed in. Jackie watched him, her stomach unsettled and jittery at the sight. She wiped at her watering eyes and sniffed. "For fuck's sake. I'm not going to cry. Not going to." Several deep, slow breaths and the moment passed. "Suck it up, Rutledge." No one would want a partner who was going to break down at every reminder of her old partner.

After five minutes, McManus returned. He handed Jackie the bag and her coffee. "That's the blackest coffee I've ever seen."

Jackie took a sip and sighed. Two weeks was far too long. "It's liquid heaven. What are you drinking?"

"Plain old latte," he said. "I got a bagel for later."

She gave him an *are you kidding me* look. "You don't come to Annabelle's for bagels. That's a total waste of money."

"I like bagels," he said and peered into his bag. "They look good at least."

Jackie shook her head. "Waste." Back out on the street, she continued their conversation. "Laurel had special gifts. She was psychic."

McManus nearly spit out his coffee. "For real? What could she do?"

"Sense and communicate with the dead," she replied. "She could tell if a vic's ghost was still at a crime scene. A few times she actually contacted them. We solved a couple of cases because of her abilities."

"Wow. The Bureau is cool with that?"

"Belgerman is very open-minded about the paranormal. He has to be."

"You guys deal with a lot of ghosts?"

"No, but it does come up," she said. "You OK with that?"

"I don't know. I've never really thought about it before. You actually saw her communicate with the dead?"

"You think I'd bullshit you on something like that, McManus?" He had skeptic written all over him. Give it lip service but won't believe until he sees.

"Hey. No," he said. "It's just . . . you don't see that in the Bureau."

"Laurel was the only active agent I know of who did this kind of work. It was the group from Special Investigations that helped us stop Drake. I need to know though. What information do you have on the Drake case?"

"Just what I got in the file. Serial killer who drained blood from his victims. He was setting up another guy for the crimes and apparently leaving very little evidence at the scene. He escaped mysteriously after Agent Carpenter's death and again when you trapped him in a funeral home that was set on fire. Somehow you managed to catch him out at the home of the setup guy, where he died at the scene."

The newspaper version, in other words. Jackie

frowned. This was not going to be easy. "You're a skeptic, aren't you, McManus?"

"Excuse me?"

"You don't really believe what I'm telling you."

"Did I say that?" He sounded offended but his answer confirmed it.

"You didn't have to. I was, too, at first," Jackie said. "But I need you to believe me. We won't be able to work together if you can't trust what I have to say, crazy as it may sound."

"Your record speaks well enough," he replied. "I was told you're a no-bullshit sort of agent."

She had to laugh at the absurdity of what she was about to say. "Well, what I'm going to tell you is going to sound like the biggest pile of bullshit you've ever heard."

"I'm all ears," he said. "I might be skeptical, but I'm open-minded. I've seen a lot of whacked-out shit in my years here."

"Not like this. None of this goes beyond this car. You want to bail after I tell you, that's your prerogative and I wouldn't blame you."

His eyes widened in surprise. "They told me this was a unique assignment. I came for the challenge, and I heard Belgerman is one of the best leaders in the Bureau."

Jackie nodded. No doubt there. "He is." She took a deep breath and ate a bite of her croissant for courage. Chocolate was the wonder of all foods. "You're gagged on this, remember."

McManus laughed. "Not a word. Christ. How bad can it be?"

"You believe in vampires, McManus?"

"What do you mean?" He brought the coffee cup

at his lips back down. "Like real, blood-sucking, coffin-sleeping vampires?"

"Yes," she said, "but they don't sleep in coffins."

"The Drake guy?" He looked at her in disbelief. "He was a vampire?"

"Yes," she said. She decided to leave out the other vampires for the moment. One step at a time. She didn't want to overload McManus's skeptical brain.

"Holy shit. You're serious."

"Completely. He could do things . . ." Jackie had to wipe the vision of the warehouse from her mind again before continuing. "Things that no normal human could do."

McManus stared at her, clearly trying to determine if she was bullshitting him or not. He turned away and looked out at the passing traffic. "I'm going to guess it isn't turning into a bat."

"You're a believer in the afterlife, McManus?"

"Like heaven and hell?" He chuckled. "What good Irish Catholic doesn't?"

"What do you think is on the other side?" He looked at her, perplexed. "When you die. What do you think happens when you die?"

He sat back in his seat, clearly unsure how to answer the question. "Honestly? I have no idea."

They came to a stoplight and Jackie laid her forehead against the steering wheel. "Fuck. I really don't want to be doing this."

"What?" McManus sounded alarmed. "What's wrong?"

Jackie sat back up, flinging her arms wide. "This. This whole damn partner bullshit. No offense to you. You seem like a good guy, but I really . . ." She put her hands back on the wheel and continued on. "It just sucks, OK? I don't want a new partner."

McManus sat in silence, staring straight ahead. After a couple of blocks he nodded, as though finally agreeing with himself about something. "I'm a good partner, Jack."

"I never said you weren't."

"I'm not Agent Carpenter," he said. "I can't be and I'm not going to try to be. I'm just Ryan McManus, an Irish-Catholic boy from Philly who believes in bringing a little more justice to this world. I'll always have your back and expect you to have mine. We don't have to be buddies either, as long as there's respect going both ways. So," he said and turned to stare at her with intense, blue eyes, "give me a chance here."

She couldn't argue with that. There was no choice really. Belgerman wouldn't let her get away with saying no to Ryan McManus. Regardless, he sounded sincere. Her gut said this was a decent agent, but decent or not, if he could not handle the supernatural then they would have problems.

"Do you actually believe in ghosts, Ryan?"

He raised an eyebrow. "Um, yeah. I guess I do."

"You believe Agent Carpenter could see ghosts?"

"Hey, you tell me, Jack," he said. "She was your partner."

"And if I told you she could, that I'd seen her do it?"

"Then I'd have to believe you, now wouldn't I?"

"But would you really believe?"

He thought in silence for a moment before nodding. "Yeah, I would. There's lots of shit out there that I believe but have never seen. Ghosts being one of them. Where you going with this, Jack?"

"I've seen them too," Jackie said in a quiet voice.

"Ghosts. I've talked to them, seen where they come from."

"No shit?" He raised a warning hand at Jackie's scathing stare. "OK. Really. I believe you. Whose ghost did you see?"

"Laurel's for one," she replied. "Others, too. I went there when I almost died in Drake's attack at the funeral home." She would leave out the part about Nick drinking her blood. Ghosts were enough for one day.

He stared out the window in silence. "Wow. I think seeing my partner's ghost would freak me out just a little."

"It was unnerving at first," she said, "but the worst thing is, after all of this, I seem to be able to speak to ghosts, too."

Ryan's eyes widened in surprise. "Serious?"

"Completely. Reason I'm helping on this case is to see just what I can do." She watched him nod his head with acceptance and breathed a small sigh of relief.

"That's pretty damn cool, Jack," he said. "Scary, but cool. Anything I can do?"

"Just keep being cool about it. Don't give me any shit, because honestly, I don't think I'd handle that well."

"You got it," he said. "Certainly going to make things interesting." He laughed and Jackie smiled. *Interesting* wasn't even the word. "So, what do we do with all of this?"

Jackie turned a corner and began to head back to headquarters. "I have no idea," she said. "I guess we do what we always do and see what happens. We work the case."

McManus rubbed his hands together. "Sounds great. Can't wait."

You're probably going to regret saying that, Jackie thought. They always do.

Chapter 15

Jackie stood in the conference room before the case board. Outside, McManus was making calls to Gang Enforcement, trying to find some connections, and collecting all of the information currently known about the gang involved. There were several pictures of the two crime scenes taped up, depicting the victims and other noteworthy evidence, like bullet holes and blood spatter. There was a list of notable gang members associated with the victims. There was a note from the crime lab indicating that the bullets found at the second scene were indeed fired from a law-enforcement weapon.

The first scene had clearly been made to look like robbery in order to cover up a vicious murder. The second was pure cold-blooded killing. Except for the evisceration. Two of the four victims were cut open. What sort of motivation inspired that kind of butchery? Vengeance? Sending a message to someone else? That was one hell of a message.

If it weren't for the bullets used in the second murders, the case would be far more cut and dry. The woman's ex-boyfriend was a prime suspect, one

Renaldo "Rennie" Vasquez, and a sticky next to him indicated he was still at large. But the bullets indicated two different weapons, which likely meant two different shooters. This gave credence to gang retaliation of some kind, except that the bullets in the second indicated law enforcement. A note under forensic information on the bullets stated that there were no reported stolen weapons or ammunition by local law enforcement. So, taking that one step further, what would it mean if the second killer was a cop? Someone had even written *cop?* underneath. Could one killer have used two different weapons? It was certainly possible, but generally unlikely.

For Jackie, it was the eviscerations that were most disturbing. Why were those particular two people targeted? Both were affiliated gang members, the first being the former girlfriend of a gang member, the second an actual member of the gang. It took a particularly twisted sort of soul to gut someone, especially if that someone was pregnant. Nothing on the board indicated anything beyond gang affiliation. It could have been gang retaliation. Wars between gangs could get extremely brutal, but that was nearly always shootings or stabbings. Taking the time to slice them open was personal.

And then there was the ghosts. A shiver ran through Jackie. This was information she clearly had no clue how to process. Had the occurrences at the two crime scenes meant anything other than spirits really pissed off that they had died? Jackie sighed and turned away from the board. Laurel might know.

Nick stood in the doorway to the conference room, watching her with a faint smile on his face. "Hello, Jackie. Come up with anything?"

After her heart kick-started itself, Jackie shook her

head. "No. The information we have now is somewhat confusing and contradictory. We need more. What are you doing here?"

"Belgerman asked me to come to a meeting this afternoon about the case and give everyone the paranormal angle on things."

"Oh." She nodded. "Good. That's good." *And here's Jack to help out because she's hearing ghosts, too.*

Nick shoved his hands into his jean's pockets. "I'll leave your situation out of my discussion if you want."

She nodded again. "Please. I'm not ready yet."

"Hey. Excuse me," McManus said, nudging up behind Nick. He stepped aside and Ryan walked in. "I didn't get much from Gang Enforcement." He gave Nick a cursory look-over. "Who's this?"

"McManus, this is Nick Anderson. The setup guy."

He stared at Nick for a moment without saying anything; Nick gave him a polite nod. "I see. Pleasure to meet you, Mr. Anderson." McManus stuck out his hand. "Anyone who saves a fed is a friend of mine."

Nick shook his hand. "Agent McManus. The pleasure's mine, and call me Nick."

"You here for the case meeting?" McManus looked down at his hand for just a second and then at Nick's.

Jackie knew exactly what he was thinking: Why the hell was the man's hand so cool? "He's going to give us the ghost angle."

"Excellent," McManus said. "Looking forward to hearing about that."

Nick cocked an eyebrow. "Glad to help any way I can. I'm going to go get a cup of that swill you all call coffee here, let you discuss case matters." He gave Jackie a nod. "See you shortly, Agent Rutledge."

"OK," she said and watched him leave. "You got nothing useful?"

"Nah, nothing new," McManus said. "No major gang warfare going on at the moment. No recent killings that might indicate someone is out looking for vengeance. If I were to guess, I'd say we have something internal going on. Someone stole some cash or drugs or slept with someone's girlfriend. Something stupid."

Jackie turned back to the board. "You don't gut people over something stupid. Someone is extremely motivated and angry."

"He killed a pregnant woman," McManus said, disgusted. "We're dealing with a sociopath."

"Maybe more than one," Jackie added. "Killers like this like to use the same weapon. They like the routine. None of this is making a lot of sense to me yet."

"We just started," he said. "I think we should go talk to some of these gang members, especially that witness who can't remember anything. You don't stand in a room and watch two murders happen and block out everything. Shock only goes so far."

"Maybe. But yeah, I'd like to talk to her, too."

"You up for a little interviewing after the meeting?"

"And deal with obnoxious gangland bravado?" Jackie smiled. "When do we leave?"

The meeting went as well as Jackie could have hoped for. Only Pernetti didn't look pleased to have her back, though he wisely kept his mouth shut about it. Nick elicited groans from everyone with the possibility of a ghost being involved, followed immediately by murmurs of wishes that Laurel was around. They were relieved that Nick and Shelby would be around to deal with it. Jackie's role was designated as an assist and liaison for Special Investigations. They were working every angle for now, from cop involvement to gang assassination, under the assumption that whoever was involved would be killing again.

Nick wanted to speak with the witness as well, so McManus called where she was staying and arranged a time to talk to her later that evening. He would meet up with them then. With about three hours to kill, McManus took them out to "chat with the locals." He wanted to see if there was any buzz on the street about what had happened. Jackie agreed, but found herself in the uncomfortable position of playing second fiddle to McManus.

"So that guy is a legit ghosthunter," he said, turning on the wipers against the steady rain that now fell. The wind-whipped clouds were particularly low, dragging their soggy fingers across the city streets. The Chicago skyline was a stunted block of concrete and steel.

"He and his business partner can both see and talk to ghosts," said Jackie. "Even their office manager is a psychic."

"Who'd have thought?" he said. "I'll be interested to see it in action."

"There's not much to see," Jackie replied. "Usually."

He laughed. "Usually?"

"A powerful ghost can make themselves seen. They look like . . . ghosts. Kind of washed out, see-through versions of themselves, I guess." Jackie shrugged. This was not something she was comfortable explaining.

"You think we'll see one?"

"McManus, how would I know that?" she snapped. "I don't see the future."

"OK, sorry. Just curious," he said.

"I don't really like talking about it. You should talk to Anderson. He's the expert."

"That guy had very weird-looking eyes. You notice that before?"

"Oh, yeah. I've noticed."

They were silent for a few minutes, listening to the soft, rhythmic thump of the wiper motor. Jackie absently rubbed her hands together, unaccustomed to the fact they were not on the wheel.

"Do you know anything about the gang landscape in Chicago?" he asked.

"Not really my area," she replied. "I think I've been involved in a couple of homicides involving gang members before, but mostly it's the Gang Enforcement Task Force."

"I should probably take the lead with these guys then," he said. "Be easier."

Lead? Who died and made you boss? "Why would it be easier? You think I can't talk to a bunch of macho gangbangers? I can hold my own against any trash-talking thugs who might think a female fed—"

"Whoa!" McManus laughed. "I'm not trying to steal your thunder here, Jack. I'm fluent in Spanish is all. I worked with gangs, so I'm more familiar with how to talk to them and get useful information."

"Oh." She gave him a halfhearted smile. "That makes sense."

"I believe partners should play to their strengths. Mine just happens to be gangs. I'll follow your lead on the homicide stuff. I'm still learning there."

"Sorry. I'm just used to being the one in the driver's seat. Laurel didn't like being lead."

He nodded. "No problem. We'll figure it out as we go. I don't want to step on any toes here."

Jackie had a feeling that was going to happen regardless. Laurel had never wanted to take the controls. She never cared about stuff like that. Likely because she had been in love with her. Jackie wondered then how much of their working relationship had been predicated on that simple fact? Probably everything. Certainly no worries about that being the case now. The world had flipped upside down and there would be no righting it. She would just have to make things work. Somehow.

Rain was coming down in swirling waves when McManus finally parked the car. They were up somewhere near Lincoln Park. Jackie was not sure exactly where. Given the few people she had seen on the street and the Spanish language signs everywhere, they were in the center of a Hispanic neighborhood. Jackie couldn't recall the last time she had been up in this part of Chicago.

They were just beyond the city's efforts at gentrification. Six blocks south and you went from poor working class to solid middle class. No peeling paint or graffiti back there. The sidewalks and pavement were at least a decade newer, and most of the businesses did not have bars over their windows. City money did not trickle down to this level.

Across the street, a flickering neon bull provided a rather unwelcome invitation to the El Toro Furioso, a dark gray-sided building at the end of the block with a brick skirting that was missing a few dozen bricks.

"This looks charming," Jackie said.

"The Raging Bull," McManus replied. "Was told this is a popular hangout for a bunch of the Kings."

"The Almighty Latin Kings? That's who we're dealing with?" Of course she had not bothered to check out who they were yet. Jackie knew of them—a large, if not the largest, gang in Chicago with chapters in many cities around the country. A very organized group as far as gangs went, with a long history in the area. Founded on Latin pride more than any desire to be an organized criminal group, they delved into it like any other gang. Jackie knew little beyond the basics, though. Gang Enforcement did most of the work.

"It's what the guy in GE told me," he said. "This will just be kind of a 'shooting the shit with the boys.' They don't know me at all, so it's more a chance to let them see I'm not an asshole."

"Need me to do anything particular?"

"Just keep eyes and ears alert. We're hoping for clues on the whereabouts of Vasquez. If we hit any nerves, it'll probably be from someone we're not talking to. Family of the victims have been interviewed already, so I'm guessing word of these murders has spread to almost everyone. Word spreads fast in these communities."

"OK, easy enough. Let's go."

They jogged across the puddled street and entered the dark doorway. It took Jackie a moment to adjust to the lighting change, and by then it was apparent everyone in the place had noticed their presence. Latino music blared from a jukebox. She caught the clack of pool balls from the back, where she could just see the edge of a pool table beyond a partition. A giant flag of Mexico graced the wall opposite the bar, where four booths were filled with mostly tattooed, Hispanic men, half-empty beer bottles, shot glasses, chip baskets, and smoldering ashtrays. A thick haze of smoke hung in the air, stirred up into drifting eddies by a pair of overhead ceiling fans.

Along with the couple dozen wary eyes burrowing into her, Jackie could feel something else, a cold breath of air that failed to stir the smoke around her. The dead. The taint of Deadworld lingered in this place.

Yeah, this was going to be fun. She followed McManus up to the bar where he spoke in rapid Spanish to the bartender and flashed his badge. The bartender did not sound pleased with their presence.

Two stools down, a weathered-looking Latino stubbed out his cigarette and gave Jackie a leering smile. One arm had a miasma of color running from wrist to shoulder, and letters decorating each finger of his hand. He spit a slew of words Jackie couldn't understand.

"No Spanish here," she said. "Got something to say, talk to the man."

"Didn't know they made *federales* so little," he said with a thick accent. "How's little girl fed going to catch big, bad Latino man?"

Jackie frowned. Guys certainly didn't change much across racial lines when it came to women. "By planting her little steel-toed boot into the bad Latino's ball sack."

He laughed and McManus turned to him, speaking once again in fluent Spanish. The smile disappeared and he replied in a far less amused tone. After several exchanges, the man grabbed his beer and walked away. In his place sat the faint, translucent form of another man, hunched over, his hands resting on the bar.

Jackie's mouth dropped open, her voice a whisper. "Holy shit."

McManus looked at her. "What?"

"You see that?" She pointed. "There, sitting on the barstool."

He glanced over at the barstool and then back. "See what?"

The ghost turned his head, eyes widening as he realized Jackie could see him. He said something, but his voice was drowned out by the din in the bar.

"It's, um, nothing." What the hell was she supposed to say? *Oh, it's just a ghost of some guy. No biggie.*

McManus stared at the stool for a moment. "Getting some psychic vibes or something?"

Jackie took a step back as the man got off the stool. "Something like that." Psychic vibes, like Laurel's little psychic radar she used to always poke fun at. It wasn't so fun now. The man, dressed in jeans and a T-shirt and sporting a wide array of tattooed artwork on his arms, much like the living man who had just left, began to speak again, his expression visibly upset. This time he was speaking loud enough to be heard.

"He's saying something about Vasquez." The man's hands were waving angrily in her direction and Jackie took another step back.

"What he say?"

She turned on McManus in a panic. "How the fuck would I know? I don't speak Spanish."

The bartender paused in the middle of polishing a glass and eyed her curiously. Others were beginning to look more intently in their direction. The ghost stepped right up to Jackie, repeating the same phrase over and over. Jackie let out a yelp and backpedaled toward the door. Barks of laughter could be heard around the bar.

McManus came up and grabbed her arm. "Jack? What's going on? You OK?"

She yanked her arm from his grasp. "I have to get out of here," she said in a rush and pushed at the door, kicking at it with a desperate lunge to get out of the bar. Jackie ran for the safety of the car, narrowly missing a car that blared its horn at her as she bolted across the road. The door when she reached it was locked.

"McManus!" She yanked on the handle until he clicked the remote and then virtually fell into the seat, slamming the door shut when she was in. McManus climbed in a moment later.

"Jack?"

Deep breaths. Deep breaths. Jackie drew in large lungfuls of air and slowly exhaled. Gradually, her heart began to slow to a sane rate. She turned and looked beyond McManus to the door of the Raging Bull. The ghost stood on the edge of sidewalk, shaking his fists in her direction, mouthing words that Jackie could not hear.

"Go, Ryan. Please. Get us out of here."

He pulled out into the street watching the bar entrance in the rearview mirror. "Care to explain? You act like you saw . . . you saw a ghost."

Jackie stared out through the rain wiping across the window. "I did. What does *matalo* mean?"

"*Matalo?* It means *to kill,*" he said, worried.

"He wanted Vasquez dead. I heard him say *loco,* too. He wants the crazy Vasquez dead."

"Shit." They drove in silence for a minute before he looked at her again in disbelief. "You really are a psychic."

"Fucking looks that way," she said. Jackie ran her fingers through her hair, clenching them into fists. "God, I don't want this. I really don't."

"You want me to take you back?"

And the chickenshit says, yes. Jackie sighed and looked back up at the steady, gray rain coating everything in a wet, dreary gloom. She heard Laurel's voice then, echoing similar sentiments from when they had first encountered the feeling of Drake. *Stay away. Get off of the case.* And Jackie clearly remembered her response. She turned to McManus.

"We have a witness to interview, don't we?"

He smiled. "That we do, Agent Rutledge. That we do."

Chapter 16

Ninety minutes later they were back at headquarters, with no further information. How did someone hypnotize a witness into complete forgetfulness with the touch of a hand? Jackie's first thought was *vampire*, but there were no signs from the victims of blood-draining. Everything in the evidence spoke to purely human violence. The only true wildcard here was the dead. There was an active and angry ghost at both scenes. She needed some expert advice and the one person she needed to talk to had been frustratingly unavailable. Shelby could reach her though.

McManus had packed up his carry bag and was ready to leave the office. It was nearly 8:00 PM and neither of them had eaten. "I'm heading out to have some drinks with the guys. They invited me out for a little first-day-on-the-job celebrating. You sure you don't want to come?"

"Thanks, but no," Jackie said. She did not feel like celebrating anything. "I've got to go talk to someone about what happened earlier."

He nodded. "Yeah, I guess that would be a good idea. You going to be all right, Jack?"

"Once I get a handle on this, I should be," she said. She sure as hell better be. She couldn't keep running in panic every time some ghost decided to have words with her. Her career would be over otherwise. "Sorry I freaked out on you today. Not the first day you'd hoped for, I imagine."

"You made it memorable." He chuckled. "Gang Enforcement was never this interesting."

Jackie rolled her eyes. "I'll take competence over interesting any day."

McManus shouldered his bag. "I've no doubts about your competence, Jack. I'll see you in the morning."

"Ignore whatever those boneheads say about me," she said. "Except the part about being a bitch. I have no excuses for that one."

He laughed and waved at her as he headed for the elevator. "Night, Jack."

"Night." He was a good guy. Motivated. Calm. And he appeared to take the psychic craziness in stride. She couldn't complain. It could have been a lot worse. Belgerman had, as always, chosen wisely. Jackie picked up her phone and dialed. It was picked up on the third ring.

"Hey, Jackie," Shelby said in her perpetually cheerful voice. "I've been hoping you'd call."

"Can we talk? I had another encounter today and I've got a question for Laur."

"You did? What happened?"

She did not want to talk about this shit over the phone from the office. Who knew what someone might overhear. "Not now. Can we meet?"

"Sure. Come on over. I'll put some tea on."

Tea. Shelby was so Laurel's girlfriend. "Thanks."

She hung up, grabbed her things, and headed for the elevator.

Shelby's presence emanated through her apartment door before she even opened it. The dead part anyway. The very living part beamed her wide, cherry-red smile, and stared at her with those iris-less, sparkling eyes. She wore a pair of Chicago Blackhawk sweatpants cut off at the knees and a form fitting top that wouldn't have pulled down past her navel if you'd hung weights on it. Her perfect, matching cherry toes reflected the light from the hall.

Her smile faded after a cursory look at Jackie. "Hon, you look like you just got steamrolled. Come in."

Jackie stepped in to the warmth of Shelby's eclectic Victorian loft. "It's sad that I always look more dead than you actually are."

She laughed. "When's the last time you put on makeup?"

"I don't wear makeup."

"And there you go," she said. "Sit down. I'll get the tea."

Jackie was about to tell her she did not drink tea, but decided against it. Let her play hostess. She sat down on one of the ornate couches, shoving the crocheted pillows aside. "This ghost shit is driving me crazy, Shelby. I need it to stop. I'm no psychic."

"I think you lost that choice when Nick and Laurel dragged your dying ass into Deadworld." She walked out of the kitchen with a tray in her hands. Besides the teapot and two cups with saucers was a dark bottle. Shelby sat down on the opposite end of the couch and set the tray on the coffee table. The label on the bottle said BAUCHANT.

Jackie eyed the tea suspiciously. "What is that?"

"Drink," she said. "It's the best tea ever."

She picked up the cup and sniffed at the steaming liquid. The vapors nearly burned her nostrils. "There's alcohol in this?"

"It's an orange cognac brandy. Lovely stuff and just what you need right now."

Jackie took a sip and was hit with a burning wave of orange citrus with a hint of tea. The warmth seeped quickly down her throat and into her gut. She nodded. "OK. I can drink tea like this."

Shelby picked up her own cup and drank. "Told you. Now, what happened today? Tell me everything." After another sip, she added, "Please."

Jackie told her, from the initial cold breath of the dead to the angry ghost following her out of the bar. Her cup was empty when she finished. "That's pretty much it. I'm not a psychic, Shelby. I'm just . . . I'm not. I don't want this ability or power or whatever the fuck you want to call it. It freaks me out."

Shelby leaned forward and made Jackie another cup of tea. "First of all, I'm sorry. I know you didn't ask for or want this to happen. It must be scary as hell. I know I was scared when I first became what I am. I was so pissed at Nick. I didn't talk to him for months. But after a while, I realized I needed it. I wanted to kill Drake and without the abilities I received, I'd have had no chance."

"I don't need this," Jackie said. "It's just getting in the way of me doing my investigations."

"Because it can't help you or because you don't know how to use it?"

"I don't want to use it."

"Why not? It's a powerful tool," Shelby said. "Didn't you solve some cases because of Laurel's abilities?"

"Yes, but that was Laur, not me. She grew up with

this shit. She was born with it. What I've got is more like . . . like I've been infected or something."

Shelby nodded. "I know, and I guess in a way you have. It's incurable, Jackie. There's no method that we know of to just make it go away. You can't go into remission. You must learn to live with it, simple as that. Claim it and make it yours. Talking to the dead is a powerful resource that very few people have."

Jackie sagged back against the couch, looking up at the whirling ceiling fan overhead. Shelby wasn't helping at all. She didn't want to claim anything. "And what happens the next time I deck someone at a scene because some ghost's idea of talking is little more than murderous rage?"

"That's not talking," Shelby said. "That's channeling, which is another ability all together. That one will take some work. It's strength of will, self-confidence, and control."

Jackie groaned with frustration. "I don't need another thing to work on, damn it!"

"I know," she replied, her tone quieter and even more serious. "You shouldn't be channeling right now. You aren't in a good place for that."

"Gee! You think?" She turned and glared at Shelby. "So, where's the fucking off switch at? Because right now I've got fucking babies and really pissed dead people just jumping into my head. How am I supposed to work like that?"

"You don't, Jackie. Right now you need to stay away from crime scenes until you can get a better handle on this."

"No fucking way." She had just got back on a case and wasn't about to let that go. "Working cases is saving my sanity right now."

"Not if your psychic abilities are going to make it

worse," she said. "You had a month off to work on yourself, to deal with Laurel's death, and get your life back in order. What happened with that?"

"Work *is* my order," Jackie said. "And I don't need another shrink, thank you very much. One is more than enough."

"I'm speaking as a friend," Shelby said sternly. "You've suffered a lot. You had a breakdown and almost killed someone, and it's been very apparent that living without Laurel has proven very difficult. You honestly think you're ready to be effective at work after two weeks?"

Jackie sat back up. "And how has living with Laurel been? Not too difficult I hope?"

Shelby looked up at the ceiling for a moment and then sighed. "Laurel can't see you yet, Jackie. Neither of you are ready."

"What the hell is that supposed to mean?"

"It means she's afraid of being with you right now. She's afraid of slipping back into how things were. We both agreed that taking those first steps to being healthy again needed to be on your own."

Jackie leaped to her feet. "Who died and made you fucking queen? You've got no business meddling in our affairs."

"Laurel asked me to," she said.

"What?"

"Because she knows herself well enough to admit that she's too weak to not help you when you should be helping yourself."

"Oh, that is bullshit!" Jackie searched for a reason, any rationalization to go along with her exclamation. "I'm helping myself. I got my fucking job back, didn't I?"

"Why?" Shelby asked, curious. "Did you ask yourself

why you were so desperate to get back? It's not because you were ready, Jackie. That much is obvious."

"Fuck you." She wanted to slap her or better yet, ball up her fist and plant it right in the middle of those faintly smiling cherry lips.

"I'm serious. You can get indignant all you want, but what've you done? Are you talking things out with the FBI psychologist? Are you reaching out to anyone for help or even a bit of comfort when you're really needing it? Nick is trying but you're too afraid of him to give him a chance."

Jackie walked away. Her hands were clenching so tightly they were starting to shake. She didn't need this, not one damn bit. At the window overlooking the street, Jackie stared at her reflection, gaunt and warbled by the rivulets of water running down the glass. "I'm not afraid of him. And I'm here, aren't I? I'm asking you for help."

Shelby's bark of laughter made her stomach clench. "You don't want my help, hon. You want me to make your problem go away, just like you'd want Laurel to do if she was here now. And don't lie to me. I see through that shit. Nick terrifies you, but unlike me, you're terrified of all men."

She spun away from the window, jabbing an angry finger at Shelby. "That's crazy. I'm not afraid of—"

"You are!" Shelby interrupted her and got to her feet. "I know about your past, Jackie. Laurel has told me a lot. And before you get all goddamn huffy about it, I'm the only person she's confided this to, besides her therapist. She's trying to get things right after being your crutch for eight fucking years, so get off your high horse and at least admit you're screwed up." She walked around the couch and stopped in front of Jackie, who tried desperately to stare her down and failed miserably. "Nobody who experiences what you did with your mother and stepfather comes out on the other side undamaged. They just don't. And I saw what happened to you when Laurel died or did you forget that, Jackie? You're not OK. Two weeks of moping around in your pj's and a tequila bottle won't fix that. Getting back on a case won't fix it either." She reached out and poked Jackie in the chest. "Take a hard look, Agent Rutledge. It's not pretty, and nobody else is going to make it better except you."

Jackie had started to interrupt her several times during the tirade, but she could find no words to countermand the attack. She knew it was true and it was a bitter pill to swallow. The finger jab was it, though. The words stung, but the poke went over the line. Jackie clenched her fist and aimed an uppercut for Shelby's chin.

Two inches from connecting, Jackie's forward momentum came to an abrupt halt, her fist suddenly clenched in Shelby's cool, firm grip."You really want to do this, Jackie? Fist fighting with a vampire is a losing proposition."

This time Jackie did stare her down, glaring into the bright depths to the darkness beyond where she could sense that doorway to Deadworld. Fucking dead people. Fucking know-it-all, meddling, Jolie-wannabe, Miss Perfect goddamn vampire. One punch. She just wanted to land one good, solid blow to that grinning Revlon mouth.

"Fuck off," she said and swung with the other fist.

It missed. Shelby let go of the fist and snapped her arm across to block the other punch away. It threw Jackie off balance, and she stepped right into the back of Shelby's hand, which struck her a stinging blow on the cheek. "Bit slow there, Jackie. Not good enough to land a single punch? Or, you know, just not good enough, period?"

The line between anger and stupidity is a thin one and Jackie had just erased it. She yelled something at Shelby, a garbled mash of expletives, and lunged at her. There was no plan of attack, no bloodying the lip anymore. She just wanted to take her down and wipe that smug smile off her face.

Shelby sidestepped with unnatural speed. One moment Jackie's hands were going to land and the next she was stumbling through open air. She had to grab a dining chair to keep from falling down completely. As she brought herself back up, Shelby's hand flicked out and stung the other cheek.

"Your energy would be better spent on yourself, you know," she said, dancing lightly away from Jackie's wild swing. "Or is it that you don't believe you deserve something better?"

"I deserve to plant my fist in your goddamned face," Jackie huffed, and this time attempted to feint with her left and sneak in a right. Shelby didn't bite and her punch was flicked away. The stinging slap to her face quickly followed. Humiliation was the worst sort of torment. She was helpless to do anything against Shelby's supernatural abilities. But rage was the best of motivators, even if it was utterly blind. Jackie yelled and leaped at Shelby, hoping to tackle her.

A subtle pivot, a sweeping block, and Jackie found herself tumbling over the back of the couch. Her feet crashed on the coffee table, knocking the tea set onto the floor.

Shelby groaned. "Damn it! Now look what you've done. Can't even fight properly, can you?" She put her hands on her hips, a scolding scowl on her face. "Can you do anything right, Jackie?"

Jackie reached down and picked up the teapot from the floor. The voice was far too reminiscent of Carl the cop; her stepfather had uttered that phrase more times than she could remember. "I can do better," she recalled saying to each and every admonition but, over time, the belief dwindled, because it was never better, only worse. And how could it get better when you watched your mother cry the same phrase only to be beaten down until she was nothing. In the end you just became nothing.

She screamed at Shelby, "Fucking bitch!" and hurled the teapot at her head.

Shelby caught it. "You done yet? I can do this all night if you want, Jackie. I can keep slapping you around and berating your poor ego, and telling you about all of the things wrong with you if it'll help. But I don't think it will. Your too stubborn to let go of that one thing that's held you together for the past twenty years, afraid you'll have nothing left."

Jackie struggled back to her feet, stepped up and sprang off the back of the couch at Shelby, hands outstretched, reaching for the bitch's throat. She had the vague notion that holding the teapot might put her at a disadvantage, slow her down just a fraction, enough to get her hands on that pale flesh.

The teapot arced away toward the cushions of the couch, and Shelby deftly crouched beneath Jackie's lunging arms, planted a hand in her midriff, turned and used Jackie's own momentum to bring her crashing to the floor. All of the air in her lungs rushed out in one big whoosh and everything went bright and white for a few seconds. When things came back into focus, Jackie found Shelby straddled over her, pinning her arms to her sides. Jackie squirmed and screamed to no avail.

Shelby reached down and firmly grabbed Jackie's chin hard enough to hold her still. The ever-smiling mouth had turned south. "You fucking done?"

Jackie tried to yank herself free of the grip, but the more she tried, the harder Shelby held her. She was a helpless child in parental lockdown, a parent who'd had it with her tantrum. Tears welled up. "Bitch! I hate your blood-drinking guts."

Shelby rolled her eyes and shook her head. "No, you don't. You're just pissed off and scared to death."

"I'm not afraid of you, Shelby."

Her face came down to within inches of Jackie's. "Yes, you are. Afraid of what I am. Afraid of Nick and what he might see if you let him into your fucked-up little world. Afraid that Laurel is going to leave you behind. Afraid you can't do your job anymore. And afraid that you're now a psychic and some kind of freak like the rest of us."

Jackie tried to blink away the tears. "I'm not afraid."

"Yes, girl, you are," she said, the anger dissipating. "At least admit that much, because when your world crashes down on your head, you have every right to be afraid."

"Shelby, get off of me."

"Admit it, damn you!"

The fingers dug into her jaw. They were going to leave marks. She didn't want to admit a damn thing to Shelby, not matter how right she was. "Fine! I'm afraid." Jackie yelled the words at her, pulling them up out of her throat, along with the plug capping the well of tears she had been trying vainly to hold back. "I'm afraid of everything, OK? That good enough for you? My life is falling apart. I'm turning into some kind of freak! And Nick . . ." She was going to say she was afraid of him, too, but that wasn't the truth and the truth was swimming up out of her along with the rush of tears. "I don't deserve a guy like that. He's too good for someone like me."

Shelby's grip relinquished. "Aww, hon. You got to stop thinking like that. You may be all kinds of fucked up, but never think you're not good enough." She slid back and let Jackie's arms go, pulling her up into a hug. Jackie held on to her until the tears finally began to subside. Shelby drew back, taking Jackie's face in her hands. "You listen to me. Everyone is screwed up in some way or another. Me, Laurel, and even Nick-fucking-Anderson. That's just the way of the world. Who you are depends on how you deal with it."

Jackie stared into the bright, glistening eyes. There were tears there, too, it seemed. "I don't know how," she said.

"Then quit trying to do it by yourself." Shelby leaned forward and gave Jackie a quick hard kiss on the mouth. "You've got people who want to help." She stood up, towering over Jackie. "Let them, you stubborn bitch."

Jackie stared up at the hand being offered to her. She wiped the tears away with the back of her hand and then took Shelby's, who pulled her up with the slightest effort. "That's the hardest part."

"It is," she said, and walked over to pick up her teapot laying on the couch. "But if you can't ask for help, then you deserve whatever end you get."

That was one harsh way of looking at it. "Will you help me?"

"That depends," she replied. Shelby patted the couch. "Sit back down, please." She waited until Jackie reluctantly moved around and sat back down. Her cheeks still stung and her jaw was beginning to ache. "What do you want help with?"

Jackie rubbed at her jaw. "Everything."

She laughed. "Be a little more specific."

There were so many other things. Jackie picked up her cup and gulped down the cognac-laced tea. "I need a life."

Shelby laughed. "Don't we all, babe. That requires being with other people. And, gee, you know someone who wants to be with you."

"I don't get why he's interested in someone like me."

"Oh, I don't know," she said with a huff of frustration. "Maybe it's because you're smart and tenacious? Maybe it's because you don't take bullshit from anyone? Maybe it's because you'll fight for what's right no matter what the costs are? Maybe it's because you're cute as hell and you turn him on."

"I'm not cute."

"I think you vastly underestimate your appeal," Shelby said. "Of course you do absolutely nothing to heighten the appeal, which I think Nick finds utterly attractive."

Jackie took another gulp of tea. "Yeah, well. What should I do now?"

"Go home. Rest. We need to figure out these psychic abilities of yours so they don't drive you batty. And you should read some of Laur's journal. I think it will help you come to terms with some things. She's really very insightful."

Shelby's face softened as she spoke about Laurel, the mischievous smile curving into something else all together. She truly did care about her. "I miss her," Jackie said. "I bitched her out yesterday like an idiot because I haven't seen her."

"Don't worry about it, Jackie. She understands.

She misses you, but she can't make any of these problems go away. That's all on you."

Jackie sighed. "I really have no idea what I'm doing anymore."

"Most of us don't, but we get support from our friends to help us get through."

"Are we friends?"

Shelby leaned over and kissed Jackie on the cheek. "Of course, unless you don't want to be."

"No, I do. I need all the friends I can get."

Chapter 17

Jackie set the journal down in her lap and took a sip from her glass of wine. She remembered little of that first day of FBI training. She had been a nervous wreck and kept to herself, too afraid to say anything that might make her sound stupid, especially compared to Bailey Thompson, the pretentious Princeton bitch. She was working in D.C. the last she had heard. Sadly, she couldn't remember much about Laur from that first day either. The first study night, though, she did. That was when she had decided they would be friends. Jackie thumbed through the next couple of pages until she found the entry. It had happened fairly quickly after classes began.

"God, Laur," Jackie said. "Nine days? How could you think of me like that after just nine days? That's crazy."

Jackie turned each page with care, picking through the entries. Some she skimmed, others she read each word. The sensation of watching Laurel's life unfold before eyes was a surreal one, much like a flower blooming through time-lapse photography. Thirty-two days into the journal, Jackie stopped at a compelling opening line.

Jackie wiped at the tears in her eyes. No more morning coffee trips. They had often been the best part of their day. Laurel had usually paid, too. Not that Jackie couldn't afford it, but it just always seemed to work out that way. Laurel took care of things, the things she didn't want to do or couldn't do or was too lazy to do. Jackie looked at the words in the journal again, her finger tracing over them. *I think there's some part of her that needs to be taken care of.*

A tear ran down her cheek. "How did you put up with me for so long, Laur? You did it all. You gave me everything and I gave you nothing."

A cold tingle washed over her, raising the fine hairs on her arms. A moment later, Laurel stood at the foot of her bed, a sympathetic smile turning the corners of her mouth. "Hi."

Jackie closed the journal. "Were you listening in or something?"

"Sweetie, I can almost always hear you, but especially when you talk to me."

"I was talking to myself, really."

"I know," she said. "You still mad at me?"

Jackie heaved a sigh. "Laur, when have I ever been mad at you for more than three seconds?"

"This last time you were."

True. This time around it had stung more than most. "I was being selfish and a bitch and I'm sorry I yelled at you. I'm terrified of my life right now, and . . ." she gave Laurel a helpless shrug, "I miss my caretaker."

Laurel looked down at the journal in Jackie's lap. "Have you read much of it yet?"

"Just a few entries. Is everything in here about me?"

"Mostly it is. Work stuff too."

"I'll read more," she said. "I think I need to. You know me better than I know myself."

"Some of it might be hard to read."

"I figured as much. I can be a real pain in the ass."

"But in a good way," she said, her effort at being light falling short of its mark.

Jackie sniffled. "I've so much to apologize to you for. I don't even know where to begin."

"You don't have to, hon." She sat down on the edge of the bed. "I have no regrets about what we had, and we still do to some degree. I only wish I'd been able to tell you how much I love you before I did."

"Not sure I would have handled that well. I'm not sure that I am now," she said with a sardonic chuckle.

"I know," she replied, "and maybe now's not the time to discuss all of that. I can't be your therapist, Jackie. Not anymore."

She nodded. "I know. I have to take care of myself and all that shit. I'm not good at that."

"Learn then," she said. "Talk to Tillie. Don't give me that look! She's exceptionally good and kind and understanding and most importantly, she cares. She wants to help you, Jackie. She told me numerous times."

"Why? I still don't get that other than the fact she gets paid good money to do it."

Laurel shrugged and smiled warmly. "Because she likes you. Because she sees what I did, even if you don't. But she can't do anything unless you're willing and believe you deserve something better for yourself."

She picked up the journal and set it on the nightstand. "What if I don't? Or what if she can't help?"

"You do and she will. Jackie, you have to try. I never gave up on you, so you can't either. And yes,

I know how terrifying it is to just lay it out there to someone, but I did it and it was because of you."

"Me? What do you mean? I never told you to seek therapy."

"You gave me the strength to do it," she said. "Because every day you'd do whatever it took to make sure the needs of justice were met, no matter how dangerous or frightening it might be."

"Yeah, but that's work."

"And why shouldn't that apply to you? You are more important than your job, hon."

"I guess—"

"You are! I want to see you happy with your life, don't you?"

A happy life. Now there was a foreign concept. Did she even know what that meant? "This may sound stupid, but—"

"Then it's time to figure it out," Laurel stated, poking a finger into Jackie's leg. "You deserve to be happy, hon. Say it."

"That's silly. I'm not going—"

"Say it, you stubborn, cantankerous woman!"

"God. OK. I deserve to be happy."

"Thank you." She grinned. "Now then. What's going on with this psychic thing? Maybe it's something I can help you with."

"You have permission for that?"

"Don't be a bitch. Tell me what's happened."

So she did.

Chapter 18

The phone pulled Jackie out of dreamless sleep. The clock read 5:37 AM. Caller ID told her it was Belgerman. Shit. That couldn't be good.

"This can't be good," she said.

"We've got another one, Jackie. Another gang member associated with Renaldo Vasquez has been murdered. You want to grab Anderson and Fontaine and bring them down here? Rest of the team is on its way."

Jackie groaned. Not really. "Where's here, sir?"

"Outside a little town called Iroquois."

"That doesn't sound very close."

"It's about two hours south," he said.

Jackie winced. "I hate you, sir." She sat up and rubbed a hand over her face. "I'll be heading out within the hour, with or without them."

"OK." There was a brief silence. "Should I ask how things went yesterday?"

Shit. It was too early for this kind of discussion. "I guess I'm psychic, if that's the answer you were looking for."

"I see." He paused again. "Do I want to know what that means?"

"It means I have no clue, sir."

"I'm sorry, Jackie. Let me know if I can help."

"Just don't fire me for it," Jackie said. "Right now, I don't know if it means anything."

"All right. Just keep me informed. Are Anderson and Fontaine helping you at all?"

"They're trying."

"Good. I'll talk to you later, Jackie."

She hung up and punched in Nick's number. It was time for the circus to hit the road again.

Five shots of espresso and a dash of cream and an hour down the road, Jackie cursed at the rain and single-lane highway traffic.

"They'll have everything bagged and tagged by the time we get down there," she said, cutting back in to her lane after passing a listing pickup brimming over with rusted-out junk.

Nick let go of the door handle as the Durango resumed its frenetic pace down the road. "They might be able to add us to the list at this rate."

Jackie gave him a sidelong glance while Shelby laughed in the backseat. "I've been driving for seventeen years with only one accident," Jackie said. "And that was in a chase. I had no choice."

"Only takes one," he muttered.

"Nick, you're such a wuss," Shelby chided. "You get nervous when anyone besides you is behind the wheel."

"After years of driving with you, can you blame me?"

She snickered at him. "Jackie, when we get there, I think you'll want to stick with one of us, just in case something happens like yesterday."

"I won't be doing much of anything other than

watching and looking, unless Pernetti decides he wants my input," she said. "It's not my case, and my only responsibility is bringing you two."

They passed through Iroquois, a blink-and-you-missed-it town on the banks of the Iroquois River. Just the other side, the GPS had them turn onto Township Road 407, which was blocked off. Jackie flashed her badge and got waved forward, but they were halted at the drive heading into the woods.

A sheriff's deputy came up to the window as Jackie eased the Durango to the side of the road. He gave a quick glance to Jackie's badge and gave her a grim smile. "Far as you can go right now with the car, Agent Rutledge. They've got tire and footprints they're dealing with right now."

"Lovely. How far to the scene from here?"

"Quarter mile into the woods there."

"Great." She turned to find Shelby handing over her jacket. "Thanks." It was her feet she was worried about though. They would be wet and mudcaked by the time they reached the scene.

They walked through the dripping wood, wet leaves swooping down on their heads. Jackie kept her gaze focused on the ground, stepping over and around puddles in the gravel drive. Shelby walked right down the middle, her feet shuffling through the long grass, oblivious to the wet strands that were soaking the cuffs of her pants.

"This is lovely," she said. "I adore the fall."

Jackie cast an annoyed glance her way and proceed to step into two inches of water. "*Gah!* God damn it! Yeah, getting soaked is one of my favorite pastimes, too."

She laughed. "Watch where you're walking then."

Nick, who had walked ahead, stopped at the point

where the wood opened into a clearing. Immediately ahead, crime-scene tape cordoned off a patch of ground outside of a double-wide mobile home. A window facing the area had been broken out and a pale, sickly yellow curtain swung against broken shards of glass. The gravel drive turned into a large circular parking area sandwiched between the double-wide and another single-wide mobile home on the other side. There were a half dozen vehicles parked in the circle, two sheriff's vehicles, and a pair of FBI cars. A van for hauling the bodies away was parked off to the side by the single.

Jackie paused next to Nick, looking up at his placid face, whose eyes were unfocused. "Sense something, Nick?"

"*Mmm,*" he said. "See if you can."

"How? I've never tried to do any of this shit. It just happens."

Shelby stopped on the other side of her. "That's what you need to figure out, how to reach out to it before it reaches out to you."

"You make it sound like a living thing," she said and scanned the scene, thinking perhaps she might see a ghostly figure walking among the crowd. Her gaze fell on Denny, who waved and began to walk her way.

"It's a force," Shelby said. "It's a matter of opening your awareness to it."

"Oh. Is that all?" She waved back at Denny. "Hey, Den. What have we got here?"

"Four dead Hispanics, three males, one female," he said. "All gunshots to the head, except the one, who's had his guts spilled all over the floor. And . . . one survivor, critical condition, was airlifted out about an hour ago."

"They say anything?"

"Something about a pissed-off black dude," he said.

"I see," she said. They needed to track down every black guy who was at the crime scene. Given the neighborhood, the percentage was likely low. Morgan was the only one she knew of and that seemed highly unlikely. Cops were too strong-willed to get possessed. Or at least they should be, and Morgan would have no connection to the vics to want revenge. Right? Jackie could not rule the possibility out and decided it would be something to check on later. "Where are the vics?"

"They're all in the van now. Pernetti, Jenkins, and Wendall are in the big mobile home there picking through things. Sheriff guys are in the other trailer packing up the weed. Think there might be heroin, too."

Nick pointed at the taped off section of grass. "Who died there?"

"That was the female," Denny said. "Shot in the back trying to run away after jumping out the window there."

He took a couple of steps toward the grass. "I think she's still here somewhere."

Shelby agreed. "Someone is, that's for sure. Jackie? Can you sense anything?"

Denny blinked at her, wide-eyed, confused. "What? You mean like a ghost. No shit? You can too, Jack?"

Jackie licked her lips, a burst of warmth rushing into her face. She could feel something, but it was too vague for her to grasp onto. "No. I mean, um . . . I don't know exactly." Why did they have to bring it up like that? Just bam! Yeah, Jackie's psychic now, how about that?

"Fucking-A," Denny said, wagging a disbelieving

finger at her. "This is why you're back early on this case, isn't it? Something happened when you . . . well, when you almost died."

"Den, don't you have something better to do?" She wanted nothing more than for him to go away and keep word of ghosts to himself.

Shelby saved her. She stepped up and kindly pushed at Denny, turning him back toward the scene. "Leave her alone, Denny. This is unfamiliar territory we're exploring here and you're making her nervous. So, shoo! Go away."

He gave one look at Shelby and nodded. "OK, I'm going. Need a pic of anything, just holler." Denny kept walking but looked back over his shoulder at Jackie several times, a mixture of awe and disbelief on his face.

Jackie pulled her hands out of her pockets and rubbed them over her face. "Shit. That's the last thing I need. Whole fucking office is going to know by the end of the day."

Shelby squeezed her arm and pulled her to a stop. "Stop that right now, Jackie."

The squeeze snapped her attention back. She looked at Shelby. "What? I'm not doing anything."

"I know that look and I know what you're thinking," she said. "Don't. It won't be like that unless you let it. Right now, you just need to focus on the task at hand. Relax. You get any more tense and you'll snap in two."

"I really don't want to be doing this."

"I know, but tough shit, babe. You need to do this or it'll end up driving you bonkers."

Jackie gave her an evil glare and pulled free of Shelby's grip. "Fine." She walked hurriedly over to where Nick stood. "What do I do?"

Nick squatted down by the string that cordoned off where the body had been. "Can you feel that general, pervasive sense of the dead? Like when you know Laurel is about to come."

"I know what it is," Jackie snapped back. She took a couple of deep breaths. The moment she envisioned Laurel arriving, the feeling clarified, like a dense, unseen fog settling over the entire area. The air took on a thicker, earthier odor along with the familiar creeping cold that began deep within her bones and radiated outward.

The density of this deathly fog ebbed and flowed, a swirling mist blown about on imaginary winds. It coalesced in places, hot or dense spots as it were, that beat with a dull, slow thrum. Jackie realized what they were as she had seen or at least had a vague sense of the same effect before when Laurel showed herself. They were the places where the dead had gone through to the abysmal cold of Deadworld.

Shelby's hand lightly touched upon her arm. "You can see things, can't you, hon? Places where the dead have been?"

Jackie pointed, though her eyes were not at the moment seeing physical reality. "There and there. Maybe further on, too. They are close together. And here, too, in front of us. Laur told me before that the space between our world and the next is thinnest at that place of death."

She gave Jackie's arm a squeeze. "I knew you'd be able to do it. This is so wild. I wonder what else you can do?"

"Shel," Nick chided, "leave her be for a minute, will you? Jackie? What about right here in front of us? What can you tell about this spot? You might have to touch it in order to get anything. And don't worry, we're ready this time."

"Why don't I find that soothing?" She walked up to the edge of the string and stopped, staring down at the matted grass. "What if I black out again and try to hurt you?" It was that possibility that terrified her more than anything. And not even the fact she might lash out at Nick and clock him in the head again. It was that loss of self that gave her hesitation. What exactly was going on there? Did she actually become someone else for a few seconds? Was she actually and literally gone in that time frame?

"We're here," Nick said. "We'll snap you out of it soon as it happens. If it does."

Jackie continued to stare down at the flattened grass as random drips of water fell from the leaves above, hitting, as she imagined, the dead woman's face, running any makeup across her face, diluting the blood staining the back of her shirt, and helping to wash away trace evidence from around the body, if the killer had indeed even come out to check on her. She squatted down to her toes, reaching toward the background glow of the doorway to the dead.

An assault of Spanish assailed her ears directly ahead, coming from somewhere inside the mobile home. Jackie sprung awkwardly to her feet, cringing in anticipation of the impending blackout, but none came. The screaming woman's voice dimmed, but now that she was aware, it continued on, barely audible above the sounds of the investigation going on around her.

Nick's large, firm hands gripped both shoulders, pulling her back against the breadth of his chest. "Jackie! You with me?"

She nodded. "Yeah." She looked over at the broken window in the mobile home. "I think she's in there, ranting in Spanish. I can't understand a word she's saying."

"Awesome!" Shelby said. "She's a fucking natural, Nick. Holy shit. You didn't even have to try, did you, Jackie?"

"I . . . I'm not sure. I don't understand how any of this works."

"It's like she's got a direct link."

Her voice was giddy, about the exact opposite of what Jackie thought of the whole situation. "You'll have to pardon my enthusiasm. I think this whole thing blows in every way possible."

"It takes a while to get used to it," Nick said. "You'll get to where you can turn it on and off at will or in your case, just off, since it's apparently always on for you."

"What in hell does that mean?" As if this wasn't freakish enough, she was going to be a unique and special freak.

"Like Shelby said," Nick replied. "It seems your trip to Deadworld and back has established a permanent link."

Jackie spun around and stared up into contact-concealed eyes that had an even eerier glow in the misty, shrouded weather. "And that means? Fuck, you guys. I don't understand any of this psychic bullshit. Put it in normal, dumb-girl terms that I can understand."

Nick stared up into the trees for a moment. "That doorway we use to go between, that Laurel uses, it's locked for most people. For someone like me, I'm holding it open through extra means. For a ghost, they can use their own energies to open it up. But for you . . ." He looked back down into her eyes, a sympathetic smile softening the normally hard lines of his face. "I think the door may swing freely either way."

"So shit can just pop through any time it wants?"

"Well, technically, I suppose that's true."

Shelby shoved Nick in the shoulder, forcing him to step out to catch his balance. "Quit sugarcoating. Yes, Jackie, shit can pop through, if they know you're here and if they have reason to want to. Which means it's very unlikely. But since it's possible, you need to be prepared to deal with that. That is the most important thing we must help you with."

"That what happened when I decked you, Nick?"

"Something like that, yes," he said.

"I don't want that to happen again. Ever." She said it with a bit more emphasis than she had planned, and she came off sounding truly desperate.

"Then you are going to have to learn how to push back when the other side starts to bleed through, Jackie," she said. "Otherwise, you'll be at the mercy of whatever decides to come through that door."

"And I do that how?"

"Well . . ." She gave Jackie a little halfhearted shrug. "That's the hard part."

"Fuck, you guys. I thought you were here to help me?"

"We are," Nick said, his voice quiet and calm. "But the best way to figure it out is to interact with the dead. If you are aware of the push and pull between the living and dead you will sense where your own power lies. Then you can tap into that and use it."

"Easy for you to say. I have no clue what you're talking about."

Shelby huffed. "Let's just go in there and see how it goes. We'll deal with things as they come."

Jackie threw up her hands and marched toward the mobile home. "Sure, why not. Let's go chat with the screaming, dead Latina."

At the screen door to the mobile home, Jackie was hit by an all too real sensation of blood and death. It was mixed with the lingering odor of pot. At least they came from the living side of things. She could hold on to that, even if it did turn her stomach.

"Well, well. How on Earth did you get out of bed so early?" Pernetti grinned at Jackie from inside. The light from the kitchen gleamed off the sheen of sweat on his bulbous forehead. God, she had not missed him one iota.

"Belgerman said I could take over the case," she said.

"What!" The flush of red, the utter look of shock on his face made Jackie smile. "You can't be fucking serious."

She opened the screen and stepped in. "Oh, for Christ's sake, Pernetti, loosen your panties. Belgerman would never play that game, fun as it might be."

Jenkins, who was on the far side of the living room, laughed. "Got you there, Pernetti. How you doing, Jack? I see you brought the Ghostbusters with you."

"The what?" It took a moment for it to sink in. She glanced back at Nick and Shelby who had come in behind her. *Ah, hell no. No, no, no.* "Don't go there, Jenkins. I swear to God—"

Pernetti barked out in laughter. "You Akroyd or Murray, Jack?

"Fuck you, guys. Damn it. Fucking *Ghostbusters.*" It would be through headquarters in days. How many weeks of pranks would it spawn?

Shelby stepped around Jackie. "I kind of like it actually. I want a Proton Pack though. That would be cool."

"God, Shelby. Don't encourage them."

Pernetti snickered. "Who ya gonna call?"

"You're going to have to call an ambulance if you don't shut up," Jackie said. "Now, someone want to tell me what happened here, so we can get to work?" She had expected Ryan to be involved here somewhere or at least to have poked his head in to say *hi.* "Where's McManus?"

"Not sure if he's coming. Had his kid to deal with. Anyway. Pretty straight forward looks like," Pernetti said, pushing himself away from the kitchen counter. "Shooter parked out on the road and came right to the door. No signs of forced entry. Took out the two guys here in the living room, nailed one in the kitchen, but not sure that one is going to make it, not without being a vegetable. One that died by the table there had a gun that discharged and we can't find any signs of the bullet. So, hoping the bastard got hit. Rain washed away any signs of injury. Then, our shooter went down the hall there to the bedroom where one vic apparently tried to hide in the closet while the other jumped through the window. Shooter then proceeded to seriously fuck up the one in the bedroom."

"Disemboweled?"

"Yep. Shot to the groin and head."

"Just like the previous scene," Jackie said, more to herself than anyone. "We have IDs on any of them?"

"Yeah, but haven't heard back yet with more info. We'll know soon. I'm guessing they're connected to the previous vics though."

"You call Hauser?"

"Of course, Jack. I've got a handle on things here. Don't worry."

"Not worried," she said. *Just hate you running lead, you swollen-headed prick.* "So, you good to have us look around?"

"Yeah. We're about done in here for now if you want to check things out and do whatever it is you guys do."

Jackie's fists clenched at her side. Her worst, nagging fear about all of this, from falling apart, to the psychic bullshit, and everything else was that she would no longer be taken seriously as an agent. While Pernetti's opinion mattered little to her, she could not help but feel like it was going to be pervasive among the entire unit. Shelby's fingers brushed her hand, lingering for a moment.

"Let's see what we find," she said.

"Go for it," Jenkins said. "I need some fresh air anyway."

The three of them stepped further in to let them out and Jackie gave Pernetti her evilest glare. She wanted nothing more than to wipe that smarmy smirk off his face.

"He's a charmer," Shelby said

"Tell me about it." She unclenched her fists and took a deep breath, wrinkling her nose at the stench. "So, what now?"

Nick stepped into the living room and looked down at the marked-off areas where the victims had been gunned down. "Can you tell where our ghost is?"

"Oh yeah." She had forgotten about her already. Jackie closed her eyes and focused once again upon the dead. The voice of the ghost sprang into her head with such sharp clarity that it made her flinch. Jackie pointed down the hall. "She's down there."

Nick nodded. "Good. Let's go see."

Thankfully, he led the way down the fifteen feet of hall to the main bedroom. A cold draft wafted into the hall from the broken window, cutting down on the reek of blood. The woman's yelling had subsided to an insistent, angry muttering, still in incomprehensible Spanish. Nick walked into the room without hesitation and Jackie hugged close to his broad expanse of protective back.

The room itself was demolished. Lamps were on the floor. The bedside tables were overturned, drawers pulled out on the floor. Clothing lay strewn everywhere, along with the shredded pages of magazines. The base of some kind of figurine stuck out from the middle of a flat-panel television mounted on the wall. The bedcovers were collected in a pile at the foot of the bed. On the mattress, Jackie could see an all-too-familiar pool of blood spread nearly from one end to the other.

Seated on the edge of the bed, face buried in her hands was the faded, translucent form of a woman, long dark hair forming a curtain around her head.

"Ma'am," Nick said with his polite sheriff's calm, "do you understand English?"

Her head whipped around, revealing an anguished, tear-streaked face. She unleashed a torrent of Spanish at them.

"Ma'am," Nick said, "I'm sorry, but we can't understand you."

Jackie found herself shuffling behind Nick a bit more, poking her head around his shoulder. *Stay right there, lady. Don't you come any closer.*

"The bastard!" she shouted with a thick accent. "That bastard took my Loopy!"

"Is this where your Loopy died, ma'am?" Nick asked.

"Vile black devil tore my Loopy up. Why?" she lamented. "Why he do that to my poor Loopy? He was a good man." She buried her face in her hands again and began to sob.

Jackie whispered, "So, what now?"

"We convince her to move on and join Loopy," he said.

"Got any brilliant plans for doing that?" Jackie stayed behind Nick. She couldn't get it out of her head that any sudden moves would have this ghost flinging objects at them—or worse, zapping her and having her attack Nick and Shelby.

"You talk to her," Shelby said. "Treat her just like you would the victim of any other crime."

Jackie stared at the distraught ghost. "But she's not like the victim of any other crime. She's dead, and what if she's pissed off?"

Shelby gave her a hard look. "She's not violent, just traumatized, and I know you can relate to that. Perfect learning opportunity, Jackie."

"Yeah, but . . ." Jackie slowly let out a deep breath. "What if she decides to . . . attack or something?"

"We're right here to help," Nick said. "Just talk to her, calm her down. In these situations, they often don't realize yet that they are actually dead."

"Great. You two are no help at all. You want me to just sit down there and have a little chat with the ghost there and tell her she's dead and should be like . . . moving on." Didn't they get the absurdity of this situation? Or the fact it wigged her out so much she could barely walk?

Shelby nodded and pushed her out from behind Nick. "Yeah, pretty much. Have at it, girl."

Jackie swatted at her hand and gave Shelby a look. "You're such a bitch. Why does Laur put up with you?"

She nudged Jackie forward. "I come with excellent fringe benefits. Now go. She isn't going to bite you."

"Biting is the least of my worries," she said, taking a couple of hesitant steps toward the bed. She could feel the muscles in her legs trembling. What in God's name did you say to someone who did not realize they were dead? Pardon me, ma'am but did you notice the hole in your head? Jackie gritted her teeth and stepped forward.

The piercing cold intensified with each shuffling step. At the corner of the bed, Jackie stopped and glanced back at Nick and Shelby, who both gave her an encouraging nod.

"You're fine, hon," she said. "Get her focus off the Loopy fella."

Fine. This was about as far from fine as Jackie could imagine. She inched closer, rubbing her clammy hands on her pants, and stopped a couple feet away. The blood on the bed was dangerously close to the edge, but Jackie realized if she didn't sit down, her trembling legs might betray her. With her hands braced on her knees, she eased herself down onto the very edge of the bed. The woman didn't seem to notice, and continued to sob and mutter into her hands.

"Hey," Jackie said in a quiet voice. "My name is Agent Rutledge. I'm here to help you." The woman gave no indication of hearing her. "We're going to catch whoever did this, don't you worry."

"Don't focus—" Shelby began.

The woman turned, arms flailing out. Her arm whirled through Jackie like a blade of ice and she gasped, flinching away. Jackie's right hand reached out to the bed in an involuntary effort to brace herself from the blow that made no contact and planted itself squarely in the blood-soaked mattress. The energy of Deadworld leaped up Jackie's arm.

"It was the Devil!" the woman said.

The air grew teeth-chattering cold. Through the thin veil between the worlds that surrounded Loopy's place of death, the opening expanded, emitting a long, violent howl of agony from the other side.

"Loopy!" The ghost turned, staring wide-eyed with both horror and relief. Her arms outstretched for her departed lover. "Loopy. My darling Loopy."

"Ahhh, Maria! Maria!" came the anguished voice from the other side.

The woman stood and turned, leaping through the open door. Jackie, finally having regained a bit of her balance, jerked back from the jolt that flashed up her arm from the bed, a rod of ice that for a moment seemed to freeze her in place. The instant she did, the veil closed, and she stumbled back off the bed, letting out a scream suitable to a seven-year-old who has been snuck up on and goosed.

"What the fuck was that?" Jackie continued to scramble away, pushing herself back against the wall.

Shelby sounded truly stunned. "Holy shit."

Nick jumped over to Jackie and knelt down, laying a hand upon her arm. "Jackie? You OK?"

She clamped onto his forearm, needing something solid to cling to while her heart worked its way out of her throat and back to its normal resting place. "What . . . what just happened?"

Footsteps came clamoring down the hall and Pernetti and Denny ran into the room. Pernetti looked around briefly and then relaxed. "What's going on?"

"It's all good," Shelby said, waving them off. "Just had a little scare is all. We're fine."

Denny rushed over to Jackie. "Jack? You all right?"

Jackie gulped down the hysteria that was threatening to burst out of her throat and nodded. "I'm OK. I think."

"What happened?"

Shelby laughed. "Just a little Ghostbuster action. Jackie was just taking care of business."

Pernetti shook his head, looking utterly confused. "Whatever. Can do without the screaming though, if you don't mind."

Shelby waved him off. "Go. Give the girl some space. Denny, she's fine. We're all fine here."

He backed off, waiting until Jackie nodded in agreement before turning away. "OK then. Let us know if you need anything."

"We will." Shelby walked him back to the door, making sure they both left the room, then leaned against the doorframe, arms crossed over her chest. "Well, Jackie girl. You're just full of surprises."

"You opened a doorway to the other side," Nick said and clasped his hand over Jackie's, giving it a firm, reassuring squeeze. "Our ghost went through to see her man, I believe."

Jackie stared at the bed, not really comprehending what had happened. "How? I don't get it."

"Honestly, I'm not sure I do either," Nick said.

Shelby walked over to the edge of the bed and reached down to touch the bloodstain. She shook her head, mouth slack with amazement. "You have a key, babe. It's like you've been given instant access. Incredible."

"No." Jackie shook her head. "No, it's not."

Nick still clasped her hand. His comforting grip was the only thing keeping Jackie from bursting into tears. She didn't want this. She didn't need it. Her shaking hands didn't need it. Her knotted stomach could certainly do without.

"Think you can stand?" Nick asked.

"Of course I can stand!" She jerked away from him and used her hands to push herself up and away from the wall, only to find her legs would barely hold her up.

"Here," Nick said and offered his arm.

Jackie gave him a defiant glare and made her way out of the room on her own, moving with careful, measured steps. She felt drunk, and the stench of blood in the mobile home was beginning to turn her stomach. Nick stayed close behind, monitoring her every move until she slammed open the screen door and stepped out onto the wooden deck, making her way over to the railing where she grasped it with firm resolve and sucked in the cool morning air. The milling crowd of law enforcement all turned to stare.

She wanted to yell at them, tell them to get the fuck away and quit staring. Jackie turned her back to them and leaned against the rail. Nick and Shelby eyed her with concern, their sympathy crawling around her like a fog, seeping into her pores. "How am I supposed to work with them like this?"

"Not your job to make them accept," Nick said. "You can't worry about that. Right now, your only job is to figure this out."

"Yeah, and that's going so well right now."

"We know more than we did before," he said. "Experience will make you more comfortable. Just give it time, Jackie."

"How about I just leave the dead alone? That would make me happy."

Shelby gave her a curious look. "You going to stop

doing crime-scene investigations? Take a desk job maybe? Quit the FBI?"

The thought didn't sound so bad at the moment. "No." She blew out tense breath. "I'd just like things to be normal again."

She surprised Jackie then and stepped forward, wrapping her arms around her. "Time to make a new normal."

Jackie hesitantly hugged her back, feeling a bit odd embracing her in front of the entire crime-scene crew, but she was glad for it. "Thanks, but—"

"No buts" she replied, stepping back and wagging a finger at her. "You kicked ass before, and you'll do it again."

Yeah, well things were sort of kicking her ass at the moment. It would be nice to feel in control of her life for change.

Nick finally looked down at her. "We need to narrow down our suspect list before she strikes again."

"If these are vengeance-inspired killings, how many could possibly be involved?" Jackie wondered.

Nick shrugged. "Who knows? But this could involve more than just those at the scene. We could be talking whole families of those involved, and if it's a cop, her ease of access to things is going to make it difficult."

"Or someone with a cop's gun," Shelby added.

A cop possessed by a dead pregnant woman. It was difficult to fathom, but the picture of Morgan on the television came to mind once again. They needed to rule him out. Detective Morgan was a good guy, a good cop. She could not imagine him going rogue on them, or being possessed for that matter. He was a tough guy.

"What?" Shelby said, laying a hand on Jackie's arm. "You thought of something?"

"I don't know. Maybe. I'll have Hauser check for me." She pulled out her phone. "It might be nothing. Hauser!" she said when he picked up the other line. "It's Jack."

"Jack? It's 8 AM. I didn't know you were a functioning human being this time of day."

"Oh, ha-ha, funny boy. I need you to check on someone for me."

"This important? Hey, I thought you were doing a vacay or something."

"I know. I'm helping out on the Rosa Sanchez case; more supernatural weirdness."

"Oh!" The excitement in his voice perked up instantly. "Very cool. What've you got?"

"Dig up anything on homicide detective Thomas Morgan. Especially if he's got any connection to the gang involved in this case. Also, I need to speak to his partner and get me a list of all African American law enforcement involved in the initial crime scene investigation."

"Sure thing. Give me an hour or so and I'll see what I can come up with."

"Thanks, Hauser. You're the man." She clicked off the phone. "Might be a long shot, but worth checking out."

Nick agreed. "If he was on the initial murder scene, it's a strong lead."

"I hope not. Morgan's a good guy."

"It's not a matter of good or bad," Nick said. "It's all about strong or weak. Possession is a difficult thing for spirits to do. It takes a certain state of mind to be susceptible to it."

She had no idea what Morgan's state of mind was.

However, it was something to go on, something that she could actually bring to the case if it proved worth pursuing. For the first time in a while, Jackie felt that familiar tingle of excitement for a case, the little surge of adrenaline she received for knowing she was on the trail of a bad guy, pursuing justice for the victim. Only this time, the victim might actually be involved in the murders.

She wondered. "So how do you deal with possessions, if it actually comes to that?"

Shelby frowned. "Good question. I've never exorcised anyone before. Nick?"

He got a pained smile on his face. "I've only encountered one possession. It didn't end well."

"Lovely," Jackie said. "You had to kill them?"

"Yes, I did."

Chapter 19

Belgerman did not sound pleased to hear they might be dealing with a possessed killer. Jackie called him on their way back to Chicago, fulfilling her duties as liaison.

"Is there any way to verify this possibility?" he asked.

"If we can find whoever is possessed," Jackie replied, "we should be able to tell if there's a spirit involved. Nick and Shelby appear to be pretty sure that's what we're dealing with."

"What about you, Jackie?"

"What about me, sir?"

"Would you be able to tell?"

Her stomach lurched at the question. "I . . . um . . . maybe. I think."

"You good for this?" The concern in his voice was clear. "This may push things beyond just being a liaison."

"I think it's beyond that already," she said. "I'm not sure Pernetti will handle this direction in the case, though."

"You let me worry about Pernetti," he said. "You

three keep pursuing this angle. I want it eliminated or confirmed ASAP."

"Working on it, sir. We'll let you know when we have more." She clicked off and punched in Hauser's number. "Hauser, it's Jack again."

"Hey, gorgeous, was just about to call you."

"You got something?"

"Maybe. Your boy Morgan is currently on an emergency leave of absence."

"Really? Since when?"

"Two days ago."

Christ. That was the day of the second murders. "The request say why?"

"Personal reasons, which may have something to do with the fact his wife filed separation papers a week ago."

"Interesting."

"There's more," Hauser said. "I wouldn't be shocked if that separation has something to do with an investigation into prescription drug abuse."

Wow. Bingo. "Anything come of that?"

"It was closed about three weeks ago. Not enough to go on, looks like. Couple other officers busted for it, though. They like their Oxycontin."

"OK, this is great, Hauser. I need Morgan's address—wife's, too, if it's different. Anything else?"

"That's it so far. Up until the past few months, it looks like Morgan was a fairly accomplished homicide detective."

"Thanks. You rock. Email those addresses and call me if anything else pops up."

She informed Nick and Shelby of this new information. They agreed with her assessment. "He's certainly a possible candidate," Nick said.

"I'm going to drop you guys off and get McManus,

see if we can track Morgan down. If we do, I'll call so you can check him out."

"You should be able to tell as well, Jackie," Shelby said.

That was what she was afraid of. "I know, but I want backup for that. Morgan I can deal with, but what the hell do I do if he really is possessed? Will it know I can sense it?"

They were both quiet for a moment, and then Nick said, "I think calling us would be wise. Your abilities are still something of an unknown, so let's not take any chances."

Jackie couldn't agree more.

After dropping off Nick and Shelby at the Special Investigations office, Jackie called McManus. "Ryan? It's Jack."

"Hey, Jack. You still down at the crime scene?"

"No, I'm back in the city now. I need your help with something."

"I've got my daughter with me," he said. "Belgerman let me opt out, which I know I shouldn't have, but this is important. It's my first weekend with her. She needs to know I won't be bailing on her."

Jackie ran a frustrated hand through her hair. "I know, and I'm sorry, but I may have a lead for us to track down."

"Shit. It can't wait until tomorrow?"

"I may know who's doing this," she said.

"What? Seriously? Who?"

"It's . . . it's kind of complicated. Can I come get you?" She held her breath waiting for his reply. If she couldn't count on him for this, what kind of partner would that make him? Sometimes sacrifices had to be made.

"Shit. Yeah. I'll need to get Amanda back home first," he said, his voice soft with resignation.

"Great. We can drop her off. Give me your address." She could hear a young girl in the background complaining already. Jackie understood the dilemma even if she had no personal experience with it. Many agents had family obligations, and she knew of several whose families had crashed and burned due to an inability to balance family and the work. She punched his address into the GPS. "Thanks, McManus."

"Yeah, well. I'll see you soon."

When she arrived, they were waiting for her outside his apartment, a manicured, suburban, sprawling complex with a swimming pool, tennis court, and pretty pond in the center, where the move-in special sign was posted year-round. McManus was shouldering a large duffle while at his side a cute, slightly overweight girl looked at her with a decidedly petulant, disappointed frown on her face. She was going to be the bad guy right from the get-go.

McManus opened the back door and tossed the duffle across. "Get in, sweetie, and buckle up. Jack, this is my daughter Amanda. Amanda, this here is my new partner, Agent Rutledge."

Jackie pasted her friendliest smile upon her face and turned in the seat to greet her. "Hi, Amanda. How are you?" She thrust her hand between the seats toward the girl.

Amanda stared at it for a moment until she caught Ryan's waiting stare from the door. She gave her hand a quick, limp shake. "Hi. Fine, I guess."

"Sorry to steal your dad away, but we've got a big case we're working on."

The girl just leered at her until McManus got into

the front seat. "Buckle up, sweetie. Agent Rutledge drives like a maniac."

Jackie grumbled. "I drive just fine."

Amanda huffed and reached for the seatbelt. "Whatever."

McManus shook his head and faced back to the front. "Sorry. She's not real happy at the moment. We were going shopping today."

"Ah." Jackie nodded. Shopping. A female pastime she never had gotten the hang of. Another aspect of her life she would have to reclaim from Laurel. "Sorry, Amanda, but we're getting close to catching a bad guy and I need your dad's help in finding him."

"You going to kill him?"

She turned her gaze to McManus, who looked skyward. "We don't try to kill them. We try to catch them and put them in jail, so they can pay for the crimes they've done."

"Mommy says it'd be better just to kill some of them. The really bad ones."

Jackie smirked at Ryan's discomforting sigh and pulled out onto the road. "And that wouldn't be right. We're about justice, remember? Not vengeance." On the other hand, Jackie tended to agree. Some of them were so bad, they had no place in society.

She watched Amanda shrug in the rearview mirror. "If someone killed you, I'd want them dead."

Jackie started to smile. "I like the way she thinks, McManus." But it brought up the vivid image of Laurel's body, lying motionless on that stainless steel table, arm dangling over the side with a thin trail of blood running down her arm. Justice had gone out the window at that point. Nobody was going to stop her then from trying to kill Drake. And that kind of motivation could lead to ruin, as she had soon discovered. The amused smile faded away.

"God, don't encourage her, please," he said.

"Are you really a psychic, Agent Rutledge? Daddy said you can see ghosts."

Jackie frowned. "Did he now?"

"Amanda!"

"Just asking. Sheesh."

She gave Ryan a stern glare. "Fact is, I can. I saw one earlier today."

"Wow, really? That's so cool. What it look like?"

McManus turned to face his daughter, clearly annoyed. "Now's not the time, sweetie. I'm sure there will be plenty of chances to ask Agent Rutledge about her work at another time."

"It's fine, McManus. Doesn't matter now if she already knows. Amanda, it looked a lot like a regular person except they were all faded out and gray. A lot like you've seen in movies sometimes."

"What happened to her?"

"She was shot, but that's all I can tell you about that, OK?"

Amanda sighed. "OK."

At least she believed. McManus gave her a pained *I'm sorry* look, which she ignored. The rest of the fifteen-minute ride went in relative silence. Jackie felt her blood pressure rise with each passing mile. You didn't chat with family about your partner, not in any intimate, revealing sense at least. Some did, but passing along this information was not cool. Who else had he told? Then again, why the hell did it matter? The entire office would be talking about her soon and everyone would know. As much as she wanted to keep it a secret, Jackie knew she would have to be willing and able to discuss it. At the very least to dispel the inevitable rumors that would spread.

McManus called his ex shortly before arrival and she was waiting outside when Jackie pulled up in the driveway. There were a few, obviously bitter words exchanged and he gave Amanda a hug good-bye. Part of Jackie felt bad for doing this to him, but most of her did not fully understand. If you had an active case, you worked it no matter what. The bad guys weren't going to wait for you to go shopping before they decided to kill again.

She waited until they were back on the road before she gave him her best *what the fuck* look. "Don't talk to your daughter about me, Ryan, unless you ask me first."

He gave her a sheepish nod. "Yeah, I'm sorry about that. Something got mentioned in passing and she just latched onto it."

"I don't care. Honestly, I'd rather you didn't mention anything related to ghosts, but it's starting to go around. Just don't make me sound like an idiot."

"I wouldn't do that, Jack. Nobody knows anything?"

"They have some vague information, but I'd prefer not to feed their infantile brains. I'm already being referred to as one of the Ghostbusters and it's . . . hey! Wipe that smile off your face. I'm not going to be the butt of office jokes every time I turn around. Someone will get hurt."

"Jack! Chill." He raised a hand to ward her off. "I won't let it happen again. If it bothers you that much, I'll keep my mouth shut until you give the word."

"I just can't handle being made fun of right now."

"Fair enough. So what are we doing?"

"We're tracking down a homicide detective by the name of Thomas Morgan."

"No shit? That whole rogue cop angle is legit?"

"Maybe. A"—she paused and licked her lips—"a ghost referred to the murderer as the 'black devil' and oddly enough Morgan called in sick after the second murders."

"That seems a bit weak," Ryan said. "What about the other murders then?"

"The theory from Special Investigations is that this person has been possessed by the woman murdered at the first scene and is seeking vengeance on her killers."

"We can work that as a legitimate lead? Don't you think Chicago PD will be all over us with that?"

"Sure, if we tell them. I just want to find Morgan. If we can track him down, I'll be able to tell if he's possessed, or I should anyway. If it's true then we call in the crew and get him off the street before he goes after anyone else."

"These murders are happening in a hurry. He could be doing that now."

"I know. That's why I wanted to get on this fast. We've got tire tracks from the scene to try and match to his car and also the ballistics evidence. We believe he may have been injured, too."

McManus stared at her in silence for several seconds, weighing what she'd told him. "All right. Do we know who he might be going after?"

"We've got a list from Gang Enforcement of people associated with Vasquez. I'd like to chat with his wife first, though. Maybe she's got some info that might lead us to him."

"You got a number? I'll let her know we're coming."

"Pernetti says that Vasquez is AWOL, too. We need

to find him. He's either involved in this or knows who did it."

"I'll talk to Gang Enforcement and see what I can find and touch base with the other guys working that end and see if there's any new developments."

"Great." She could do this. He was a capable, smart guy. It felt completely awkward, like one of those first couple of dates where you're still trying to figure out the other's rhythms and the ebb and flow of things. Nobody would ever be Laurel. Jackie had to keep reminding herself of that fact. Somehow that would have to be all right. "And get me directions to Morgan's wife. I have no idea where she works."

After receiving an address and plugging it into the GPS, they found Beverly Morgan worked as an office manager for a small accounting firm just west of downtown Chicago. She was smartly dressed, perfectly coiffed, and very aware of what a visit by the FBI might entail. They didn't even get a chance to introduce themselves.

"What's he done?" Her tone held equal parts fear and worry. "Is he dead?"

"Mrs. Morgan," Jackie said, "I'm Agent Rutledge and this is Agent McManus. We don't know if your husband has done anything at this point. As far as we know he is still alive, but we need to find him so we can speak with him."

"I haven't seen him in three days," she said in a hushed voice. "We've been having . . . marital difficulties. I filed separation papers a week ago and he has not taken it well."

"Do you know where he's been staying?"

She shrugged. "Friends, hotel, I don't know and, honestly, I don't really care. Until he gets help, I don't want him in my life. If you can get him to stop coming by the house while I'm at work, that would be a big help. The cops won't do a damn thing."

McManus said, "How often does he do that?"

"He stops to get food, clothes, whatever. I don't know how often. He could be there now for all I know."

"Ma'am, we need to check on your house. It's urgent that we find your husband."

"I'm off at five. I can let you in then," she said.

"Mrs. Morgan," Jackie replied, fighting to restrain the tone of her voice. "Your husband is working on an ongoing murder investigation and may be in some danger. Determining his location quickly is very important."

Her hands dropped to her sides. The tight line of her mouth went slack. "Is someone after him?"

"We really don't know anything at this point," Jackie said quickly. She did not want Beverly going down that path at this point. "He has information vital to our investigation and nobody has been able to locate him for the past two days."

"He hasn't been at work?" Now she was beginning to panic.

"He called in for a leave of absence two days ago," McManus said.

Jackie inched forward, easing into Mrs. Morgan's personal space. "Please, Beverly, we just want to check out your house to see if he has been there or if he's left any clue as to his whereabouts. Hopefully it won't take long. We'll vouch for your need to leave work if need be."

"No, no, that's fine," she said, shaking her head. "I can take a couple hours off. I'll meet you there."

The wide-eyed panic said it all. She knew he was in trouble or worse, knew he was capable of making it.

"Thank you, Beverly," Jackie said. "Your cooperation is greatly appreciated."

At the Morgans' house, Beverly stood on the front steps; it was a brick and wood suburban home in a subdivision where every third house looked like a reversed floor plan of this one, with the same chemically green lawns and perfectly shaped shrubs. Jackie parked on the street, leaving the one Nissan Sentra alone in the driveway. No other cars were parked by the house. Morgan's absence was immediately confirmed by his wife as they walked up the driveway.

"He's not here," she said, "but the door was unlocked, so he must have come by earlier."

Jackie picked up her pace. "OK. I'd like you to stay by the front door if you can, Mrs. Morgan. We'll try to be as quick as possible."

"Stay by the door?" Her hand came up to her mouth. "Sweet Jesus. He is involved in something, isn't he?"

Jackie laid a hand on her arm. "Mrs. Morgan, we honestly don't know. Our only goal here is to either confirm or deny some information we've received."

"What information is that?"

"We can't divulge that at this time," she said.

She nodded. Thankfully, cops' spouses understood this. "All right."

Once inside, they got the layout of the house and Jackie asked McManus to take the upstairs. "See if anything has been used recently, change of clothes, computer, or whatever. I'll check out down here."

"Sounds good." He nodded once and headed up the stairs.

Jackie left Mrs. Morgan standing in the entry worriedly working her hands together as she watched strangers begin to poke through her house. The living room and dining rooms appeared to be in perfect order, immaculate even, magazine quality in their arrangement down to the artfully placed coffee-table books. In the kitchen, Jackie found the first signs of use, a single glass perched on the edge of the sink. While it could have been left from Mrs. Morgan's morning routine, she had the suspicion that nothing got left out of place in this household. Moving into the kitchen, Jackie picked up an odd sound, a low vibration she felt in her feet.

"Mrs. Morgan," she called out, "is the washer and dryer in the basement?"

"Yes. The laundry and playroom are down there."

Washing machine cycles were typically around forty minutes. Could they have missed him by such little time as that? Or possibly he was down there now. Jackie pulled out her Glock and walked over to the basement door in a short hall running between the kitchen and dining room. As quietly as possible, she opened the door and listened. There was no other sound other than the churning rhythm of the washer.

"Detective Morgan?" No sound. She heard McManus come to the landing of the stairs directly above her.

"You got something, Jack?"

"Washing machine is running down here," she said.

His footsteps thumped in rapid fashion down the stairs.

"Thomas!" Mrs. Morgan called out in a shrill voice.

"Stay right here, Mrs. Morgan," McManus said to her. A moment later he was with Jackie at the basement door. Seeing her gun, he withdrew his. "Anything?" he asked quietly.

"Just the machine."

He looked down the stairwell. "Lights are still on."

"Yeah."

"Stay here, I'll take a look," he said and started down the stairs.

Jackie grabbed his arm. "I'm quite capable—"

"Liaison, Jack. Keep back unless it's necessary. Don't want you getting in trouble."

She let go. "Shit. OK, go."

McManus went down. She watched him disappear around the corner of the stair. "Detective Morgan?" he called out. "This is Agent Ryan McManus, FBI." More silence. He came back to the stair and went in the other direction before returning a moment later. "It's clear, Jack."

Jackie went down, following the sound of the washing machine. The laundry room was to the right, a squeaky clean, finished room with shelves, a folding table and a long bar to hang clothes on. A hamper sat beneath a shoot leading up into the house. She stepped up to the washer and opened the lid. It was in the spin cycle. The timer said there was ten minutes left on the cycle. "He was here within the last thirty minutes."

The load inside was only a few items. What caught her attention, however, was the bright smear of blood on the lip of the washer's bowl. Blood. Fabulous. "McManus, look here."

"Blood? Well, shit. Look at that." He peered into

the bowl to check out the clothing. "Think we better get the scene guys over here."

Jackie let out a deep breath. "Yeah, we better. I want to check something first." *God help me, please be ghost-free.* She flipped her gun around. "Take this."

"What? Why?"

"I'm going to test the blood sample there for signs of . . . ghost stuff."

He took the gun, eyes wide, unsure. "Need me to do anything?"

Jackie ran a hand through her hair, staring down at the simple red smear, so full of potentially bad news. "Get behind me and put me in a restraining hold."

"Seriously? What the hell for?"

"In case I flip out and try to claw your eyes out," she snapped back, nerves beginning to chew like ravenous wolves through her stomach. "I decked Anderson the last time I did this."

"Wow, OK. We don't need that." He stepped behind her. "Give me an arm." He turned her right arm up behind her back and wrapped his arm across her chest. Her left arm was only free from the elbow down. "That work?"

She nodded, her eyes still riveted on the blood. Jackie's mouth had gone dry as bone. She rasped out, "Yeah, good enough."

Jackie closed her eyes and took a couple of deep breaths. As her mind turned its focus toward the dead, the smear of blood took on substance. It radiated beneath her hand, a faint but discernible presence. She did not have to open her eyes to tell exactly where it was. Her fingers hovered inches above it, quavering with dread anticipation.

"Here goes," she whispered.

The glow of the doorway to Deadworld sprang to life upon touching the blood, a soft nimbus of pale, gray light enveloping the washer. The biting cold wind of the other side came through, carrying with it a thunderous bolt of anguished rage that flowed up her arm like water down a funnel.

"Jackie!"

Something fierce had a hold of her, clamping her down into submission. She turned and twisted against it, desperate to break free of the thing she knew had intentions to kill.

"Jackie! Jesus Christ! It's me. Ryan!"

Her eyes fluttered open, staring up at a row of baskets sitting upon a shelf, full of neatly folded clothes. Shirts hung from a rod overhead. The light of Deadworld had vanished. "McManus?"

"You want to get off of me now?"

They were sprawled on the floor and he had her pinned on top of him. Jackie turned and rolled off, getting up on her hands and knees. Her elbow was throbbing from smacking into something, while the bitter cold of Deadworld faded from her bones.

"What happened? What'd I do?"

McManus rubbed at his jaw. "Besides elbowing me in the face and threatening to kill me, not much. What the hell was that, Jack?"

"Thomas!" Beverly Morgan yelled from the top of the stairs.

"He's not down here, Mrs. Morgan," Ryan yelled

back. "Just a little scare down here. Nothing to worry about."

Jackie grabbed the washer and pulled herself up and then offered Ryan a hand. "Sorry about that. I haven't figured out how to stop it yet."

"And what exactly was that?"

"The rage of the woman who's got a hold of Morgan," she said.

Ryan pulled himself up. "That's one pissed off lady."

"Look what happened to her. Wouldn't you be just a little peeved?"

"Yeah, guess I would be ready to kill."

"We need to get the evidence guys out here for this stuff," she said. "And I need to get Nick and Shelby out looking for this guy. He's going to be looking for the next perp."

"I'll ring Pernetti and get an APB out on Morgan's car."

"Good. Then I want to get back out there and hit up neighborhood hangouts for this gang. Someone has to know who Vasquez's men are. We just have to hope Morgan doesn't have too much of a head start."

Chapter 20

They left a distraught Beverly Morgan sitting on her front step with her head in her hands, hair whipping across her face from a blustery October wind, waiting for the crime-scene crew to arrive. Nick and Shelby were on their way up to the north end of Chicago to look for Detective Morgan, with a clear warning from Nick to avoid direct contact with the suspect. Jackie hoped that would be the case. She had no desire to interact with Morgan if he was filled with what she had felt from Deadworld. McManus was now in his own vehicle.

They needed as many separate bodies on the street as possible, because as it stood now, Morgan was only a person of interest. Jackie was not about to have Pernetti start a manhunt based on her sensing a ghost. They needed some kind of direct, physical evidence. But more importantly, Morgan was working with the advantage of knowing whom he was going after. Their only real hope was that he didn't know where the next perpetrator was at and they could catch up to him. There was a chance Morgan was doing something entirely different, but Jackie had a gut feeling that was not the case. The ghost of Rosa Sanchez was on a very single-minded mission and would not stop until she was done.

After much internal debate, Jackie decided to call Belgerman. She still had no real idea how all of this supernatural stuff sat with him.

"Belgerman," he said. "How you doing, Jackie?"

"Following up on a lead from Iroquois," she said. "We encountered another ghost."

"What have you got?"

Jackie took a deep breath. "I think that homicide detective, Thomas Morgan, may be possessed by the ghost of Rosa Sanchez."

There was a slight pause as he took that in. "Damn, Jackie. That's not going to go over well at all. You have any way to confirm this possibility without turning it into a shit storm?"

"Not 100 percent, sir. We're close. I found blood at Morgan's house that, uh . . . indicates the presence of Rosa Sanchez, and that we may be looking for an injured suspect. We missed him by less than thirty minutes."

"You got Pernetti in on this?"

"Mostly," Jackie replied. "The crime-scene crew is on its way there. We've got an APB out on Morgan's car, but I haven't told him we might have a possessed cop on our hands."

"No other evidence connecting him specifically?"

"Tire and foot tracks at the scene. We've got the ballistics, but we need him or his car to confirm. McManus, Anderson, and Fontaine are out with me hoping to track him down."

"You need more bodies?"

Yes! Just like that. He didn't even question. "We do, but I was hesitant to tell Pernetti what we're doing. This is kind of out there, sir. What we really need is to track down this Vasquez guy ASAP or find some information on his known associates. That's who Rosa is after."

"OK. I'll get more resources on that. I'll tell Pernetti to get some bodies out looking for Morgan. His actions are suspicious enough to warrant questioning. We need a tighter connection though, Jackie. I'm very hesitant to be chasing down a respected detective without some solid evidence."

"I know," she said. "I'm just worried we don't have time before she finds her next victim."

"You find him; I don't want you getting involved, Jackie. You aren't officially on this case."

You mean you don't think I'm prepared to be involved. "I'll do my best, sir."

"Jackie, I mean it," he said. "You're a liaison on this, not an agent. Confirm your suspicions and get the team on it."

"Sir, I get it."

"All right. Good. And be careful, please. This is untested ground you're covering."

"Yeah, no kidding." She hung up and slowed the Durango down to the speed limit. She was in gang country now.

And severely wishing she knew some rudimentary Spanish. McManus would have far more luck than she talking to the locals. Regardless, they were searching on a wing and a prayer. Their only hope lay in the fact that the killings were in the news and whomever else was involved had found a safe place to hide. Rosa would have to do a little digging to find out where they were at and Jackie hoped they could find her doing just that.

She drove up and down several blocks, keeping her eye out until she spotted a bar with a name printed in bright, green lettering. Jackie pulled into an empty space at the curb and was about to get out when her phone chimed. It was Nick.

"Hey," she said, "any luck?"

"Can you tune into police radio?" he asked.

"Not in the Durango. What's going on?"

"They're responding to an assault call at The Raging Bull," he said. "You know where that is?"

"Shit! McManus and I were there. I think I remember where it is."

Nick gave her the address. "We're on our way. Five minutes."

She called McManus while she wheeled back into the street and then skidded around the next corner. "Ryan, we've got a police response to an assault at The Raging Bull. Meet you there." Jackie clicked off and blared her horn at the traffic to get out of the way. The bar was only a few blocks away.

A pair of Chicago PD cars were pulled up to the curb in front of The Raging Bull. Two uniforms were standing outside on the sidewalk with a Hispanic man seated at the curb between them. He held a bloody white towel to one side of his head and was waving his other vehemently at one of the cops. Jackie came to a lurching stop behind the nearest police car. At the same time, the roar of a motorcycle engine came up from behind and Shelby came sliding to a stop behind the Durango. Even as she was swinging off, Nick's car slid to a stop on the opposite side of the street.

One of the cops turned to Jackie, anger written all over his face. "This is a crime scene, lady. You'll have to—"

"FBI," she said, pulling out her badge. "We need to question the victim here."

"Whoa! Hold on a sec." The cop raised his hand. "What's going on?"

"We believe the perp is a suspect we're trying to track down. A few questions and we'll be out of your hair."

He waved at the bleeding man at his feet. "Have at it. Hope you speak Spanish."

Yeah, great. Shelby solved her problem in seconds. She knelt in front of the man, her tight T-shirt hiked up to reveal even more midriff than usual. She pushed her sunglasses up on to her head and gave him that huge, disarming smile that turned most men into slobbering idiots.

Spanish flew out of her mouth and the man snapped back an incensed retort. Her hand reached out, fingertips resting on the man's knee. Jackie couldn't follow a word of it. Nick arrived in the middle of their interchange.

"We know what's going on here?"

The cop shrugged. "Someone barged into the bar and assaulted our compadre here. Still haven't determined what it was about. These guys don't tend to be very forthcoming."

Jackie gave him a hard look. "These guys?"

"The gangbangers. They tend to settle their own disputes. Unless weapons are involved we aren't going to do much."

The man on the sidewalk had changed his tone. The anger was gone. He gave Shelby a begrudging smile. She had him pull the towel away to inspect the wound. It was a nasty lump at the hairline on his forehead with a half inch long split that was still seeping blood.

"That's going to need a couple stitches," Jackie said.

Shelby patted the man on his knee and kissed the bare side of his forehead. "Hector here was smacked with the butt end of pistol. Says a big, pissed off black guy came in and started grilling him about the whereabouts of 'Steel-Toe' Juarez."

"Did he know who it was?" Jackie asked.

"Never seen the guy before, but he knew poor ol' Hector here. Sounds like our guy."

"Did he tell him where this Juarez guy is at?"

"Aunt's house on Oaktree Lane."

McManus came running up the sidewalk then, badge in hand. "You guys were quick. What've we got?"

Jackie pointed at him. "Call Gang Enforcement. We need an address for 'Steel-Toe' Juarez's aunt on Oaktree Lane. Morgan was just here looking for him."

He was on the phone before she finished. "Anyone know where Oaktree Lane is?"

One of the cops pointed in the direction behind the bar. "About eight or ten blocks west of here."

"Thanks," she said. "Nick, Shelby. Head over from the south. Ryan and I will circle over from the north and hopefully the address will be between us. I'll call you soon as we have it—and let me know if you spot his car, a green '05 Cadillac."

She didn't wait for their reply and ran for her Durango. Ten minutes, maybe fifteen. They couldn't be any farther behind him than that. A little luck and Morgan would be waiting until night time again, but she wasn't counting on it. Rosa was not acting with patience. The dead didn't need to wait for a damn thing.

Six blocks later, McManus called in. "Four-six-three-three Oaktree. That's north of us I think."

"Great! Thanks, Ryan. I'll tell them. You see his car, get on Pernetti right away."

"Yep. You got it."

Jackie flipped on her wipers. The wind-whipped clouds were starting to fling hard little pellets through the air, snicking off the Durango like the nails of a hundred tiny claws. She reached Oaktree and had to slam on the brakes to get around the corner. Fortunately the sleet had just started and the streets were still dry or she might have found herself kissing the grill of the Ford F150 that blared at her as she straightened out and gunned it north up Oaktree Lane. McManus was already there, turning a careful circle on the sidewalk.

She put down the passenger window as she approached the unassuming, small brick house and leaned over. "Ryan! I'm parking up at the corner to block the road off. Give me a sec."

He groaned and looked skyward. "Shit. Should have done that myself. Sorry."

"Just in case," she said, and drove half a block up, stopping angled across the road. A person would have to drive over someone's lawn to get around. Jackie kicked the door open and stood on the runner to jump down, when the she noticed something from her extreme height advantage: a green car parked behind an SUV half a block farther up the street. Suspicious for sure, except when she looked in the immediate vicinity, Jackie caught sight of a man, a tall black man with a limp, walking up the steps to a house, but it was definitely not 4633 Oaktree.

"Fuck!" Jackie hopped down and began to run. She fumbled at her phone, trying to hit McManus's number again and then managed to drop it. "Motherfu—" Jackie hesitated. Morgan or someone looking very much like him from a distance was on the porch of the house. Stop to pick up the phone and lose what might be precious seconds or yell for McManus and alert Morgan to her presence? Jackie kept running, tiny pellets of sleet stinging her face. Fifty meters.

At forty, the man reached into his coat and rang the doorbell with his other hand. Jackie reached into her own and grabbed a hold of her Glock. "Morgan!" He turned his head in her direction, just enough to see her coming out of the corner of his eye. "FBI, Morgan! You need to stop right there."

Twenty-five meters and the front door opened. The screen came off, pulled free with one swift yank. The move was so abrupt and absurdly out of the ordinary that Jackie did not realize until too late what the possessed Morgan was doing.

At fifteen meters she dove to her right, down into the grass, but the corner of the door caught her across the back. It felt like a knife had been jabbed into her. There was a scream and Morgan's voice said something in Spanish.

Jackie sprang to her feet, ten meters away just as Morgan's gun went off, the steely crack stopping her heart for a brief second. Someone in the doorway fell back into the darkness of the house. "Rosa! Stop!" Jackie yelled. She pulled out her Glock sprinting the last few meters to the front step. The arm pivoted back around and Jackie realized there wouldn't be time. She fired once, hitting the side of the chest as she turned. Again, dead-on center. And a third in the right shoulder, hopefully disabling the shooting arm.

Three point-blank shots, all in good locations, with enough force to drop a man in his tracks, or certainly to knock him back off his feet. All it did was knock his aim off a few inches.

Morgan's Glock flared, booming in Jackie's ears from two meters away. In those life-threatening moments when you see everything with pristine clarity,

Jackie swore she could see the bullet coming out of the barrel, a hot, pointed hunk of lead screaming directly at her head. A flare of fire then erupted above her left eye, streaking across the side of her skull, leaving a shallow groove, searing like lava.

Jackie's momentum carried her into Morgan, her shoulder burying itself in his gut, and they stumbled through the doorway, landing on the contorted, groaning body of whomever he had just shot. Her vision was blurring, stung with blood running into her eye, but she did see Morgan's hand, raising up his Glock, and rolled onto her side, putting a bullet through his wrist. His gun clattered across the floor and bounced off a wall.

Through the raging fire that seemed to be engulfing her skull, Jackie could hear someone screaming. There was yelling going on somewhere in the house. Morgan had sat up, staring at the ragged hole in his arm. His gray T-shirt had blossomed a dark red stain. Jackie had seen this before, that look of disbelief, that it could not really be happening, that they really were about to die, and for a moment that is what she thought she was seeing in Morgan.

A smile crept across his dark lips, spreading to reveal teeth tinged with the pink of blood. "Agent Rutledge," he said, this time in heavily accented English.

"Hands on your head, Morgan," Jackie said, trying vainly to squirm her way out from beneath Morgan's legs, but the body beneath was making it too difficult. She blinked at the blood flowing into her eye. A minute tops and McManus would be here. He had to have heard the gunshots.

In the space of a blink, Jackie found herself going from pointing a gun at Morgan's face to being pushed down to her back, gun pinned to the ground with her hand under such force her knuckles were grinding into the hardwood beneath. His eyes looked down at her with the bottomless void of the dead. Jackie continued to struggle, but her head was about to explode from pain and she was feeling the warm rush of lightheadedness.

Morgan's weight crushed down. "Sweet Mother Mary," Morgan's voice hissed into Jackie's ear. "You're broken."

Laughter bounced around in Jackie's head, chased by scorching, bursting flames. She could taste the blood in her mouth. Broken? What the hell was that supposed to mean? How long had it been? Twenty seconds? Thirty maybe? Where were they?

Morgan's eyes were wide and bloodshot and Jackie could feel his fist balled up around her hair. His voice wasn't sinister or even angry or filled with pain. Of all things, he sounded surprised.

"You're broken," Morgan said again.

The fist picked up her head and snapped it back against the floor, bringing a final fiery explosion of pain to Jackie's skull, followed by the extinguishing, howling wind of Deadworld. In that last moment of awareness, Jackie felt that doorway swing wide, pulling at her like the vacuum of space, cold and empty, and then the darkness consumed her.

Chapter 21

Nick pulled up to 4633 Oaktree to see McManus at a dead run, sprinting up the street. Shelby straddled her BMW just in front, watching the same scene. When he looked outward with his otherworldly senses, it was then he realized where he was headed. They had got the wrong house. Jackie's Durango was parked sideways across the street at the end of the block, the driver's side door flung open to the sleet. She was nowhere in sight.

Two muffled pops, like firecrackers set off indoors, made Nick flinch. Panic bloomed in his chest, a dark, storm of wings beating into the sky.

Shelby must have had the same reaction, as they both gunned their vehicles up the road, cutting up over the lawn of the corner house and bouncing off the curb. McManus had crossed the street and was bounding across the lawns toward the fourth house from the corner. Shelby raced up the sidewalk. A screen door, torn from its hinges, lay in the grass. Nick skidded his way back onto Oaktree and then slid to a stop in front of the house, door flying open before he had stopped completely. Shelby had laid the BMW down in the grass, jumping from it in one smooth motion to reach the door at the same time McManus did.

There were two bodies lying on the floor in the doorway, and Nick could see blood splattered against the opposite wall. *Please, not Jackie. Please, God, no.* The phrase repeated over and over until he reached the door and realized that her life force was still here. Shelby and McManus had just stepped inside.

"Jack?" McManus yelled. "Where you at . . . Jack! Fuck! Man down! Man down."

Nick grabbed his phone, but Shelby could be heard already shouting at the 911 operator. On the floor in the entry, two bodies lay unmoving in spreading pools of blood, one of whom looked to be Detective Morgan. Around to the left in what was apparently the dining room, McManus and Shelby were knelt over another prone figure. Nick recognized the hiking boot right away and leaped over Shelby's back and landed on the hardwood beyond Jackie's bloodied head.

The entire left side of her head was soaked in blood. Other than that, her body looked surprisingly peaceful, half curled onto her side, head resting on her arm. Shelby's deft fingers were digging into Jackie's hair.

Nick tried to stare around the fingers. "How bad does it look?"

McManus had a hold of her wrist. "Praise be Christ, she's got a steady pulse."

"Looks like the bullet grooved her skull," Shelby said. "Bleeding like a stuck pig. See if you can find a hand towel or something in the kitchen."

"Right." Nick sprang to his feet and went into the next room, where another body lay slumped against the back door. His hands were clasped over his groin and a black circle anointed the center of his forehead, centering the splash of blood across the door and wall. He gave a quick, furtive glance around the kitchen and spied a dishtowel hanging by a hook next to the sink. Nick folded it, soaked it in cold water, and rang it out, dripping water across the floor as he hurried back in and handed it to Shelby. He could feel the surge of energy from the other side coming through her and into Jackie. The wound at least would be sealed off in a matter of moments.

"I'll get those bodies out of the way so we can get her out of here."

McManus raised his hand to stop Nick. "Slow down, Mr. Anderson. We've already compromised the scene stomping in here to get Jackie. Stay right here until the paramedics arrive. I'm going to go secure the area."

Even as he spoke, Nick heard sirens off in the distance. He heaved a sigh of relief. "All right. Yes. I hear them now." Kneeling down by the dead, black man, Nick looked him over. The wide, glassy eyes were sunken in, surround by dark, purple smudges. He looked a lot like a heroin junkie who'd overdosed. If his spirit still hung around, he had wandered off from this place, perhaps in search of his home. They would have to check later, on the off chance he had not moved on. It would be very interesting to find out his side of this story.

A moan escaped from Jackie's lips then, and Nick's stomach nearly sprang into his throat. An instant later he knelt by her head. "Jackie? You with us?"

Shelby continued to dab at the blood on her face and head. It had stopped at least. It was all she would do for now, given the paramedics were coming. "She's still out, babe. Relax. We're under control here. You should go see if McManus needs help with anything."

Nick stared down at Jackie, blood still streaked into the lines and crevices of her face. She looked nearly childlike with all of the stress removed, but the fact was, she'd been a centimeter from her life being drained away. She had promised to not go after him by herself. "What I need is to find out what the hell happened."

"Nick, chill. Now is not the time. Your girl is going to be OK. That's all that matters."

"My girl?" He tried to give Shelby the stare-down, but she only gave him a wide-eyed little smirk. He blew out his breath and stood. "She promised not to face this thing alone and she did anyway. That's going to be a problem."

"Likely good reasons," she said.

"Which is why I'm going to go find out what happened. Did you check her for any other injuries?"

"Yes, I did. A nasty contusion on her back. Looks like it might have been that screen door in the yard. Otherwise, she's all right. So go. Make merry with the FBI."

He rolled his eyes at her and stepped carefully back over to the front door, making sure not to move or touch anything he didn't have to. The wail of sirens indicated they were close, and stepping out onto the front steps, Nick could see McManus waving them over while he talked on his phone. People were starting to gather on the sidewalks on either side of the street. Even wind-whipped sleet would not keep the gawkers away, not when the bullets and blood were flying. Getting the story from McManus would have to wait.

By the time Jackie was loaded onto a stretcher and

into the ambulance, FBI were beginning to arrive. Pernetti was in the first car. He winced at the bandage around Jackie's head.

"Christ, Jack. You're going to get killed one of these times." He nodded at Nick. "Anything I should, um . . . know about, Mr. Anderson?"

"No, we're clear in that regard. I'm going to follow Agent Rutledge in and make sure she's OK. I'll let McManus know once doctors give the thumbs up."

"Thanks. Where is that little Irish newb at?"

Nick pointed. "On the steps."

"Great." He turned toward the door. "McManus!"

Nick made for his Porsche and followed the ambulance to the hospital, hoping they had seen the last of that ghost. Perhaps now she would see to her babe. And it hit Nick just then, like a slap to the head. The babe was the key to tracking this ghost. Why hadn't they considered it before? Laurel could find it. It might take a few hours, but she would, and then it was wait until the woman showed herself or try to talk her down from this rage-filled vengeance she was inflicting upon them all.

He dialed up Shelby, who said she would pass the request along. It made sense, she said, and stupid of them all not to think of it. They arrived in less than ten minutes, and the paramedics wheeled Jackie in. Nick was forced to wait in the lobby, which he would for now. He called Belgerman to let him know what was going on, and got an earful for not making sure someone was with Jackie at all times. His heart sank for her. She would be on leave once again while they investigated the shooting, and this would not be so easy to dismiss.

"How are you going to handle the supernatural

element of this when the Internal folks come asking questions?"

"I don't have a fucking clue," John barked back. Nick hoped he mellowed before seeing Jackie. "I can't exactly tell them she shot a cop because she thought he was possessed by a ghost, now, can I?"

"No, I can't imagine that will go over well at all," Nick replied, mustering his calmest voice. "Let's hope there is sufficient other evidence."

"We'll make some goddamn evidence if need be," he said. "Is this ghost, or whatever the hell it is, gone now?"

"I don't know," Nick said. "I hope so, but we don't know if she was done. I'm hoping to find out."

"How you planning on doing that?"

"Honestly, John? It's better you don't know."

He chuckled in Nick's ear. "Figured as much. Jackie's going to be all right, though? You're positive?"

"She'll have a hell of a scar on her head, but otherwise I think she'll be fine. Physically at least."

There was a moment of silence between them, both understanding what those last three words implied. "You'll keep an eye on her, Nick?"

"Much as that's possible."

"Yeah." Again there was a few seconds of silence. "Let me know when she's available over there."

Nick hung up and waited. It took ninety minutes for them to patch up her scalp and get her into a private room. He looked through some magazines, got a cup of bad coffee from the in-hospital McDonalds, and tried to avoid noticing all of the little things that kept reminding him of one centimeter. The distance between life and death could be very small. Then again, it might as well have been a mile. Jackie was alive and that was all that mattered.

That life still ebbed and flowed in his veins. In quiet moments, if Nick turned his senses inward and he focused upon that energy that fueled his continuing existence in this world, he could catch fleeting moments of Jackie, taste her soul as it were. She reminded him of good coffee: strong, dark, and complicated, with hints of many wonderful flavors hidden within if you paid close enough attention to notice. He wanted to continue savoring that drink.

Nick finished his coffee and glanced at his watch. Jackie had been in her room for ten minutes. He did not want her waking up by herself. He made his way down the labyrinth of tile hallways, sidestepping the occasional ghost he found wandering the halls. Hospitals were horrible places if you could see the dead. They were everywhere, lingering in rooms and halls and parking garages. One could counsel the dead for endless days and never see the end of them, and by now Nick had spent enough time in hospitals over the years to avoid them unless absolutely necessary.

At the third floor nurses' station, Nick walked up to the counter and leaned on it, smiling down at the nurse seated at the computer. "Pardon me, ma'am. I'm looking for Jackie Rutledge's room. I believe she was just brought up a short time ago."

Her hard, worker's gaze melted away when she caught his eye. "Are you a family member, sir?"

"Someday, perhaps," he said, throwing in a bit of drawl. "We haven't got that far yet."

She gave him a knowing smile. "Ah, I see. Well, I wish you the best, sir. Let me see." She shuffled through a few charts. "Here we go. She's in three twenty-four. Down the hall there and on your left."

"Much appreciated, ma'am. Thank you."

Her cheeks began to redden. "Any time, sir. Let us know if she needs anything."

He found Jackie mumbling softly in her sleep, white gauze creating a cap on her head. An IV ran down to her arm, dripping clear fluid into her veins. Nick pulled one of the chairs over from the opposite wall and seated himself beside her. Jackie's head turned back and forth, the murmuring growing more intense. He couldn't make out what she was saying but the tone did not sound pleasant.

Gently, Nick reached up and placed his hand over hers. "*Shhhh*," he whispered. "It's all fine, Jackie. You're safe here. *Shhhh*."

Her hand involuntarily grasped his and her body settled itself. She remained quiet for some time after that, but Nick kept his hand on hers, until at some point he began to drift himself.

She woke him abruptly by squeezing his hand. "Broken," she said in a raspy voice. "I'm not broken. I'm not. I'm not broken."

"Jackie," Nick said, leaning in close. "Jackie, it's Nick. You're safe in the hospital."

"What?" Her eyes blinked rapidly. "Hospital? Nick?" Her eyes finally focused on him. "Nick. What happened?"

Her voice held the drunken, groggy remnants of anesthetic and painkillers. "Morgan shot you," Nick replied. "Grazed your skull."

Jackie closed her eyes. "God, my head hurts. I shot him, Nick. Did he make it?"

"No. Morgan is dead."

The eyes squeezed even tighter. "Fuck. I'm so screwed. I had no choice."

"I know. They'll see that."

"Shit." A moan escaped her lips, but then she

opened her eyes to look at him. "The ghost. What about Rosa?"

"She was gone by the time I got there."

"Is she really gone?"

"Wish I knew. If that was the last guy, then maybe," he said.

"Oh." Her eyes closed and Jackie was silent for a while. Nick said nothing, but kept a hold of her hand. "What time is it?"

"It's been about two and a half hours since the incident."

"Any news?"

"Nobody's called me," he said. "I talked to Shelby about thirty minutes after getting here and she just told me the place was crawling with FBI and CPD. She wanted to make sure you were all right."

"Am I? OK, I mean."

"Looked a lot worse than it was. You know how scalp wounds bleed, but you'll have a nice scar to show for it."

"As if my hair didn't already look like shit. Lovely."

"Least of your worries now, Jackie. You'll have people in here asking questions soon."

"Yeah, I know." She turned away, looking out the window at the rain running down the window. "I killed a fricking cop." She let out a long, slow sigh. "I knew Morgan. We weren't friends, but I knew him. He was a good guy. He has a daughter."

"I'm sorry, Jackie. This kind of thing is never easy."

"They'll all say I should've waited, but how could I?" Her rough voice was cracking. "He just blew away the guy in the doorway without hesitation. Was anyone else in the house? Did my foolishness save someone at least?"

"There was another body in the kitchen," he said,

wishing like hell he had something good to say to her. There was no decent way to spin this story.

Jackie nodded and was silent. Then her head turned back to him. "Wait. How? Wasn't Morgan dead in the doorway?"

"Yeah. I don't know." Nick envisioned the scene again, Morgan and the first victim in the entry and Jackie lying on the floor in the dining room. She was the only one with a clear view of the second victim. "He must have staggered around the corner and shot the guy and fallen back into the entry."

Jackie gave him a blank look for a second. "I guess. Last thing I remember was Morgan slamming my head into the floor, and . . . that's it."

"Maybe you pulled him back into the entry after that. Your memory is likely a little skewed after what happened. Blows to the head will do that."

"I guess," she said and sagged back into her pillow. "I really could use something to drink."

There was a pitcher and plastic cups on the bedside table. "Here let me get you some water." He poured out half a cup and held the cup up to her lips.

"I'm not an invalid, you know," she said, the hint of a smile on her lips. "But thanks."

"Hungry at all?"

"God no. My stomach feels like hell. I bet the coffee here is horrid too."

"I'll bring you a latte later."

"Thank you." She closed her eyes once more. "That'd be great."

"Get some rest, Jackie. You need it." She nodded but did not open her eyes. "You want me to hang around for when the others start rolling in?"

Her voice was a murmur now. "That could be hours. You don't need to do that."

"Sooner than that, I think." He stood up and gave her hand a squeeze. "I'll be around. Get some more sleep, and I'll give you warning when they start to arrive."

She made an agreeable sound but was already fading out. Nick looked down on her for several minutes, watching her sleep, the slow rise and fall of her stomach, the bandaged head that made her look far more frail than she was. When he was sure she was out, Nick turned around and left.

Chapter 22

McManus sat in the dining room of Javier Johnson, cousin of Manuel "Steel-Toe" Juarez, his head propped on his hand. The evidence crew had finally left with their plastic bags and collected items detailing what they figured had happened. They had it wrong, however. They took the convenient answer.

He couldn't exactly knock Pernetti for accepting it. The guy was a decent agent, but he didn't want to accept the unlikeliest of scenarios. They had stopped the bad guy in a less-than-ideal manner, but when it was all said and done, they had stopped him and that was all that mattered. All they needed was a confirming report from Jackie and they could file it away: Agent Rutledge tracks down rogue cop and kills him after two victims are killed and he fires his weapon at her. Justified response. Unfortunate. End of story.

Only the more he had looked at it, the less likely it seemed the scenario played out that way. The others either didn't see it or had collectively decided not to look at the evidence. Protect your own. The Chicago PD didn't like it either. One of their own had gone astray and was gunned down by the FBI. That never went down well no matter how you played it. But even they had glossed over what seemed plainly possible to McManus.

Detective Morgan had not shot the second victim.

The first shot fired had been victim number one. He clearly remembered hearing that first distinct pop and turning to see Jackie sprinting across the lawns in the next block. Who would have thought those short, slender legs could move a body so fast? He had started after her when he saw Morgan. Then another gunshot followed by three in rapid succession as she charged him. That was when she had been nearly killed. They had blood evidence from the yard for that. Jackie had then barreled into Morgan, taking him down in the entry of the house. McManus just reached the house's yard when two more shots went off.

Three seconds. It couldn't have been any more than that before he got to the front door. Morgan and Johnson were dead in the entry and Jackie lay unconscious in the dining room. In the initial chaos of dealing with Jackie, he hadn't even considered what had happened. By the time he got a moment to breathe and had come back in from securing the area, the rest of the crew had arrived and Pernetti had taken over. Nobody had asked the disturbing question: Why was Jackie the only one in sight of the second victim?

Ballistics would tell a clearer story. If she had fired more than three shots, people might then begin to wonder. Her gun, though, had been on the floor, lying between her and Morgan. There may or may not be prints from Morgan on her weapon, but that wouldn't be conclusive. He knew how they would write it up. Morgan had grabbed her gun and shot the second victim before collapsing himself. Perhaps he had shoved her into the dining room where she collapsed. Any number of potential scenarios could tell the story, but the facts didn't really add up. How did a guy, shot twice in the chest, stagger around the corner into the living room and get off two perfectly aimed shots? It had been mere seconds, so Morgan, even if alive, was at the end of his rope and not in any shape to get off any kind of clean shot, much less two bull's-eyes.

So, however improbable, Jackie had or most likely had shot the second victim. Why would she do such a thing? It made no sense.

McManus got up and walked back to the front door, playing through the scenario in his head. He ignored the television crews on the street who turned their cameras in his direction. There would be plenty of time for questions. He would play out the events over and over again for many. The Bureau of Professional Standards guys would be all over them, going over the events until he was sick of them. Jackie would have it ten times worse. Poor Jack. Helping on a case to get back in the swing of things and she winds up killing a cop. No telling how long she would be on leave for this one.

"What the hell happened, Jack?" McManus said, trying to put himself in Morgan's shoes, being shot in the doorway, bleeding out, shoving Jackie into the dining room, putting two rounds into a guy in the next room and then stumbling back to collapse in the entry. While physically possible, McManus could not wrap his brain around the second victim. If you're in your dying moments, you aren't moving around blowing people away with pinpoint accuracy. But trying things from Jackie's point of view made even less sense. Tackling Morgan, staggering into the dining room after he's died, likely light-headed and woozy as hell from the head wound, and then shooting an unarmed guy in the next room.

It made the scene look like Jackie had taken out Morgan's last victim for him. Unless, by some miraculous turn of events, the second victim was actually the first and Morgan happened to run into the first coming out of the house. That didn't explain the screen door though.

McManus sighed and thrust his hands into his pockets. This was getting him nowhere. He needed to speak with Jack before the Standards guys came down on her.

He pulled out his phone and dialed up the hospital and got routed to Jackie's room. After four rings a male voice answered.

"Agent Rutledge's room."

"Mr. Anderson? This is Agent McManus."

"How are things over there?" he asked.

"Winding down here. Is Jack available to talk? How is she?"

"Groggy but all right. She's got company at the moment. Something you needed to ask her?"

"Lots of things, actually," he said.

"You and a dozen other people," came Nick's agitated reply.

"Yeah, I figured. This is going to be one big cluster fuck. Tell her to call me as soon as she can. I really need to chat with her about what happened."

"I'll do that, Agent McManus. Oh, hold on," he said and there was a moment of muffled conversation. "Call her tonight. She insists she will be home in a few hours."

"Will she?"

"Unless they chain her to the bed."

McManus laughed. "Yeah, all right. I'll try her around nine or so. Thanks, and wish her luck for me."

"I'll do that."

He shoved the phone back in his pocket and headed back outside. There was little for him to do at the scene now, and he needed to figure out what the hell to put in the incident report on this. For now, at least, he would keep his absurd notions to himself. Things were enough of a mess already without throwing suspicions toward Jackie, and it would look bad for her if they had different accounts of the events.

Stepping down onto the front walk, McManus recognized a familiar figure standing on the sidewalk beyond the scene tape. Belgerman had decided to come and see for himself, and given the beckoning shrug of his head, he had been waiting for McManus to come out. So much for syncing their stories together.

Chapter 23

Jackie prayed it was time for another Percocet. Her head felt like a sculptor was going at it with a hammer and chisel. Nick stood at the window, staring out through his reflection. Laurel sat weightless on the end of her bed, legs dangling through the footboard. Shelby had contacted her after leaving the scene, and the hospital was a place she had been to before, so she could travel directly. Her presence had helped alleviate the stress of two hours of endless questioning, made worse by Belgerman.

He had come by twenty minutes after she woke up. After assuring himself of her health, the first words out his mouth about the case had been simple and direct. "Jackie, you need to consider yourself gagged when it comes to anything supernatural involving this case. Don't even hint at anything odd."

Not that she had any desire to do so, but her involvement in the case was entirely supernatural. "And what was I doing on this case then?"

"Investigative backup. Research. Background on potential suspects. You were looking into the rogue cop angle after Morgan went on leave after the second murders. Spin it however you like, Jackie, but leave the ghost out of it. I know it will be difficult, but you will manage it."

Nick, who was sitting against the windowsill, arms crossed over his chest, sounded more curious than angry about the news. "If they look into us, they may start to wonder."

"Don't worry about that, but I need you on board with this, Mr. Anderson. If you're asked, you were investigating a prescription drug ring, involving illegal Oxycontin prescriptions. Your client is confidential and shall remain so."

"This is a bit unusual, John," he said.

"I know, but we can't afford the supernatural angle to get public on this one. It's already a mess with a cop getting killed."

"So, I'm on leave again I take it?" Jackie asked.

"Until this gets investigated, yes. The case, as far as everyone is concerned, is over. The killer was stopped."

Nick unfolded his arms and hooked his hands in his pants pockets. "We don't know that Rosa is done. We still don't know everyone she was after."

"We'll keep looking for Vasquez, but as far as this case is concerned, once these loose ends are tied up, we're done."

Two hours later, Jackie felt nowhere close to being done. More than anything, she felt done in. The cops had been first, a grim-looking female detective with her hair pulled up into a tight little knot on the back of her head and an even tighter frown. She spoke in a rock-hard staccato voice, but Jackie couldn't muster the energy to be annoyed. Drugs and the mild concussion made the world beyond the confines of her body inconsequential. Pernetti had followed, but was mercifully brief, realizing quickly that she was in no state for prolonged questioning. Denny had stopped by more to see how she was doing, followed by the doctor checking up on her, then someone from Professional Standards, who only took a brief statement of events and stated they would need to speak with her as soon as she was able.

In between, Jackie dozed in and out of consciousness, full of hazy dreams smelling of blood and Morgan's grinning, bloodstained teeth. When she came out of the last dream to the touch of the nurse looking to take her blood pressure, Jackie felt the overwhelming desire to get out.

She reached for the water on her bedside table, but it was empty. Nick, stoically patient in the corner chair, got up to fill her cup. After taking a couple of sips and waiting for the nurse to leave, she said to him, "I'm ready to go home."

"They want to keep you overnight for observation," he said, but his tone was perfunctory.

"I need to get out of here, Nick. I hate the sterility and the smell."

He nodded with a knowing half-smile. "All right. I'll make the arrangements."

"Thank you." Jackie sagged back against the pillows. Once again, Nick was there to help out. Quiet and subtle as a mouse, he had stepped up his presence in her life. Even when she had not really asked or wanted him to be around, he had wormed his way in, refusing her complaints in that ever-steady, unruffled voice. And obviously, she didn't mind that much or she would have fought him more. The fact was, having him around outweighed how nervous he could make her feel.

Shelby walked in with a duffle-shaped suitcase slung over a shoulder. It took Jackie a moment of sluggish awareness to realize it was hers. "Hey. That's my duffle. How did you get that?"

She cocked an eyebrow at Jackie. "How do you think?" Shelby unzipped the top and removed some clothes. "I took the liberty of grabbing a couple of things for you to wear, since the other stuff is covered in blood."

"You knew I was going home tonight?"

"Hon, I'm surprised you made it this long." She patted Jackie on the leg and gave it an affectionate squeeze. "Nick asked me to get you some things to wear a couple of hours ago."

"Oh, OK. Thanks." She turned and pushed herself up into a sitting position, head swimming around like it was free-floating atop her neck. After grabbing a T-shirt from the pile, Jackie reached back to undo the tie on her hospital gown, but found her fingers bogged down by the Percocet. They would not work properly.

Shelby slapped her hand away. "Stop. Here." A moment later, the ties were lose and Shelby was assisting Jackie out of her hospital gown and into clothing: sweatpants, T-shirt, jacket, socks. It was like a mom getting her daughter ready for school in the morning.

"I could've done that, you know," Jackie said.

Shelby's fingers stopped in the middle of pulling up Jackie's second sock. She looked up at Jackie for a second, those bright green eyes curved in sympathy. "Do you ever let anyone just do something for you?"

"Of course."

"Without letting them know you were quite capable of doing it on your own?"

"I . . . what is that supposed to mean?"

"It means just say 'Thanks, Shel.' That's it. No addendums or rationalizations. I don't think less of you or think you're weak or unfit or whatever it is. You don't need to be independent every single moment of your life, Jackie girl."

"I know that—"

"No." Shelby shook her head and finished tying off her running shoes. "I don't think you do. There. Good to go, babe. Let's get you home and in a proper bed."

Jackie looked down at the shoes she likely had not put on in two years. Laurel had bought them for her after a chase in her hiking boots had failed to catch the perp. "Thank you," she said, overenunciating each word. "Did Laur head out?"

"She's off to see if Rosa has gone back to her babe or not. We need to find out if she's done."

"And if she's not?"

"Then we need to figure out a way to stop her and keep her over in Deadworld until she can move on."

"Why do I really not like the sound of that?"

"Because we've no idea how to go about doing that other than crossing over and confronting her."

"Screw that. I'm not going over there." Jackie shuffled over to the bathroom to pee and caught the sight of her bathing cap of a bandage. "Oh, my God. I look like a fucking Q-Tip."

Shelby snickered. "Notice how I politely said nothing about that."

"I can't go around with this thing on my head," Jackie said. "Nobody will take me seriously." She pointed out at Shelby. "Don't say it, bitch. I know you were."

"Did I say a word? I was only going to tell you that I will take it off when we get you home. Or Nick can, if you prefer."

Jackie slammed the bathroom door closed. "It doesn't matter."

"Thought so," came the amused reply.

The doctor reluctantly let her sign out, warning her to rest and not do much for the next day or two. She got another prescription for the Percocet and they were home by eight-thirty. It was going to be a cold night, and Jackie felt all thirty-eight degrees of it biting into her as they hustled into her apartment. She was practically shivering by the time she got inside.

Jackie sniffed the air when she walked in, finding the faint whiff of blood and corpse still following her. Maybe it was the bandage and wound on her head she was smelling. Bickerstaff distracted her annoyance by running up and rubbing for food. "You a hungry boy, Bickers?"

Shelby waltzed into her bedroom to put the duffle away, and Nick stepped into the kitchen. "I'll get a can out for him," he said. "Just sit down and relax, Jackie. You want a coffee?"

She held the cat against her chest, rubbing at the soft fur. "What I want is peace and quiet actually. I'd like to be alone for a while."

"You want that bandage off before we go, Jackie?" Shelby called from the bedroom.

"No, I can—" She dropped Bickerstaff when he reacted to the can being opened on the counter. "Thanks. That would be great if you could."

Shelby gave her a big, cheesy grin. "Scissors?"

"Kitchen drawer."

Jackie found herself sitting on the edge of her bed, looking into the mirror over her dresser as Shelby looked to be jabbing scissors into her head. The metal was cool against her scalp, and Shelby made quick work of snipping through enough of the gauze to peel it slowly off the side of her head.

"Well . . . it's healing well," Shelby said. "Have to get you a sock hat to wear though, because it's—"

Jackie turned her head away from Shelby's probing fingers and glanced sidelong into the mirror. Someone had taken a pair of sheep sheers and shaved a two inch wide strip off the left side of her head and painted a mottled pink strip down the middle of it. She sucked in her breath. Looks never ranked high on Jackie's, but she knew she wasn't ugly. Plain maybe, but this? This was horrible. "Ahhh, shit! What the hell? I'm the bride of Frankenstein."

Nick stepped in to the doorway. "How's it look?"

"It's fine, Nick. Go away," Shelby told him and took a step in front of Jackie. "You've seen one scar, you've seen them all, so shoo!"

"It's just hair," he said, but Jackie heard him walk away.

"He's right, you know," Shelby added. "Most of this will grow back. You'll just have to wear it long enough to fall over that scar. Just think of the stories you'll be able to tell your grandkids about—"

"Stop, Shelby," Jackie said. She didn't even want to look at the mirror. "It's just hair and it's also fucking hideous. I don't need any interesting marks to show off to people." She kicked off her shoes toward the closet, bouncing them off the door. "Plain ol' Jackie doesn't need a war wound or something for people to point at or wince at or do any fucking thing at. Just give me the goddamn Percocet and let me go to sleep."

Shelby sighed heavily beside her. "OK, hon. I'll get you a glass of water."

Two minutes later, they were mercifully gone and

the apartment was shrouded in blissful silence. Jackie flopped back on her bed, still clothed in sweats and T-shirt. The mutant, freaky scar-girl didn't have the energy or willpower to undress herself. Her fingers wandered up and lightly touched the stitches along her scalp. The wound was a good six centimeters long, running from above her left temple clean across the side of her head.

Bickerstaff walked up from the end of the bed to sniff at her hand. "Scary shit, huh, Bickers?" He licked her finger and Jackie pulled it back down. They were starting to tremble.

Death had come and left her a little calling card. One measly centimeter and her brains would have been oozing out into the grass. Jackie pulled her cat in close and clung to his furry warmth. She squeezed her eyes shut, trying to hold back tears. The worst of it was, she couldn't even take solace in knowing that all of this was over. Rosa could still be out there, planning to take over someone else to finish her deadly vengeance.

Bickers began to purr with contentment in her grasp and the gentle motor along with the creeping haze of drugs lulled her off into sleep, where the doorway to Deadworld yawned open and Rosa's words pushed her along. "You're broken. You're broken."

Chapter 24

A perk of being dead was that you never got tired. You could walk for hours and hours and not feel a thing. If you knew where you were going, it did not even require walking. All you needed was a reference point and you could will your spirit to that place. If one were so inclined. Most spirits had no such inclination. Why bother? There were no crosstown barbeques to attend. You could not go see a movie. Church services were not held. Dying had the tendency to sap all the fun out of life.

Laurel continued walking. It had been a couple of hours, she guessed. Telling time in Deadworld was difficult given that it did not seem to flow in the same manner as physical reality. She had an address, had looked at the map on Shelby's phone, and shuffled off to find Rosa. She had wanted to stay with Jackie, be there when she woke up, and assure herself that she was recovering. When Shelby had informed her that Jackie had been shot, panic gripped her, sending her instantly to the hospital before Shelby could even tell her the room number.

But determining if Rosa was finished took precedence. If she wasn't, then she would be looking to possess someone else in order to finish the job. When Shelby had told her Morgan was dead, her first thought had been to see if Jackie had become a victim of Rosa's wrath, but her presence had been gone, only the lingering taint leftover from the fight with Morgan.

She continued to walk, up avenues of empty businesses and through silent neighborhoods, cloaked in the perpetual hanging fog that continually shifted to obscure and reveal the colorless landscape. Laurel made careful note of the places she went. Solid reference points would make traveling much easier in the future. A detailed knowledge of the city was what had allowed Nick's friend Reggie to move almost unimpeded throughout Chicago. That ease of movement had saved Cynthia against Drake's goons.

On occasion, she would find other spirits walking aimlessly through the streets, looking right through her most times, oblivious and lost in their own laments, but once in awhile someone would look at her and offer a nod of acknowledgment or stare at her with wide, hopeless eyes. Many, she expected, had been lingering here for so long that they had forgotten why they remained. The times she had made an effort to strike up a conversation had generally been met with stony silence. If they did speak, it was almost always plaintive requests if she'd seen someone. So many souls unable to let go of their lives.

It would have been easy to get depressed, but thank the Great Mother, Laurel had a purpose still. Jackie needed her—to help nudge her life in the right direction and keep her from spiraling down into ruin, where she continually teetered on the brink. As much as she wanted to, Laurel knew the decisions were not hers to make.

And then there was Shelby. What sort of relationship did they have? They could not be together in a physical way, other than the few blissful moments when she would pull Shelby across for a brief kiss goodnight. Even then, the contact was dulled, not quite there, and more often than not left her wanting. She would give almost anything to have a bit of real, physical time with her. Shelby had more life in her than a dozen living people. Funny, smart, giving, and a walking poster girl for sensuality, Shelby was a girl's wet dream. Or dream anyway; the dead had no physical response to desire. She would take what she could get, having lost so much in her dogged love for a woman who would never feel the same for her.

But her only regret was in failing Jackie by not helping her face those things that continued to pull her down and keep happiness always at arm's length. For that she would linger until Jackie was gone, if it came to that.

Rosa's neighborhood was not unlike the previous miles Laurel had walked, an endless, gloomy tract of buildings, seeping into the mist, lifeless structures coming out of the featureless, stony ground. Laurel wondered why this world presented itself as it did, how there were buildings but no trees, as though someone's architecture class had built models of everything in Chicago and failed to accessorize. Worst of all, perhaps, there was no sense of the Great Mother here, no vastness to the universe or feeling of greater power existing within and around all things. There was power in this place. It permeated everything, and Laurel could only guess that it was this power that formed the landscape in which she traveled, that gave her the energy she needed to travel to the living world.

It was then she realized she had no sense of anything at all in this area. No ghosts wandered these streets or lingered in the homes nearby. It was as though nobody had ever died in this neighborhood, as if they had all been well-adjusted souls who moved on, or for some reason had all left the area. It was a ghost town for ghosts. With a growing sense of unease, she continued on.

Laurel had street names and an address. It was all she needed to find Rosa's home, but within a few blocks, Laurel realized an address would not have been needed at all. The keen of Rosa's baby echoed through the fog, a ceaseless wail of fury and fear. Even the blanketing sky needed respite from the onslaught, drawing away from the power of the babe's spirit to leave a clear, pristinely detailed group of houses centered around the glow of Rosa's. The whole area had a light of its own, radiating from the core, a tiny sun in a dark sea of the dead. The empty neighborhood now made sense. Who would want to linger in the presence of this anguish and anger?

The baby's spirit had the intensity of innocence and burned with the rage of having it stolen before it had even begun. She could not feel Rosa's presence, though perhaps it was buried beneath the power of the babe's. Laurel continued to approach, cutting between houses now, making a direct line for the source. The wail continued, fueled by spiritual strength not air, so that it sounded more like a never-ending siren. It reminded Laurel of a tornado warning.

There was no way to hide or disguise her approach. The babe would sense her, but there was no way to judge what his reaction would be. If Rosa was there, obscured by the power of her child, Laurel realized she might not know until she actually reached them. Would she be viewed as a threat? She would have to assume that was true until proven otherwise.

Three houses from her goal, Laurel began to sense another presence, but it was not Rosa's. It had a different quality all together, a familiar taste upon her senses that she knew all too well. Laurel stopped in the middle of the street.

"Jackie?" How was that even possible? Jackie could not be here. "Jackie!" she yelled and began to run. There was only one reason she could be here. "Sweet Mother, no."

Laurel willed herself to the front of the house and was instantly whisked over to the front door. It stood half open. Jackie's presence was clear now, in sharp relief to the more diffuse, radiating energy of the baby. She pushed the door open.

"Jackie!"

From up above, a hesitant, confused voice answered. "Laur?"

And then she was gone. The cool rush of wind signaling the opening of the door to the living world blew through her and then Jackie's presence abruptly vanished. In her place someone else had come.

Laurel paused at the foot of the stairs. This taint was familiar, too. Rosa had returned.

She stood frozen, hand clenched on the banister, staring up the stairs. It took Laurel a moment to let this turn of events sink in, to process the meaning of what had just happened. Jackie had been in Deadworld. She left at the same moment Rosa arrived. Had they somehow switched places? It did not make sense. Possession didn't throw you into the other side, not as she understood it anyway, but then Jackie was different. Something had happened to her here, where no living soul should be able to come. She had been changed by the experience. Was it possible to possess someone by literally swapping out their spiritual energies? She had possessed Jackie to get her out of Deadworld before.

There was no other conclusion Laurel could find. Rosa had possessed Jackie and forced her spirit self to the other side. Rosa would have free, unfettered control of Jackie's body. And now she was back. Had she felt Laurel's presence approaching her babe?

Rosa's frenzied, roaring voice answered her. "Stay away from my baby!"

"Rosa," she called. "My name is Laurel Carpenter. I was—"

"Get away from my baby!"

Behind her, the door slammed shut, blown shut by the force of Rosa's voice. Laurel decided she had better run. She knew that tone of voice. It was the voice of someone past the threshold of reasoning. Nobody was going to get near her babe, whether good, bad, or indifferent. She was a threat, pure and simple, and Rosa would likely do whatever she could to neutralize that threat.

The door would not open. Laurel exerted more force of will upon it, but she could do little more than budge it. Laurel began to draw her will to go to Jackie. She needed to warn her, but the door to the living got closed before she could even try to open it. Too late, Laurel turned to face the charging whirlwind of Rosa Sanchez.

She barreled into Laurel, hands outstretched, with the speed of a rampaging bull. Laurel slammed into the door and blew it right off the hinges, sending her tumbling across the stony ground. Being dead, the blow itself did no harm to her body, but the blast of energy that coursed through her felt like she had stuck her finger in a light socket. For a few precious moments, Laurel lay on the ground stunned. Before she could get her bearings again, Rosa was on top of her, hands clasping for her throat.

"You leave my baby alone! You can't have him!"

Laurel clamped her hands around Rosa's wrists, but there was strength there beyond a single person. She was drawing from her babe. "Ro . . . sa. I . . . don't . . . want . . ."

She could not get the words out. Rosa kept pounding her head against the ground, holding her throat in a viselike grip. Each blow sent drowning waves of energy through her body. Her soul was literally getting blown out of her body with each shock of her head against the ground.

I've got no chance against her, Laurel realized. It was the Drake situation all over again—pitted with a foe that completely outmatched her and at their utter whim. This time, however, there was no holding out for the cavalry. Nick and Shelby had no clue she was even in trouble. Her only hope lay in letting Rosa believe she had won, think that she was truly dead.

Laurel ceased fighting against her, let her body get beat against the ground over and over. She turned her focus inward, concentrating down to that small core of her being from which all of her spiritual energy sprang, pulling herself down, deeper and deeper. All of her remaining energy condensed down to a tiny, protected point, a hard shell of energy that, she prayed to the goddess, would remain impervious to Rosa's rage.

Her sense of body drifted away to nothing. The world of the dead evaporated into darkness, and

Laurel braced herself for the inevitable assault. She could only hope this tiny slice of herself that remained would disappear beneath Rosa's blind anger, and she would be left with the sliver of hope that Jackie, Shelby, or Nick might find her and give her enough energy to come back from the brink.

Laurel quieted her mind—emptying it of all thought, focusing on nothing—and waited while somewhere out there her spirit bled away, one violent slam at a time.

Chapter 25

Jackie covered her ears. The baby's wailing was incessant, a droning, endless cry born of injustice and pain. Her hands did little to quell the sound. The gray fog of Deadworld drifted through the sky above her, cold and unforgiving.

"Great," she muttered. "Another damn Deadworld dream."

Only this time she got to be the ghost. Her flesh gave off the familiar soft light and was gray as the ground beneath her bare feet. At least the pounding in her head was gone. She reached up and felt the long stitched welt on the side of her head. Dreams apparently could only do so much.

She turned around to get her bearings and recognized the home of Rosa Sanchez, clear and colorless, appearing quite unlike what she had seen here before. It had a glow to it not unlike her own flesh, throbbing in syncopated time to the infant's cries. Somewhere in there, probably writhing on a bloody mattress, was the source of the awful sound. Jackie thought for a moment to tell her dream to fuck off and just walk in the other direction, but she knew how dreams worked. No matter what direction she went, the house would reappear. Jackie went to shove her hands in her pockets only to realize she had on her sweats, and so huffed in annoyance and began to walk toward the house.

"Stay out of my house."

The voice came from all around and inside her head. Jackie stopped and turned in all directions. Nobody was in sight.

"Rosa?" She was fairly sure that's who it was. The voice was rushed and low, bordering on a growl. The accent was certainly Latino.

"You keep away from my house," she said, "or I shall make sure you stay broken. Do you understand?"

Jackie winced. There was that phrase again, in all its awful simplicity. "What are you talking about?"

"Just keep out of my house!" Her voice was an intense whisper around Jackie, almost like she did not want other people to hear.

"Yeah, whatever. It's my dream. I'll go in there if I want to," Jackie said to the air. "Besides, I'm dead. Doesn't fucking matter now, does it?" For a brief, stomach-clenching moment, Jackie wondered if perhaps she was indeed now dead, having drifted off into some drug-induced coma while she slept. What a shitty way to go that would be. But she was in front of Rosa's house, which would not have happened if she were really dead. She would have been at her apartment, looking down on her corpse with half its hair shaved off and a wretched football lace running along the scalp. Nick would surely want to kiss her now. And she cared about this, why?

"To kiss or not to kiss," Jackie said and began to walk around the house, the wail pushing against her with literal force, forcing her to lean toward the house as though she were walking in a strong wind. This was one of the most intensively tactile dreams she could ever remember having. Her previous dreams of Deadworld had been very muddled, full of swirling images, violence, and cold that caused your bones to break into tiny shards. Of course now she had a screaming babe to deal with.

Jackie wondered how she would feel about this if she were a mother. Would those cries sound different to her? Probably so. But she did know about innocent lives stolen in the worst of ways, and this was just an extreme example of that.

"What was his name going to be, Rosa? If you're going to be talking to me I may as well see how I answer."

She was in the backyard when the answer came. "Antonio."

Jackie nodded. "OK. I like that name; good, strong, male name. After the father? Or was Rennie Vasquez the father?"

A string of Spanish clapped down around Jackie like a sonic boom and knocked her to her knees. Likely, the words were not kind ones for Rennie Vasquez.

"Wow." Jackie got back to her feet, more surprised than hurt. "So we don't like Rennie." She was coming back around to the front door. She stared up at the upstairs windows where somehow the wailing siren of Antonio continued to blare, his rhythm and intensity perfectly constant. "What is little Antonio saying, I wonder?" Jackie stepped up to the door and turned the handle. "Is he crying for mother or screaming for vengeance? What do I think?"

Rosa said nothing until she was near the top of the landing. "He cries for blood."

Jackie stopped and looked around, half expecting

to see Rosa. Her voice had gained a sudden clarity, but this time there were tears. There was rage for sure, but behind it, Jackie could hear the voice of someone on the verge of tears. "Maybe he's crying for you, too." As all children do for the parent they have lost. Jackie felt her throat clenching up. "OK, let's get this conversation going in a different direction. I am really curious and a bit petrified of just how I think Antonio must look here on the other side. Will he be a normal crying infant or something . . . else I really don't want to see."

"You are in my house?"

Jackie chuckled. "You mean you can't tell? How does that work?"

"Get out! Get out now."

"Rosa," Jackie said, more flippant than she might have been had this been real, "fuck you. I want to see him."

Spanish expletives faded into the backdrop of the baby's cries. Jackie walked forward and grabbed a hold of the master-bedroom door.

"No!" Rosa yelled. "Stay away from my baby!"

"I'm not going to touch him, Rosa. I swear," Jackie said. "I just want to see." *And hopefully not turn this dream into a nightmare.*

"Jackie!" The voice was faint, barely discernible over Antonio's, but still instantly recognizable. Laurel.

Jackie turned away from the door. "Laur?"

"Damn you, you broken bitch," Rosa's voice sounded dangerously close.

She spun around to see the yawning bright door between worlds, and Jackie felt herself being sucked through. And it had just been getting interesting, too.

Jackie gasped awake, sucking in a huge lungful of air

as though she had been suffocating. She lay sprawled over the end of her bed, covers thrown aside. Her head played a horrid techno-beat on a big bass drum in time with her pounding heart. Roughly ten miles away, the bottle of Percocet sat on her end table. Jackie flopped over and fumbled for the bottle, focusing at last on her alarm clock. It read 7:12 AM. She lolled her head over and could indeed see the sky was getting lighter, even if it was soaked with rain.

"Shit. No way." Jackie groaned. She felt exhausted and lay on her back until her body calmed itself from the shock of jumping through that doorway. Apparently even in dreams it fucked you up. Bickerstaff leaped up on the bed and poked his wet nose at her face. "Hey Bickers. Give me a minute, would you? Mommy is still out of it." He gave her a lick and then proceeded to jump down and trot back toward the kitchen.

Jackie realized she had to pee about thirty minutes ago. Her bladder pleaded no matter how she turned. A moment later, the phone rang. It could be any number of people trying to reach her. She reached over and picked it up, rolling painfully over on her bladder. Caller ID said it was McManus. Jackie remembered now. He was going to call last night, but she probably had slept right through it.

She clicked the TALK button. "Hey, McManus. I just woke up."

"Finally," he said in an exasperated tone. "I called twice last night, but figured you must have been pretty much drugged out. How you doing, Jack?"

"Percocet party," Jackie said. "Sorry. I had to. My

head is still throbbing. Hard to believe a couple of smacks against the floor can do this."

"Don't mess with a concussion, Jack," he said. "Just get some rest."

"Trying to," she replied. "I slept all night, but feel like shit right now. Anyway, I have to pee and get coffee in me. Let me call you back in a few minutes."

Jackie struggled to the bathroom and relieved herself. It took a great deal of effort just to flush and get back up. The toilet wasn't all that uncomfortable really. She could lay her head against the counter on her arm and doze for a bit longer. Bickerstaff nudged the door open and meowed.

"OK, fine. I'm coming."

She opened the can and let him eat off the kitchen counter while she put some coffee on. It was then she remembered Nick had bought her cold coffee drinks. There were still two Doubleshots in there. She grabbed one and went back to take a shower and another Percocet. Once naked, Jackie caught sight of herself in the mirror and realized how much of a beating she had taken. There were bruise marks from Morgan's fingers around her throat and a huge purple and brown patch in the middle of her back where the screen door had hit. Her left elbow ached, her knees were scraped, and her feet felt like she had been walking for miles. Of course there was her head, a tender welt the size of a damn golf ball on the back and shaved down the left. She could handle the cuts and bruises. That was just part of the job, but the exhaustion and the throbbing made it difficult to think, and an FBI agent who couldn't think was pretty much a dead one.

The shower felt so good, Jackie stood beneath the hot spray until it ran out and cold water snapped her back to being half-awake. The phone rang again the moment she sat down on the couch with her coffee. It was 8:01.

Jackie clicked the phone on. "Hi, Nick," she said, attempting to sound more chipper than she felt. "I'm still sore, tired, and my head hurts. But I'm clean and I have coffee. How are you?"

"Not as sore or clean," he replied. "How's the head? No signs of major concussion?"

"No, Dr. Nick. It seems to be just a normal, minor concussion."

His soft, deep chuckle rumbled in her hear. "Sorry. Habit. You tend to just ignore things when you shouldn't. So I'm playing it safe."

"I can't ignore a concussion," she said, wondering if he was being just a little bit patronizing. "It makes it difficult to function. Not that it matters. I won't be doing much of anything for a while."

"Perhaps. I can bring you something from Annabelle's. You hungry?"

Do I really want him over here right now? "Sure, that'd be great." *Thank you, mouth. You're a big help.*

"One or two?"

Not all that hungry really, and don't want to sound like—"Two. I need to call McManus, though. Told him I'd call him back a bit ago about the case. See you soon."

Jackie dialed McManus and laid back on the couch, sipping her coffee. He was already at headquarters, and if the speed of his voice was any indication, his nerves were rattled. They had to get their story straight, make sure there were no inconsistencies or errors in logic.

"The Standards guys aren't out to get us, McManus. You realize they're on our side."

"Yes, I know," he said and blew out a deep breath away from the phone. "Sorry. They stress me out, and they will get on us if our stories don't match."

"Why wouldn't they?" Jackie felt the gnawing worm of worry in her stomach. "They find something there, Ryan? Did something . . . weird happen?"

"You mean besides killing a Chicago detective who was offing gang members who may or may not have been responsible for the deaths of Rosa Sanchez and her husband?"

"Yes," Jackie said. "Besides that."

There was a pause, maybe half a second before he replied. "Isn't this case weird enough without all the ghost shit getting in the way?"

The ghost shit. Jackie frowned. It did not sit well with her. "Yeah. Well, Ryan, why don't you give me the official run down of what's in the report and I'll just make sure my story matches up. OK?"

"Sorry, Jack," he said. "I didn't mean it that way. It's just the Standards guys aren't going to like the sound of anything weird."

"Didn't Belgerman gag you on talking about ghost stuff?"

"Yes."

There was a lingering "but" in there. Jackie could feel it. "But what, McManus?"

He paused for several seconds. "I've got the impression you don't always do what Belgerman asks."

Jackie wasn't sure if she should laugh or be pissed. "From who? You've been here for, what, a week? Who gave you that impression?"

"Um . . . everyone, really. Don't get me wrong," he added hastily. "I actually find that refreshing. Bosses don't always know everything."

She laughed. "This one does. Don't cross John. You're not a pigheaded bitch like me, so you'd never get away with it. Speaking of which, has he come in yet?"

"Yeah. He was here before I got here at seven thirty."

"Great. Shit is hitting the fan already," Jackie replied and closed her eyes. *John really must love me right now.* It would be a good idea to make sure their knowledge of events didn't contain any inconsistencies. "All right, Ryan, tell me what you've told anyone so far about what happened. I had a few in to see me last night but my answers were all the same. I saw Morgan about to enter the house, I approached, he shot whomever it was that answered the door. I tried to tell him to stop and he attempted to shoot me. I returned fire and then tackled him in the entry of the house. In the struggle to subdue him, he got his hands around my throat and slammed my head against the floor until I blacked out. No memory of anything after that."

"That's about what I figured," McManus said, but Jackie could hear that wasn't all he had to say about the events. He told her his side of things until he got to the part about finding her in the dining room. "Wait a minute. How the hell did I get from the entry into the dining room?"

"I'd hoped you had an explanation for that," McManus said. "I'm guessing you were delirious from the concussion and crawled over there before passing out."

"OK, maybe, but Morgan was dead in the entry?" She was in the dining room? The other victim was in the kitchen. It didn't make any sense.

"The presumption is that he staggered around the

corner to kill the second vic and then fell back into the entry."

"Oh. I didn't actually see him die, so that's possible. That must have been what happened." Had to be. She was going to have to look at the evidence soon and verify what the hell had gone on there. "I'll be in later today so I can go over the evidence. We can get some official paperwork written up for this."

"That would be great, Jack. Thanks." He sounded clearly relieved. "Be nice to get this case out of the way as soon as possible."

"We still have to find Vasquez," she said.

"That's still a different case," McManus replied. "He's not who you and I were after."

Jackie let out her breath, chin sagging to her chest. How ironic was this, to be explaining supernatural case elements to her partner? *I miss you, Laur. I really, really do.* "If Rosa's ghost isn't done and she believes Vasquez was a part of her death, then this case isn't done, McManus. I'll bet Vasquez is hiding because he knows someone is killing those involved in Rosa's death. He just doesn't realize that it's Rosa that's after him and eventually, if she wants to, she'll find him and spill his entrails all over the floor like everyone else."

"Thanks for that," he said with a pained sound. "So much for breakfast."

"Vasquez is gang stuff, Ryan. This is your gig, isn't it?"

"I don't know Chicago gangs very well, but I should be able to help out."

"Then find him before Rosa does, because she's only got one goal and doesn't give a rat's ass who gets in the way."

Nick arrived about ten minutes later, a white bag in

his hand, the familiar brown with gold trim lettering partially obscured by his hand. Jackie snatched it from his hand and stuck her face in the bag. "Damn it! I can still smell blood even through the chocolate. This is so gross."

"It should hopefully clear with your concussion," Nick said. "Is it really strong?"

"Other than wondering if there's a beheaded body stuffed in my piano, no." She took the bag over to the couch and sat down. "You can have one of these if you want. I'm not all that hungry actually."

He shook his head. "Keep it for later then." He sat opposite her on the couch. "Are you going in today?"

"They've all got questions. The sooner it's out of the way the better, and I'd rather they didn't come out here."

"Any more memories of the events come back?"

"Nick, it was a mild concussion. I've got the headache from hell, not amnesia."

"OK. You just look really tired. Will it be safe for you to drive in?"

"Nick!" His concern was actually kind of endearing, but too much was going to drive her batty. "If I need a ride, I'll let you know. OK?"

"All right. Sorry." He sighed and gave her a wary smile. "It's just you come up to a gun fight and see a head wound and nine times out of ten, it's not good."

Jackie swallowed the lump in her throat. Christ. It really had freaked him out. What did that mean? Was it just sweet or should she be worried he was stressing over her getting shot? These weren't questions she had needed to consider, except with Laurel. She had not needed to worry about wanting to sleep with

Laurel either. "You're right. You're right. I was this close to being dead yesterday. It was reckless and—"

"Brave," Nick finished. "It was brave and foolish and, for the most part, worked. I don't think you could have stopped Morgan without killing or seriously wounding him. It's just unfortunate Rosa kept him going long enough to kill the other guy."

Jackie held her breath and chewed on the chocolate-filled croissant. If she did that, at least she could enjoy the flavor without it being tinged with the metallic, pungent flavor of blood. "Would Morgan's ghost be there, you think?"

Nick gave a noncommittal shrug. "I didn't feel his presence, but he could very easily come back, too. Shelby and I will check it out again today."

It was time to change the subject. The creeping nerves of the situation were working their way in. Jackie knew she had killed someone, someone who didn't deserve to die, a victim of circumstance and caught in the crossfire. It happened in law enforcement. You just hoped it never happened to you. The worst of it was, everyone else figured Morgan was the bad guy, and she was in no position to tell anyone what the truth of the matter was. It was not a subject she could afford to deal with right now.

"What have you reported about the incident? McManus is all nerved out wanting to ensure we have consistent stories. He's not sure how to deal with the ghost business, though I guess I'm not either. I still don't understand what's happened to me, Nick."

"None of us do," he said. He laid a hand across one of her ankles. "But we've figured out some of it and we'll figure out more until we get a firm grip on your abilities, Jackie. It's just going to take a little time."

She gave him a disheartened smile. "Prefer it was

sooner than later. Seeing and talking to ghosts is one thing, but this channeling bullshit can go away."

"Pick up your feet," he said.

"What?"

"Lift your feet up. You're stressed. I'm going to help you out a bit here because you've got a shit day ahead of you."

Jackie narrowed her gaze at him but lifted her feet. "What are you going to do?"

Nick slid over until his lap was beneath her feet. "Pressure points. You familiar with that?"

"I've heard Laur talk about them," she replied.

"If it makes you feel better, think of it as a glorified foot rub."

He pulled off a sock, her bare toes staring up at him, unpainted and in need of a trim. "My feet aren't much to look at right now. I haven't—"

"Your feet are fine, Jackie. I haven't had a pedicure in months either." His hands weren't overly large, but they easily wrapped around her foot. The coolness of his hands was soothing on her aching feet. "If I do this right, it'll help. If not, it's no loss because it's still a foot rub. Shelby used to swear by them, but I haven't given her one in about thirty years." His hands relaxed for a moment as he stared at her. "You look unsure. It's not going to hurt. Trust me."

Jackie shifted her gaze from his hands up to his face. Perhaps she looked as dumbfounded as she felt. "I know. It's just . . ." *You really want to rub my feet? Seriously?* "Never mind. Go ahead."

"Good," he said. "Just lay back and relax. Try to think about something unrelated to anything going on here. Walk in the woods or swim in the ocean. Something you find peaceful, and in thirty minutes you'll feel much better going into the rest of your day."

Walking sounded like a very bad idea just then, so Jackie opted for sitting in the woods on a large, moss-covered stone near a stream that rushed and tumbled over the rocks below. A groan involuntarily escaped her lips when Nick's fingers began to work their way into the muscles and tendons of her feet. She could feel herself sinking into that fresh, earthy-smelling moss, the cool mist from the water hitting her legs, and a warm sun caressing her face.

"OK. You seem pretty relaxed now," Nick said.

Jackie tilted her head back down to look at him. "Thirty minutes already?" It barely felt like five.

"Thirty-five," he said. "I was feeling generous."

She wiggled her toes and rotated her feet. The bones had all turned to mush. Best of all, her headache had receded to a manageable, dull throb. "Damn, Nick. Shelby was an idiot to leave that."

His face eased into a pleasurable smile. "My hands weren't the problem. I was a depressed, grumpy, sonofabitch."

She could certainly relate. "You might have to come over every morning and do this."

One corner of his mouth turned up even more. "Perhaps I shall."

Not serious! Hello, cowboy. I didn't literally mean it. Not really. But I kinda sorta did maybe. "As long as you stop at Annabelle's," she said, trying to cover up the warm flush flooding her cheeks, and reached over to grab the other croissant from the bag on the coffee table. "I actually feel capable of going in now. Thanks, Nick. Really."

"Anytime," he said and shifted himself out from under her feet. Before he got up, Nick stared at her very seriously, his bright, brown eyes dancing, and said, "Really."

Jackie felt the squirmy worms of nerves wiggle into her belly. Nick's subtle, or perhaps they never had been subtle, cues about his interest in her were growing by the day or so it felt. They had not even had a real date yet and a couple of kisses did not count. Nothing would happen until they had gone on a real date. There had to be some sort of normalcy to them if it was going to happen at all, and nothing to this point had been anywhere close to that. Regardless, a small part of her grinned at the thought of reaching up and hooking her fingers in that six-shooter buckle of his and pulling him down on top of her.

"So, what are you doing today?" she asked instead, and managed to stand up on loose, wobbly legs.

"Shelby and I are going to see if we can track down Rosa or Vasquez. At this point, either one will do. We'll keep in touch with McManus."

"No word from Laurel about what she's found over . . . there?"

"She'll have walked, since she had no reference points to travel to in that area of town. Hopefully she finds something."

"Yeah," Jackie said, remembering Laur's voice calling out to her at the end of her dream. "Hope she knows to get out if she finds Rosa."

"She'll leave her alone and discuss it with us if that's what she finds," Nick replied. "My suspicion is we'll find her here, controlling someone else to get this Vasquez fellow."

"Let's hope they can avoid Morgan's fate."

Jackie," he said in a low voice, "you can't blame yourself for events you don't have a lot of control over. Trust me, I'm an expert. The point is, you can't, and—"

"I know. I know." She waved off his words. She knew what they were going to be. She had told them to others and herself. Still, when it came down to brass tacks, all of that went out the window. The haunting specter of doubt would be nagging at her for days or weeks to come. "I'll get over it, but right now I still am not even sure what happened."

Nick nodded. "Understandable." He began to make his way toward the door. "OK if I call you later, see how you're feeling?"

"Not sure how available I'll be with the Standards guys crawling all over me, but sure. I'd um . . . I'd like that." And there it was, an open invitation. For better or worse Jackie had just put it out there for Nick to run with. She followed him to the door, knowing full well he could let himself out.

Nick opened the door but then turned and nearly bowled Jackie over. "Call Shelby or me if anything odd comes up."

"I will. I just want to go in and tell them what happened and then get back home and sleep for fifteen hours. That's all I plan on doing."

"Uh-huh," he said and his hand came up under her chin, tilting her face up toward his. "Plans tend to go astray around here most of the time."

Jackie gave him a little shrug but didn't pull away. "Shit happens. What can you do?"

His lips came down, soft and quick, just a light brush of a kiss. "Please, be careful." He stepped out into the hallway. "I'll call if we find anything useful."

Jackie smiled and closed her door. She felt so good at the moment she wondered if Nick had worked a little more than just his fingers into her feet.

The mood took a sharp right turn into Shitsville in about the time it took for Jackie to dress and drive over to headquarters and park her butt in her chair. Just getting from the parking garage to her chair had felt like it took undue effort. A Post-it was stuck to her monitor from Belgerman, reminding her of the meeting with the BPS guys at eleven-thirty. McManus had left to track down leads on Vasquez, but at least he had left her a copy of his report on her desk, along with a copy of the morning paper turned to an article about the incident.

Tillie had left a brief but kind message to drop by her office in the afternoon if it was convenient or to call and set up an appointment in the next couple of days. That wasn't about her issues. That was regulations. She had been involved in a shooting and the visit was mandatory. In some ways it might be preferable to talk about her issues instead of about killing Morgan. Maybe she would not be going home early after all.

It was only a few minutes after ten, so Jackie had some time to deal with getting all her facts straight and go over what she wanted to say to the Standards guys. They would be thorough, more so than usual because Morgan had been a cop. Every damn *i* had to be dotted and every *t* crossed in these situations or you could end up with a public relations disaster. Jackie picked up the paper and skimmed through the article.

FBI STOPS ROGUE COP'S VENGEFUL GANGLAND KILLING SPREE. Poor Morgan. Jackie felt even worse for his wife and daughter. It looked like he had gone insane. Nice legacy. There had to be a way to inform the family and keep it hushed. Maybe in a couple of weeks when the media frenzy had died down over it. Or a couple of months. Sometimes these things would drag on and on. She would have to ask John what his thoughts were. Damned if she would let psychic politics ruin the family. They would be screwed on benefits, too, without any way to prove what had happened.

Jackie threw the paper hard into her wastebasket, which sent it spilling into the aisle. "Damn it." She wheeled over and reached down to pick it back up and was greeted by familiar-looking shoes and crisply pleated pants.

"Got my note?" He pointed at her monitor where the Post-it used to be.

"I'll be ready, sir, much as I can at least. I had one question, though, related to all of this." He raised an eyebrow but said nothing and took a sip from his coffee. Jackie lowered her voice to barely above a whisper. "What happens to Morgan's family in all of this? Morgan, the real Morgan, was as much a victim in this as everyone else. He wasn't a murderer."

Belgerman gave her a pained smile. "I know, but we can't let that be public knowledge. It would be a disaster for the department. The best we can do, which is all that we are going to do"—he motioned with his coffee cup at her—"is make sure that whatever pension and insurance he had coming in case of death on the job is correctly and fully paid out."

"You don't think Beverly Morgan will wonder about that?"

"Would you want to lose a twenty-year vet's benefits?"

Jackie shrugged. "Nope, guess I wouldn't. I suppose that'll have to do. Which sucks by the way. He had a thirteen-year-old daughter."

"I'm sorry, Jackie. That's the best we're going to be able to do. You good with that?" Which was John's kind way of asking if he could be assured she wouldn't go behind his back and do something stupid and the complete opposite.

"I'm good, sir."

"Great. You have any questions about the BPS before your meeting with them, feel free to ask. I'll be in my office until lunch."

Sure as hell the sky would fall if the public found out the FBI used psychics. She understood though. It was a credibility issue. Ironic that she was now becoming one. Jackie scooted back to her desk and picked up McManus's report. "My whole fricking life has credibility issues."

After reading through the report, and then a second time to make sure she had got everything, Jackie sighed, closed the report, and leaned back in her chair while rubbing at her temples. They would be all over this case. Things just did not add up well. The biggest problems were a perp three seconds from death who managed to stumble around a corner and fire off two perfectly aimed shots before falling back to die, and an agent lying unconscious with a direct line of fire on the victim. Shooting Morgan was clear self-defense, but what the hell had happened after that? No matter how hard she tried, Jackie could remember nothing after that death grip around her neck and having her head slammed against the hardwood. There was just no way she could have done anything, right?

Jackie sat back up and called down to the forensics lab. There was one easy way to find out. She got herself transferred back to one of the lab techs. "This is Agent Rutledge up on five. You guys were running ballistic tests on the guns brought in from yesterday's shooting incident?"

"I didn't run them, but I can check for you right

quick, Agent Rutledge," the tech said. Jackie could hear the quiet clicking of a keyboard in the background. "Yeah, here we go. Two Glocks."

"That's it," Jackie said. "Can you tell me how many rounds were fired from each one?"

"Looks like three from one and five from another."

"Which was which?" she asked.

"Oh, um, five from the perpetrator's weapon and three from—Hey! This is your gun, Agent Rutledge."

"Yeah, I know. Thanks for the info though. Big relief."

She hung up. So despite the coroner's evidence, which suggested that Morgan likely could not do what he did, he had fired five rounds. Rosa had managed to keep him going long enough to finish off her target. That woman was very dedicated to her revenge. Jackie could appreciate her as far as that went. It was the callous disregard for everyone in her way that put her over the line. Jackie supposed having your baby cut from you and being shot in the head would do that. You would not stop until you were done. Was Rosa done, though?

Jackie did not think so, unless Rosa had no choice. Without Morgan perhaps she could only stew in endless frustration over in Deadworld. Last night's dream came back to her, disturbingly real in its vividness. Dreams like that were always unsettling. Rosa had spoken to her. The babe had screamed in her head, and Laurel had been there. Somewhere. It would have been good to see her, even in a dream.

Head propped on her hand, elbow on the desk, Jackie had started to drift, but then a metallic bite slathered her tongue and the scent of blood clogged her nostrils. She jerked back upright, coughing and reaching for her cup of cold coffee. "God! Gross." Her pockets were empty of change to buy some gum, which would force her to go beg some from Belgerman, since the office was virtually empty. She decided to pass. If anything could, the office coffee would kill the taste.

Back at her desk, sipping on bitter coffee, Jackie worked on something she had done almost none of for at least three years. Incident reports. Laurel had taken that responsibility. She had done practically every bit of paperwork they had to do, and Jackie knew it was a lot. Government bureaucracy was rife with it. How did people do this kind of thing on a daily basis? Why did Laurel let her get away with never doing this crap? Groceries, paperwork, clothing, and even working the damn GPS. All of the annoying detritus of life, Laurel had constantly worked at, to keep it away from Jackie's life so she could "focus on the job."

Jackie sniffed away a tear, and made a face at the bile in her throat. She had to dab at her nose to make sure it wasn't bleeding. How selfish could she have been or just bloody ignorant of what was going on around her? Either one was bad. *Fuck.* Did she have to have a moment now? At work of all places? The phone rang and Jackie glanced at the clock on her computer. It was eleven-twenty. No doubt a reminder call from John. But it was one of the BPS people, calling to say they were ready if she wanted to come down a few minutes early. Jackie let out a deep breath and told them she would be there at the allotted time.

Chapter 26

"Sleep in today?" Cynthia asked. She wore emerald green, a form-fitting skirt and jacket over a cream silk blouse. A simple thick band of gold adorned her neck and, contrary to her usual fashion, Cynthia had her hair down, gentle waves of walnut brown tumbling down her back.

Nick smiled. "Good morning, Cyn." He paused. When was the last time he had seen her with her hair down? Not within the past couple of years. "What's the occasion? You look . . . good."

"I'm sleeping in my own bed tonight," she announced, beaming up at him. "My house is finally livable. Be another couple of weeks before it's all finished, but I'm just glad to be able to sleep in my own house again if I want."

"You have everything you need?"

The smile faltered a bit. "I'm fine, really. You've spent too much on me already."

"Nonsense." Nick reached out and laid his hand upon her arm. "I have more money than I will ever be able to spend, and you're family. You need anything else for the house, just charge it to the account. Honestly, Cyn. You deserve to get anything you need."

Her cheeks flushed a soft shade of pink. "Thank you, Nick. You . . . that means a lot. So," she continued and turned back toward her desk, "what was that message all about? This about that FBI case you're helping with?"

Why would she be so embarrassed about that? He had made it clear in the past that SI would take care of anything she needed. Nick watched her form-fitting skirt pivot around the corner of the desk and Shelby's words about her crept back into his mind: *Like she would ever say no to you.* Did her feelings really go there? Nick pushed the question aside.

"Yeah. I want to find out if a certain spirit has moved on or not."

"Sounds fun," she said

"And we need to find the guy she's after."

"This guy kill her?"

"Believe so."

"I'm in. Just tell me what, where, and when, Sheriff."

Nick's smile broadened. "Thank you. I'll be in my office having some coffee. Come on in with Shelby when she gets here and I'll tell you what we're doing."

"You seem . . . different today," she said, giving him a curious eye. "I can't even remember you having a smile like that on your face."

He paused, the smile vanishing. Why was that? "I'm not sure exactly. Perhaps just the promise of new things. I'm out of the rut and can see the road again. I've turned a corner. There's a light at the end of the tunnel, or whatever you want to call it. Maybe I'm just hopeful again after a very long time."

Cynthia's eyes were glassy with tears. "That's really good to hear, Nick. You deserve it."

He gave her a casual, one-shoulder shrug before heading down the hall to his office. "Not as much as some."

An hour later he and Cynthia were off in his Porsche while Shelby headed up into the Lincoln Park area to work the locals with a little bit of the vampire voodoo, as she so lovingly referred to it. Completely off-the-record of course. It would be considered coercion in any court, and get the case tossed in a heartbeat.

Nick wanted to see if Rosa Sanchez might now be with her babe on the other side before he went to help Shelby, and so he found himself again at the scene of Rosa's murder, with another woman in hand.

Cynthia stared out at the house through the car's window. "This looks too nice for the kind of violence that happened."

"It does," Nick replied. "McManus should be here in a few minutes to let us in."

"That's who replaced Ms. Carpenter, isn't it?"

Nick nodded. "Strikes me as a good man."

"And what about Agent Rutledge? I heard Shelby say she was having a rough time of it. I can just imagine after everything she went through, but to think she might be psychic. That just boggles my mind."

It did boggle the mind. Deadworld had irrevocably altered Jackie. How could he have known? All he could do now is help her make the best of it. "I'm not sure what to make of what's happened. Actually, I've been considering having her talk to you about all of that."

"Me?" Cynthia laughed. "That woman does not like me one bit."

"You were my office manager and I was a murder suspect," he said. "That's all in the past now, but I'm very curious what your take on her abilities might be. We don't know the scope of what she can do."

Cynthia turned and stared at him. "Seriously? She's that strong, just like that?"

"She can hear and see the dead. She's channeled them also, quicker and stronger than I've ever seen anyone do. She has no control over it, which is what has me concerned. Think you might be able to help her?"

"The poor woman needs someone to work with her. She'll go crazy just getting dumped into something like that. If she is willing, I'll talk to her at least."

Nick gave her a faint smile and glanced up in his rearview mirror. McManus had arrived. "Ah, here we go."

Cynthia followed his gaze. "Well, time for the fun stuff."

McManus walked up and shook their hands, and gave Cynthia a very appreciative look-over. "Mr. Anderson. No Ms. Fontaine today?"

"She's up in Lincoln Park area doing some looking around for our elusive Mr. Vasquez." Nick motioned at Cynthia. "And this is my office manager, Cynthia Forrester, who is a medium. She's going to see if Rosa Sanchez is residing on the other side or if we've still got a hunt on our hands."

"Excellent," McManus said, smiling at Cynthia, and holding her hand for a moment or two longer than the handshake. "Can't say I miss the motorcycle lady at all."

Nick watched Cynthia freeze for a half second, catching her breath before letting it out through a brilliant smile. "Nick, you didn't tell me the FBI were such flirts."

McManus took a half step back and assessed whether he had just crossed a line or not. Nick watched McManus flick his glance toward him for an instant before coming back to Cynthia. "Flirting Bastards Incorporated, Agent Ryan McManus at your service."

They laughed and Nick offered an appreciative smile before McManus led them up the walk and into the house of the screaming babe.

Cynthia knew before even walking in the door. Nick could see her tension grow with each approaching step. When she turned to look at him, a tear eased down her cheek. "Oh, Nick. This is horrible."

He reached out and lay a hand upon her arm. "Cyn, if you'd rather not, I understand."

She shook her head. "No. I've seen rage and pain before. This is just so . . . intense." She sniffed and wiped at the tear. "And innocent."

McManus unlocked the door and let Cynthia walk into the foyer. His gaze followed, far more intrigued, than lustful. "She can really hear the dead baby in here?"

"The scene of death is very thin between this world and the next," he said.

"Give you guys one thing—you don't lack for interesting conversation." McManus shook his head, as though knocking out the cobwebs, and went inside. "The murder location is upstairs at the end of the hall, Ms. Forrester."

"I know," she said, her eyes staring up at a blank spot in the ceiling. "Please. Call me Cynthia."

"You ready to go up, Cyn?" Nick asked.

"As I'll ever be," she said. "You sure you don't want me to try and talk to Rosa if she's there?"

"Certain," Nick said forcefully. He would take no chances with Cynthia. Just a quick peek and out, that was all. "You look and check and get out. If you're there more than sixty seconds, I'm snapping you out of it."

"Well, shit, Nick, that barely gives me time at all. Sometimes it takes a minute just to get settled once I cross."

"I know, but this woman is looking to possess, and I'm taking no chances even if you are strong enough to resist. Agent McManus, stick close to me until she's done."

McManus laughed. "You're worried I might get possessed by an evil spirit?"

"She's not evil," Nick replied and followed Cynthia up the stairs. "She just wants revenge on those who killed her and her child. If she's with her child now, at least she is not actively possessing someone, so we know we have some time to get Vasquez and find out who else was involved in her murder."

"OK, I can get my FBI brain around that one," he said. "What if she's not there?"

"Likely she's gotten hold of someone and is looking for those left on her list."

"But wouldn't it benefit us to try and reason with her if she is over . . . there?" McManus wondered.

Nick could see he would have to do some more training on the FBI if he was going to consult with them in the future. "Spiritual energy by itself is different than the combination of it with the material world. It's difficult to explain clearly but suffice to say, spiritual energy is far easier to be single-mindedly focused with. That's why you can get ghosts haunting the places where they died for decades or longer. So, reason is not always the best option."

McManus nodded in agreement, though Nick was not sure he understood or believed it. Cynthia was entering the master bedroom now, hand held over her mouth.

"So much blood," she said, muffled through her fingers. "Rage and blood." She paused and looked back at him in the hall, her face melting down from its usual bright cheerfulness to something akin to despair. "Nick, this is awful, what happened here." Her hands had come down over her abdomen, rubbing softly at her belly.

"If it's too much, just back out, Cyn. Don't push it." Nick stepped up and put a firm hand on each arm. "I mean it. This is a bad spot. If it's going to overwhelm, don't do it."

She shook her head. "No. I'm fine, Nick. Thanks. Just worse than I thought it would be." She took a deep breath and let it out. "Holy Mother, it really reeks of blood in here." She smiled at them. "Good thing I've got a strong stomach. Well, let me get prepared and we'll see what happens."

The bed in the room had been removed and Cynthia proceeded to step into the middle of that previously occupied space. Hands clasped lightly in front of her, she closed her eyes. Her lips moved but she voiced nothing. Nick knew she spoke prayers to the Great Mother.

McManus leaned in close and whispered, "Is there a reason I don't smell a damn thing?"

"That smell comes from the other side. It will fade from here eventually, but nobody will sleep very comfortably in this room for some time to come."

"Place creeps me out, that's for sure," he said and remained hovering in the doorway.

Nick leaned against the opened door, watching Cynthia prepare. It would only take her a couple more minutes to get into that trancelike state where she could take her spiritual self into Deadworld and get a clear picture of what existed there.

"What is she doing?" McManus said.

"Not now." Nick held up his hand to quiet him. "Just be prepared."

McManus was quiet for a moment, opened his mouth to say something and then closed it again. Nick gave him a nod of thanks and continued to watch Cynthia. Her prayers finally stopped, which was an indication she was ready, and slowly her chin sank toward her chest. For a few seconds she appeared to be sleeping, but then her head came up and her eyes were wide open.

"It's very empty here," she said. "Not a ghost in the area except for the baby and . . . Rosa, I suspect."

"Are you with the babe?"

She shook her head. "Outside. Too much blocking me inside. He's really strong, Nick. Unborns close to birth are quite . . . oh, hold on. I sense something else over here."

Nick's eyes narrowed, though he could see nothing. "What is it?"

"Not sure. It feels like . . . yikes. I can hear Rosa. She doesn't sound happy."

"All right. Come back, Cyn. We know. I don't want you risking yourself with her."

"Just a minute. There's someone on the ground over here."

"You probably don't have a minute, Cynthia. Get back now or I'm going to slap you out of it."

Cynthia gasped. "Shit!" Her hands began to wave frantically in the air. "Rosa! No, I'm not here . . . stop . . ."

Her body twisted and fell to the floor. Stretched out of the ether, Nick could see two ghostly hands wrapped around Cynthia's throat. He leaped into action, dropping to his knees at Cynthia's side and reached for the arms coming through Cynthia's door. They were strong, absurdly so. They might not just strangle Cynthia, but crush her windpipe as well.

"Rosa," Nick said in a loud, firm voice. "If you don't let go now, I'm going to destroy you and your babe will be alone." Nick had no idea if he could draw in a spirit from this side of the veil, but he could sure give Rosa something to think about.

He could not pry her hands away, and Cynthia was making rough, gargling sounds. Behind him he could hear McManus yelling in panic. There would be no noble counting to three on this. Nick gave Rosa all of one second to comply and then began to open up his door and draw upon the other side, pulling upon the reserves he still retained from being filled with all of those souls. Rosa's reaction was instantaneous. With a bitter screech, the hands withdrew and vanished as quickly as they had come.

Cynthia coughed and spluttered, her hands rubbing at her throat. There would be some fine bruising there later.

McManus's voice cut in. "Never mind. Cancel that. The situation is under control. No, no, it's fine. Sorry. It looked worse than it was." His cell phone clicked shut. "What in God's name was that?"

"You all right, Cyn?" Nick scooped his hands under her and picked up Cynthia like she was stuffed with straw. "Let's get you out of this house first. McManus? Can you find us a cup of water?"

"Yeah, sure." He bolted out ahead of them, and was waiting with a cup filled with tap water when Nick got Cynthia downstairs. She eagerly grabbed at the cup and gulped down half of it before coughing several times again.

"She's . . . wow. She's bad news."

"Don't talk," Nick said. "Drink some more water when you can."

Cynthia nodded and then shook her head. "Agent Carpenter." She was wracked by another fit of coughing and finally drank down some more water.

"She was there?" Damn. Laurel would have no chance against Rosa in her current state.

"She was on the ground, Nick. Not moving. I think Rosa already got to her."

Nick closed his eyes and took a step back. "Ah, hell."

Chapter 27

Jackie let her head droop forward. She closed her eyes and took a deep breath, partly out of frustration and partly to keep from throwing up; the air in the closed space of the interview room was stifling, warm, and compounded by the ever-present smell of blood.

"Is something wrong, Agent Rutledge?" The woman, dressed in a very smart charcoal-gray suit and blindingly white blouse, tapped her pen on the file folder next to her laptop. Any sort of agitation activated the pen. She had been polite throughout, asking questions in a calm, even manner. She did not push or cajole or attempt to influence Jackie's answers in any way. At times, Jackie thought she might be talking to a robot.

"You realize this is the third set of questions aimed at asking me about the same course of events and the same set of actions taken. Do you really need me to tell it again?" She looked up and stared hard at the prim woman. "I understand how this works, and my story is going to be the same each and every time. I know you have more investigating to do. Go do it and get back to me. I'll answer more questions then, I promise. But right now, Agent Patterson, I'm about to throw up all over your pretty black leather pumps."

The tapping pen stopped. She opened up the folder and marked something and then typed in a quick note on her laptop. A glowing review no doubt. Jackie knew they did not particularly like her answers. Ghosts had turned into hunches and going after a detective based on a hunch did not sit well. They would have more questions. What had happened out at Iroquois? What went on in Beverly Morgan's basement? Why exactly was she on this case to begin with if she had been on leave for her partner's death?

All excellent questions. Fortunately, they would have no idea to ask why Rosa, through Morgan, had gleefully told her she was broken in the moments before he died. Jackie wanted to ask that one herself. She tried to ignore it, forget about it, and just plain leave it alone, but it would not go away. It mattered more in the way the words had been spoken than the words themselves. It had not been an insult. Rosa had been rather pleased it seemed with the discovery, whatever it was. The words gnawed at her and something about them she found deeply disturbing.

"Agent Rutledge." The woman closed her laptop and folded her hands over the top as though to protect it from Jackie. "You've been very helpful. Thank you for cooperating so quickly after your ordeal. As you know, we'll be continuing our investigation until all parties are satisfied with the results. There are still a number of unanswered questions in this matter, which I'm sure you're aware of. You'll be available for us to contact with further questions?"

"Of course," she said. "If my head hasn't exploded."

The agent gave Jackie a pained smile. "Great."

No sense of humor, Jackie decided. Though, she

imagined, if one's job involved looking into bad agents all of the time, she would have lost hers, too. And speaking of no humor, she had to now attend an hour of the *I Told You Show*, emceed by everyone's favorite host, Dr. Matilda Erikson.

Three floors up, Jackie pasted her fakest friendly smile on her face and told the receptionist she was there to see Tillie. She gave Jackie a sympathetic and worried stare.

"So glad you're all right, Agent Rutledge," she said. "I heard you almost got killed."

"Almost, but turns out I'm too hardheaded to die."

She looked confused, but Jackie was not going to explain, not with her head beginning to throb to the beat of a high school marching band's bass drum. Tillie saved her from the awkward silence, opening her door from behind the reception area.

"Jackie! I thought that was you. Come in," she said, and waved her toward the door. She left it open and went back inside.

"Fuck," Jackie muttered and marched toward Tillie's door. "Can't have a minute to wait and collect my thoughts, the few that haven't been beaten out of my head?"

Inside the fastidiously comfortable office, Tillie was making tea. Jackie flopped down into the overstuffed chenille chair and let her head sag back. She closed her eyes. "I'm apologizing in advance in case my head explodes all over your pretty office."

"I think you'd still manage to get yourself in trouble," she replied and set the tray down on the table between them.

Jackie rubbed at the stitches on her head. It was beginning to itch. "Can concussions mess up your sense of smell?"

"Pardon?"

"Sense of smell," Jackie said, and finally looked back at Tillie. "I keep smelling blood everywhere I go. I can't get rid of it and it's making me nauseous."

"Hmmm, I'm not sure, Jackie. I can check into that for you, though. How you feeling otherwise?"

"You mean other than seeing dead people and killing a cop?" Tillie gave her a sour look. "I'm having a shitty day."

"What about the killing the cop? Wasn't Detective Morgan on the Homicide Task Force?"

Jackie closed her eyes again. "I knew him. He was a good guy and the fucked-up part of the story is, nobody will know. Everyone is going to think he was a painkiller-addicted cop who got strung out and snapped when he found himself on a really bad murder case."

"Why won't anyone know? I'm not sure I understand that. And drink your tea, dear. It'll help your headache."

Jackie picked up and sipped the tea. Maybe Tillie had spiked it or laced it with Percocet. It was warm and actually soothed her upset stomach. "It's ghost crap. Is this off the record?"

"It's not in a record anyone can see," she said.

"No, I mean is it off the record? I want no recordings of this stuff in any way, shape, or form."

Tillie frowned for a moment but then nodded. "All right. No record."

"You really believe in this, Tillie?"

"I do. In spirits at least and the belief that there is something beyond us."

That would do just fine. "I'm under a gag order on this but I don't think you count."

She nodded. "Everything stays here, Jackie. You know that."

"Morgan was possessed by a really pissed-off ghost. He took a shot at me when we caught up to him and I killed him. He was stuck in the corner of his head somewhere trying to kick this thing out and I had to plug three rounds into him. The poor guy never had a chance to defend himself. I killed an innocent man and I'm going to get praised for it. How fucked-up is that, Tillie?"

"Have you been getting praise for it?"

"Well, no, not really. Not yet," Jackie said. "OK, praise is the wrong word. Nobody will know the truth, which is that I took down an innocent cop."

Tillie sat back, staring thoughtfully at Jackie over the top of the cup raised to her lips. "Is this any different than an officer being taken hostage and then killed in the effort to get the kidnapper?"

"Of course! The hostage and the kidnapper were the same person. Maybe I shouldn't have shot him."

"Wouldn't you likely be dead now?"

"I know!" Jackie was on the verge of yelling. The headache and nausea were doing wonders on her patience. "It's just . . . I killed an innocent guy."

"Sometimes we're put in untenable, no-win situations, Jackie. You know this. Everyone in law enforcement knows this. Does it bother you more that nobody is going to be blaming you for killing him?"

Jackie threw up her hands. "I don't know. I guess. Even worse is I don't think we've stopped her."

"The ghost?"

"Yeah. I think she's still out there somewhere. Morgan died and it's time for her to find someone else to help her finish the job."

"You can tell this?" She was genuinely curious now, leaning forward in her seat.

"I can tell when she's nearby. I could feel her inside Morgan. She said . . ." Jackie took a sip from her tea. She wasn't sure if she wanted to tell Tillie this, but what the hell? She knew this much of it, and hadn't called up the mental hospital. "She said, right before she bashed my head against the floor, that I was broken."

Tillie shrugged. "Could be nothing more than a reference to what she was about to do to you."

"No." Jackie shook her head. She knew it went beyond that. "I saw the look on Morgan's or her face when she said it. She was happy about something. It wasn't something about to happen to me. It was like she suddenly realized it when she had her hands around my throat. She felt something and it pleased her."

Tillie eased back into her chair again, perplexed. Her brow furrowed. She tapped a finger against her pursed lips. "Do you feel broken?"

"In some ways, sure," Jackie said. "This has been a hellish couple of weeks. But this was something else. I don't know why it creeps me out so bad, but it does. In what sort of way would a ghost want you to be broken? Maybe they can see some deep-seated flaw that I can't. Maybe the dead can see things that we can never see. But the way she said it, it was something important. I just can't put my damn finger on it."

"This is really worrying you, isn't it?"

"Tillie, what if there's something fundamentally broken in me? What if something happened when I went to the other side and almost died? Maybe I'm damaged in some way that can't be fixed."

"Nonsense." But she did not sound thoroughly convinced. "You aren't broken, dear. Hurting? Yes.

Recovering? Yes. But you are not damaged beyond repair."

Jackie sagged back and settled her head on the cushion, stretched her mouth with an enormous yawn and closed her eyes. "Feels that way at times."

"You know what," she said, and Jackie could hear her standing up. "Rest there for a few minutes. I'm going to write you a prescription for some sleeping meds. They'll help you sleep, even with the headache, and you won't get loopy like you do with Percocet."

"Will they make the blood odor go away? I might have to love you for that."

She laughed softly. "Not that I'm aware of, but I will look into the blood smell. If it's a sign of something more harmful, I will call you."

Jackie turned her head and looked at Tillie. "More harmful? Like what?"

"Like that concussion you got is more than mild," she said.

"Oh. Guess that would be better than some kind of new ghost cancer."

"Ha! Funny girl." She walked back around her desk and handed Jackie a slip of paper. "Fill this on your way home," she said. "You are going home now, aren't you?"

"Straight away, Mother. Promise." She took the slip and stuffed it into her pocket.

"You OK to drive, Jackie?"

"Yeah. I got here didn't I? It's just a bad headache. Another day of rest and I'll be fine."

"Looks like you could use three." She reached down and gave Jackie's shoulder an affectionate squeeze. "Get someone to drive you home if need be."

Just to prove her wrong, Jackie got to her feet and

nearly threw up on Tillie's shoes. "I'm just tired and have a headache. Not a big deal."

"Will be if you don't get some rest. Now go. Doctor's orders."

Jackie shuffled out. She really was ready to crawl back into bed. "Night-night, Doctor Erikson."

Despite the effort, she took the stairs back to her floor, worried the elevator might throw her stomach off just enough to make her puke. A quick update for Belgerman and she would head home. Jackie paused by her desk and gripped the cubicle wall to fend off a warm wave of nausea. She yawned again and then rubbed at her eyes with the palms of her hands. When was the last time she felt this out of it? Even the candle to the head at Cynthia's house, when they had fought off Drake's goon, hadn't put her out this badly. Perhaps she should just put her feet up at her desk and doze for an hour before going home? The thought tempted her. A cold fire was beginning to chew through her gut.

Jackie stood up and took a step toward John's office when that cold flame blossomed into a raging maw that clamped down on her insides. Her chest constricted, heart skipping a beat, and Jackie fell to a knee. Her breath suddenly could not move through her frozen lungs.

It was the chill wind of the dead screaming through her body, blowing from the inside out. Upon that lifeless current, Jackie heard or rather felt a faint, desperate voice.

"Laur?" she gasped.

Then it was gone, leaving Jackie shivering with the force of it. She crawled over to the waste basket by her desk and proceeded to retch the contents of her stomach into the crumpled papers in the bottom.

"Jackie?" Belgerman's worried voice came from behind. "You all right?" He pulled back the chair and was beside her, hand lightly on her back as her stomach clenched and spasmed several more times before finally subsiding.

"Just . . . just give me a sec," she said, and spat out the sour bile and fluid that remained in her mouth. *What the fuck was that?* Jackie had no clue, only that something about it spoke of Laurel and it was not good, not at all.

"Let me get one of the cots out and you can lay down in the conference room," Belgerman said, and handed her a wad of tissue from her desk.

Jackie sat back on her heels and wiped her mouth. "No. I need to get out of here. I have to go."

"Not like this you aren't. I'll find someone or drive you home myself."

She shook her head. "Call Nick. He'll take me." Jackie reached for her chair and clasped the arm to pull herself up. Belgerman's firm hands helped get her back in the seat. "I'll get you some water. Just sit tight."

Jackie laid her head back against the seat cushion and closed her eyes. She needed to tell Nick. Something had happened to Laurel. Something terrible.

Chapter 28

Nick's Porsche screeched to a halt outside the elevator doors in the parking garage. Jackie had meant to call him, explain what she felt, but Belgerman and Tillie, plus struggling to keep her gag reflex under control, had kept her from using the phone. He reached over and pushed open the door for her. He looked grim.

Jackie sagged into the seat. "Nick, Laurel—"

"I know," he said. "I'm sorry."

Jackie sagged into the seat. "Oh, thank God! Thought I might be losing it."

John gripped the door and leaned down to look at them both. "Nick. Be nice to meet you under pleasant circumstances one of these days."

"Agreed," he said. "I'll make sure she's actually going to rest."

He laughed. "Thanks. You read my mind."

Jackie frowned at them both. "I'm not a child."

"Stubborn as one," Belgerman said, giving her shoulder a soft squeeze. "Get some sleep, Jackie. You look like something out of a zombie movie."

He closed the door and Jackie leaned the seat

back. The throbbing eased the more inclined she became. The softly humming engine revved up and launched them out of the parking lot. "What happened, Nick? Is Laur OK?"

"We don't know, but I don't think she is," he said. "She found Rosa's house, but Rosa is apparently not welcoming anyone near her baby. From what Cynthia said, it looks like she attacked Laurel and left her on the ground outside of the house. That was all she got to see, however, before Rosa attacked Cynthia."

"Holy shit! She OK?

"Bit bruised, but she'll be fine."

"How do we get Laur out of there?"

"Working on it," he said, but his voice did not sound very hopeful. "Right now, though, you need to rest. You look asleep on your feet, Jackie."

"I slept like seven or eight hours last night. Stupid fucking Deadworld dreams to prove it. I'd be better without the stench of blood everywhere. I didn't know concussions could mess you up like that."

"Very odd for a mild concussion to have a serious side effect like that," he said, looking her over while they were stopped at a light. "Could just be your contact with Rosa, but I've never heard of it lingering on like it's doing for you."

Jackie turned her head and pressed her forehead against the cool glass of the window. "Be nice if you could make it go away."

"I might," he said, "or at least make you able to handle it better."

"You're talking vampire mojo crap, aren't you?"

His answer was a simple "Yes."

Jackie didn't answer. When Shelby had done it to her so she could walk on a banged-up knee, the side effect had her nearly tearing Nick's clothes off. She had no energy for that right now, even if she might be more inclined to give in to the inclination.

"Don't worry," he said. "I can make it more subtle than Shelby did."

"How do you manage that?"

"It's a matter of will," he replied. "Shelby wants us to sleep together. She put that energy into you along with healing your knee."

Jackie pivoted her head and half-opened her eyes. "So, does that mean you can avoid putting that energy in or you don't want to sleep with me?" She gave Nick a halfhearted smirk.

The Porsche swerved over and stopped. They had arrived at her apartment. Nick's smile was vague. "I suppose I'll let you decide that one." He walked around the car and opened her door by the time she sat up straight.

Jackie wobbled on her feet when she managed to get up out of the car. Nick's hand was right there at her elbow to offer support, and Jackie suppressed the urge to yank her arm away. It would make getting up the stairs easier and safer. "How can we help Laur, Nick? Will she be OK until we can get to her?"

"Getting to her is not the problem," Nick said, as he followed one step behind her going up the stairs. "Rosa is the problem. I don't know that we can handle her. I was able to scare her off, but I don't believe I could drain her away even if I wanted to. Not with her babe there. On her own, we'd have a much better shot."

Drain her away. Goose bumps snaked up her spine. Jackie unlocked her door and stepped inside. The stench of blood was even stronger in her apartment. "Fuck. OK, the vampire mojo wins. Juice me up, Sheriff," she said. "I can't handle much more of this."

"You'll want to change into whatever you're sleeping in, brush your teeth, take pills, or whatever," Nick replied. "Once I do this, you're done until you wake up."

"Really? That good, huh?"

"Or," he said, with the slightest cock of his head, "I could hang around and wait to see how well it works."

"Lucky for you, I'd fall over if I took a swing." Jackie shuffled off to the bathroom to get ready.

Twenty minutes later, Jackie was buried up to her neck in downy softness, a shot of espresso warming her belly, while it dissolved away a Percocet, since she had failed to remember to pick up Tillie's prescription. Nick sat on the edge of the bed next to her. On the far corner of the mattress, Bickerstaff gave them a wary eye.

"You all set?" He gave her a warm smile, accentuated with the touch of crow's-feet around the eyes, which now glowed with eerie brightness. Nick had removed his contacts.

"I think so. You'll call me if something comes up with Laur?"

"Yes. I don't think you need to worry. She's no longer a threat to Rosa, and as long as she remains that way she'll be safe."

"You're totally bullshitting me, aren't you?"

Nick winced. "More or less. I haven't seen her, Jackie. I'm going by what Cynthia said. She could be dying. She could be fine and waiting for a chance to get away without Rosa noticing. I just don't know."

"You'd have been a good politician." Jackie rolled her eyes at his little smirk. "You were, weren't you?"

"I was mayor for a year," he said. "Long time ago. It didn't suit me."

"And apparently my rough edges do." It came out far more snide-sounding than she had planned.

"Indeed they do, Agent Rutledge." Nick reached out and cupped her face with one large, firm hand. The hand was warm.

"Do I have to do the whole *look into my eyes* bit for this to work?"

"It'll help." The other hand came up and Jackie found her face held firmly, fingers running back into her hair. One was close to her stitches and the mere thought of it made it start to itch. "Don't worry. That'll go away too," he said.

The warmth began to radiate inward. It was like the lovely heat from a steam bath without all the sweat. "You reading my mind?" Her thoughts were getting syrupy, turning to mush. She got the disturbing sensation that his fingers were sinking into her head.

"Just your face. Now then," he said, voice deeper, more melodious than usual, "look at me, Jackie." She did and found, surprisingly, that his eyes did not frighten her as before. "You trust me?" She nodded and said nothing. "Good. I want you to pretend you're sitting at Annabelle's. What do you smell?"

"Pastries. Donuts. Coffee." The scents of her favorite eatery filled her nostrils. "Could I have more coffee?"

"Soon. That fresh-roasted coffee smell fills the room, seeping into everything. Your clothes, your furniture, your sheets, they all emanate the essence of fresh-roasted coffee. It overpowers everything."

"Mmm. This is great. You smell good enough to drink."

"All you can smell is the coffee. Everything else is quiet, soft, and far away. The pounding in your head is gone. The itching is gone. Your body is floating on clouds, comforted and relaxed."

Jackie tried to keep her eyes open, but the lids were too relaxed to make the effort. The throbbing drum in her head had faded to a distant, mellow thump, keeping time with her heartbeat. Her body sank into the cottony softness of clouds, enfolding her with a caressing, downy touch. Nick's hands had become little more than warm, velvety pads that stroked her cheeks.

"Kiss me goodnight," she said, her voice distant, not even part of her body.

Nick's lips brushed hers, a feathery touch of skin, and sleep finally carried her away.

Minutes or hours later, Jackie had no way of knowing, the cold breeze of death woke her up into the same Deadworld dream. She sat up and looked around, watching the gray, wispy tendrils of fog skim low overhead. Up the street, Rosa's house loomed, its siren, infant wail echoing through the neighborhood, pushing the fog away in a circle several houses wide.

"Again? Really?" Jackie got to her feet and flipped everything the bird. "I was sleeping quite well, thank you very much. I hate you, brain." Perhaps if she could get the babe to shut up, she might be able to just lie down and fall back asleep and just dream of being asleep.

The cold stone of the road provided for a charming, cold ache in her bare feet, threading its way up through her heels and into her ankles. Jackie ignored it. That was as bad as it would get. Everything was dulled in this place, gray, washed-out, a shadow of its former self, which Jackie realized was appropriate for her. She did feel like a shadow of her former self. Was this her subconscious's way of telling her she was fucked? Or maybe it was what Rosa had meant by broken.

At the edge of Rosa's property, Jackie stopped. There on the smooth stone of the yard was a faded, translucent body. It was so faded, Jackie could easily see through it.

"Hello?" Only the babe's cries answered. The figure did not move, so Jackie walked forward.

"Stay away from my baby." Rosa's voice swirled around and through her. "Stay out of my house."

Jackie paused and looked up into the fog, as it was where it seemed the voice came from. "Or what, Rosa? What are you going to do to me here that could make things any worse? Huh? Going to make me more dead? Can't get more broken than that." She shook her head and marched toward the body. "Stupid fucking dream."

Rosa was silent as Jackie came upon the prone, ghost figure. It was then she realized who it was. Laurel had been attacked by Rosa, and now her paranoia was going to find her here, deader than dead. Standing over the body, Jackie discovered she was right. Her eyes were closed. She looked as though she were sleeping.

"Laur?" Jackie knelt down. "Come on, dream, wake her up for me. Least we can do is get to talk."

She brushed away a stray strand of hair from Laurel's face. The skin was icy cold, but she felt something else too. There was a tingle of warmth, of life from within. Jackie put both her hands on Laurel's face, much like Nick had done earlier. It occurred to her then, in a moment of gut-clenching panic, that perhaps she was not dreaming after all. What if

Laurel had actually been attacked? What if Rosa had drained her away? And if she was here with her?

"Shit. Laur? You there?" She gave her head a little shake. "Come on, Laur. Wake up. This is only a stupid nightmare, right?" The panic spread and her arms began to shake as they held Laurel. "You're not dead. No, no, no! It's a dream. You're there, I know it." She had to be. Laurel could not be dead. This was not how it was supposed to happen. She said she would be there for her.

"You come back right now!" Her voice quavered, on the verge of tears. Jackie pulled Laurel's head to her breast and kissed her forehead. "This can't be happening. Not like this. You can't leave me, Laur."

She kissed the cold skin again, lips lingering, and that was when she felt her. Deep within that cold body, Laurel's life force pulsed with the faintest warmth. The tension flooded out of her in a wave. "Laur, come on. How do I get you back?" The panic began to change to anger. Was this what Rosa had done to Laurel? Drained her down to nothing and left her to lie forever on the ground of Deadworld?

"What did you do to her, Rosa?" Jackie stood back up and approached the house. "What did you do to Laurel?"

Rosa's voice came back, sliding around her in a soft, urgent hiss. "Stay out of my house!"

"And if I don't?" Jackie demanded. "If I march up there and take your baby?"

There was a pause of a few seconds. "Then I shall destroy your body and you will rot in this hell forever!"

On the verge of grabbing the front door handle and storming in, Jackie stopped, her fingers inches away. "What did you say?" She looked at Laurel and then backed slowly away from the door. A scrambling panic began to claw its way through her insides. "What do you mean, destroy my body?" Part of her already knew, however. This was no dream. Jackie slapped herself. "Wake up, Jackie. Wake your drugged ass up!"

Nothing happened. The baby's wail droned on. Jackie scooped up Laurel's body in her arms. It was surprisingly light.

"Stay away from my baby!" Rosa said. "I will destroy you both."

Jackie continued to back away, Laurel's head sagging against her shoulder. Rosa did not come, did not say anything else in fact, and Jackie walked backward down the street until the shroud of Deadworld found its way back to the ground. With Rosa's house out of sight, Jackie turned and began to run.

The nightmare had become real. Rosa had her body and she was now stuck in Deadworld.

Chapter 29

Shelby paced back and forth in Nick's office. Cynthia sat in the corner chair, sipping tea. Nick ran a hand over his short hair in frustration. "I have no good answers for this one. Reasoning with her is not going to work. And we can't get to her from a defensible position. She would likely kick our asses."

"Can you just suck her up, like Drake did with the others?" Shelby asked.

Nick shook his head. "She's strong enough to resist. I just scared her earlier, and I'm not sure how I'd feel leaving the babe's spirit to wail there for eternity."

"Maybe she doesn't care that Laurel is there," Shelby said. "Maybe we could just go in, and get her away from Rosa. You create a distraction while I grab and go."

"And what then?" Nick leaned back and opened up his hands. "You got some powers I don't know about? We get in a fight with her, we might not be able to get back out."

"What about Jackie?" Cynthia said quietly from her corner.

Yes, Nick thought. There was always Jackie, the great unknown. "We're still a bit clueless about what it is Jackie can do. We still don't understand what happened to her over in Deadworld."

"Laurel possessed her before, when we got Drake," Shelby said, shaking a finger at Cynthia and nodding in agreement. "If Jackie could coax her into possession, she could take her back over to Deadworld."

"Jackie is in no position to be going anywhere," Nick replied. "And we used Laurel to get Jackie through before. I'm not sure we could do it without her."

"But Jackie has her own power and abilities now," Shelby insisted. "I'll bet the three of us could open the door wide enough to get us through."

"Shel . . ." Nick sighed. No reason would be good enough right now. She wanted something hopeful to cling to and would not stop until she had it. It was odd to see her this attached to someone. It had been a long time. "We can see how Jackie is doing later. Maybe she'll feel better and be willing to try. I'm sure she's just as worried as you are." And utterly terrified of doing anything with Deadworld.

"All right!" Shelby said. "We'll do that. First thing," she added.

"I should've had her stay at my place," Nick said. The more he thought about it, the more uncomfortable he felt about Jackie's safety in this whole situation. "Too many unknowns going on with this."

Shelby's smile drifted away. "You think she's susceptible, don't you? Because of what happened with Laurel."

"I agree," Cynthia added. "Her body has been used

once, which will make the next easier, and she is weak. I wouldn't put her anywhere near an angry spirit."

"You're right," Nick said. "Foolish of me. I should have stayed with her or brought her home." He started to get up and noticed Shelby's arched brows and faint smile. "Don't give me that look. It's her safety I'm worried about, not whose bed she's sleeping in."

"Awfully nice to have both, though," she replied.

Nick grabbed his coat off the back of his chair. Cynthia gave him a bemused smile over the top of her tea cup and he pointed an accusing finger. "You could take my side once in awhile, Cyn."

"But I am," she said, lowering her cup. "I thought you wanted to sleep with her."

"You know what?" He forced the zipper on his coat together and yanked it up. He didn't know what, actually, but was tired of them pointing out the obvious. "Whatever happened to chivalry? It used to be a noble aspiration."

Nick opened the door and strode out into the hall, not waiting for the answer.

Behind, Shelby's voice yelled after, followed by her and Cynthia's snickering, "I'd rather get laid, Nick!"

Fact of the matter was, he did want her, in a way he hadn't wanted anyone since Shelby. Perhaps it was because Drake was dead and he had saved her life. He was trying to move on and she was the most obvious connection to move on with. The thought had crossed his mind more than once that he wanted Jackie due to convenience. As the days wore on, though, Nick had discovered she was far from convenient. She had a troubled past that continued to plague her. Her best friend had died. She drank too much and, to top it off, some fair part of her was still terrified of what he was. It was enough baggage to sink just about anyone.

Nick rolled down the windows of his Porsche and let the chill of the early evening air assault him. He cranked up his stereo when, coincidentally, Sinatra's *My Way* came on. He could easily let Jackie go. The part of her that cringed at his touch would breathe easy and say good riddance. Then what of that part that came to life beneath his lips? That had not been his imagination. They were both lost souls hoping to find a way to reconnect with life, and that was really all that he needed to know. Everything else was just icing.

As the minutes rolled by, Nick's worry grew. He shouldn't have left her alone. The shooting incident had been nagging at him from the moment it occurred. Something had not been right about it all. He had dismissed the idea that Jackie had been used by Rosa. After all, Jackie had woken up in the hospital as herself. What if Rosa was not so utterly single-minded, though? What if she was smart enough to leave and come back at a more opportune time? What if Jackie was as susceptible to possession as he suspected?

Nick picked up speed, weaving through evening traffic that was heading into town, cruising by the solid line of cars heading out.

The most damning evidence of all, however, was the one Nick had glossed over. The smell of blood. Rosa's murder scene had been ripe with it, cloying and dense, so much so you wanted to wash yourself after leaving. Jackie had not been able to get rid of it. Rosa was lingering on her in a palpable way. And maybe it was all just paranoia and the simple desire or excuse to be near Jackie. Nick decided he would gladly take that alternative if it meant Rosa was not interfering with her. Possession was the last thing in the world she needed after all that had happened.

He had to park two blocks away from her apartment. People were just getting home and taking all of the spots. Nick walked briskly down the sidewalk, providing an imposing enough presence that people eagerly sidestepped out of his path. Half a block away, he reached out, trying to sense her, feel her sleeping, buried in the soft down of her comforter. Jackie's blood would tingle in his veins when he got in close proximity to her, a bond he would have with her no matter what might happen.

At the downstairs entry, Nick grabbed the handle and focused some of his energy upon it until the lock released. He still could not feel her. Up the stairs three at a time and still nothing sparked his senses. All of this he could have brushed off except that he found the front door to her apartment unlocked. He was sure he had locked it, and Jackie would never leave without locking. She kept the chain hooked even when answering the door.

"Jackie!" he shouted, moving quickly around through the living room and marching down the hall to the bedroom. "Jackie?"

The bed was empty.

Bickerstaff sat on one corner, staring apprehensively, ready to bolt. Nick looked in the bathroom and checked the rest of the apartment. Nothing looked disturbed. It had been three hours and a normal human being would not have woken up from what he had done for at least eight—ten if you were lucky. And Jackie had proven she was far from that.

Nick took out his phone and hit speed dial. "Shel?"

"Hey, babe," she said. "Snuggling up with your girl?"

"Get your cycle. She's gone."

Chapter 30

Jackie came to a stop at last, sitting down on an embankment beneath a bridge with Laurel in her lap. It had been several minutes or maybe an hour, she could not tell. Time did not run properly in Deadworld. She had not stopped because she was tired or out of breath. Being a spirit rather alleviated that problem, but Jackie figured if Rosa had been chasing them, she would have caught up or given up by now, if she had even chased them at all.

Laurel's face had not changed. She still looked as though she slept peacefully. Somewhere in there, however, her pulse or life force or whatever it was beat ever so faintly. Rosa had left it alone or been unable to reach some part of her. Jackie brushed her hand across Laurel's cheek.

"Laur? Can you hear me? Are you there? It's safe now. Please. I need you. You have to come back for me." As she expected, Laurel continued her unresponsive slumber.

Jackie turned and set her down on the incline, carefully folding her hands over her belly and straightening her clothes. If she was aware in there, at least she would be comfortable. With arms crossed over her knees, Jackie set her chin on top and stared out into the dense and shifting gloom beyond the bridge, eyes scanning from one side to the other at quick, regular intervals. There had to be something she could do. She had to find a way to contact Nick or Shelby or even Cynthia and let them know what had happened. Then again, it would be helpful if she knew just what the hell had happened.

Assuming for the moment this was not still a horrid nightmare, it meant Rosa had booted her to Deadworld and taken over her body. It also meant she had done it the night before, which explained why she had been so utterly exhausted. She had never actually gone to sleep. Rosa had been out there trying to track down Rennie Vasquez. It meant she was out there now, driving around in Jackie's Durango, hoping to pick up those needed clues to go finish him off. And then what? Would she come back to her babe so Jackie could return? Or, what if like Morgan she got caught in a shoot-out and her body died? Then Deadworld would be her new home.

"Fuck no," Jackie said. "No way that's happening." She reached down and laid her hand on Laurel's. "Wake up, Laur. I really need your help with this one."

Jackie took a deep breath and counted to ten. Her brain was beginning to turn into frazzled mush. Her piano would have been good right about now. The first step any good investigator took was to look at what you already knew. Primary fact: she was now a ghost. What did she know about ghosts? They could possess people. They could move back and forth between the real world and the dead one. With a point of reference, they could will themselves to another place in a fraction of the time it took to walk. Laurel had done this. Nick had, too. She had tried and failed. *But I wasn't a ghost then. So, I should be able to now.* Crossing over would be the trick. Jackie hadn't the foggiest idea how one went about doing that.

If she could travel, where should she go? Nick instantly came to mind. Nick knew how to cross over. Laurel had helped him. If he could sense her presence like she could with Laur, then maybe he could let her know how to get out of this Godforsaken place. Jackie tried to recall what it was Laurel had explained before, about moving as a ghost, but then her focus was interrupted by someone running by along the stone streambed.

He looked like an Amish man, given the conservative attire and the beard, but he paid her no mind. He just looked over his shoulder once and continued to run like a bat out of hell. The first thing that popped into Jackie's mind was the smarmy, pretentious smile of Cornelius Drake. There were other vampires, though Nick told her he had only ever seen one other. What were the odds another vampire was roaming around in Chicago's side of the dead? Of course, Nick did not know how things were here, not for sure. Her first trip over had been his, too. Maybe there were a lot of soul-slurping vampires running around over here.

Whispering voices moved quickly overhead on the bridge, fading on the other side. Maybe it was Rosa on the warpath or some other royally pissed-off ghost? Jackie decided it would be best not to wait around and find out. She scooped up Laurel's body and walked out in the direction the Amish man had gone. Up the embankment on the other side, Jackie paused to try and figure out where she wanted to go. It was not an area of Chicago she was familiar with.

Ahead of her, it was turning into a mix of old business and residential. Across the dry creek-bed, it was purely residential, neat rows of 1920s and 1930s homes, of which Jackie could only get glimpses of the nearest ones. Two more people ran across the bridge, one leaping down to the bed below and continuing on past her. By the expression on her face, Jackie would say she was terrified.

"What's happening?" she called out as the woman passed her.

One furtive glance was all she afforded Jackie. "Run!" she yelled.

Still not seeing anything, she pulled Laurel tighter against her chest and stepped over between two buildings. It was not much cover, but when your visibility was one hundred feet with favorable Deadworld winds, it would do.

Jackie half expected some sort of Godzilla to come stomping through, but the air remained silent. The wispy blanket above continued to eddy and shift, reaching down with tenuous fingers toward the ground. About to give up and start walking, Jackie felt a shift in the breeze, a subtle change in direction, from blowing into her face to coming at her back. She watched the dangling fog, drifting toward her abruptly bend and twist and begin its quest in the opposite direction. What sort of thing would cause the wind to shift? Something that scared the shit out of people, no doubt.

It was not Godzilla that came to the foot of the bridge on the opposite side, but it might as well have been for the imposing presence it radiated. Jackie first saw something dark moving through the gray, not much bigger than a person. It might have been a person for all she could tell, except that nothing in this place had any sort of crisp color. Deadworld was a washed-out palette of grays. This was black, night-sky darkness. It moved slowly, and because of the cottony strands of fog that were being drawn to it like the eye of a hurricane, Jackie could not tell if it walked on two legs or just floated across the ground.

The thing had arms, long and spindly, with sharp joints that gave the appearance of tree limbs, which swung with smooth grace next to its body. Without getting closer, Jackie could not tell for sure, but it looked to be covered in something, stiffer than fur, maybe quills, that ran vertically over its body, flowing right up into its head, which gave it a ragged paint-brush look. Well, it wasn't human, of that Jackie was certain.

The black creature began to move over the bridge at a very casual pace, its head turning back and forth. It seemed to be looking for something. Jackie turned away to gain protected cover from the corner of the building. *That's not human, whatever it is. So why is it in this place?* Of greater concern was the fact people were running away from it frightened for their lives. *Maybe it's time I got the hell out of here.*

Jackie gave it one last look and froze. It stood in the middle of the bridge, facing her with silver-dollar-sized eyes distorted by the wiry hair that grew over every part of its body, glowing with a luminescent emerald-green stare. The head cocked to one side as though perplexed or confused by what it saw. *It wonders why the hell I'm here, just like I do.* But Jackie did not think that little cock of the head was curiosity in a puppy-dog sort of way. She got the panicky feeling its curiosity tended toward the "how many different ways can I cook it?" side of things. This was where humans came when they died, so what in

God's name was that? The panicky feeling bloomed into full-on dread. When it turned and continued to cross the bridge, Jackie spun back between the buildings and fled, hoisting Laurel up over her shoulder in a fireman's carry.

"Shit. Holy shit. Laur? Now would be a good time to wake up. Something really bad is after us." Jackie sprinted down the street, watching the gauzy fingers of fog make their sluggish turns in the other direction toward the gathering storm that had to be named Death.

Jackie ran until the wind shifted back to its usual direction. Then she ran some more, praying that she was not somehow running in a circle back to that dark, swirling storm. She wanted to get to Nick's. If she was going to be safe anywhere in this chill world, it was Nick's house, but she couldn't leave Laurel, and Jackie had no idea if she could pull both of them along. Maybe it would work, but she could not risk failure and leave Laurel within the clutches of that black thing.

She reached a park, a smooth open field of stone, likely soccer fields in the real world, and decided to stop. She could not hide here, but nor could the thing sneak up on her. The first hint of changing wind and she would be off again. Jackie laid Laurel on the ground and cupped her face in her hands.

"Laur? I know you're in there. Can you hear me? If I can help you somehow, you need to let me know."

She came back to Deadworld to recharge. Laurel had told her that much, but how? Did it happen naturally or did she have to do something? More importantly, maybe she could do it for her? Jackie closed her eyes and tried to relax, hard to do when green eyes were somewhere behind them and swirling in their direction. It was all a matter of relaxing and focusing, like with her piano. The piano was her meditation or so Laurel had proclaimed.

Jackie tried to let her mind drift to those memories, blocking out the edgy panic that gripped her and the unknown danger that closed in. Imagined sitting at her piano, Bickerstaff parked on top, eyes half-closed while she played, churning through clues or just playing out frustration or depression. If she could get to that place then maybe she could bring Laurel what she needed. Jackie had no idea how it was supposed to work. She was not a psychic, but she could play those notes in her head, feel herself seated at the bench, her fingers stretching, pressing, lifting, and floating over the keys, filling her with lush sounds that dulled and pushed away all the things that threatened her being.

Something began to pull at her, like the suction from a straw, drawing upon her insides.

"Hon? What? What are you doing here?"

Jackie opened her eyes and found Laurel blinking rapidly up at her, trying to focus her gaze. A wave of dizzy exhaustion swept through Jackie and she let go of Laurel's face, bracing a hand on the ground. "Damn, it worked." She laughed, unbelieving. "You don't know how glad I am to see you."

Laurel looked around and sat up, still shaking the cobwebs out. "Where are we? Rosa was beating the crap out of me . . ." Her hand came up to cover her mouth. "Oh, Sweet Mother, Jackie. Why are you here? How? Oh, please, no!"

"Oh! I'm not dead. At least I don't think I am." She reached out and hugged Laurel, whose arms enfolded her, the first embrace she had received from her best friend since before she had died. Jackie began to cry. "God, Laur. You don't know how good that feels. I've missed you so much."

Laurel held her for a moment longer and then pulled back, taking Jackie's face in her hands. She leaned forward and gave her a brief kiss. "Why are you here?"

"I think Rosa took my body while I was sleeping and booted me over here."

"But . . . when, Jackie? I don't understand. It doesn't work like that."

Jackie shrugged. "I don't have a fucking clue either, but we don't have time to discuss this now. There's some . . . thing out there following us."

"A thing?" Laurel's forehead wrinkled up with confusion. "What sort of thing?"

"I don't know! It was black and had these big, freaky green eyes," Jackie said. "Everyone was running as fast as they could in the opposite direction, so I figured it would be good to stay away. Maybe it was the Grim Reaper or something."

Laurel got to her feet, turning slowly in a full circle. "How do you know it's following us?"

"Because it saw me, and gave me this cockeyed *who the fuck are you?* look and started walking our way."

"It came after you, particularly?" Laurel said, still gazing out into the dense fog. "But why?"

"Eating ghosts for breakfast? I really don't want to hang around and find out. I was going to try that teleport thing you tried to teach me before, but I was worried I'd leave you behind."

Following her cue, the wind abruptly switched from the left side of her face to the right. Laurel perked up and turned around. She had noticed it, too.

"Teleport or run?" Jackie whispered in a rush. "It can't be far."

"Let's go to Nick's," she whispered back. "Don't feel like running."

"Just focus on his place?"

She nodded. "Imagine it and you will arrive." Laurel took Jackie's hands in hers. "Close your eyes, hon. Easier that way."

Jackie did and imagined Nick's living room with its enormous, comforting, river-stone fireplace. The perfect place to curl up on a cold Chicago night. There was a pull on her, like wind pulling sand off a dune, digging deeper and deeper into her, until they were drawn away, fired across the gray like an arrow. A moment later, stillness enveloped them and Jackie opened her eyes. She was greeted by the familiar expanse of stone and heaved a sigh of relief.

Laurel, on the other hand, stared in shock, her mouth agape. "Sweet Mother, that thing was definitely not human."

"I know," Jackie replied. "Now then, how do we cross over? Because the broken girl here wants her body back before Rosa gets it filled full of holes."

Chapter 31

McManus could not believe his ears. A hundred, or so it seemed, gang members and not a peep or clue, and then this random old man walking down the sidewalk from the liquor store to his house, which happened to be across the street from the bar he had been visiting.

"You speak decent Spanish for a fed," he said to McManus. "Suppose you're looking for who killed that Rosa Sanchez girl. Or who's left of them."

"I am, sir," McManus said, "and thank you. Eight years of Gang Enforcement in San Francisco. Moved here to be near my daughter." He looked up and down the sidewalk and then back over to the bar. "Nobody's going to mind you talking to a fed?"

"Ha!" He waved his cane toward McManus. "Nobody round here is going to fuck with me. Gangbanging little shits know better, unless they want to end up minus a few body parts."

"I see. I suppose I should know who you are then."

"And I'm supposing you don't," the old man replied. "You're looking for Rennie Vasquez and whomever is left of his crack-smoking little posse."

"That I am, sir." McManus got the feeling the man had to be related to a gang member, likely a leader of some sort if he had no fear of retaliation. "You know he killed Rosa Sanchez?"

The man looked taken aback. "Boy, you know that saying, 'Not a jealous bone in his body?'"

"I do."

"Rennie Vasquez is the goddamn opposite of that," he said, emphasizing his words with taps of his cane on the cement. "Rosa got pregnant with some rich boy's kid, left Rennie after he tried to kill her. She got even by ruining his bid to become leader of this part of town, cost Rennie a lot of drug money and made him look weak. One thing you don't want to do to a crazy little shit like that is make him look weak. He gathered up some boys and took her down. Sad," he said with a shake of his head. "Rosa was no saint, mind you, but killing a pregnant girl ain't right for any reason. And now looks like he stirred up someone's righteous fury from what I seen on the news. Hope he gets his."

"Would prefer if we could put him behind bars for the rest of his life and let him rot away a little bit at a time," McManus said. "I can't let a vigilante keep running around killing people, sir."

"From what I saw, you all got the boy who was doing that. Cop wasn't it?"

"It was. You happen to know where Rennie is hiding out, sir? That would go a long way toward helping us if you did. Think there might be a reward out for information leading to his arrest."

"You don't say?" The man smiled. "Guess I could use a new TV. I like them new flat ones you hang on the wall. It's like looking through a window."

McManus dug out his pen and pad. He loved

when grinding things out paid off. You talk and talk and talk until someone you didn't see wants to talk to you. "You tip us off to Rennie, and I'll take you shopping for it myself, sir."

He laughed. "I'll hold you to that—Agent . . . ?"

"McManus. Ryan. And I'm certainly pleased to meet you today. The gang boys are a silent bunch."

He shrugged. "Sticking together is what they do well, even if one of their own is gone bad."

"Mind if I ask how you are privy to all of this information?"

"I helped run the damn thing, back when it was more about Latino pride than what they've turned it into." He shook his head in disgust. "Enough said, boy. You let me know if I'm shopping for a new TV. I live right up there on the left, in the blue bungalow."

McManus took down the address the old man figured Rennie might be staying at. It wasn't an address that had been on their search list. "You take care, sir. I'm much obliged for your help," McManus said, and he truly meant it. Hard to find anyone these days that didn't either fear or loathe the FBI.

The sound of screeching tires turned him around toward the bar. A familiar, black Durango had just lurched to a stop at the curb. At the wheel, he could see the tousled mess of auburn hair that immediately identified Agent Rutledge. "Jack?" McManus rocked back on his heels for a moment in disbelief before crossing the street. What in God's name was she doing out here?

Jackie slammed the door shut and hopped down to the sidewalk as McManus trotted up to her. "Jack! What are you doing here?" She ignored him, marching toward the door to the bar. He hurried up to her and reached out to touch her arm. "Hey, Jack. Shouldn't you—"

She wheeled around, eyes wild and bright. "Hands off, asshole!"

McManus noticed the clenched fists and took a quick step backward. "Shit, Jack. Calm . . . down," he began, but then stopped. The wild-eyed look remained. She didn't recognize him. "I thought you were home sleeping off that concussion?"

The tension dissipated. Her fists unclenched. "Oh, yes. I was, but the painkillers started working so, I wanted to come out and see if I could track down Rennie."

She looked like hell, her eyes sunken and dark. The bandage on her head was gone, and the pink, stitched welt marking the side of her shaved head made her look like someone escaped from the psych ward. "You should be resting, Jack. You look beat to hell."

"I'm fine!" she snapped. "Don't you have something better to do than stand around and harass me?"

Man! She was in a fine mood. "Sorry. Christ. You don't need to be out here though. I think we finally got a good lead."

"What?" Her hand shot out and grabbed a handful of his shirt, thumping his chest with painful force. "You found Rennie?"

McManus stared down at the fist clenched in his shirt, so tight the knuckles were turning white. She really was starting to lose it. "You mind letting go?"

"Where is he? Where's Rennie?" Her hand shook against him, refusing to release.

"I'm not going to tell you shit if you're going to go ballistic on me," McManus said. "So why don't you let go and maybe we can discuss what we're going to do next?"

For a moment, McManus didn't think she was. Her mouth drew into a tight, bloodless line, as if the subject was actually something to debate, but then finally let go. "There. Happy? So, where is he?"

McManus reached into his jacket and pulled out his notepad. He was going to have to call Pernetti in on this first. No way was he taking Jack out there like this. She was in no state to be confronting a murderer. "You know, Jack. You're probably not in the best state to be going—"

The rest of his sentence rushed out with the air from his lungs as Jackie's fist buried itself into his solar plexus. He dropped to a knee, a swirling wave of nausea overwhelming him. "Jack!" he managed to gasp out. Her face was twisted into smiling, wicked sneer, but it was in the eyes that McManus saw the truth. Jackie no longer stared down at him. "Rosa."

She reached down and snatched the notepad from his hand while he sucked air like a beached fish. What was she doing?

"Huh," she said from somewhere above him. "I'd have never guessed, the little shit."

McManus turned and looked up. "You have to . . . stop, Rosa."

She bent over until her face was only inches from his. "Thanks, Agent Whoever-you-are, but I need your gun now."

"Rosa . . . no." He clamped his hand down on his holster, a feeble effort at best without any breath to fuel his defense.

McManus turned just in time to see her steel-toed hiker come sweeping through the damp air, and he kissed it goodnight.

Chapter 32

Nick thrust his keys into the ignition of his Porsche outside Jackie's apartment and then froze. The whisper of Deadworld blew through him, tingling his blood. The scent of it was all too familiar, as her blood still coursed through his body.

He glanced up, looking around at the street. "Jackie?" But no, she was not close. Nick closed his eyes and took a slow, deep breath, focusing on the feeling of her spirit touching him. He turned until the sensation, faint and subtle though it was, became strongest. Home. What had happened? How could he be feeling this?

Nick's heart leaped up into his throat. Dear God, could something dreadful have happened to her?

The ring of his cell startled him back to reality. It was Shelby. "Nick! Laurel's back! I can—"

"The house," he replied, and swallowed hard. "I think they're back at the house."

"What? But . . . how? Jackie? Shit, Nick. What the fuck's going on?"

"Rosa. God damnit! Rosa got to her." Nick gunned the engine, his hand suddenly clammy with sweat fumbled at the shifter before he launched the Porsche out into traffic. "Meet me there."

The normal thirty-minute drive took nineteen minutes. A million panicked thoughts raced through his brain during that time—what had happened to Jackie? Could Rosa have possessed her, taken her out somewhere, looking for Vasquez and been killed? If Rosa still had her, then how could her spirit be roaming around freely? She should have been locked away, forced into submission by Rosa's dominant force. He had feared it might happen, suspected Rosa has done something to her when Morgan was killed, but there had been no way to know. Jackie was certainly in no state of mind to be dealing with Rosa. Her will had been battered and beaten down to nothing. He should have never let her stay in her apartment alone.

Whipping through the curves up to his house, hands clenched around the steering wheel slick with sweat, Nick knew for sure Jackie was there. He could even feel Laurel, much weaker, but definitely present. A single light flashed behind him as Shelby's BMW flew up behind him, hugging the curves with physics-bending force. They slid to stop in his driveway together, running to the door side by side.

Once inside, Nick crossed the foyer and came to a stop in the archway leading to the living room, his breath locking up inside his lungs. He knew what he was going to find, but it still stunned him. There on the hearth of stone stood Jackie's gray, translucent figure. Laurel, far less visible, reclined on the sofa beside her.

Jackie gave him a feeble wave and her voice cracked. "Hey. Got a small problem here."

Shelby rushed over to the couch and knelt down

beside Laurel. "Baby! Thank-fucking-God. I thought you were dead. I mean, really dead."

"I'm OK now," she said, "but we need to help Jackie before it's too late."

Nick staggered into the living room toward Jackie, his legs loose and rubbery. "Too late for what?"

"Rosa said I wouldn't get my body back." Jackie shrugged and sat down on the slate apron of the fireplace. "Think she plans on wasting my body once she's done with me." Her voice quavered. "How does this even happen? It's because I'm fucking broken, isn't it? Goddamn Deadworld bullshit." Her voice rose an octave. "What the hell is wrong with me?"

Relief flooded through him. Rosa still had her body. She was alive and yet somehow her spirit roamed freely. A choked laugh escaped his lips. "You're not dead." Her fists were clenched together in her lap. Nick walked over and sat down beside her. He wanted nothing more than to wrap his arms around her. "There's nothing wrong with you, Jackie." He rubbed his hands over his head. "And thank God you're not dead."

She cocked her head and looked up at him. The fear and anger in her face melted away. "You thought . . . oh. No, Nick. I'm not dead, not yet anyway. I'm just, um, I'm missing my body." She tried to smile but failed. "So, how do I get my body back?"

He heaved a sigh of relief, regaining his composure. A monumental failure had been averted, at least for now. "We need to get Rosa out first," Nick said. "Then you can go back, just like crossing over. That part should be easy. I just don't get why you're here and not trapped in your body."

"Me either," she said.

"The bonds are broken," Laurel replied.

"What?" All three of them said in unison.

Laurel sat up straight. "The bond between her body and spirit has been broken. Rosa didn't trap her because she didn't have to. She just shoved Jackie over to Deadworld."

Jackie's fists clenched in her lap. "She came while I was sleeping. The bitch invaded me while I slept."

"Ah," Nick said, nodding. It made some sense now. That was why she could open the door to Deadworld so easily. "Well, we need to encourage her to come back home then."

"Her baby," Jackie said, shoulders slumping. "We have to go threaten her baby again."

"Worked before. No reason to think it won't work again."

Shelby looked skeptical. "Can you handle her, Nick? You said before that she might be stronger than we can deal with."

"Before?" Jackie wondered. "What before?"

"Cynthia went to see if Rosa was at home," Nick said, "and nearly got strangled. This must have been before she came and took you."

"Oh. Can you handle her?"

"Between Shelby and me, we should be able to hold her for the few seconds you'd need to cross back."

"And after that? How do we keep her out?"

Nick gave her a grim smile. He had no ready answer for that one because he honestly had no idea if Jackie could hold Rosa off. "We'll keep an eye on you until this Vasquez guy is tracked down and caught. Speaking of which, I should call McManus and warn him that you're out there looking."

Jackie shook her head and then put her face in her hands, mumbling something Nick could not quite understand. He punched in McManus's number, who sounded like he had just woke up when he answered.

"McManus? Nick Anderson."

"Hey . . . Nick? We've got a big ol' cluster fuck going on here. I'm pretty sure Rosa has Jackie."

His stomach tensed. "You've seen her, then?"

"You could call it that. We need to find her quick. She sucker-punched me and took my gun."

Jackie's head snapped up. She had heard McManus's message. "Oh, shit. I'm so screwed."

Nick raised a finger to her to be quiet. "Do you have any idea where she was heading?"

"Jackie!" Laurel shouted or tried to, but her strength was not up to it. "We'll figure this out."

"Yeah, she got me right after I told her where Vasquez might be," said McManus.

Damn. "You found him?" asked Nick.

"Maybe. Reliable source, but still have to check it out."

"How long ago was this?"

"Ten minutes, maybe," McManus replied.

"Try and find her," he said. "I'm going to see if we can get Rosa out, so she might be back to the same old Jackie we know and love."

There was a pause on the other end. "Get her out, Nick? Where you at?"

"Home."

Another pause. "OK, then. I wouldn't mind being clued in a bit more on this."

"Soon. Call me if you find her." Nick hung up. "We need to act fast. Jackie, I'm going to need you to help pull Shelby and me across. Think you can do that?"

Laurel sat up. "I'm not sure that's a good idea, Nick."

"We go after Rosa's babe, she comes back. We

need to do this now before Rosa kills someone else. She may know where Vasquez is."

Shelby stood up. "Nick's right. Five minutes ago would've been better."

"You want my help?" Laurel said.

"No," Nick replied. "Stay here. This shouldn't take long and I don't want to risk you with Rosa again."

Jackie waved her hands in warning. "Wait a sec. Laur, what about that thing we saw?"

The nervous, wide-eyed look concerned Nick. "Thing? What thing?"

Laurel shook her head. "No idea what it was. It wasn't human, though."

"What?" Nick and Shelby asked simultaneously.

"It was black with these long spindly arms and covered in something . . . spikes or quills, I don't know, but it had these huge, green eyes and gave me the damnedest look when it saw me."

"It come after you?" Nick wondered. There was something non-human in Deadworld? How was that possible? What could it be? At the moment though, it did not matter. They had to get Rosa out of Jackie's body immediately.

"Yeah," Jackie replied. "Freakiest thing I've ever seen."

"All right," Nick said. "We'll deal with that later, since I'm not even sure what to say about that. This won't take us long, if the last time is any indication."

Jackie sighed. "It freaks me out more knowing my body is out there being used by someone else."

A clap startled him. Shelby grinned and rubbed her hands together. "Let's do this. Jackie, you know how to open the door?"

"You could say that," Laurel said quietly.

"Apparently I do," Jackie said with a shrug. "But I didn't actually do anything. It just happened."

Nick raised an eyebrow with surprise. "You must have done something, Jackie."

She motioned with her hands, flustered. "Not really. I just . . . um . . . closed my eyes and pictured the door and it was there."

"Seriously?" Shelby said. "Show us, Jackie."

"But I don't"—she started and then shrugged—"OK. No guarantees. I have no clue what I'm doing."

She closed her eyes and let out a deep breath. Nick watched her intently, focusing his senses on the space around them, ready to add his own strength to hers, but it was not necessary. It only took seconds. In the air behind Jackie, the world cracked open and the rush of Deadworld's air hit him in the face. It wasn't a door being cracked open like he was used to, a heavy weight to be forced open with great expense of energy. This was a sliding door, wheeled back on greased rollers, effortless and opened wide.

"Good God," Shelby whispered in awe.

Nick couldn't agree more. "Incredible."

Jackie turned and stared through the opening, arms folded across her chest. "Yea for me."

Nick laid a hand on her shoulder. "We'll figure this out. Don't go anywhere once we're over." Nick stepped forward wincing at the pain of transition, the instant cold ache in his bones. A moment later they were all through, standing in the monotone gray, Deadworld version of his living room. "Now then. I imagine this is going to be quick. Jackie, I don't want you inside. Stay out of her house." She nodded in agreement. "Once Rosa comes back, you should be able to go right back to your body."

"How?"

"Rosa won't be blocking your way," he replied. "Just keep trying once we get over there. Once you've gone we'll leave."

"Don't you think she'll attack?"

"She will. Rosa thinks that I can drain her. She might be angry but she's not stupid."

Jackie appeared worried. "Can you? Drain her, I mean."

"Honestly, I don't know," Nick said. He hoped it did not come to that. "I'm counting on the threat being enough to get us out."

Shelby took a hold of her hand. "Important thing is getting you back, and making sure she doesn't get to you again."

"You going to keep me awake for the rest of my life?"

Always the smartass. Nick gave her a fleeting smile. "No. We'll just keep you under watch until Vasquez is caught. I think Rosa will be done once the source of her rage is dealt with. You ready to go over there?" They were wasting precious time. Nobody knew how close Rosa was to confronting Vasquez.

"No, but let's do this. I want my body back," Jackie said.

Nick reached out and took her hand and offered his other to Shelby. Jackie's cold hand felt incredibly small and frail in his grasp. If Rosa proved a problem, he would have to take her out. He would not let her get close to Jackie. "Here we go."

They arrived together on Rosa's front steps, engulfed immediately by the baby's keening wail. Was it any wonder Rosa was driven to kill those responsible? Jackie flinched and pulled away from his grasp. "What is it?"

"She knows we're here," Shelby said. "And not happy about it."

Nick walked up and opened the door. "Stay here, Jackie. Be ready. I'll get a hold of you as soon as I can after we're done."

She nodded, arms folded over her chest. She looked like a lost, homeless waif, battered and shrunk in on herself. "Be careful," she said.

Shelby followed him and they went quickly up the stairs. He figured it would not take Rosa long to jump back and she proved him right. Her presence lit up the bedroom even as he was opening the door.

"Get out!"

"Rosa—" he began, but it was as far as he got. She leaped at him, hands extended like claws, reaching for his throat. The speed at which she moved took him by surprise and she was on him before he could even get his hands up to protect himself.

"Stay away from my baby," she screamed. Her legs clamped around his waist and the momentum carried them tumbling backward into the hall.

"Nick!" Shelby cried out, leaping to his aid.

The hands at his throat were digging in with ferocious tenacity, cutting off his air. "Rosa," he gasped, but it was all he could muster. Shelby's arm came around and hooked around Rosa's throat, trying to pry her loose, but even her blood-fueled power could not pull the vengeful woman free.

"Goddamn, Rosa," she grunted. "We're not after your baby."

Nick felt the power of a doorway opening nearby and then abruptly close. Jackie's presence was no longer nearby, which hopefully meant she had returned to her body. Rosa noticed, too, and the pressure around his neck abruptly subsided. She reached up with one hand and grabbed Shelby by the hair, flinging her down the hall to crash on the floor.

"No!" Rosa let loose a tirade in Spanish and turned her burning gaze back to Nick. She balled up one small fist and cocked it above his face.

"Shel! Go!" Nick turned and brought up a forearm to block. The force of her blow snapped his arm back into his face hard enough that he heard something crack in his nose. Out of the corner of his eye, he could see the hallway was now empty. Rosa pivoted and brought her other fist down, but Nick was ready for this one and caught it in his hand, diverting the blow away from his face. "Don't force me to drain you, Rosa. I don't want to."

She yanked her hand free, face twisted up into rage, but her eyes widened with fear. "Devil!" Her body sprang back, one moment clamped around his body, the next several feet back, crouched to attack. Nick took a defensive stance.

"She's not yours to use, Rosa," he said. "We'll stop Vasquez."

She shifted around to his left and Nick turned to counter. "I will kill him. He must die."

"Not by your hand," he replied. "We'll take him down. You need to take care of your babe."

"He wants his blood! I will get it," she hissed, and jumped at him once again.

Nick took the momentum of her jump, pivoted, and threw her to the ground, coming down on top of her. He summoned up the energy from the souls within him and began to draw upon Rosa's spirit. Her eyes turned wild, her body bucking against him, nearly throwing him off, but Nick kept her arms pinned to the ground. She screamed at him, cursing in Spanish, her head thrashing side to side.

Nick could feel her pulling energy from her baby. "Rosa, you will destroy him. Stop."

"Let me go," she yelled. "Rennie must die."

"Rosa!" He dug his fingers into her shoulders and slammed her against the floor. "Stop this! Or I will take your soul."

Finally, fear seemed to take over. The bucking stopped. She began to cry. "My boy needs justice."

"And we'll get it," he said. "Let us do this. If you can't, I'll be forced to take you. I won't let you use Jackie again."

Rosa went limp and began to sob. "Devil. It's not fair. It's not fair."

"I'm sorry." He knew how she felt, knew how deep-seated that need for vengeance could be. He had been there. "Take care of your baby. He needs you. Let the living deal with its own, Rosa. Let it be." He let go of her at last and swung himself off of her body. "I'm going to go now. If I come back, Rosa, this will be finished."

She sat up, chest heaving with sobs. "Go, Devil! I hate you."

Nick sighed. Was it enough? Would she stop? He hoped the threat was serious enough, but he wasn't going to count on it. He would still need to keep an eye on Jackie.

"Goodbye, Rosa. I hope you find peace." He focused on his home and a moment later was gone.

Chapter 33

Jackie came around to familiar surroundings. She was seated in her Durango, slumped against an inflated airbag. In front of her, a minivan parked along the curb was mashed into the crumpled hood of her SUV. Sirens wailed nearby. She fumbled for the handle and opened the door, falling to her knees as she stumbled out of the vehicle. The immediacy of her exhausted body was overwhelming and for a moment she just remained on her hands and knees, trying to get her bearings and strength to get back to her feet. The pain was a welcome relief. She could feel things again. Her body was solid and living. Tires screeched to her left.

"Rosa!" It was McManus. He ran up. "Don't move, Rosa. Just . . . stay right there."

She could see him from the waist down, his creased slacks and polished leather shoes, but she could not motivate her head to peer up to see his face. His hands moved over her, patting her down and Jackie tried to pull away, but she only sat down on her butt. It hit her then he was looking for the gun Rosa hand taken.

"It's the real me, McManus. Look in the car," she said. It had to be in there. God, how was she going to explain this? The BPS people were going to be all over her.

McManus stepped around her and a moment later came out. He held the gun at his side, grip firm and ready. "Jack, is it really you?"

She nodded. "Is your daughter named Amanda? Do you come from Gang Enforcement in San Francisco? Are you a divorced guy trying to make this whole agent-family thing work?" His grip relaxed somewhat. "Sorry, Ryan. I'm really sorry." His left eye was swollen and darkening into quite the shiner.

He knelt down beside her. "Thank Christ you're back. Are you hurt?"

"No more than I was." She swallowed hard. "Put me in the back of your car."

"What?"

"I need a safe place. In case Rosa comes back."

"Oh, yeah. OK. Here, let me help you up." He gripped her arm and Jackie dug her fingers into his jacket and struggled to her feet. Her legs shook with the effort.

She shuffled with him back to his car and flopped down into the seat. At that moment, her cell rang. She dug it out and sighed with relief. It was Nick. "Hey. You made it out OK?"

"We did," he said. "Hopefully Rosa will stay put. How's it going there?"

"Ryan's here," she said, "and I crashed the damn Durango."

His voice tensed. "You weren't hurt, were you?"

"I hurt all over Nick, but not from that. I don't think my body has slept for three days, and my head is still killing me."

"No meds, Jackie," he said. "You need to stay awake until we can get out there. Rosa is probably waiting for her chance to come back."

That was news she wanted to hear. "Thanks for that. You can take me home after I get fired."

"You won't get fired. Belgerman won't let them fire you for this."

"Nick, I punched a fellow agent and took his weapon. Even if I can tell the BPS the reason why and they actually believed me, I don't think it would matter. I'm screwed." Another car pulled up alongside McManus's car. It was Pernetti. "And now the fun really begins. Just . . . hurry, Nick. What if Rosa tries to come back while I'm awake?"

There was a pause, long enough to tell Jackie that he was not sure of the answer. "I think she would have tried already if she could. She's weakening, Jackie. Her strength comes from the babe and it's waning. You're too strong for her while you're awake, Jackie. Remember that."

Strong. That was so not true. She had never felt weaker, entirely at the whims of things she did not fully comprehend, like the sadistic stepfather who tortured and tormented her mother to the point of suicide. How or why did such things exist in this world? "I'll see you soon?"

"We're on our way now."

Jackie clicked off and lay back against the seat. They could not get there fast enough. All she wanted to do right now was curl up and go to sleep. Better yet, if Laurel could show up, that would go a long way to alleviating her stress. She muttered quietly to herself, "Red Rover, Red Rover, send Laurel right over."

Pernetti rapped his knuckles on the window. "What

the fuck, Jack? Have you lost your mind? Why are you locked up in McManus's car?"

"Pretty much and long story," she snapped back. "Go away."

"What were you doing? Chasing ghosts again?"

"Not now, Pernetti."

He stared at her through the window. "Yeah. You look like shit. McManus!" He walked away, thankfully leaving her alone.

Something swelled and stretched the fabric of space around her and Jackie lurched up.

You tricked me.

The air froze in Jackie's lungs. "Rosa," she whispered.

Let me in, so we may finish this. My little boy needs justice!

Jackie could feel Rosa pushing at the door, nudging and prying with her throat-clenching fingers. Once the moment of utter panic had subsided to a dull quaking in her boots, Jackie realized a different tone to Rosa's rants. She was desperate. "We'll get Vasquez. We'll get your justice, Rosa." *I'm strong. I am strong.*

Jail? That's your justice? Fuck your justice! The desperation was pure anger again. *Rennie Vasquez must die. He will be killed like he killed me and my poor little boy! And I don't care if your Devil destroys me.*

A sudden cramp gripped Jackie's stomach, twisting it into a violent knot. She doubled over in the seat, sucking in her breath. "Oh, fuck. Rosa, stop!" A kaleidoscope of images tumbled through her brain, drenched in a sheen of red: a flashing knife thrust between her thighs, plunging into her womb, unzipped from sternum to navel with everything fumbling out through panicked fingers, all at the hand of the psychopathic Rennie Vasquez.

Jackie fell over in the seat, swatting at the imaginary knife, kicking at the drug-fueled insanity of Rennie, and then covering her head as the pistol aimed itself at her forehead. "No!" she screamed. "No, stop!"

The car door jerked open, and McManus grabbed Jackie's ankle as it thrust out into the open air. He pushed it over against the seat, pinning her legs and then leaned in, folding his arms down on top of hers and sandwiching them to her chest. "Jack! What's going on? You with me, Rutledge?"

Jackie opened her eyes, half expecting it to be Rosa, and half choked out a sob or a laugh, it was hard to tell which. "It's Rosa," she said in a hushed voice, hoping Pernetti couldn't hear them. "The bitch is trying to come back."

McManus heaved a sigh. "This is Twilight Zone sort of weirdness, you know that right?"

She nodded. "No shit. Need Nick and Shelby to hurry up and get here. Not sure how long I can last against her."

His eyes widened. "Seriously? It's that hard to keep a ghost away?"

"Rosa's got some help," she said, "and I'm beat to hell, and I have no fucking clue what I'm doing." She laughed, a cackling, hoarse sound that likely did nothing to dispel the notion of her mental breakdown. "Just keep me locked up until they get here, OK?

Jackie Rutledge, get out of this car! Do not fail my little boy. You know what true justice is. You know what he deserves! Help me kill him. Please. You're my last chance.

Jackie scrunched her eyes closed, trying to will the voice away. If only she knew how. The anger had gone back to desperation, and desperate for justice was a feeling she had years of experience with. Part of her sympathized with Rosa, but this was not the way to help her.

"She won't shut up," Jackie said. "Sad thing is, part of me wants to help her kill this guy. She's showing me what he did."

"Sweet Jesus," McManus said. "We need to get you a sedative or something."

"No!" She pushed at him, but was so weak he would barely budge. "Can't sleep, Ryan. She'll come right through the drugs and take over. It doesn't matter."

He shook his head in disbelief. "OK. Shit. I'll just keep you locked up then." He pushed himself back up.

"That's one way to break in a new partner, Jack," Pernetti said with a bark of laughter. "So, do we know where this Vasquez guy is or not?"

McManus pushed himself off of Jackie. "Sorry, Jack. I'll send Nick over soon as he gets here." He closed the door, but she could still hear him talking. "Yeah, here's the address I got from the tip. Let's get some guys over there."

Rosa began to push and pound on the space around her. Jackie felt as though something was trying to pry open her head and climb inside. *They're going to get him! Let me in! You want justice too, I can feel it. You want to spill his blood.*

Jackie flinched with each blow, feeling herself give and buckle just a hair each time. How could she deny the feeling, if it was there? She did want Vasquez's blood for what he had done. And Drake's and Carl's too. Her own anger synched with Rosa's. She had lived that rage for a long time, but had learned to channel it. The images of Rosa's revenge kept filtering into her head. The sweet feeling of letting that rage loose coursed through her blood.

If Rosa kept it up, eventually she would collapse. "Killing him is not justice, Rosa. It's revenge." Even to Jackie, the words sounded hollow.

My little boy needs revenge!

Jackie clutched at her head. She needed help now and Nick was still minutes away at best. She was slipping fast. "Laur? Please! I need you now." To her surprise, Laurel actually appeared, stepping through the car door and sitting down by her head.

She gasped. "What's happening? Rosa?"

"Rosa's winning," Jackie moaned. "Not sure I'm . . . ow! damn it. Not sure I'm going to make it until Nick gets here."

Laurel's hands brushed her face, a cool, soothing whisper of sensation. "I'm not back to my usual strength," she said. "But I'll try and help you hold out." Rosa came after her now like a charging bull, and Jackie could feel herself getting pushed away from her body. Both of them flinched. "Sweet Mother! She's strong."

Jackie tried to laugh but it came out far more tearful. "I know. I don't want her in my body, Laur. She's going to get me killed."

Look at what he did to us! We must kill him.

Rosa's presence pushed at her, rattled, bent, and bowed Jackie's will, exerting more and more pressure on Jackie's soul. And the bloody onslaught of images, screams, and gunshots skipped and rewound themselves in a jagged refrain of horror. Jackie had no place to turn in order to not see them. She covered her ears. "Fuck, Laur. Make it stop. I can't take this."

"Let me in, hon. Now, before it's too late."

"What? Why?"

"Because I can help you better from the inside, and she's coming through, whether we want her to or not."

"No," Jackie yelled. "She can't have me. I won't—" She ground her teeth together in agony and doubled up once again, as something sharp and cold pierced her between her legs. Tears burst out of her. "I'm not strong enough for this."

In the background, McManus's fist pounded on the window. "Jack? You OK in there?"

"Then let me in," Laurel whispered.

"But won't you be trapped too?"

"It's OK. Do it now."

"Jack!" McManus yelled. "Fuck. I'm calling in the paramedics."

Jackie let go, letting herself slip away, and Laurel's spirit swept in. Unlike Rosa, her cool, calm presence brought relief. On Laurel's heels, however, came the tidal wave of Rosa's rage and desperation, burying them both. Jackie did the only thing possible at that moment. She held on to her friend for dear life and crashed down in to the darkest depths of her being.

Chapter 34

"Rosa! You can't do this. Innocent people are going to die."

Pernetti's car darted through traffic, lights flashing. Jackie felt as though she sat in a dark room, watching things happen through a first-person POV camera. Most disturbing was seeing her hands on the steering wheel, but having no direct sensation of them. She was her own bad movie. Laurel had tried to help them get through to Deadworld, but Rosa was too strong, and no amount of focus would make those curtains part between worlds.

"None of them are innocent," Rosa said.

This isn't justice. The law will deal with him, Rosa. We know where he is now. He'll get the death penalty, I guarantee you.

"I am the death penalty," she said.

Jackie, you can't reason with her, Laurel said. *We need to figure out how to stop her.*

How? I couldn't even keep her from taking over. I don't know how to do any of this shit.

Laurel's voice continued its soothing calm, which eased Jackie's panicked nerves. *But you do know things, hon. You can sense the dead. You can channel spirits. I would not be with you now if you couldn't. You can cross over to the other side, with the uncanny ability to open that door with no effort at all. You have amazing abilities. You are not broken, sweetie. It's just . . . your body and spirit, which are one unit in everyone else, can now come apart. You're truly unique.*

Jackie wanted to throw up her hands in frustration, but they remained locked on the steering wheel. *How does any of that help us to throw the bitch out?*

Rosa turned onto a neighborhood street, clipping the front of a parked car with the rear end of Pernetti's. "Who is in there with you?" she demanded.

Like I'm telling you a damn thing, Jackie snapped back.

"How did they get in there?" Was that actually a hint of worry in her voice?

Unlike you, Jackie said, *I invited her.*

The car sideswiped a pickup turning another corner and knocked off the side-view mirror. Jackie watched her hands grip the wheel so tightly the knuckles turned white. Her hands, and she could not even feel them. It was disconcerting.

"You should be grateful," Rosa shouted, and then her voice grew eerily quiet. "You're helping the dead get justice. You should be helping me, Agent Jackie Rutledge." Jackie could feel a calmness wash through her, blurring her vision, making her wish for sleep. She was so tired, her body being dragged along by Rosa's strength. "My baby needs your help."

Jackie! Laurel shouted, burning off the cool breeze of sleep with a mental slap to the face. *She's messing with you.*

But the baby—

Rosa's vengeance is draining it to nothing, remember? Come on, hon. You have to fight this.

Jackie struggled back to alertness. *I'm trying, Laur. Damn it!*

Then do what you've always done, she said. *Get pissed and kick some ass. I always loved that about you.*

That's great, except for the fact I have no body to kick ass with. What the hell was she supposed to do trapped in the depths of her own mind? Insult Rosa into leaving?

The car slid to a stop in the middle of the street. Jackie watched herself turn and look up at a huge, rundown, converted Victorian. She recognized the address nailed in large, metal numbers to a post on the sagging porch as the same one from McManus's note. Rosa's cold, furious excitement smacked her like a gust of wind. Jackie knew that feeling. When they were about to take down a killer, that same excitement would flow through her veins. There was always that dark, barely veiled hope that she would get to pull the trigger on him. She completely understood Rosa's drive.

"Mama's going to get him, baby. Don't you worry."

The words struck a chord in Jackie. She had said something along those lines after her mother's suicide. She had promised her that Carl the cop would die for his crimes. The death of Carl had motivated her for years, occupying her dreams, and coloring every aspect of her life growing up. But if she could have asked her mother, what would she have wanted? Would killing Carl have been her sole desire? Maybe, but she might have wanted nothing to do with him at all.

The tires smoked as Rosa pulled the car back and then lurched up the drive and onto the front lawn. Jackie cringed when the Glock appeared in her hand. Shit was about to hit the fan.

Laur, what if the baby was gone? You think Rosa would still need to do this?

Gone? What do you mean? How? Rosa won't let us take him, and she's too strong as long as he's around.

What if we don't have to take him? What if . . . maybe he doesn't want to do this, she said in barely a whisper. *What if he just wants comfort and solace? Maybe if I invited him, he would just come with me.*

Invited? I don't . . . oh. Oh! Jackie felt the excitement as Laurel understood. *Invite him here. Inside, with me.* Their train of thought got brought to an abrupt close.

Rosa did not bother knocking. Feds were coming soon, so no time to waste. Jackie watched her own steel-toed boot kick the door open, splintering the door jam. Through an archway to the right, someone was scrambling up from a sofa. Rosa made no hesitation. No questions. Not even a *Where's Rennie?*

With appalling, gunslinger speed and accuracy, Jackie watched her arm swing the Glock up and fire. Rosa had her vision focused squarely on the man's forehead. It was hard to tell if Rosa was actually guiding the bullets to their mark, but there was a definite coursing of power going on in the process. The man dropped to his knees and then keeled over on the coffee table.

The sounds of shouting could be heard upstairs and the thumping of feet upon the wooden floor. Someone appeared in the kitchen doorway at the end of the entry hall. It was hard to tell if the silhouetted figure was male or female, but Jackie watched once again as Rosa guided her hand up and squeezed off two more shots. The person screamed and spun backward into the kitchen. Female. That scream had been female.

Rosa, stop! You're killing innocent people! Jackie

pleaded, desperately wanting to get control of her limbs again. Though she knew Rosa was killing these people, part of her could not escape the fact that it was her body, moving through this house and ending innocent lives. They saw her, not Rosa. They all watched the psycho agent rampaging through their house, a psycho with a gun. When . . . if they got through this, they would all believe Jackie Rutledge had murdered everyone. And there wasn't a goddamned thing she could do about it.

"They're harboring a murderer, a serial psychopathic murderer! They all die." The last was said with such quiet, angry resolve, that Jackie had no doubt that every last person in this house was going to get a bullet in the head.

Jackie, stop. Stay with me and focus. We might only have one chance at this.

Chance at what? Jackie wondered. Rosa was moving quickly up the stairs now, Glock aimed at the railing above. Jackie felt ill. If given her body back at that particular moment, she might be puking all over the floor. It was difficult to dissociate herself from her body doing these murderous things.

In the now disturbingly quiet upstairs, Jackie heard the distinctive *snick* that told her someone had just cocked a gun. *Rosa? They've got guns up there. You might want to think this through a little bit.*

"Not to worry, Agent Rutledge. We can take a few," she said, and as she reached the point where her head would be poking above the rail, Rosa leaped up the last third of the stairs in two bounds, turned around the banister and squeezed off a shot at the man just starting to swing open a bedroom door to shoot at her. The door slammed shut and someone slumped down against it on the other side.

"Rennie! Get out here you sonofabitch. I've got a few words for you." She cooed the last in a sing-song voice.

A second bedroom door off of the landing burst open, followed a moment later by the sound of steps from behind. Jackie would have immediately dropped into a roll toward the stairs, hoping to catch the attackers from behind. But when you weren't too worried about getting shot, because, well, your body was disposable, you just kept going in the direction you thought necessary.

Shit, Jackie said. *We're so dead.*

Jackie! We need to open the door. We can trick her to go through, said Laurel.

How? I thought we weren't strong enough?

When she uses her power on something else, her will to hold us weakens. If we really focus, I think we can open the door. If we time it right, maybe we can trick her into going through.

When? Now?

No. Anticipate her moves. Just be ready.

Got it, Jackie said and steadied herself in expectation of Rosa's next move.

Rosa rushed the two coming out of the second bedroom. The first got his gun up, but her uncanny speed got Rosa inside that shot before he could wheel his arm around. The blast fired harmlessly into the wall behind them. The second went into the floor, when Rosa blocked his arm with such force Jackie heard the bone snap. If she had been able to, Jackie would have flinched with every muscle. As it was, the man screamed and stumbled sideways, heading for the railing, which Rosa helped him through by burying two rounds in his chest. He went crashing through, slamming into the wall and then continuing down the stairs.

Now that she knew, Jackie could feel the walls around her ease, their strength begin to wane. She began to focus, pulling her energy together to open the door.

The next had a gun as well, but didn't get a chance to bring it up, as the attacker from the rear tackled Rosa into him. The view suddenly went dark as Jackie saw her face smashed up against the man's chest. It was in that moment, when Rosa began to push back and swing her elbow around toward the other attacker's head, that Jackie saw, along with Rosa, a familiar figure at the top of the stairs.

Chapter 35

McManus had given Nick and Shelby the address. Five minutes. They were five minutes from the crash site when Nick felt Rosa come barreling back to the world of the living. Shelby confirmed it with a sharp gasp and a sideways glance at him while he wheeled the Porsche back and forth through city traffic.

"Shit," she said. "I guess the threat didn't work."

Nick hit the steering wheel with the palm of his hand. "Call McManus. Warn him."

A few seconds later, she shook her head. "Not answering." She threw the phone up on the dash where it rattled around and then tumbled to the floor. "Damn it! Should've rode my bike."

"Hold on," Nick said through gritted teeth, sliding the Porsche around a corner through a red light and narrowly missing a pickup. Somewhere behind them, Nick could hear the wail of a siren. Someone did not appreciate his driving skills.

Just a couple more minutes and they would be there. A lot could happen in such a short period of time and he doubted, even with the heads-up, that

McManus and Pernetti were ready to handle Rosa, not when she looked like an agent dead on her feet.

His fears were confirmed two minutes later, as he screeched to a halt in the middle of a two-lane residential street. The Durango was angled into a van parked at the curb. An FBI car was angled at nearly ninety degrees across the road, and two men moved sluggishly in the middle of the street. Half a dozen gawking bystanders milled around in the neighboring yards, half with cell phones aimed at the scene, the others texting madly. Shelby was out of the car before it came to a complete stop.

"Ah, fuck," she said as she ran up to McManus and Pernetti.

Pernetti was not just struggling, he was writhing in pain, swearing up a storm. "She fucking shot me! The fucking bitch shot me."

Nick realized there was blood on the street beneath them and a pair of handcuffs joined them. It became apparent that Pernetti had been shot in the foot. McManus just looked pissed.

"She got away," he said. "I should've cuffed her. I need a phone. Got to call this in."

Nick pulled his cell out while Shelby reached down and grabbed the cuffs in her hands and snapped the chain between them. Pernetti rolled away and grabbed his foot, groaning loudly. McManus made his call.

"What happened?" Nick closed his eyes to focus and turned until he got a sense of where Rosa was. "She's heading north."

"Fucking bitch shot me is what happened," Pernetti yelled.

"Said she needed some air," McManus said, "was going to puke. Pernetti let her out. I should've done it." He turned his attention back to the phone. "Pernetti is down, sir. Yes. It's Jack again, sir."

Nick winced. This was not going to go well for her. "Where's she heading?" They needed to get moving again quickly.

The siren sound swelled as the cop that had been chasing finally caught up. Pernetti kept his tirade going while Shelby tried to get his shoe off.

"Shut up and be still, you big, fucking baby," she snapped, swatting his hands away from his injured foot.

McManus gave Belgerman an address as the cop came running up, hand on his holstered gun. "Officer," Nick said, voice unruffled and smooth, "we need an ambulance here for this injured federal agent."

The cop had been about to lay into him, until he saw Pernetti and the blood spattered on the pavement. "You need to . . . feds? Christ. I'll get paramedics out here."

Nick nodded. "Thank you. We'll just be on our way now."

The cop agreed. "Just get out of the way, sir."

"Shel, leave it. No time." He moved quickly back to the car.

Nick gunned the engine and honked, turning the car up onto a lawn to get around the parked cars.

"How far?" Shelby wondered.

"Couple minutes," he said, blowing through a stop sign. "Gun's in the glove box."

"I'm not going to shoot her, Nick." She reached in and took out the Beretta anyway.

"If we reach her before she gets to Rennie Vasquez, we take her down any way possible," he said. He could not believe he was saying that. Last thing in the world he wanted to do was hurt Jackie.

"Nick, that's nuts."

"Rosa doesn't care what happens to the body," he said. "If Rennie Vasquez is armed, if he has friends who are, then she's likely to get filled with so many holes before she gets to him that we'll never save her."

"She's just as likely to shoot us as them," Shelby added.

"I know." Nick was not too worried about that possibility. A bullet or three would not be a big deal, as long as he avoided a head shot, which nobody else had seemed able to do up to this point. "We'll have the feds there right behind us, too."

"Fuck, Nick. This is going to be a mess."

"A little luck and maybe Jackie will be able to do something from the inside when the time is right. I hope she's aware enough to be watching." He pulled sharply to the right, sliding on to the street McManus had given him. A light spatter of rain had begun to fall, making the streets slick and more difficult to handle. The houses were getting larger, older, and more rundown as they went down the street, Victorian homes with sagging porches, broken up into three or more apartments.

"There!" Shelby pointed.

"I see it," Nick replied. A dark sedan was half off the street, sitting on top of a section of wrought iron fence. The door hung open.

Nick slid the Porsche to a stop behind the car and even before he got out, the air cracked with the sound of gunfire.

Voices were yelling inside. There were screams. Of the two doors leading in, one sat wide open. Nick stepped out at a run. Shelby was already crouched, gun drawn, creeping quickly up to the front steps. He approached with her, hugging her right side, turning his focus outward, searching for Rosa. Shelby stepped through the doorway, leading with the Beretta. It was a large, open foyer with stairs leading up and a hallway stretching toward the back of the house. An archway to the right led into a living room. A body, dark-haired, male, lay slumped off a couch, his upper body resting on a coffee table in a spreading pool of blood. His eyes stared at him, wide and unblinking, a neat, black circle in the center of his forehead.

Somewhere above, a male yelled in Spanish, followed by a short burst of gunfire. More yelling followed, different voices this time, and then thumping and scuffling of several people. Nick turned and leaped up the stairs four at a time.

Then an all-too-familiar voice rang down. "Think you can kill me, Rennie! Think bullets will keep me from gutting you like you did to me?"

Through the railing posts on the landing, Nick could see a struggle going on. Three pairs of legs jostling around. Then one set abruptly left the ground and the railing shattered next to his head. A male crashed into the wall of the stairwell, indenting the plaster before tumbling down in a shower of splintered wood. Shelby leaped straight up in the air, but a flailing leg cut across her ankle and sent her sprawling down on top of the guy. Nick reached up and grabbed the banister post at the top of the steps and swung himself around onto the landing.

Rosa was busy burying her fist into the other guy's face, already a bright smear of blood. At their feet was Pernetti's Glock and at the other end of the landing, a door flung open, banging against the bedroom wall. A man stood in the darkened entry, silhouetted against the light coming through the blinds on the opposite side of the room. His features were too shaded to make out clearly other than the wild whites of his eyes, but it didn't matter. They were washed out by the sharp clarity of what he held in his hands, a pair of snub-nosed machine pistols.

"Jackie!" Nick had no weapon with which to respond, and despite Rosa's recent claims to the contrary, bullets could keep her from gutting Rennie. The number of bullets about to fly in their direction would stop almost anyone, maybe even a vampire.

Nick summoned all his strength and sprinted down the hall.

Chapter 36

Nick! Jackie's concentration broke.

"Devil!" Rosa hissed at the same moment.

The distraction cost them. Something heavy and big snapped her view sideways, and Jackie caught the glimpse of a fist trailing away from her face. The Glock clattered to the floor.

Jackie! Come on! Now. Do it now.

But Nick . . .

At the end of the hall, the sound of a door slamming open echoed in her ears. Off balance from the blow that would have knocked a normal person out, Rosa stumbled into the attacker at her back. She threw an elbow into his gut to push herself off and there at the end of the hall appeared the prize.

Dressed in a pair of black boxers and white t-shirt was a man much smaller than the others out in the hall. Wiry, with long, black hair whipped about down past his shoulders, like he had just woken up. The wide-eyed look had as much confusion as crazy in them, and in his hands were two, snub-nosed machine pistols.

Rosa raged. Her Glock was on the floor and there

was her killer. Jackie watched her vision turn red, pulling up power from the other side. Rosa dropped for the gun.

At the same moment, Jackie felt the swelling of energy from behind. Nick was coming. "Jackie!"

Open the Mother-loving door, Jackie!

The machine pistols raised and the solid, flying figure of Nick brushed past, arms outstretched. Apparently, Rennie Vasquez did not care that his own friends were standing in the hall. He was prepared to take everyone down.

Jackie reached out for the other side as the first burst of the pistols went off. Rosa picked up the Glock, Nick's body providing a shield from the initial spray of bullets. Once again he was putting himself in the line of fire to save her.

Damn it, Nick. You're going to get yourself killed.

Laurel pushed at her. *Jackie, open it in the doorway. Now!*

Jackie pushed open the way to Deadworld, and the wind howled at them through the bedroom doorway. It drew Rosa's attention immediately.

"What are you doing?" she screamed.

Plaster erupted from the wall, inches from her face. Rosa made an instinctual duck away from the danger or perhaps it was her own effort to not get shot, and ducked toward the bedroom doorway. For the first time in more days than she could remember, luck smiled down upon Jackie. Rosa had stepped directly into the Deadworld door.

Jackie! Hold on to your body, said Laurel.

She felt as though she were flailing, poised on the top of a cliff, whirling her arms to keep from toppling over, until Laurel's hands clasped around hers and guided them, helping her hold on to and reinforce that bond between her spirit and body. She could see it now, that soft, glowing energetic force, twisted strands bound together, which she could now simply pull apart.

Rosa staggered away from the door, frantically trying to keep a grip on Jackie. Her hands pulled at those same strands, but Jackie and Laurel had the benefit of more pull in their direction. Rosa was keeping herself in the living world. It was not her place and the open door pulled at her as well. And when Rosa's fingers slipped free at last, Jackie found herself filling up her body once again, with the unnerving, woodpecker *pop-pop-pop* of the machine pistols in her ear. Nick was on top of Rennie, sending them back into the bedroom at the end of the hall.

Jackie called out *Nick!* But her voice was dragged away by the bitter wind of Deadworld. It dug into her bones with frozen claws and a moment later the doorway closed upon the world of the living.

Rosa's! Laurel yelled from within her head.

Jackie barely had time to acclimate herself to Deadworld before she closed her eyes and focused on Rosa's. No front yard this time. Straight to the master bedroom and a screaming, bloody mess of a baby. She would have three seconds, if she was lucky, to make it work before Rosa came stampeding back to keep her away.

Imagining Rosa's room was not difficult. The image still burned in her mind from the first time, with the babe's scream piercing her skull, the metallic, nauseating smell, and a mattress soaked with an unconscionable amount of blood. It took a second, perhaps two, as moving her physical body in Deadworld required more effort, and it might have been longer without Laurel's extra push. Rosa's voice followed almost immediately.

"Get away from him!"

Jackie felt the door opening. Rosa was coming through. No time to think or prepare, only time to act. She leaped across the bed, just beyond Rosa's grasping reach, landing on her elbows right over Rosa's baby. His scream was barely louder than a normal speaking voice, with eyes scrunched closed and tiny little hands curled loosely into fists. His fragile, doll-sized body was smeared with the dark stains of blood.

Part of Jackie, a large part really, desired nothing more than to cringe away from it, put up her hands and shy away. The thing was alien. More significantly, Jackie had no clue what to do once she picked him up. How did you hold it? What did she say? How did you invite a spirit in who could not even speak? This plan, if one could have called it such, had not been thought through. Regardless, Jackie took the only possible course left to her. She scooped her arms beneath the listless body, cradled it to her chest, and rolled off the opposite side of the bed. Jackie landed on her back with a soft thump.

Rosa was on top of her a split second later. She straddled over Jackie, hands hooked around her wrists. Jackie had never seen a face contorted with so much rage in her life. It was misshapen, turned and curved at wrong angles, and the snarl of her lips seemed to stretch halfway around her face. "Give him to me!"

From within, Laurel fed Jackie extra power to hold Rosa off. Her voice was soft, cooing. *It's OK, sweetie. It's going to be all right. We'll keep you safe. You can come in and be safe.*

"He's mine, you bitch!" Rosa yanked over and over, bouncing Jackie against the floor.

"You're going to kill him, Rosa! Is that what you want? He's going to be gone. Forever!" She was losing the battle. This could only go on for so long before she lacked the strength to keep her arms locked around her chest. And Rosa had passed listening to reason long ago.

Jackie looked down at her chest, at the baseball sized head pressed to her shirt. His mouth formed a tiny *O*, reaching out, wanting, yearning. *Dear God, you poor, little guy. You don't want vengeance. You just want to crawl right back into mother's womb, don't you?*

Yes! Laurel said. *That's what he needs. Invite him in, Jackie. Be his mother.*

But I'm not.

Pretend, you nit! Or Rosa is going to drain him to nothingness.

The decision was made for her as Rosa began to peel one of her hands away from her body. "Give . . . him . . . to me."

Was it her imagination or had the baby begun to fade? *Christ! OK, little guy. Come on in. Be with me and I'll keep you safe. It's warm and safe inside. No more cold . . . just . . . come on, sweetie. Please! You don't need to go out this way.*

The babe's crying stopped and he slowly sank into Jackie's body. Laurel gave a triumphant shout. Rosa let go of Jackie's arms and sat back with a thud on the floor, scrambling back with her hands and feet, eyes wide in shock. Her mouth hung slack in horror.

Rosa pointed at her, hand trembling. "What have you done? What have you done to my baby?"

Jackie gritted her teeth. Safely within the protection of her body, the baby had settled precisely where she had offered. Though her physical body looked unchanged, her entire midsection now felt distended and stretched. "Damn, Laur!" She moaned, placing her hands on top of the still and quiet form. Her entire midsection felt as though it was going to tear apart.

Well, was all Laurel could say. A radiating warmth emerged from her, enveloping Jackie in a soothing glow. *This should help. Mother of us all, hon. Look at that. Look what you've done.*

Rosa sat back on her heels at Jackie's feet, fists balled up, poised to attack, but tears were running down her cheeks. "What have you done?" she asked once more, but the anger had clearly dissipated. "Give him back."

Jackie pushed herself up and tried to scoot back toward the wall. It hurt like a sonofabitch, but she was still filled with a sense of awe. How could something like this happen? She looked up to Rosa, heart clenching at the look of sorrow and defeat on her face. She reached out to her.

"Rosa," she said. "You see? He never wanted revenge. He just—"

"Give him back!" Rosa wailed and scrambled forward until she was upon Jackie again, fingers clawing at her stomach. "Give me back my baby!"

Rosa was significantly weaker now that she no longer had her baby to draw upon. Jackie grabbed her wrists and rolled over until she was on top, pinning Rosa to the floor, who continued to squirm and buck to get free.

Only now her voice did not hold rage so much as despair and fear. "Don't take my baby! He needs revenge."

Jackie leaned in close, until Rosa's wild eyes finally

locked on to hers. "No, Rosa. You need revenge. Your boy just needs you." She pulled Rosa's arms up and pushed her hands against her stomach. "See? No more crying. He just wanted to feel safe and secure and you nearly destroyed him. This madness ends now. Do you understand?" Jackie pushed Rosa's hands away. "Do you?"

The tension in Rosa's body melted away. "Please. I just want my baby."

"I don't trust you, Rosa." Jackie sat up straight and stared down at the broken woman. She wondered though. *Laur, will you be able to keep them with me if I take Rosa in, too?*

What do you mean? Why?

I'm going to invite Rosa in, but I don't know how long I'll be able to stay awake once I cross back over.

Maybe? I think so.

It would have to do. "Rosa? You can join him if you wish. You can be with him. Maybe it's time you put this behind you and moved on. I'll get your justice. Rennie will be put away for the rest of his life."

Rosa's shoulders slumped. "He deserves to die."

"And he probably will," she replied, "but it will be through the laws of Illinois. No more innocent people will die, Rosa. I'm going back to the living world. If you want to be with your boy, come with me, but you must swear upon your boy's . . . soul, that you will make no attempt to take me over. If you do, my partner, who is with me now, will see to it that you never see him again."

Jackie? I can't do that. It's—

It's an empty threat. Don't worry.

Rosa nodded. "Promise me he will pay?"

"I guarantee it, Rosa." She let go of Rosa's wrists

and took her hands. "Come and be with your boy. He still needs you."

Her fingers clenched Jackie's clasping tightly and Jackie opened herself to Rosa, inviting her in. "I'm sorry," Rosa whispered, and her form faded gradually away to nothing. Within her body, Rosa's arms curled themselves around her babe and the cramping pain within her abdomen receded to a tolerable, dull ache.

You did great, Laurel whispered. *Incredible, hon.*

"Yeah, well," Jackie said, reeling from the fact she had three people's spirits residing within her body. "Let's hope they move on soon. I feel stuffed to the gills."

Laurel laughed. *Practice for later.*

"God, don't even go there." Jackie sat up and groaned. She was swollen and chilled with the aching cold of the dead. She would kill for fifteen minutes in Nick's steam bath. "Oh, hell. Nick! We've got to get back."

Chapter 37

Nick began to heal himself the moment he leaped down the hall. He had the element of surprise and confusion on his side. Rennie Vasquez had a pair of machine pistols on his. This was going to likely test the limits of his ability to take a few rounds, the previous record being fourteen. That was courtesy of the Reardan brothers, three gun-happy bounty hunters in post–Civil War Arizona, who had the tendency to shoot first and verify their target second.

Jackie went by on his left, scrambling to get to the Glock on the floor. Shelby had managed her way over the stair diver and hopped up the stairs five at a time. Nick noticed that things tended to slow down in those times near death, but it may have only been that the world came into a particularly sharp focus, when one was faced with the fact that his life might soon be gone.

The bullets began to spray as soon as Vasquez raised his guns, sweeping across the floor and up the wall on the one side and shattering the railing posts on the other. There was no stopping these first few bullets, likely ten or a dozen in the half-second it took

Nick to close in on the murderer. Perhaps a good thing, too, as Nick realized if he had met Vasquez head-on with those guns properly aimed, he might have been sawn in half, and no amount of vampire mojo would fix that.

Nick did not aim for the guns. He moved quick enough that fractions of a second were not going to make a difference. His sights were set just over the raised guns, where the arms joined up at the shoulders. The first bullet hit Nick high on the right arm, then wrist, hand, and finally chest. Coming from the other side, the first zinged by his ear, but the next caught him in the cheek, then his jaw, neck, and finally chest. There may have been other bullets, and Nick was not really counting; his focus was upon the spot he wished to strike.

Vasquez made it one step back into the bedroom before Nick reached him, his fists plowing into and snapping Rennie Vasquez's collarbones in half. The guns fell to the floor and Vasquez flew back, indenting the Sheetrock in the opposite wall. He slumped to his knees and then toppled over, face down on the floor. Another foot over and Nick would have had sent him on a cinematic death fall through the bedroom window.

Momentum carried Nick halfway across the room before he landed, feet first, then one hand down before dropping into a roll and coming to a stop against Vasquez's head. In the hall, the brief sounds of a scuffle met his ears, followed by the sound of flesh meeting flesh in unfortunate ways. A moment later, Shelby was at his side.

"Nick! You dumb sonofabitch. What the hell were you doing?"

"Jackie?" he asked, but the word came out jumbled.

Nick winced. The bullet must have torn out part of his jaw.

"She's gone," Shelby replied. "Poofed out to Deadworld."

"But . . . I thought Rosa . . ."

Shelby pushed him over and the expression on her face told Nick his wounds probably were as bad as he sounded. "Aww, Nick! Look what you've gone and done." She reached out and touched his face, coming away with a bloody hand. "This is going to be rough, babe. You've got blood running out all over the fucking place."

He brought up his own bloody hand and placed it high up on his chest, attempting to focus more energy upon the wounds. "Worst . . . here."

"What?" She shook her head, tears watering her eyes. "Just shut the hell up. I can see for myself." Her hands came down over his, power flowing through her fingers.

Shelby's face blurred, then doubled as one of his eyes drifted off in another direction. He was feeling faint, not a good sign. His chest was in bad shape. Several wounds there, one in the throat, one in his jaw. He needed to get everything closed off internally first, and it would not happen if he was out cold.

"You need some blood, Nick," she said.

He shook his head, his voice burbling through the blood in his mouth and throat. "No."

"You want to die here on this floor? You've got like twenty wounds here. I can't get to them fast enough and you're fading quick."

"No."

"Tough shit, hon." She reached over him and

grabbed Vasquez's unconscious arm. "Besides, you know how bad off Jackie is going to be if you die saving her?" She pulled a blade from her pocket, a thin, switchblade razor and opened up a two inch slice in Rennie's wrist. "Drink cowboy. Heroes deserve to live."

She held the wrist over Nick's mouth and he tried to turn away from the gush she squeezed out over his lips. The fire of it in his mouth was immediate, a sudden burst of spiritual energy blending in with his own, but it quickly dissipated. Perhaps Jackie did need him, and he wanted her, wanted to be with her. Yes, Nick felt certain about that. Dying on her now would be a travesty if it was because he refused to drink from a psychopathic murderer. He turned his head back and closed his eyes, clamping his mouth around the wound.

"There you go, babe. I'm sorry." Her hands continued to work over his face and chest, feeding him with the much needed healing energy. With the blood, it would probably be enough. "Nobody is going to hold it against you. The guy deserves to drop a couple of . . . she's back."

Nick opened his eyes. He'd felt it to, the opening of the Deadworld door. He lifted his head and sure enough, Jackie stood in the hall, staring down the corridor at them.

"Nick?"

He tried to shift a bit behind Shelby's form and let the arm fall away from his face. Shelby motioned for her to come.

"Get in here! You can help me."

She took a step forward and stopped. "You OK?"

She knew. He could tell by the look on her face that she knew, thinly veiled horror at the thought of someone drinking another's blood. He had to give her credit, though, the pause did not last even a second before she was trotting toward them. She favored her left leg.

Jackie looked down at him from over Shelby's shoulder and her eyes went wide. "Oh, my God, Nick! You're . . . Jesus Christ! Nick, there's a hole—"

"Jackie! Shut up and help out," Shelby ordered. "Keep that arm bleeding out into his mouth so he can use both hands." She turned and looked up at Jackie's shocked face. "Now!"

There were sirens nearby. Nick could hear several. Police. Paramedics. McManus would be there any time. Jackie moved and knelt by his head and picked up Vasquez's arm. She stared at it for a second before moving it over Nick's mouth.

"Drink," she said. "If you die saving me, I'm going to kill you myself."

He wanted to know what happened. He could sense Rosa, Laurel, even the baby. They were all near.

Shelby nudged him with her knee. "Calm down, Nick. Keep your heart rate down so I can close this shit off."

Jackie lay a warm hand on his brow. There was energy there as well, flowing from her finger tips. It was then that Nick realized. They were all inside her. She had channeled Rosa and the baby into her and trapped them. He stared up at those hard, hazel-green eyes with the crinkle of concentration between them. The circles under her eyes were so pronounced it looked like someone had smudged makeup under them. She was pale, extremely so. She hadn't slept in three or four days.

"Jackie," he said. "You're amazing, you know that?"

"What?"

Shelby rocked back on her heels. "OK, patched up the fucking arteries. Rest should be cake."

McManus's voice could be heard downstairs. "Paramedics. We need paramedics here now!"

Jackie stood up, swaying on her feet. "Upstairs, McManus." She looked back down at Nick. "You going to be OK, now?"

"Soon enough, thanks," he said. "You better sit, Jackie. You look like you're going to pass out." Something else about her was different. She looked a bit off.

"I should," she said and nodded slowly. "Feel a bit lightheaded."

Shelby reached out and grabbed Jackie's leg. "Is that your blood?" She swiped it across her tongue. "Christ, Jack! Did you get shot?"

"Um, I don't think so," she said. She turned, inspecting her body.

Nick saw it then, on the back of her thigh below the right butt cheek. A dark stain streaked and spattered its way down the back of her leg and was trickling out on to the floor. "Jackie? Back of your thigh."

She twisted to look and Shelby reached up and ripped open the hole in the back of her jeans. "Yep. Bullet wound right here. Jackie, you need to sit your ass down." Her other hand shot up and pushed against her stomach. "Oh, wow. What did you do, babe?"

McManus stepped up to the room at that very moment. "What the . . . Jack? Is it the real you?"

Jackie laughed, and Nick thought that there was nothing amusing in it. She looked more than a bit frightened and glassy-eyed. "Yeah. We're all here now." She swayed and took a lurching step to the side. "Hey, Ryan. Looks like I got shot."

McManus ran forward. "Shot? Sit your . . . whoa! OK then." Ryan caught her as she began to collapse and eased her to the ground. His hands pushed and prodded at her. "Where?"

"Back of her thigh," Shelby said. "Think it's stopped bleeding now."

"There's a lot of blood here," he said.

"Mostly Nick's. He's OK now, too. Need to patch up psycho-boy there. He cut himself on something."

McManus glanced around at everything with a skeptical eye. "Nick. You look like you got . . . you know what, never mind. We'll deal with reports later."

Shelby patted him on the knee. "Good boy, McManus. Get Jackie to the hospital. Again." She reached over and caressed Jackie's belly, shaking her head in disbelief. "Think she needs fluids more than anything, and to be knocked out for about twenty-four hours."

"Is the um . . . the ghost?" asked McManus.

"Think it's been taken care of," Shelby said.

Nick nodded at Ryan with a grim smile. "Except for Jackie. I don't think her troubles are near done."

"Right about that," he said.

Chapter 38

Jackie struggled and slogged her way out of drug-induced sleep. Her eyes, crusted with sleep, were difficult to open. She dug at them with her fingers, finding something tugged at her hand. When her vision finally swam into focus, she noticed the IV tube trailed from the back of her hand up to a clear bag hanging on a metal tower. Hospital. Again. She was truly getting tired of finding herself here.

And her body felt surprisingly empty. Jackie reached down and found her stomach once again soft and flat. The only presence within her body was her own. Thank God. She turned her head and looked about the room, identical in appearance to the one she had graced before, right down to the sleeping sheriff in the chair. Nick looked whole once again, not the blood-soaked, shredded thing she had last seen sprawled on Rennie Vasquez's floor. She attempted to swallow and found her mouth and throat to be a bed of dry gravel. Reaching for the glass of water sitting on the bedside table elicited a groan. Her body was stiff and sore and a horrible itch crawled across the back of her thigh.

Nick opened his eyes and sat up at the sound of her voice. He smiled, stretching a thin, pink and jagged scar that now ran from chin to ear. "Welcome back," he said. He pushed to his feet and retrieved the water from the table and then used the automatic adjustments to raise Jackie to a sitting position.

Jackie took the water and gulped down the entire cup. "Ah, thank you."

"How you feeling?"

"Better, I think. We need to stop meeting like this."

"Agreed," he said. "The furniture is incredibly uncomfortable."

She reached up toward his face and touched the fresh scar. "You OK? You scared the shit out of me."

Nick took her hand, holding it lightly in his. "Might have some issues with setting off metal detectors, but otherwise I'm all right."

"How long have I been out? I seem to have lost everyone that was with me."

He glanced at his watch. "About seventeen hours. Laurel said she convinced Rosa and her babe to move on." He gave her hand a soft squeeze. "That was an amazing thing you did."

Jackie withdrew her hand, comforting as it was. "Yeah, I guess. Not going to do much to save my job, though. Can't exactly put any of this in my report."

"No," he agreed. "I suppose not. Things are going to be different."

She sighed, throat constricting. "They're going to fire me, Nick. Without knowing the truth, they're going to think I'm a complete nut job. Be lucky if I'm not charged with anything."

"You aren't going to be charged with anything," he said.

"I assaulted two agents," Jackie exclaimed. "I shot Pernetti in the fucking foot. They have every right to charge me."

"I talked with John this morning. He said there will be no charges."

"Oh." That was something at least, but it didn't change the fact she was going to be out of a job. "Still. No law enforcement agency is going to hire me after this."

A corner of Nick's mouth turned up. "Hopefully that won't be necessary."

"What? How could they not fire me over this? The BPS is going to fry me for what happened."

He shrugged. "I don't know what's been arranged. John will have to fill you in."

"John told you all of this?" That made no sense. "What's going on, Nick?"

"Better if John talks to you. I don't think it's my place to say anything yet."

What the hell? "Seriously? Come on, Nick. You can't lead me on with that and then take the fifth."

"Sorry," he said. "I really don't know all the details. How about some food? You must be starving."

"Nick!"

He stepped away. "I'll go get you something. Sandwich sound good?"

"Nick," she shouted at his back, but he did not answer and Jackie was left fuming in her bed.

He returned a short time later with two sandwiches, chips, Jell-O, cheesecake, coffee, and a Coke. Part of her wanted to not eat just to irritate him into spilling the beans, but after a few bites, Jackie realized she was ravenous and thirty minutes later the tray was empty, bad coffee and all.

As she was washing down the last bites of cheesecake, McManus came walking in, knocking softly on the door before he entered. One eye was swollen shut and he had a bandage across the bridge of his nose.

Jackie scrunched up her face in pained sympathy. "Shit, Ryan. I'm so sorry. I really nailed you good."

He waved her off. "Teach me to be more on my toes. And when someone claims to be ready to puke in my car, I'll just let them." Ryan stuck out his hand toward Nick. "Mr. Anderson? Good to see you so quickly recovered. Still wrapping my brain around that one."

Nick gave him a wry smile and shook his hand. "I'll show you one of these days."

Ryan laughed. "Looking forward to it. So," he turned to Jackie, "you look far better than the zombie they hauled away yesterday. Do I get to know what actually happened?"

"You don't really want to know do you?"

"Maybe after a few beers," he said.

She gave him a pained smile. "How much shit has hit the fan over this? Nick is under the impression that I'm neither fired nor under arrest. Pernetti want my head on a platter? The BPS hanging outside in the hall?"

Ryan held up his hand. "Slow down, Jack. Everything is cool and quiet right now. Belgerman clamped down on the whole thing about thirty minutes after I got there. No reporters, no interviews, no nothing. We aren't even allowed to write up any reports on this yet. Anything and everything about this case has to go through him for now."

Damn. How could he do that? She would have to

sign something saying she would discuss this with nobody after she left. Which was fine. Jackie had no desire to talk about what had happened. Ever. "What's the official line, then?"

"Distressed federal agent tracks down heroin trafficking operation," Belgerman said, coming in through the door. "Three killed in ensuing gun battle."

"Sir," Jackie said, "don't you think 'distressed' is a bit of an understatement?"

"The press can debate the semantics of it," he said with a shrug. "I'm not worried about them. I am worried about you, though. How you doing, Jackie? You look slightly less dead than yesterday."

"I'm feeling a bit better," she said. "Still kind of weak and tired."

"Too tired for the BPS?"

"Sir, I'm always too tired for them." She tried to give him a rueful smile and surprisingly he returned it. What was going on here?

"Then I'll make sure you don't see them today. Maybe ever."

"How's that?"

He offered her a wry smile. "I have your resignation papers here," he said

The air froze in her lungs. She spluttered, "Resign! Sir?" Quit the FBI? It really was as bad as she had feared.

"Hey folks!" Shelby called out, walking in shoulder to shoulder with Cynthia. "Not too late, am I?" She beamed at Jackie and walked over to her, planting a big, wet kiss on her forehead, but without an enormous lipstick mark, Jackie hoped. "Hi, babe. You're looking much better today."

Cynthia had come too? All at the same time. Jackie tried to look cheerful, glad that everyone was there to see her, but it struck her as just a little bit more than suspicious. "Tell me it's just a bizarre coincidence that everyone is here at the same time to see me."

"Agent McManus," Belgerman said, "would you get the door, please."

"What is this?" Jackie demanded. "If I'm resigning, why is everyone here?"

The whisper of Deadworld blew through her head. *Can I come in, hon?* Laurel's voice echoed quietly in the back of her head. *I'd like to hear what John has to say.*

Jackie reached out and let Laurel across. *Sure! Everyone else is here. Do you know what's going on?*

Sort of. Shelby was talking about it last night. Said we would find out today if it was going to happen.

What's going to happen? Be nice if someone told me what the hell is going on.

Shelby reached out and grabbed Jackie's chin, staring her in the eye. "You just invited Laurel in, didn't you? Easy as that?" Jackie stared at her, surprised. Then Shelby grinned and brought up her hand to wave in Jackie's face. "Hey sweetie."

McManus shuffled back against the wall. "Am I missing something?"

Belgerman pulled one of the two chairs over next to the bed and faced Jackie. "Not yet, Ryan. Jackie? We're meeting here, this morning, before anything else might interfere."

She scooted back up in the bed, feeling surrounded. "Interfere with what?"

"Your decision on this." He held up his hand to stay her response. "Let me explain. Then anyone else can chime in with what they think or ask any questions. This is the one time we'll be doing this. Then, I expect an answer within twenty-four hours. OK?"

Jackie nodded. "Sure."

"About a year ago," he began, "I and a couple other regional heads from around the country had a little meeting about what to do with people like Laurel. She was special, unique in her abilities to help the FBI in certain rare cases. There are a handful of people around the country with similar abilities, though Laurel, I must say, was likely our best or at least most consistent psychic agent."

I always loved that man, Laurel said happily.

"We decided it might benefit us all if we got a special unit together to deal with such cases, a paranormal crime-unit you could call it." Shelby huffed and John raised a finger to her. "Whatever it's called, we were going to have Laurel head up this unit and we were about a month away from offering her the position when everything crashed down with Mr. Drake."

Laurel gasped inside Jackie's head. *Awww, well damn. That would've been really cool.*

"The project got canceled, and funding got redirected somewhere else," Belgerman continued. "We have another opportunity now, or so it seems, as you have inexplicably inherited or learned Laurel's abilities and then some. We also have the Special Investigations team on our side, which is an asset any of my compatriots would kill to have access to. The funding for this will take some time to reacquire, and this isn't an operation we want in the public eye as you can imagine."

Jackie nodded. No disagreement there. Publicity for a ghost-chasing FBI operation would generate a shit storm.

"So, to begin with, this unit will be a private operation. You all will be on your own. We'll be considering you special consults. We'll do this for six months to start, Jack, and then I hope to have things in order to make this an official unit within the FBI. If not, then you'll hopefully have the option of getting hired back to your old position."

Hopefully? Lovely. "If it's not FBI," Jackie wondered, "where's the money coming from?"

He turned and gave a thankful smile to Nick. "Nick has generously offered to fund this, which is really little more than an extension of his current business. You'll be employed by Mr. Anderson."

Inside her head, Laurel was clapping and jumping up and down like a school girl. *Yes! Yes! You have got to do this, Jackie. Please! Oh, Sweet Mother you just have to.*

Would you be quiet! God. I can hardly hear myself think. "Sir. That's . . . well, it's an interesting offer to have me help you with something like—"

"Jackie," he said and waved a hand at her to stop. "I don't want your help."

"But I—"

"I want you to lead the unit. You'll be running Special Investigations."

For a moment the room stood in silence, all breaths held at precisely the same time, every movement paused, and all eyes on Jackie. She looked around at them all, one by one. *Me? Lead them? Was he insane?*

Do it, do it, do it! Jackie, honey. This is your chance to get a fresh start on things, regain perspective and figure this all out without the pressure of being in that office. It's perfect for you.

You don't know that. This is crazy. "Sir? That's . . . that's, um . . . wow. I don't know what to say."

"Take a day to think about, Jack," he told her, patting her leg through the blanket. "I'll need an answer tomorrow morning, though. We do this or we don't. I've got people waiting on answers."

"She'll say yes," Shelby said. "We're good."

"Hey!" Jackie proclaimed. "I wouldn't assume that."

Shelby gave her a snarky little smile. "Babe, if you had wanted to say no, you'd have said it right off the bat. Now you're just looking for a good reason to say yes. You can't turn this down. Besides, you need a job." She cocked her head to the side, the smile getting broader and snarkier. "Anyway. I've got shit to do. Cyn, you want a ride home?"

"Sure." She gave Jackie a little wave. "Good to see you're feeling better, Jackie. I think you'd be great, for what it's worth."

"My sentiments exactly," Belgerman added. "I'll let you rest, Jackie. I know this is a lot to swallow, but in my opinion, you can't afford to pass this up. Six months. That's all I'm asking for. If you want to come back, your spot will be here. I'll get you back in."

Jackie watched him leave and then turned to Ryan. "What's your role in all this, McManus?"

"Liaison," he said. "I'll be your in-house contact for whatever you may need."

"You want to do this?"

"Are you kidding me? A paranormal unit? How could I not do it?"

Yeah. How could she not do this? *I have to, don't I, Laur?*

Always a choice, hon. But we both know how you did without a job for two weeks, much less six months. This is a once-in-a-lifetime opportunity. It will be amazing and great for you. You are a leader, Jackie.

It's the psychic shit that scares me. I don't know what I'm doing.

Then we'll learn. We'll help you figure it out. You won't have to do it on your own, hon.

Jackie heaved a sigh. It was difficult to comprehend the abrupt right turn her life was about to take.

Shelby was right. If the answer had been *no,* she would have said it right away. She had to convince herself that it would be the right thing to do. "I see your point, Ryan. In your shoes, I'd do it, too."

"Say yes, Jack. Six months you can come back and punch me in the face again." He smiled at her and the Irish clearly came through. "I've got some things for this case to do. I'll see you later. Take care, Mr. Anderson."

"You too, Agent McManus." Nick walked over and sat down in the chair John had been in next to the bed. "So, Agent Rutledge."

"How long have you known about this?"

"Since last night. John called me and asked if I might be interested in helping out."

"You realize how expensive funding something like this is?"

"I'll cover it, Jackie. Money isn't the issue," he said, and his eyes were locked in on hers. "I'll go to bat for John in this if you're on the team. I think it's a great idea. I think it could help a lot of people and save some lives. I also don't want to do it unless you're there, too."

"You do realize what a rookie I am in all this?"

He shrugged. "Doesn't matter. We take cases we think we'll be able to handle. We work on refining and understanding your abilities. We experiment. It's a short-term operation for now. Six months. If it's not working the way we want, if we're all nipping at each other's heels, then we call it and you can come back to doing homicides. My biggest question is," he said and paused, laying a broad hand over the top of hers, "are you OK being around and working with me on a regular basis?"

Not a question she had come close to thinking about. Laurel fidgeted with anticipation inside her head. Hard to hide your thoughts from someone who was right there to listen to them. *This is exactly what you're hoping for, isn't it? Who are you more afraid of here, hon?* Laurel asked. *Him or yourself?*

I'm not afraid of Nick, not anymore. A little intimidated maybe.

Laurel huffed at her. *Look at him. The guy wants you. He likes you, a lot if I were to bet, and he respects you. When is the last time that happened?*

That's what is freaking me out. I don't think it's ever happened before.

Jackie could feel her frowning. *It's happened at least once before.*

I know, but . . . She had been about to say Laurel did not count, but that would not be fair. *Fine, OK? I get it. I just . . . it scares the shit out of me.*

And when did scary shit ever stop you before? Where's the woman I love who just says "Fuck it," and jumps right in with both feet?

Jackie knew she could keep coming up with rationalizations, excuses, or reasons to justify her fears, but in the end it came down to whether she was going to be a chicken shit or not. For the past month she had been running away from everything. Fear and guilt had been pushing her in all of the wrong directions. It was time to jump in with both feet again.

She held Nick's gaze, staring into those bright Deadworld eyes. "I'd be OK with that."

Nick smiled, clearly pleased. "Good. It's settled then."

Chapter 39

Much like her apparently altered body and spirit, Jackie felt frazzled, pulled apart, and definitely separated. She was no longer an FBI agent. At least, it felt that way after handing over her gun and badge to Belgerman. There had been no fanfare upon her departure. No office going-away party or drunken revelry at the bar rehashing stories and cases. Everyone figured she would be back in six months. Jackie Rutledge leave the FBI? Yeah, right. But packing up her things from her desk had given her a certain note of finality. After six months, would she want to come back? Life had turned in a new direction and maybe the FBI was no longer the destiny she had thought for so many years.

Everyone had been polite, and even McManus, who after a couple of days was still sporting a nice shiner Rosa had given him, kept his trap shut. No good-byes. Enjoy the vacation. Everyone was appropriately jealous. Even John treated it like she was just off to do a "side project." With her small box of belongings, Jackie had gone down to talk to Tillie. At the least, she wanted say good-bye and thank her for being supportive in the face of her animosity. Except now she sat in the soft, chenille-covered chair, sipping on Tillie's tea and struggled to keep the tears at bay.

"What's wrong, Jackie?" She had set her tea down and folded her hands in her lap, giving over to that sympathetic, motherly expression that broke her resolve with Jedi-like effectiveness.

She shrugged. "Can't help but feel this is the end of things. I know it's not necessarily true, but I wonder if I will even want to come back in six months."

"Try not to think of it as an end, but as a beginning," she said. "Your life is moving in a different and hopefully positive direction."

"Hopefully. I hate that the truth hasn't been told. I wish I could say what really happened and have people believe. I don't like being in this position."

"The alternatives would be far worse, I believe."

"I guess." Jackie sighed and finished off her tea. "You'll be happy to know I have a date tonight. You can check that box off in my little file."

"You do?" She grinned. "That's fabulous! Is it with Mr. Anderson?"

Jackie nodded. "Some fancy dinner thing, fancy people in fancy clothes, raising money for something."

"You seem less than enthused," she said.

"That's not my scene." She waved absently toward her head and the garish scar on the side. "I mean, look at me. I'm going to have to wear a damn hat or something. I have nothing to wear. I'm going to look like the ugly stepchild."

"So buy yourself a new outfit, dear. Heaven knows you deserve it."

"Shelby is getting me something, insists I'll look fine. I have to go over later and try it on."

"That sounds like fun."

"Whatever." It did not sound like fun. It sounded like a royal pain in the ass. Nothing she could wear would make her look like date material for an event like this.

"It's a positive step, Jackie."

She shrugged again. Nothing about any of this felt positive. She was jumping into the deep end and had no idea how to swim in these waters.

"Well, speaking of positive steps," Tillie said. "Are you still willing to come see me? Even though you're no longer officially here, you are still welcome to come and talk with me about things."

"We had a deal," Jackie said. "I'm not going to bail on that."

Tillie shook her head. "Regardless of the deal. Do you want to?"

Did she want to come spill her guts to this woman on a regular basis? No, but Jackie knew that she needed to. Tillie understood her and knew what was going on, for the most part. More importantly, Jackie had come to see that she was more than just another client that Tillie had obligations toward due to her job. Tillie cared about what happened to her and that was not something she could turn away from.

"I do," she said quietly. "You are . . . helpful."

Tillie laughed. "Thank you for the boost of confidence. Do I get to find out what happens on your date?"

Jackie rolled her eyes. "Given my track record? I'm sure something will happen that will be worth therapy."

After agreeing to return within a couple of weeks, Jackie got in her rental car and left, watching headquarters shrink in her rearview mirror until the surrounding buildings swallowed it up. She drove around aimlessly for an hour, killing time, not sure what to do with herself. She hated feeling at loose ends. The new job had yet to be worked out. Everyone would be meeting in a couple of days to start sorting through things. She had no idea what she would be doing or how this new unit would work. Six months seemed like such a short amount of time to begin such an endeavor, if *endeavor* was even the right word. Insanity was more appropriate. Finally, Jackie got tired of waiting and called Shelby. Maybe she would be ready early. Even trying on new clothes was better than this stomach-gnawing aimlessness.

Jackie discovered she was ill-prepared for Shelby in makeover mode. Five minutes past, "Hey! You're looking much better," Jackie found herself stripped down to bra and panties trying on four different outfits and various combinations thereof.

An hour later, that decision was finally made. Shelby was all smiles. "When he sees you, he'll be drooling into his boots."

"We're going to some fundraising dinner," Jackie snapped back. "I think drool will be low on the list."

Laurel, who had stepped out of her head and now drifted around the apartment, approved too. "Hon, you look beautiful."

Shelby stepped by her and walked into the bathroom. "If I know our Nick, he's got more in mind than some stuffy fundraiser."

The squirming worms of nerves in her stomach seized up into a giant knot. "What's that supposed to mean? Like what?" She wriggled into the skirt while Shelby pulled things from her bathroom drawers.

"No clue," she replied with a laugh. "He's a romantic though, a very sneaky one at that."

Now she was worried. Sneaky? How in the hell

could that be a good thing? "Do I want to know your definition of a sneaky romantic?"

Shelby pulled open the door and gave her a once over. Her full, cherry-red lips spread into a grin. "Put that six or seven pounds back on you've lost the past few days and you will be so 'fuck me' gorgeous in that. Good enough to eat, don't you think, baby?"

Jackie turned to Laurel in an exasperated panic, who gave her a pained smile. "You'll be lovely, hon. Quit worrying."

"God, Jackie. Get that 'doe in the headlights' look off of your face. I can't have any fun if you're terrified." Shelby shook her head and turned back into the bathroom. "Come on. Sit your ass down here so I can get your face and hair into shape."

Jackie sighed and stared at the ceiling. "I feel like an idiot, a sixteen-year-old, blubbering, virgin idiot."

"Got to start somewhere." Shelby chuckled and tipped Jackie's head back to level. "Now be still and quit verklempting on me. It's all good, Jackie. Nick is likely just as nervous. Trust me. You don't need to stress this much."

She took a deep breath. "I know. I know. I'm sorry. I just don't want to fuck this up. Which is stupid. I'm thirty-two and it's a damn dinner out with a guy I like, for crying out loud, and he said he likes me. He wouldn't lie about that, would he?"

Shelby rolled her eyes. "Oh, dear gods and goddesses. Should I mojo you up, Jack? I could mellow you right out if you want."

"What? No! No way."

"Then calm down. This is supposed to be fun. Pretend it is, for all of our sakes. Please?"

Jackie nodded and said nothing. She could pretend. It was just like girl's night out: getting dressed up, having drinks, and flirting with guys. She could do that. She had done it before, sort of. If half a dozen shots of tequila counted for getting warmed up. Maybe a couple of glasses of wine would chill her out once they got there. But not too much. What if she did get drunk? Jackie cringed at the thought.

Her inner battle continued while Shelby worked her magic. Every five minutes, Laurel would sigh heavily and give her a stern look, and Jackie would take a deep breath and let the tension out of her neck and shoulders and sooth the squirming worms in her gut. After about an hour, Shelby finally stepped back.

"All right." She put her hands on her hips and pursed her lips. "Think that will do. We still have a couple hours before Nick picks you up, so we can have a beer or two and then touch up the lipstick before you go."

Touch up the lipstick? Jackie never thought to hear that term in relation to her mouth. It was a very odd feeling having it there, coating her lips. Oddest of all was the hat. She looked herself up and down, wondering who the person standing there might be. A stranger straight out of the 1920s or 1930s. That was the hat mostly, a black, short-brimmed, rounded top thing with a purple silk ribbon embroidered with flowers running around it. The blouse and skirt gave her a fluid, undulating look, making her look as though she were moving even when still. Shelby had made her put on black nylons, something she had not worn since high school. At least she had been nice enough to get her flats instead of heels, though something on them shimmered in the light, which would just draw people's gaze.

The last thing Jackie wanted to was to draw people's

attention. "Couldn't you have picked something more subtle?"

Laurel moved next to her, admiring the outfit in the mirror. "Compared to what other women will be wearing at this event, you are being subtle, hon. You look beautiful."

It didn't look bad at all. Not something she would have ever chosen for herself, but Jackie felt she could not really complain. "Seems rather demure, don't you think?"

"See!" Shelby said, pointing a finger at Laurel. "I told you. Demure is perfect. Nick loves that look. He'll be all over . . ." She stopped and shook her head. "He'll think you look gorgeous."

Jackie reached out and touched the image of her lips in the mirror. How could they look so full? Perhaps Nick would want to kiss them again. She could handle that. No risk there, right? Why did something so exciting have to be so utterly terrifying at the same time? It was so unfair.

"OK, you're getting that 'lost in the woods' look again, babe. Let's get a beer or two in you before you go out and settle those nerves."

If anything, the nerves got worse. Two hours was a long time to fritter away on two beers. Her stomach had become so knotted it hurt. Puking in Nick's Porsche would be a wonderful way to start the evening. Shelby told some stories of her times with Nick back in the thirties, fun times, before Drake came along and ruined everything, and Nick became a guilt-ridden, depressing shell of his former self.

"He needs you, you know," Shelby said at one point. "He needs someone who understands and wants him, too. The man desperately wants to live again. He's been trying to get back to the Nick of old, and you can help him do that, Jack."

"I don't want to have the burden of making or breaking the man," Jackie replied.

Shelby threw up her hands. "Holy shit. You both are putting way to much drama into this. If you two would just fucking relax and be yourselves, things would be hunky-dory. Throw all the paranormal bullshit aside for tonight. Just be a couple of people out on the town, having fun. Is it really that goddamn hard?"

"Easy for you to say," Jackie muttered.

"It is easy!" she yelled back. "Fuck. I need another beer." Shelby got up and stormed back to the kitchen and didn't return for several minutes.

"She means well," Laurel said quietly from the other side of the couch they were seated upon. "She wants this to work."

"I know. Wouldn't mind seeing it work too. I think that may be what scares me the most, Laur. He's going to see past all this . . ."—she waved a hand at her outfit—"stuff, and the real me is going to be a huge disappointment."

"Nonsense. I hate when you do that." She leaned over to Jackie and whispered in her ear with kind urgency. "You aren't your mother and you never, ever will be."

Jackie sniffed. "Damn it. You're going to make me cry. Stop." She let out a huge breath of air. "I'll be fine. I can face down a dead raging mother and her baby. I can do a stupid date."

At that moment, Shelby's doorbell rang, and she came striding out of the kitchen, beer in hand. "Thank the Mother, he's here." She waved her beer bottle in Jackie's direction. "And for fuck's sake, look happy to see him. Please?"

Jackie stood up and straightened out her skirt. "OK." She turned to Laurel and smiled. "Calm and relaxed. I'm calm and relaxed." Her eyes drifted toward the front door. "You really don't think this is too much purple, do you?"

"You're perfect. Now hush and go say hi."

Chapter 40

"I don't think I've ever seen you carry a purse," Nick said, glancing over at the purple leather handbag in her lap.

"Shelby bought it," Jackie said, the third time now she had used that excuse on their way to the Arts Center. "I don't actually own a purse." *Or, you know, anything else that makes me seem much like a woman.* "No, wait. Laurel gave me one for Christmas a few years ago, but it's stored in a closet somewhere."

"You can leave it here in the limo if you want. No reason to take it in, unless you want to show it off."

Jackie spluttered. "A purse? That's ridiculous."

"Oh, you'd be surprised at the things people want to show off. Money brings out the worst in shopping. Should be worth a few laughs at least."

"I'm going to feel like an idiot out there," Jackie said, setting the purse down on the floor.

"Why?" Nick looked at her in disbelief. "You're smart, you give as good as you get, and you look absolutely stunning. Nothing else is needed or required at these. And we can leave as soon as the dedication is done if you wish."

"How long until that?"

"Hour at most," Nick said. "It's all drinks and schmoozing after that."

Stunning. She looked stunning. It sent a little, pleasant flutter through her "I think I can handle that."

He reached over and took her hand, giving it a light squeeze. "Trust me. It's not nearly as bad as you think, and we'll do something hopefully kind of cool after we're done."

"Oh? What? I thought we were just doing the party thing."

"No." He smiled, with something more than amusement in his eyes. "That wouldn't be much of a date, now, would it?"

"Please tell me," Jackie said. "So I have something to look forward to besides trying to be social with politicians and lawyers."

He leaned back in the seat, the perfectly fitted black suit and gleaming silver tie giving him an air Jackie had not expected to see from Nick. He looked debonair, and rather striking with the fresh scar along his jaw. "It has to do with music, but that's all I will say."

Music. A piano bar maybe? A recital? "That's a shitty clue."

"Wait and see, Ms. Rutledge. You'll just have to wait and see."

Jackie huffed and crossed her arms over her chest. "You suck."

"Shelby was right. You really are cuter when you're mad."

She glared and fumed for all of ten seconds. Calm and relaxed. Having fun. He's smiling. He's enjoying himself. Just picking on the little purple girl with her leather purse. That was OK. She'd get back at him at some point. She would.

The limo had an espresso machine built in and Nick made them shots of espresso to sip along the way. It was Bloodwork's limo apparently, built to suit its owner. Nick talked about the Center where they were going, what he had donated to, and what to expect at the party in general. It was useful and remotely interesting information, but more importantly it kept Jackie from having to carry on a conversation. She could smile and nod or ask the occasional question and it was all good.

They arrived like all the other limos and Mercedes and Bentleys, pulling into the parking turnaround at the Center's front door. Jackie scanned the people on the grand front steps, two hundred feet across, and she and Nick did not stick out. If anything, they were underdressed. Tuxedos and flowing evening gowns abounded. It was a goddamned Cinderella ball. The driver closed the door after she stepped up onto the curb and waited until Nick came around.

He looked her up and down again, with the same wide-eyed, surprised gaze. "Don't go far, Marcus. We'll be less than an hour."

"Yes, sir." He nodded and moved quickly back around the car.

Nick stuck out his arm toward Jackie and it took her a good three seconds of staring at it to understand what he was doing. *God, I really don't belong here.* Maybe if she pounded on the window, Marcus would let her back in now.

"Ready, Ms. Rutledge?"

"No." But she threaded her arm through his and let him lead her up the stairs.

The trip to their table, which was up on the stage of a grand ballroom, took at least fifteen minutes. It seemed that every other person knew who Nick was. Representatives, socialites, business executives, and a slew of other professions waved Nick over or made their way to him as he guided Jackie through the tables arranged throughout the ballroom. Off in a distant corner, Jackie could hear a string quartet playing.

She kept her mouth shut unless someone specifically said hello. Most treated her as though she wasn't even there, especially the women, until Nick began to introduce her to everyone as a matter of course. Her mouth was beginning to hurt from smiling so much by the time they reached their seats. It was there that Nick actually made an effort to talk to someone. She was elderly, likely in her seventies, but still obviously sharp. She dressed like a baroness and chided Nick for not being more present in Chicago social life.

She was also the only woman they had run into who gave her equal attention. "And who is your lovely companion tonight, Nicholas?" She stepped forward and wrapped her arms around Jackie, who found herself hugging in return. "Have you managed to snag this wonderful man while our backs were turned?" She beamed and laughed, full of mirth.

Jackie felt the heat rushing into her cheeks. God! Please no blushing. "No, ma'am. My name is Jackie Rutledge. I'm a friend of Mr. Anderson's."

"Call me Gladys," she said. "Well it's a pleasure to meet anyone who catches this wary man's eye, and who can dress so adorably." She turned and gave Nick a hug. "Sit and enjoy. I expect you to say few words, Nicholas. No slipping out the back."

After she walked away, Nick leaned over. "That was Gladys Wainwright," he said. "We go back a few years."

"Wait. Senator Wainwright's wife?" Jackie turned to stare after the woman. The senator's wife had just hugged her? Nick went back with a senator's wife? "Man, this is so out of my league."

"Bullshit," he said. "They just have money. That's all. Let me get a bottle of wine. I'll be right back."

He returned and poured them each a glass. "Here's to everyone ignoring us the rest of the evening."

"Yes, please!" Jackie said and smiled, clinking their glasses together.

Nick made small talk with the others at the table, and Jackie did her best to just smile and nod and sip her wine. Dinner was served, delectable in appearance, but Jackie only picked at it. There were several speeches about the new institute, dedicated to art created by cancer survivors. There was a standing ovation for the last, by a young female artist in a wheelchair who was missing her hair from chemo and spoke passionately about how art had saved her life. A screen set up on stage behind the speakers, which had been flashing pictures of various pieces, showed hers last. Jackie gave a little gasp when she saw it. The title of the piece, "Journey Back from Death," struck a deep chord in her, beyond the intensity within the piece itself.

"Oh, my God. That one is phenomenal," she said.

Nick leaned over. "Would look good on that wall by your piano."

Without thinking about what he might be saying,

Jackie readily agreed. "That would be amazing on my wall."

After the ovation, Nick took Jackie's hand again. "Come on. I want to check on something before we go."

Thank God they were leaving. "What?"

He didn't answer and led them over to the stair leading up to the stage.

"What are we doing?" They were going up on the stage, where several hundred people would be able to stare up at her to their heart's content.

Nick's hand pulled her along until they reached Gladys Wainwright, another elderly man and woman, and the wheelchair-bound woman. To their right, the slide of her art loomed larger than life.

"Nicholas!" Gladys said spreading her arms in greeting. "So glad to see you being social. This is Adam Parker, the director of the new institute and his wife, Dorothy." Nick smiled and shook their hands. "And this is our special guest of honor, Melanie Armond."

He took her hand, burying it in his. "Pleasure, Ms. Armond. Your work is quite impressive."

Pink flushed her cheeks. "Thank you, Mr. Anderson. This is all rather overwhelming."

"Unbelievably, I'm sure." Jackie could see the woman was clearly enthralled and Nick had dropped his voice to a smooth, smoky sweetness. She imagined that would enthrall nearly any woman. Did he practice that voice? "This is my good friend, Jackie Rutledge. She's also quite taken by your piece here."

She turned and smiled up at Jackie, who found herself spluttering in reply. "Oh, hi. Glad to meet you." She took the thin hand and shook it gently. "It really is amazing. I um . . . connected to it immediately." What the hell were you suppose to say to artists about their work?

Melanie's hand continued to hold hers, her eyes intent. "Are you a survivor, too?"

Jackie's hand involuntarily squeezed Melanie's. One could say that. She swallowed the lump in her throat. "Yes, actually. I suppose I am."

She smiled, both pleased and sympathetic. "I'm happy that it speaks to you."

"We'd like to buy it, if the piece is going to be for sale," Nick said.

"Really?" Melanie's face lit up. "I, um . . . I don't know if it is."

She turned and looked up to Adam Parker, who beamed at her. "It will be on display at the institute for six weeks, but then, if you desire, the decision is yours, Ms. Armond."

Jackie stared at Nick. *We are going to buy it?* He gave her a little half smile. "You aren't interested in it?"

"Sure," she said. What was she going to say? The artist was sitting right next to them. The fact was though, she would love to have it. "But, I mean, you're going to buy it? Just like that?"

Melanie answered for him. "I'd be happy to sell it to you, Ms. Rutledge. Knowing it's going to someone who can truly relate would make me happy."

"Oh. OK then. Thank you very much."

And just like that, Jackie found herself the likely new owner of the piece of art. Nick got them out of there as quickly as possible afterward, another fifteen minutes of handshaking and hugs, hellos and smiles. By the time they plopped back down in the limo, Jackie felt worn out.

"God. How do people do that for hours on end?"

Nick laughed. "Tiring, isn't it?"

"It is," she said. "How much is that painting *we* bought, anyway?"

He shrugged. "Does it matter? You can afford it. You have a good salary as head of the new Special Investigations Unit."

Jackie rolled her eyes. "Oh yeah? What's a ghost-hunter pull in these days?"

"You'll have a company card to get whatever you need."

"Like art for my apartment?"

"Whatever you want," he said. "Money is not going to be issue for this endeavor."

"OK." She sighed and sagged back into the seat. "This is just all so strange."

Nick's hand covered hers, cool and comforting. "We'll figure it out. I'm rather excited about it actually. Something to really sink my teeth into."

She flashed him a startled glance, finding him looking halfway serious except for the smirk. A smile crept across her mouth and then laughter finally bubbled forth. "That was really bad."

"Trying to take myself a little less seriously now," he said. "I can milk vampire jokes for a few years I imagine."

Jackie laughed harder. "Please don't."

Nick pulled out his cell. "Michael? Yes, it's Nick. I'm good, thank you. We're running just a few minutes late, but should be there shortly. Sounds good. See you then."

"Now what are we doing?"

"I told you. It's a surprise."

"Oh, come on," she insisted. "Tell me."

"Nope. Not a chance."

Jackie huffed. "You're a prick."

"I know. Great, isn't it?"

"Ugh. You're worse than Laur."

Jackie watched the skyline of downtown shift by them to the north. They were over by the lake, near the University of Chicago. What possible music-related venue could they be going to by the university? A concert perhaps? No, not if Nick was talking to someone about being late. It sounded more personalized than that.

They rolled by the university on Fifty-ninth Street, groups of students strolling along the sidewalks, going about their evening activities, actually knowing what they were doing. Nick sat in silence, a smug little smile upon his face. She wanted to smack him. Finally the limo slowed and turned up Woodlawn Avenue. It stopped and turned into a narrow circle drive.

Jackie stared out the window at the gothic stone edifice rising several stories above them. "A church? We're going to a church?"

"It's the Rockefeller Chapel," Nick said.

She had heard of the place, but was she supposed to know its significance? "I'm still not getting it."

An elderly man, short gray hair ringing his head and a priest's collar around his neck stepped out of the shadows of a doorway at the edge of the drive. The limo stopped next to him. Nick opened the door and stepped out to greet him. "Michael! A pleasure to see you again."

They shook hands and then embraced. "Likewise, Nicholas. Now tell me," he said and leaned over to peek into the depths of the limo at Jackie who stared back with blank confusion, "who is your organ-loving companion?"

Nick motioned for her to get out and Jackie slid across the seat and stepped out. Organ-loving? Her brain was taking that in all the wrong directions for being in proximity to a church. "Jackie? This is an old friend, Reverend Michael Chambers. Michael, this is my good friend, Jackie Rutledge."

"A pleasure, Ms. Rutledge," he said, grasping her hand in both of his. "By that look on your face, I'd say you've never been to our fair chapel?"

"No," she admitted. "I've heard of it, though." She gave him a nervous smile. What in the world did Nick have in mind?

"Well then. Come." He waved them toward the door. "You're in for quite a treat."

Nick smiled, clearly happy with himself, and waved a hand toward the door. "Please. Let's go see."

The door opened into the south side of the narthex, where stairs went up to the balcony overlooking the nave. To the right, double doors were swung wide to the nave, and the warm air, smelling of oak and incense brushed across Jackie's face. Reverend Chambers stood in the doorway, arms stretched wide. "Welcome to the home of the greatest twentieth-century pipe organ in the world, Ms. Rutledge." With that he turned and opened his arms to the interior of the chapel.

Nick had a broad smile plastered across his face. "Go," he said.

Oak pews spread across the floor in neat rows 150 feet into the distance. Mosaic tiles, warm, soft, and colorful spread across the ceiling nearly one hundred feet above, between majestic, arching beams. Grand forty-foot stained glass divided up the nave with muted pastel colors. It overwhelmed Jackie with a sense of invitation. It made you want to come in and stay for a good, long while.

"God," she whispered, "it's gorgeous."

Reverend Chambers chuckled. "Let's hope He feels the same."

Then Jackie's eyes found the chancel, situated beyond the nave. Her heart skipped a beat and her breath stuck in her throat. Carved wooden supports held row upon row of metal pipes, towering toward the ceiling. There were dozens, hundreds of them even. In the center of it all, a wooden bench sat before a four-tiered keyboard, surrounded by rows of stops. It was an ancient computer of sound, symphony, and choir breathing through hundreds of feet of metal.

"Oh, wow."

Nick hooked his arm around hers. "Come on. Let's play."

"What?" Her gaze snapped back to him. "Play? You serious?"

He pulled her down the aisle. "I didn't give to the good reverend for an empty chapel to stand around and stare at it."

"Wait," she stammered, moving quickly to keep up. "We have the whole place to ourselves? You can do that?"

Nick glanced over at her, a brighter than normal sparkle in his eye. "When you donate to restore this glorious instrument, you earn special privileges."

"Enjoy yourselves," Reverend Chambers said, and Jackie looked back to see the double doors shut, closing them in.

At the end of the nave, Jackie stopped, disengaging from Nick and stared up into the warm glow of the chancel. The pipes gave the sense of rising to the heavens, built to project their sound to the angels and God above. *If only that were the case,* Jackie thought. Nick continued into the chancel to the organ itself and sat down on the bench. Dressed in his tailored suit, he looked the part of the church's organ player.

Nick turned back to her. "Awe-inspiring, isn't it?"

Jackie nodded. "I don't even have words for it."

"You ever played a pipe organ?"

"No. I have no clue." She walked up to the bench, marveling at the four separate keyboards layered one above the other and the array of dozens of stops on either side to turn the various pipes on and off.

"Join me then. I'll give you the basics," he said.

Seated on the bench, Jackie felt incredibly small. She was within the confines of one of the largest instruments in the world, a work of art on a grand scale. It was difficult to not feel like a child in a museum crossing the ropes to touch the display.

"Ready?"

She gave him a sideways look and a soft bark of laughter. "No."

"Good. First off we have the keys here. Each row is called a manual," he began. For five more minutes he went through the various parts, explaining diapasons and mixtures and how one affected the sound coming from the pipes through the various adjustments of the stops.

"Nick," she said. "I'm not going to remember any of this. Just play something."

He chuckled. "Sorry. Easy to get carried away with this. So, any requests?"

Jackie shrugged. "Anything. Make the roof shake."

After a moment of thought, Nick pulled and adjusted some of the stops and put his hands up to one of the manuals. When his fingers lighted upon the keys, Jackie felt sure the roof likely was shaking. The floor, the bench they sat upon, and the very air around them came to life, vibrating into her bones with a deep resonant sound.

She reached out instinctively and gripped his thigh, fingers digging in. "Holy shit." Nick laughed and continued to play, the sound lightening up to something that didn't threaten to send every cell in her body flying off in all directions. Her heart thumped hard in her chest. God, what a glorious sound it made. She closed her eyes and let the music course through her and goose bumps rose upon her arms. Her little Steinway did nothing to compare. After five minutes or twenty, the piece came to an end. Nick's hand covered hers, still gripping his thigh.

"That look says it all," he said, his voice whispering inches from her ear. "I'm glad I brought you here."

Jackie opened her eyes to find Nick's, bright and depthless, staring down at her, the smile upon his face faint but pleased. "What look is that?"

"Happy," he said. "I think it's the first time I've seen you actually look happy."

"Oh." The breath hitched in her lungs. Happy. When was the last time she had been able to say that? Months? Years? "I guess, yeah. For a moment there, I felt . . ." The creeping worms of nerves began to make their way back into her gut. No, no, no! She wanted that feeling back, just for a bit longer. Could Nick do that? Could she let him do that? "The song . . . was lovely."

"Much like the company," he said.

The nerves melted away. Jackie pulled her hand free from his and reached up to brush her fingers over the thin pink scar along his jaw. "You don't have to say that."

His face moved imperceptibly closer. "Even if it's the truth? I'm the sheriff, Ms. Rutledge. I'm only after the truth, and you . . . are lovely."

Jackie blinked several times for her watering eyes. *Not crying, not doing it. Damn it, you idiot. Do not . . .* Jackie tightened her grip on Nick's chin and pulled his mouth down to hers. She let her lips part beneath his, fingers cupping the cool skin of his cheek. The nerves in her stomach took on a whole different quality, tingling and warm, a feeling tequila and bars never let her have before. In their own way, more terrifying than having no feeling at all. She gripped his chin more firmly to keep her fingers from trembling.

Nick sucked on her lower lip for a moment, then nipped it lightly between his teeth. His hand had found its way up to the back of her head, cupping it in its broad expanse, fingers twining into her hair. And in the quiet solitude and warm glow of the Rockefeller Chapel, Jackie discovered something beyond the supple play of his mouth upon hers and the quivering flutter in her belly.

Safe. She felt safe with this man who had to drink blood to stay alive and had dragged her to the realm of the dead in order to save her life. A tear squeezed out through a closed eyelid and Nick backed off.

"Jackie?"

She laughed softly and shook her head. "No, it's OK. I'm good."

He leaned forward and kissed the tear off of her cheek. "Yeah? We're good?"

Jackie nodded and kissed him again. "Yep. I think we are."

"Great. Why don't you try playing. There's really nothing like it."

She brought her hands up and slid them around his neck. There was nothing like him. How could there be? Tillie was right. This was a new beginning, a chance to get something right before it got all shot to hell. "In a minute," she said, and pulled his head back down.

Jackie has encountered a startling new presence and she and the rest of the Special Investigations team will be tested as never before in the next book of the *Deadworld* series, a Kensington paperback on sale April 2012.

Turn the page for a special preview!

Prologue

Jessica Forsythe's face was numb. The motorcycle helmet provided little protection against the cold October air, but she did not care. Hunkered down in the sidecar of Charlie's roaring machine, her gloved hands gripped the lip of the shell, and she squealed with fearful delight every time Charlie took a curve too fast and the wheel of the sidecar lifted off of the ground. She was miles from nowhere with the coolest girl in the world, and no clue where they were going. It was glorious, terrifying fun.

It sure beat the hell out of shooting up on Petey's dilapidated old couch that smelled like piss and vomit. There was more warmth in this wind-whipped sidecar than she ever got from his rusted-out charcoal hibachi. Not to mention the bonus of being miles away from his grimy hands and a mouth that tasted like rotted ass. Wherever Charlie was going, it had to be a million times better than that wretched dump.

The tree-lined highway gave way to another small town. Charlie eased off of the accelerator and they came to a stop at the single stoplight in the center of the town. Her pert, red mouth spread into a grin, and she stared down at Jessica through the gleaming, mirrored lenses of her aviator goggles. If the light was just so, Jessica swore she could see Charlie's otherworldly eyes behind them.

"Doing OK down there, Sis?"

Jessica nodded. "This is so fucking great! I love you." God! Where had that come from? But what else could this tingling, energized feeling be? No boy had ever managed to spark these sensations in her before. Warmth, comfort, desire. The feelings had been almost instantaneous. Charlie oozed cool out of every pore, and that little blonde curlicue on her forehead was to die for. And the whole "Sis" thing made her smile inside. They would be just like sisters.

The corner of Charlie's mouth curled up. "Good. We'll be home soon. Mom's making us lasagna."

"Sounds fabulous. My mom can't stand up long enough to cook anything."

Charlie's hand reached down and covered hers. "Well, mine will just love having you."

The heat from Charlie's hand seeped right through Jessica's glove, sending goose bumps up her arm. "Cool. I'll just be happy to have a place with heat."

She gave Jessica's hand a squeeze. "You'll love it here." The smile softened. "Trust me."

The light changed to green and Charlie turned off the highway toward the edge of town, winding back toward the oaklined hills. Jessica sat up straighter, watching the rustic old brick buildings rush by. It looked quaint, almost old-fashioned, and a far cry from the burned out, South-Side Chicago tenement she had been holed up in. Even in the frigid, dying light, the town looked peaceful.

On the back edge of town, an entire three blocks

off the highway, Charlie brought them to a drive heading up into a stand of oak and maple, a stark, black web of limbs shielding the lighted windows of a house. A simple, wooden signpost next to the mailbox read in white block letters THATCHER'S MILL.

"You live in a mill?" Jessica shouted.

"A house next to the mill, silly," she said. "My family has lived here for over a hundred years."

"Oh, wow." Jessica nodded and stared up the drive at the looming, two-story house. Over a hundred years. She couldn't remember ever living in a place longer than two. This was a place with real family. People who cared.

They rolled to a stop in the gravel drive that circled in front of the wood-sided house. A shingled roof overhung a wide screened porch running the length of the house. Jessica had barely managed to get her helmet off when the porch lights flooded the drive and the front door flew open.

"Charlie!" A woman came bustling across the porch and knocked open the screen door, the hem of her ankle-length dress balled up in one hand. A face-cracking smile reached nearly to the edges of the white bonnet on her head. "You brought her home!"

Charlie pushed the aviator goggles up onto her head and swung off the motorcycle. "Of course, Mama. I always do."

Home. Her home. How did that work? She returned Charlie's irresistible smile. "Brought me home?"

"Yes," Charlie said and reached down to take Jessica's hand. "My home is your home. You belong here now."

A corner of those still perfect red lips curled up, and in the bright halogen glow of the porch light Jessica stared into those bright, iridescent eyes and knew the absolute truth of her words. The momentary knot in her stomach melted away. "I really do love you."

Charlie squeezed her hand, but then the exuberant clapping of Charlie's mother interrupted the moment. "Come on, girls. This is just so wonderful. Dinner is almost ready. Do you want to change, Charlie?"

"Um, yeah. We better. Becca is smelling a little ripe." She reached down and hooked her hands beneath Jessica's underarms and lifted her out of the sidecar.

Before Jessica had an opportunity to say a word, Charlie's mother embraced her. She smelled of soap and garlic and a hint of lavender. "You had us so worried, Rebecca, love. I thought you'd died."

The hug left her breathless, and then Charlie's husky whisper blew into her ear. "Just roll with it. I'll explain later." Charlie took her hand again. "Ma-ma, chill out. I told you everything was fine. So go get the table ready. We'll be down in, like, fifteen."

Her mother sobered up. "Of course, sweetie. Everything is almost ready, just the way you like it."

Charlie nodded toward the house. "Come on, Becca. Let's go clean up."

Jessica followed, Charlie's hand pulsing with warmth around hers. Inside, she was hit by a wall of heat from a woodburning stove in the corner of the living room that carried the scent of baked bread, garlic, and pasta sauce. A grandfather clock chimed that it was now five-thirty. The place was immaculate and so . . . old. Jessica marveled at the furnishings. It looked like she had just stepped into a Norman Rockwell painting.

A male voice yelled out from the kitchen. "Charlie? That you?"

"Yeah, I'm home, Pa-pa," she yelled back. "Just getting cleaned up. We'll be down in a few."

Across the dining room, where slender candles burned and a setting for four adorned the table, the kitchen door opened and a tall, fortyish man in a simple black suit smiled at them. His sleeves were rolled up and there was a dishcloth in his hand. "Rebecca?"

Charlie pulled her toward the stairs. "Yep. Just finish up. We'll be down in a minute."

Jessica leaned toward Charlie. "Who's Rebecca?"

"It's you, of course. Now come on. I'm hungry."

The bedroom took up one end of the upstairs, two expansive Persian rugs covering most of the floor. Parked on each one was a full-sized canopy bed draped in silky, gauze curtains. An ornate, gold-inlaid chest pushed up against the foot of each. Tiffany lamps gave off a diffuse glow from the nightstand of each bed. A faint scent of lavender suffused the air.

"Holy shit," Jessica said. "Is this really your room?"

Charlie walked over to a walk-in closet, disappearing inside. "Duh. But it's our room now. Your bed is on the left." She came out a moment later, a floor-length, deep blue dress in her hand. "Bathroom is at the end of the hall. Wash up and then change."

Jessica stifled a laugh. "Into that? But it's so . . ."

"What?" Charlie brought it over and tossed it on her new bed and then stepped up to Jessica, her face inches away. "Old? Is that what you were going to fucking say?"

The depthless eyes intensified, freezing Jessica in

place. "N-no, not that. I'm sorry, Charlie. It's just not the kind of thing I usually—"

"It's Rebecca's," she snapped back. "It's yours. You are Rebecca now."

Jessica swallowed and nodded. "Okay. That's cool. Is it because—"

Charlie grabbed her arms and walked her over to the bed. Jessica's toes barely brushed the floor. "Ow! Fuck, Charlie. That hurt."

The slap came out of nowhere, snapping Jessica's head sideways, and then was forcefully pulled back by Charlie's hand gripping her jaw. "You don't talk like that, not ever!" The twisted mouth abruptly softened. "Rebecca is a good girl. She doesn't talk like that. Got it?"

Jessica whispered, blinking away the tears, "Got it."

Charlie let go of her chin and sat down next to Jessica on the bed. "You are Rebecca while you're here. No more Jessica. You," she said and smiled, leaning over to kiss her on the cheek, "are my sister now." Charlie reached into her pocket and pulled out the switchblade Jessica remembered from earlier in the day when Charlie threatened to castrate Petey if he mouthed off any more. The blade flipped open.

Jessica stared at the keen, shining blade. "What's that for?"

Charlie held out her other hand and drew the tip of it across her palm. A thin, dark line of blood oozed out. "Blood," she said. "We're sisters now, you and me. Now and forever, I swear upon this oath in blood."

"What do you mean?" Jessica stared in lurid fascination at the trickle of blood slipping down Charlie's wrist.

"Give me your hand." When Jessica hesitated, Charlie heaved a sigh. "Do I have to ask again?"

This was crazy. Jessica could not believe she was going to do it. She held out her hand. "Like blood sisters or something?" Charlie took her hand, the point of the blade pushing at the skin. Jessica wanted to watch, but could not pull her gaze away from Charlie's. Her hand seemed so far away.

Charlie's face softened. "Exactly. My sister, my blood."

She felt the knife score her palm but could feel nothing. "You really want me to be your sister?" Their palms pressed together and Jessica gasped at the rush of tingling heat that washed through her, much like that moment when Charlie had first touched her, only this time it went right to places she had not expected it to go.

"Now and forever," Charlie whispered. "Our blood is one." She squeezed and Jessica felt a cold chill brush across her face. "Say it, Becca."

Her voice struggled up out of her throat, hollow and distant. "Now and forever. Our blood is one."

Charlie grinned and lifted Jessica's blood-smeared palm between them. "We'll be together. Always."

Jessica returned the smile. She was perfect. How could she feel so well-suited to this girl? It was fate. It had to be. Then, Charlie's tongue brushed the skin of her hand, the lightest, feathery touch that traced its way across her palm. Jessica closed her eyes. It should not have felt so good. It made no sense, but nothing had ever felt so right as this. Charlie was her sister, now and forever.

When Jessica opened her eyes, the wound upon her palm was gone, barely a pink line, and her skin shone white with a glistening sheen.

Chapter 1

Jackie walked back to the kitchen area of the new Special Investigations office to make herself yet another espresso, the third one in two hours. What else was there to do? Cynthia had everything in perfect order. She had spent the entire previous day nodding in agreement to every suggestion Cynthia made about setting up the office. It was a showroom office straight out of *Architectural Digest*, and Jackie wasn't even sure how to operate half the shit around her. All funded, of course, by everyone's favorite millionaire vampire, Nick Anderson.

Worst of all, they weren't actually doing anything yet. Belgerman was having the "special flagged" cases sent over at some point during the day. Cynthia had offered to train her on the needed software programs, but the last thing Jackie wanted was to start her first full day on the job as the head of Special Investigations with lessons in just how underqualified she was to do it. She could not even handle sitting in her own office.

From a cubicle with barely enough room to turn around in, to a three-hundred-square-foot cavern with its own bar and big-screen television. Nick had even had them put in a floor-to-ceiling corkboard along one section of wall to mount her case info upon. The space completely overwhelmed her. She felt like a child invading her parents' private space.

"Agent McManus!" Cynthia's voice rang throughout the office.

Thank, God! Jackie made her way toward the front, around the dividing wall to where Cynthia's grand, curving slab of mahogany greeted all who entered.

"Ms. Forrester," McManus said, with a more-than-friendly smile. "How are you today?"

He leaned against a dolly stacked four high with file boxes. Jackie's greeting froze upon her lips. "Shit, McManus. Tell me those aren't all full of files."

Laurel's voice interrupted her shock. *Look at that! I can't wait to see what's in there.*

"Nobody asked you," Jackie muttered.

McManus stood up straight. "What?"

"Nothing," Jackie said. She needed more practice at the whole keeping internal and external conversations separate. It was getting really old.

"You talking to Agent Carpenter?" When Jackie rolled her eyes, McManus grinned and waved at Jackie. "Hey, Agent Carpenter. How are things going, um, in there?"

I'm good, thanks.

Jackie sighed. "Just quit, OK? It's too damn weird. How many files did you pack up?"

He shrugged. "Going by weight, I'd guess a few hundred at least."

"Lovely," Jackie said. How many hours would it take to sort through all of that crap?

Days. We'll need to build a database. Laurel was clearly far more excited by the prospect than Jackie.

"Just put them over there against the wall, Agent McManus," Cynthia said and pointed. "We'll figure out where we want them later."

At that moment the door opened again, and in walked Nick, carrying a cardboard box with Annabelle's label emblazoned upon it. Shelby was on his heels. At least there were pastries.

"Morning, everyone," Nick said. "I bear gifts. Agent McManus. Good to see you again." He set the box down on Cynthia's desk. "Help yourself if you like. Looks like we've finally got something to work on around here."

"*Pfft!*" Cynthia huffed, and opened the box. "Speak for yourself, cowboy. I've been busting ass all week long getting things ready for you guys."

Nick reached in after Cynthia and looked at Jackie. "Croissant?" The chocolate-filled pastry was offered before she had a chance to reply.

She wanted to turn it down for stubbornness' sake, but her stomach was rumbling. "Thanks."

"Take a breath, Jack," Shelby said. "This'll be fun. Aren't you at all interested in seeing what kind of craziness we'll find in those boxes?"

Through a mouthful of croissant, Jackie replied, "Do I have to answer that?"

Shelby walked by and patted her on the shoulder. "Relax, babe. This is where the real work begins." She held the bear claw in her mouth and picked up a box, heading around toward the back.

"Agent McManus? You're welcome to stay," Nick said.

"Much as I'd prefer the company, I've got to head uptown to meet with some Gang Enforcement people." He stared at Cynthia as he spoke. "You all have fun, and try not to work too hard. This place looks real rough."

"It's pure hell," Cynthia answered with a soft laugh.

McManus backed toward the door. "Good to see you all again. Good luck with this stuff, Jack. Let me know what you come up with."

Jackie waved while she washed down her croissant with the latte. When the door closed, she eyed Cynthia. "Pretty sure he likes you."

"He's easy on the eyes, that's for sure," she said.

Shelby's voice rang from the back. "Ask him out for fuck's sake, Cyn. He was practically drooling on you."

Cynthia shrugged. "We'll see. I can wait."

"Waiting's for losers," Shelby yelled back.

Jackie turned away and walked back to find Shelby before anyone noticed the capital *L* glowing on her forehead. She had put Nick on hold for nearly a month now. Things had felt so great in those moments after their date at the pipe organ. And then?

Yeah, and then what? Laurel wondered along with her. *You're going to lose him if you keep this up, girl.*

Shut up, Laur. Nobody asked you.

Hey! Not my fault you keep forgetting to block me out. And don't get snippy. You know it's true. Unless you want to lose him of course.

No! I don't want to lose . . . Jackie sighed. *Forget it. Can we not talk about this now? I'd rather bury myself in a bazillion weirdo cold case files, thank you very much.*

Oh, me too! This is going to be too cool.

Jackie bit off her response and stepped into their conference room, with its seemingly football-field-sized table, where Shelby was already digging into the file box. Nick and Cynthia were close behind.

Jackie stared at the stacks of manila folders Shelby was heaping onto the table. "OK, so what have we got here?"

"Filed by date," Shelby said. "This box goes back to the year 2000."

Jackie picked up the folder from the nearest stack. "Which means we probably have thirty to forty years' worth of this shit to sift through." The first sheet of paper inside was a form indicating nothing more than a phone conversation. "A Ms. Rose Shumway believes her next door neighbor is a vampire and disposing of his victims in the weekly garbage. Local authorities contacted. No further information." Jackie turned the page over, then checked the next sheet to make sure there was no continuation. "What the fuck? That's it? We get forty years of this?"

Nick grabbed a handful of folders and set the donuts down on the table. "I'm sure it's not all as bad as that. We'll find something, I'm sure."

Shelby waved her file at Jackie. "Bitch, bitch, bitch. Get up in the wrong bed this morning?"

"You know what?" Jackie's jaw clenched. God, she could be an ass. Shelby stared back, eyes wide with anticipation. It was not a fight Jackie would win. Ever. "Just read your fucking files. Find something useful."

She grinned. "Ooo! She's being all bossy. I likey."

Jackie's hands gripped the file so tight they began to shake.

Let it go, hon, Laurel said with calm assurance. *She's just picking on you.*

"I'm fine," she mumbled and grabbed a stack of files. "I'll be in my office if you find something." She stormed out without waiting for a response.

Five minutes after slamming her office door closed and tossing the files across her desk, Jackie was kicked back in her chair with her eyes closed. First real day on the job and she was already getting a headache.

Someone knocked quietly on the door. "Jackie?" It was Nick, ready to tell her to relax no doubt.

She wanted to ignore him. A pep talk was the last thing she needed.

Yes, you do. Let him in. Laurel's motherly tone was both kind and stern.

"You know what?" Jackie snapped. "Why don't you go bother someone else?"

A sigh whispered through Jackie's head and Laurel stepped out of her body. Laurel gave her a sideways glance, walked out through the wall toward the conference room, and was gone.

"All right, then," Nick said.

"No." Jackie groaned and sat back up. "Come in, damn it." Nick opened the door and entered the office. "I wasn't talking to you."

He walked up and placed his stack of files down on her desk. On top was another chocolate croissant. He sat down in one of the plush chairs across from her. "Sorry about Shelby there. She was just being—"

"A bitch?" Jackie cut in. "But no more than usual. Everything's getting on my nerves today, that's all."

"Anything I can do to? Something else you need here to make things—"

"No! God, no. More than enough, Nick. Really. This is all kind of overwhelming. I mean look at this place." She waved her hand at the office space. "You'd think I was the CEO of Chrysler or something."

"Any reason we can't have the best for this? I mean, I could have them come back and set up a cubicle for you."

The slight twitch of smile, stretching the long scar along his jaw, dissipated Jackie's annoyance. "Don't get me wrong. This is an amazing space. I just feel . . ."

She picked up the other croissant and took a bite. "I feel like I'm out of my element. This isn't me."

"Then make it yours," he said. "You do have a say, you know. You're the director of this operation."

Jackie sagged back in her chair. "Yeah. I know. Wish I knew what the hell that meant."

"It means what you make of it, Jackie. We're a team here, at least I hope we are, but as director, you get final say on things."

Final say. What they did, what these powerful, nerve-wracking people did was on her shoulders. "You do realize how weird it is having me order you guys around."

He shrugged. "Not really. You're more than smart and capable enough to do it."

Jackie sighed and sagged back in her chair. He didn't get it. "Thanks, but I have no idea what I'm doing. You guys are far more expert on this stuff than I am."

"Then we'll be the experts. Look, Jackie." He leaned forward, elbows resting on his knees. "I think you're right for this job because one, you're a leader. You know how to take the reins on something and lead it where it needs to go. Even when you don't know, you have great instincts. Two, you have the guts to make hard choices when they need to be made. You won't back down when shit hits the fan. Trust me, you'll be fine. Give it some time."

She avoided his gaze. Her guts turned to mush if she looked him in the eye for long. "You must have a lot of time on your hands, then." When his smile broadened, Jackie laughed. "Fuck. You know what I mean. Right now, I don't think I could decide my way out of a paper bag."

Nick sat back. "OK, I have something easy for you to decide on then."

"What?"

"Thanksgiving," he said. "What do you want for Thanksgiving dinner?"

Thanksgiving? Shit, that was in two days. The previous eight years had been with Laurel's parents, which was kind of out of the question now. She had not given a single thought to it this year. "I hadn't really planned on doing much."

"You don't have to do anything," he replied. "All I need are your preferences. Turkey and stuffing? Ham? Rack of lamb?"

"So, I'm coming over for Thanksgiving dinner?"

"You had other plans?"

"Well, no, not really," she said. "It's just . . ." It sounded great and potentially intimate, which cranked down the screws on her stomach. "OK. I guess I'm coming over. Do I need to bring anything?"

"No. Just your appetite. Cyn and Shel are coming. We usually do Thanksgiving together. I only need to know what you'd like."

The paranormal freak-show Thanksgiving. What could be better? At least there would be other people. "Is it possible for you to cook something I won't like?"

"I could try," he said. "Maybe bull's testicles or something."

Jackie snorted. "You've actually had those?"

"Among other things. Not my preferred body part, I'll admit."

And there it was again. Normal conversation turned disturbing because the guy drank blood to stay alive. She caught his gaze, wondering if he noticed the look on her face, and Jackie realized his reference may have had nothing to do with food. "Great. Surprise me then. You know I'll eat anything you cook. Think I'm ready to dig into these files now. How about you?"

Nick picked up a file from his stack, doing little to conceal the smirk on his face. "You're the boss."

After six hours, Jackie picked at a box of Chinese takeout, her eyes glazing over with weariness and frustration. The conference room table had been papered from one end to the other, stacks of notes and forms piled up by year. Some were far bigger than others, but they had potential cases going back to 1971. Many were ridiculous notes like Ms. Shumway's, certain to be nothing, but others had a definite creep value, that made Jackie wonder. Everyone had pulled aside those they thought might hold some kind of value. There were dozens, perhaps over a hundred. Jackie gave it her best unfocused stare and continued to eat her shrimp fried rice.

Shelby plopped the rest of a pot sticker in her mouth. "So. Any ideas on how you want to sort through those, Jackie?"

"No. How about random number?"

"I saw a few interesting ones," Cynthia added.

Shelby reached up and pulled one out of the middle of the stack, floating it across the table toward her. Jackie watched it drift to the floor. "Well, that's one down. Any other ideas, anyone?"

Nick sipped on a beer, his booted feet crossed upon the end of the table. "It would make sense to either start with the most recent or ones that are closest to us."

"I think we should go through this stack of good

ones and rank them from most to least likely to be legitimate paranormal incidents," Cynthia said.

Jackie nodded. Cynthia, ever the practical one, was probably right. She leaned over and picked up the sheaf of paper on the floor. It was one she had come across during the blur of afternoon reading. Unlike all of the other ones she had read, this one had actually come from a former FBI agent. The note was handwritten, dated August 12, 1993. It stated, rather simply:

> *Thatcher's Mill. I was traveling to Chicago for a workshop when I drove through this little, rustic town on the border with Indiana. This place had more ghosts in it than I've ever felt before, by a factor of ten to one. Remarkable and completely unnerving. Will have to investigate this if opportunity arises or we ever decide to look into paranormal events.*

FBI Agent. If they were going to get any kind of reliable source material, what could be better than a fellow agent? "Laur?" She moved over from the corner of the room behind Shelby. "What do you make of this one? You recognize the name?"

Laurel took a moment to read the note. "No, but we should contact her. I know there are other agents with abilities. It's just not common knowledge."

Jackie slapped the paper down on the table. That was good enough for her. "There we go. Thatcher's Mill. It's full of ghosts. Should be great fun."

Shelby threw her arms up in the air. "The boss has spoken!"

"Shelby?"

She grinned at Jackie. "Yes, babe?"

"Bite my ass."

"Now you're getting the hang of it."